The Other:
The Linotype Legacy

Best + Bob,

Enjoy The sequel!

MRWolf

by

Michael Robert Wolf

FLP Editions

a division of Finishing Line Press

Georgetown, Kentucky

The Other:
The Linotype Legacy

To my late brother Harry, my childhood partner in building, inventing, and all-around creative endeavors—and my sister Donna, who shares my passion for writing that reflects a compassion for people.

ACKNOWLEDGMENTS

Thanks to Deborah M Wiater, M.S., P.A.-C, MPAS, for technical medical input—
and to Mindy Salkind for the long hours dedicated to meticulous proofreading.

Editor: Leah Maines
Cover Art: Pexels aerial view and grayscale photography of high-rise buildings-
       Tatiana Fet
Cover Design: Lisa Hoop

Printed in the USA on acid-free paper.
Order online: www.finishinglinepress.com
            also available on amazon.com

Author inquiries and mail orders:
Finishing Line Press
P. O. Box 1626
Georgetown, Kentucky 40324
U. S. A.

TABLE OF CONTENTS

THE
SECOND WINTER

Chapter One

Manhattan's Flatiron Building was constructed in 1902. Its builders expected it to last forever. The twenty-story steel-skeleton structure marked the end of nineteenth century Victorian architecture, and heralded the age of the skyscraper. After its construction, nothing in New York City would be the same.

That fact would be lost on most present-day tourists, just as the Flatiron Building itself can get lost among the many buildings in the surrounding Flatiron District—despite its odd wedge-like shape. And indeed, on one gun-metal grey mid-winter day, it seemed quite hidden to a certain young man whose parents had legally emigrated from Pakistan before he was born. Omar Shehadulah expected something taller—more imposing—as he stood at the intersection of Fifth Avenue and Broadway. He sported a closely-cropped head of black hair, a neatly trimmed beard, and an L.L. Bean black winter coat. He turned three hundred sixty degrees twice before he was sure the right building stood before him. And when he saw it, he was disappointed.

Omar had been told in a text by a certain party that this building would make a more reliable target than the more prominent Empire State Building, or Chrysler Building. There was less of a chance that the attack would be discovered before it could be executed—as was the case with some of the attacks over the past few years. He had also been told that it would still shake the city for blocks around and send a devastating message to the infidels, *Inshe'Allah*…God willing. Still, as he scanned its height, length, and width, the structure seemed as oddly inconsequential as it was oddly shaped. Nevertheless, Omar had already decided that he would detonate the belt under his L.L. Bean jacket in the most advantageous place possible. He would know that place once he studied the building more carefully—not just in readily available blueprints, but in person as well. Soon after that, he would either construct the vest himself, or receive it through a yet-to-be-specified contact. The belt would present its own challenges. But he was confident things would go reasonably well…again, *Inshe'Allah.*

Before returning to his small apartment in Queens, Omar decided to have lunch. *Even soldiers of Allah get hungry,* he mused. He chose the 2nd Avenue Deli on East 33rd street. He knew there would be no pork products there, as it was a kosher restaurant. Therefore, it would meet at least that specific requirement of his Islamic *Halal* diet. But, of course, the deli was owned and frequented by Jews. How he wanted to blow it up—that is, *after* eating a Reuben sandwich with some kosher pickles and potato chips on the side. But he knew that such an attack would be a strategic mistake—at least for now. He headed toward 2nd Avenue, and the satisfaction of his appetite.

Chapter Two

Forty-nine year old observant Jew, loyal daughter, and hard worker Naomi Kaplan had graduated to a higher position at her workplace—sort of. That is to say, she had moved up in the world—technically. To put it another way, it would be accurate to describe her new position as a higher one—literally.

Specifically, several months earlier she and the whole Macy's housewares department had moved up from the basement level to the eighth floor. This move did not include a change in salary. It did, however, include a change in the use of escalators. Instead of riding the moving stairs one floor down, she now had to travel eight floors up. And every time Naomi traversed from one floor to the next, she unconsciously compared her upward journey to her growing love for her beloved blonde gorgeous NYPD detective boyfriend, the Gentile committed Christian Darrin Brock. She had spent the entire year trying not to fall in love with him, and vice versa. And then, at the magnificent flower-blooming Channel Gardens at Rockefeller Center, they finally professed their love for each other and shared their first kiss—and each of their first kisses. Their devotion had only risen higher and higher since then—like her travel up the escalators, or perhaps more accurately like a hot air balloon rising above the observant Brooklyn home she shared with her father David. Indeed, sometimes their devotion for each other seemed more dizzying than elevating, or in this case escalating. And as in the example of the hot air balloon, who knew where she and her non-Jewish beloved might land? Still she had to admit, the ride made her feel more alive inside than anything she'd ever experienced.

Just one year before, during this very month of January, she had abandoned all decorum—as well as all reason—to follow a man she had met just once in the housewares department to the Times Square subway station and through the train doors. Her wandering feet had taken her up the station steps, only to watch him enter the *New York Times* building—making her late for work in the process. She didn't know his name then. She called him "Peter," as she imagined introducing him to her father and convincing him to convert to Judaism.

So much had happened since then. And none of it had turned out as she had imagined on that subzero winter day a year before. "Peter" didn't end up converting to Orthodox Judaism under the watchful and approving eye of her beloved father. And of course, his name didn't turn out to be Peter. Unbelievably, as the seasons came and went, she did indeed fall deeply in love with him and he with her—to the amazement of her less observant sister Lisa and the distress of her dear father, David Kaplan.

On this unusually mild January day, Naomi stood at the housewares counter and surveyed the stainless steel cooking pots in an adjacent aisle. Here she was, now forty-nine years old, and she had no idea how those pots could ever end up on her bridal list. After all, David Kaplan had said he could never bless a marriage to the man she loved. And without his blessing, how could she marry the only man in the whole world—besides her father—that she adored with her whole heart, the only man she had ever met in whose eyes dwelt the same knowing gentleness and wisdom as David Kaplan?

As the slightest hint of moisture dampened her eyes, a subtle quick buzzing sound emanated from the pocketbook stored under the counter—and then another short buzz. She knew it was forbidden to even *look* at one's cell phone while on the job—let alone talk or text on one. But there was no one in the department, or even on her part of the floor. *It's so dead this morning*, she thought. *It couldn't hurt to take a peek.* She stooped down, quickly unzipped her bag, and unfolded the cheap little device. A short text from Lisa stared up at her.

Dad rushed to Maimonides emergency. Looks like bad stroke. Come quickly.

CHAPTER THREE

Police detective Darrin Brock was sitting in his cubicle on the second floor of the Manhattan Midtown South Precinct station. Margaret came from around the corner and peeked in, winking in the process. This startled him. She hadn't been this playful since she tried and failed to catch his attention several years before. He sat upright in his chair, trying to ignore the wink.

"Yes, Margaret?"

"Nothing. It's just that the boss wants to see you. *That* can't be good."

Darrin couldn't hide his irritation. He got up and mumbled as he walked past her.

"It might not be bad either."

That comment proceeded from his on-again-off-again decision to quit his job and embark on an entirely different path, one of being a mentor to troubled youth. He grabbed his cane and limped down the aisle of cubicles and desks, ending up at Inspector Ralph Lewis' office door. He flirted with the idea of just walking in, but then decided a quick knock would be better. He gently tapped the door twice in rapid succession. The inspector shouted through the door.

"Come in!"

As Darrin walked in, he recalled the time months before when he entered the office while Inspector Lewis was out. The audacity of that act helped him relax this day. The inspector was leaning over what appeared to be a large full-color map of downtown Manhattan, complete with three-dimensional depictions of the major landmarks. He spoke without looking up.

"Sit down."

Darrin sat down in his usual seat, which was—as always—lower than the inspector's. Now it was made even lower by the fact that Inspector Lewis was standing up as he surveyed the map. Lewis continued.

"Looks like you're healing pretty well from that Russian bullet last fall."

"I wish it would go faster. Everything is slow…including my walking. Not great for a detective. I wouldn't blame you if you just…"

"Bored, Brock?"

Lewis looked at him for the first time. Darrin didn't quite know how to answer.

"What?"

"I said, Bored?"

"Well…"

"Not with that Kaplan woman, I suppose."

"Well…"

"Well what, dammit? You haven't answered *one* question I've asked."

"Well, sir. You only asked one question. The other one was a statement."

"Very good, Brock. Very good. So you *are* bored."

Darrin sat up in his low chair.

"I don't know."

"You either don't know or you do know!"

"Well…maybe a little. Yes…I am…to a certain extent, now that the mob boss I was tracking, Prima, is dead…and I must say, sir, that… maybe I should just move on and…"

Inspector Lewis slammed his hand down on the map.

"Good! Because I just received a call from Homeland Security and something is up. You know what Homeland Security is, don't you?" he said facetiously.

"Well…"

"You're damn *right* you do."

He lowered his voice to a half whisper.

"Of course something is *always* up. But maybe something is *really* up now, if that's possible."

Then he raised his voice again.

"Come here. Over here."

He beckoned to Darrin to come to his side of the table. Such an invitation was rare. Usually, Inspector Lewis kept to his side of the desk, or traveled over to Darrin's side and stood over him—or next to him if Brock was standing. Darrin arose slowly from the low seat and walked over to Lewis' side, holding onto the desk as he did. Lewis stood close to him and pointed at the map.

"Look at this. Do you know what this is?"

"Um...a very nice map of Manhattan?"

"*Very* nice. You see these buildings?"

He randomly stabbed at one structure after the other with his finger.

"Empire State, Grand Central, Met, Chrysler, Flatiron, Madison Square..."

He looked up.

"Which one would you target...that is, if you were a terrorist, Brock?"

"Well, sir, I'm not a terrorist."

"Come on! You're a detective, for God's sake! This is easy. Come on. Guess."

"Well...I'm sure the Empire State...or...I don't know. Maybe the Flatiron, just to throw us off."

"That half-baked wedge of nothing? Take my advice. Don't join whatever remains of ISIS anytime soon. They'd fire you."

"I'll keep that in mind, sir."

Inspector Lewis plopped down in his chair and pointed at Darrin.

"Sit down."

Darrin slowly and carefully returned to his lower-than-Lewis' seat. The inspector leaned over the map.

"I'll keep you closely informed. I may put you on this case as one of just a few of New York's finest men in blue...without the uniform, of course. You interested?"

Darrin didn't even have time to nod yes or no.

"Forget that question. You are interested. Tell no one about our conversation. Wait. I take that back. You can tell your mother, if it makes you feel better. She's so demented, she won't be able to understand you anyway."

"Is that a joke, sir? Because if it is…"

"I never joke about things like that. I know you'll be tempted to tell Naomi Kaplan, so…"

"I would never do anything…"

"Don't interrupt me. You'll tell your mother, and you won't tell anyone else. I know my detectives."

Darrin began to rise.

"Yes, I guess you do. But if you don't mind, I have some unfinished business in regard to that Mandy Mendel murder case from last year. I know you've got some other people on the case. And I realize that the same Russians who attacked me might have had something to to with his murder. At least that's what I understand."

He leaned over the desk and boldly drew close to the inspector to make his point.

"But…I do have some investment in the solving of that crime. After all, I *am* somewhat close to the widow's youngest boy Natan. So…"

"I *do* mind, Brock. How many times have I told you to stick to your assignments and let other divisions handle other investigations? Look, I'm bringing you in on this HS thing because you're a good man, and I trust you. So get out of here and I'll keep you informed."

Darrin tried to hide not only his disappointment about the Mendel affair, but also his disinterest in the terrorist end of things. Consequently, he backed down and prepared to leave.

"Okay. Thank you"

"Don't mention it, Brock. It's good to have you back full time, by the way."

"Yes, sir."

Inspector Lewis' compliments usually came at the very end of conversations. Darrin Brock grabbed his cane and walked out of the office, returning to his cubicle.

CHAPTER FOUR

As Naomi rode the D train from 34th Street toward Brooklyn, she had two wishes. The first was that the text from Lisa was just part of a bad dream she had had during a momentary doze on a slow housewares day—in which case Mrs. Lazar shouldn't have let her leave her post, and David Kaplan would be perfectly healthy when she arrived at the Maimonides Medical Center. She'd find him full of life, visiting one juvenile cancer patient after another.

The second wish was that she had brought a pair of sunglasses to work that day, so no one on the subway could see her teary eyes. She covered them with her hand, imagining that she could render herself invisible to the other riders. That simple act triggered a recent memory that was far more pleasant than her present experience. She could just about hear Darrin Brock's gentle voice behind her, and feel his warm hands covering her eyes.

"No peeking, Naomi. No peeking."

A tingle shivered through her body as she felt his perfect lips kiss the back of her neck.

"Oh, that tickles. Stop! You're driving me crazy, Darrin. I'm liable to turn right around and kiss you like I did at the Channel Gardens, just to get you back. Okay, okay. I'm not looking."

She remembered his hand lifting off her left eye, as he stretched it out to pick something up.

"Not yet. Not yet. Okay. Now!"

He removed the other hand. Naomi's now open eyes gazed down on a little black velvet box. If her heart had been jump-started seconds earlier by the feel of Darrin's lips on her neck, it started beating wildly now. But this was not passion's beat. It was fear's. If that box contained an engagement ring, she would have to say "yes." And if she said "yes," she would have to tell her father. And if she told her father, he might have a—a stroke.

That memory—one from such a recent past—propelled her straight back to the present. The prophetic nature of that thought, which crossed her mind just a few weeks earlier, startled her. The fact that the box had contained not an engagement ring but a small solid-gold Jewish star pendant—along with a note that said *I love you so much, Naomi. This star expresses one of the things I love most about you*—didn't allay her fear. She hadn't yet worn the pendant in front of her father. She didn't want to unnecessarily disturb him. And yet apparently, if indeed her father really had a stroke, her relationship with Darrin must have disturbed him enough to have given it to him—with or without the pendant.

If was the operative word. Symptoms were one thing. Diagnoses were another. Her rational self knew that Lisa's text wasn't a bad dream. But what if the word *stroke* was a bad call? What if all symptoms disappeared by the time she got to the hospital? She could always hope—and recite the traditional *Mi-Shebeirach* prayer for healing. She began whispering it under her breath in Hebrew, and then recited the English translation—as if she wanted to make sure God heard her in both languages.

"May the One who blessed our ancestors—Patriarchs Abraham, Isaac, and Jacob—bless and heal the one who is ill...

Naomi recited the *Mi-Shebeirach* prayer at least ten times during her journey to Maimonides. When she finally arrived at the emergency room, Lisa was sitting at David Kaplan's bedside, holding his hand and squeezing it intermittently. She looked up at Naomi, who tried to interpret the look in her eyes. Was it hopelessness, anxiety, grief?

The fact was, it wasn't any of those—at least the majority of it wasn't. Lisa was in the middle of fulfilling a deep need for intimacy with her father—an intimacy she never felt she had while growing up, and that she always envied in her sister. Now here Naomi was, ready to play her usual role—and Lisa wasn't ready to give up her new-found place.

David Kaplan lay there—still and seemingly oblivious to all of this. His eyes were closed, and his mouth was contorted and drooping. Lisa turned back toward him as she spoke to Naomi.

"They say his left side is paralyzed. But they're hopeful it will come back…his speech, mobility, everything…they hope. Right now they have him sedated so he won't become agitated."

Lisa put both hands to her mouth, and then lowered and wrung them.

"Oh my…."

Suddenly, she fell to her knees by the bed, right next to Lisa. Her hands reached above her bowed head and grabbed David's arm.

"Oh my God! Oh my God!"

She began to weep, trying to restrain herself from totally breaking down. Lisa kept her place by David Kaplan's side. Then Naomi turned toward Lisa, gesturing toward her chair.

"May I…just for a minute?"

"I…I…no…I need to…no. *No*, Naomi."

She emphasized the point again.

"*No.*"

Naomi quickly interpreted the "no." So *that* was the look in Lisa's eyes. Why hadn't she picked up on it right away?

"Of course, Lisa. He needs you."

Lisa's eyes began to fill with tears.

"No, I need *him*, Naomi. I need *him*. Can I please just have him to myself for at least a few minutes more? Can I…*please*?"

"Oh, *yes*, Lisa. *Absolutely.* I'll…I'll leave. I can come back later… whenever you say…tonight. I'll come back sometime tonight."

Lisa shook her head.

"No, Naomi, stay. But please just for once just let me be the one that's there for him…just for a little more time. We may not have much of that left. I just want to be the…the…."

She began to weep openly.

"…the beloved daughter…beloved…the…beloved…daughter…for just a few more…more….minutes. Let me just have that…just…"

Naomi, still on her knees, reached out and put an arm around Lisa's waist.

"Of course, Lisa. You *are* his beloved daughter. He's told me that many times. He really has. He loves you, Lisa. He's always loved you. And he needs you now, just like you need him. He's yours. Take all the time you need."

Lisa chuckled through her tears.

"I'm afraid I need too much of that…like a lifetime."

Naomi stood up and dried her eyes. She took a deep breath.

"Can he hear us?"

"I…I don't know. Maybe not…not yet, anyway."

"I…I see. Well, I'm sorry, Lisa. But I *have* to do just this one thing."

She leaned over her father, practically touching his nose with hers. Then she began to call out to him.

"Dad? Dad? Can you hear me? Abba? It's me…Naomi. I'm here with your…your…beloved daughter Lisa, whom you love."

She glanced over at Lisa and then back. Then her voice took on a more frantic tone.

"Dad! Dad!"

He just lay there, silent. Her hands retreated and covered her mouth again. Then she spoke through her closed fingers.

"I did this to him, didn't I? *I* did it."

"What are you talking about?"

"You know. You know."

"Oh, come on, Naomi. It has nothing to do with you and Darrin, and you *know* it. He loves Darrin."

Naomi dropped her hands to her sides, and then put them on her hips.

"Yes, like he loves the sick Christian children here at Maimonides during his December 25th *mitzvah*. Like he loves *the other*, as he calls them. People of other religions. That's not like loving a future son-in-law…not even a *possible* future son-in-law, let alone a probable one."

Lisa rolled her eyes and raised her voice.

"Will you just for once stop beating yourself up? You know, it's not a crime that you fell in love with a wonderful man, Naomi. You don't *always* have to be David Kaplan's perfect little observant older daughter.

Maybe you can just be yourself for a change."

Naomi felt the old anger rise up—anger she hadn't felt for about a month, since the Chanukah party at the Kaplan home, when Lisa and she experienced a joyous reconciliation. She pointed at her.

"Stop judging me, Lisa! Just stop it! I happen to be myself when I'm David Kaplan's older daughter, for your information...Darrin or no Darrin."

Lisa paused, closed her eyes and took a deep breath.

"What are we doing, Naomi? I want my only sister with me during this time—the sister who cried with me at the Chanukah party, the sister who I missed growing up. I need you now as much as I need Dad. And you know what? You need me. Okay, I'm sorry if I said anything that upset you. But let's not fight."

Naomi instantly regretted that things had gotten out of hand. Shame replaced anger.

"You're right. I'm so sorry. I really am."

Lisa let out a nervous giggle.

"Well, okay then. Let's just be there for Dad."

"I agree. But Lisa...I know I gave Dad this stroke. I'm *convinced* of it. I broke his heart. And now that's just what I deserve...a broken heart. So I've just decided I'm breaking up with Darrin. There's nothing more to say about it."

Lisa felt like she'd been slapped in the face. She didn't know exactly *why* she felt that way. After all, Darrin wasn't *her* boyfriend. She just knew she felt that way. She got up and came close to Naomi, just a few feet from David Kaplan's apparently deaf ears, and pointed her finger in Naomi's face.

"No, you are *not* breaking up with him! I won't let you!"

"I've made up my mind. I'll tell Dad when he wakes up, *if* he...well, I'm telling him."

"That's ridiculous, Naomi! What good are *two* broken hearts?"

Ignoring her, Naomi bowed her head and began to pray.

"God of Abraham, Isaac, and Jacob, if you wake Abba up, I promise to..."

Lisa's eyes widened.

"Stop! Stop! Don't you *dare* take a vow. Don't you *dare*! Promise me you won't. *Promise* me…now!"

Naomi lifted her head and they locked eyes. Lisa stared her down.

"Well?"

After a pause, Naomi responded.

"Okay, Lisa, I promise I won't talk to Daddy yet. But I've made up my mind."

As a young African-American nurse with short dyed red hair walked into the room, Naomi walked to the other side of the bed and held David's left hand. The nurse smiled as she checked their father's vitals and medication drip.

"With all the familial love in this room, he can't help but get better. And he will."

She lowered her voice.

"Don't tell anyone this, but my whole church is praying for him. Sometimes—with some patients—I just can't help but ask for prayer."

"Thank you," Lisa responded appreciatively.

"Yes, thank…thank you so much," Naomi haltingly followed suit.

Chapter Five

Even after seeing her father with her own eyes, lying on the hospital bed with visible stroke symptoms, Naomi's mind still couldn't quite grasp the seriousness of the situation. It wasn't until she unlocked the door to their Brooklyn home and entered the hallway that the reality hit her. David Kaplan wouldn't be coming home that night. He wouldn't be eating dinner with her, or sleeping in his own bed. That Shabbat—just a few days away—he wouldn't be walking to synagogue with her. They wouldn't have their special lunch discussion after services. And they wouldn't be ending the Shabbat with their own private *Havdalah* service.

She glanced around the dining room. It was deathly quiet and unusually dim. There on the mantle was the Kiev menorah—as still as her father. It seemed to radiate a substance that was the opposite of light—something like a black hole in Naomi's universe. She sat down at her usual dining room chair and put her head in her hands.

"Oh my. Oh my."

Those words replaced the silence with a sort of bell jar sound—a muffled smothering vibration—a flat dead noise. She didn't repeat it. Instead, she got up and began pacing the room as tears trickled down her face. She knew that whatever of her world hadn't fallen apart, she was about to dismantle with her own hands. And she wasn't looking forward to trying to kill her very much alive love for Darrin. Along with that inconvenient reality, she also had memories that wouldn't be easy to erase. For one thing, she had come to look forward to their times together reading the New Testament, the rabbinic writings, and the Jewish Bible. She felt no pressure from Darrin when they would sit together at a Manhattan Starbucks with open books, and she was enjoying the education she was getting about *the other*, as her father called Christians. On the other hand, Darrin was quickly learning the most treasured details about the religion she held so close to her heart.

Besides all this, she also knew that there were at least a few people who would try to talk her out of breaking things off. She guessed that chief among those would be Aunt Ida, who was not actually her aunt, but she called her that. Of course, there were also others who would support her decision—for example, Marvin, Ida's real nephew. However, she wasn't planning to contact either Marvin or his aunt Ida.

She walked over to the dining room table and picked up her cell phone. Her hands began to tremble as she flipped it open and slowly punched in Darrin Brock's number. She could have speed dialed it, but she wasn't in a rush to get through. In fact, she was hoping he wouldn't answer. But she was quickly disappointed. She pulled a chair back and sat down, trying to calm herself so she could sound emotionless. He answered.

"Naomi?"

She quickly breathed in and out.

God will be pleased, she thought to herself. *God will be pleased*.

"Naomi?"

"Yes, it's me, Darrin."

"What's up?"

His voice was bouncy—a stark contrast to her flat affect.

"Well...bad news.

He jumped in immediately.

"What's the matter? Is something wrong?"

"Yes it is, Darrin", she responded with an unavoidable coolness, as if he was personally responsible for her father's condition—which she at least partly believed he was. What a contrast with the kiss on the neck and the velvet box. Impending death enveloped her words, directed more at her relationship with Darrin Brock than at David Kaplan's present medical condition.

"My father had a stroke. They have him sedated now. They don't know...they can't say...if he'll pull through. I need to talk to you, Darrin...soon."

He had been standing in the kitchen of his Teaneck house. Now he too sat down. His parents Lester and Velma were in the living room, out of earshot. Still, he lowered his voice.

"My goodness. That's terrible, Naomi. I'm...I don't know what to say. I'll visit him in the hospital as soon as I can. I'll...I'll drop everything and just go."

She answered immediately.

"No."

There was a short pause as Darrin absorbed the shock of her abrupt response.

"But...but...he visited me when I was recovering from the gunshot wound. It would only be right if..."

"That's beside the point, Darrin. Not now. I need to see you soon. When can we..."

Tears began to form, and she choked on her words—which she tried to conceal.

"...we...we...meet...as soon as possible?"

"Anytime. Anytime, Naomi. Immediately. Where would you like to meet?"

"Not at the Channel Gardens...please. Not there."

"Oh...okay. It's wintertime anyway."

Suddenly, he felt out of breath—and strangely feverish, although he had no fever.

"Oh...well. Are you home now?"

"Yes, I am."

"Now...as soon as I can. I'll hop in the car right now."

Naomi was not expecting that. But he sensed the urgency of the moment—based on the strange aloofness he sensed—and he ached to immediately be by her side. She hesitated for a few seconds, and then agreed.

"Well...well...I suppose so. Yes, you can come over...for a few minutes. I'm tired, so just for a few minutes. I...I want you to understand that I…I wouldn't normally have a man alone in this house. But in this case…"

Her formality further disturbed him, notwithstanding the fact that he understood her Orthodox Jewish standards in this area.

"Of course. I'll be over as soon as I can."

He hung up before she could change her mind. Naomi spent the next forty-five minutes lying face down on her bed, experiencing periodic waves of fear—or more accurately, terror—that she would back down from the task at hand. She wished she could just fall asleep, as she had when she took just a bit too much Advil during the summer. But there was no time for medication to take effect. So she just repeated the only phrase she could think of that would steel her resolve.

"Not next Yom Kippur, but while Abba can still hear me, if he can…I must inform Darrin it's over between him and me. Now!"

Then fear of her "weakness" for Darrin Brock overtook her fragile emotions again. Deep tender feelings for Darrin began to rise up, to which she responded with the same phrase.

"Not next Yom Kippur, but while Abba is alive and can hear me…I must tell him. Now! Now! *Now!*"

The fifth time around, she just detected a knock on the front door. She purposely hadn't fixed her hair or her face. She wanted to look as unattractive as possible. She ran down to the front door and opened it. Darrin stood there and waited for her to speak. She didn't.

"Hi Naomi. I've so missed your beautiful face. You're so beautiful."

They stood at the threshold for several seconds. Then Darrin spoke again.

"May I come in?"

For a second, she hesitated—as if his expectation to enter after coming all the way from Teaneck wasn't reasonable—as if he was selling storm windows, and the only appropriate conversation was at the door. She knew she was being rude.

"Of course. Why not?"

She went over and flopped down on the couch where she had found her father sick with fever the winter before. She knew that was inappropriate, but she didn't have the strength to stand or even sit. Darrin entered, shut the door, and limped over to the sofa, the rubber tip

20

of his cane making subtle impressions in the worn but well-vacuumed off-white living room rug. He stood over her, his coat and scarf still on. His heart rate rose, as he sensed that something terrible was about to happen.

"I'm…I'm so…so sorry about your father…about Abba."

That marked the first time he had ever used her affectionate term for David Kaplan—and it rankled her. Was he trying to become the Jew he could or would never be? She looked up at him—not even bothering to take his coat or offer him a chair—let alone a hot drink. Just then, he fell to his knees right next to her face, throwing his cane on the floor. She quickly turned her face the other way, so she wouldn't have to look into his electric blue eyes or be tempted to kiss his soft perfect lips. Then she spoke words she had been rehearsing since she realized what she had to do.

"We can't see each other anymore. I must tell my father that. That's all."

There was silence for what seemed like a few minutes—although it was somewhat less. She could hear his erratic breathing. Finally, she sat up. When she finally looked at him, she noticed that his head was bowed, and several tears were dripping off his face and staining the couch.

"What?" he barely breathed out. She got up and walked into the bathroom. When she came out, she had a few tissues in her hand. She sat back down and gently lifted his head up with one finger on his chin. Then she quickly withdrew her hand before she lost control and ended up kissing him passionately, like she had in the Channel Gardens.

"Take these tissues and dry your eyes, Darrin. I have no choice. I gave him this stroke. It's the least I can do."

Darrin wiped his eyes. He had a puzzled look on his face.

"The *least*?" he finally asked.

"Well, I meant the *only* thing. It's time to face reality. I know what my father needs to hear. I broke his heart, and I'm the only one who can heal it."

Darrin sat down next to her, still wearing his winter coat and scarf.

"What…what if it was just a stroke, Naomi? I mean, older people do have strokes."

"I know my father. He wouldn't just have a stroke. It's not like him."

"Naomi, it's not like *anyone*. But it does happen."

He drew close to her.

"Please don't leave me...*please*. Don't do this, Naomi. Don't do this. I'll talk to him when he's better. He'll understand. I know he will. He knows my heart. He told me so. He said he was thankful for me, that he appreciated who I was as a person. He called me a mensch. I'll...I'll do anything. We'll pray. He'll get better. *Please*! I can't lose you now. Maybe I love you more than you love me. But...please..."

Part of Naomi wanted to say, *You're being just like Marvin, begging me like that*. Marvin was always begging Naomi to marry him. The other part of her wanted to scream, *No, I love you more than you love me!* But neither of those things passed her lips. Instead, she stood up and walked over to the door.

"Darrin, I just need to be there for my father. I can't afford to stay in love with you. I can't. I would never *ever* forgive myself if he died this way...God forbid. He must know he hasn't lost me. He must *know* that."

Darrin stood up and trembled as he leaned on his cane. Seeing him wince with pain almost caused her to break down and run to him. But she just managed to restrain herself. He stood there, fresh tears filling his eyes. His lips quivered.

"Okay. Okay. I understand. I really do. After all, he's your father. I see that. But...but still...how can you just...just stand there...dry-eyed? How can you...while I...I make a complete fool of myself because I love you so much it hurts, and now I'm losing you? How could you...?"

She tried to flatten her affect even more.

"Don't you understand, Darrin? I can't afford to cry. I can't afford it. I need to move on. I have to. I have no choice."

He silently walked to the door and opened it. She watched him as he passed her by and slowly limped toward his car without looking back. She shut the door and tried to continue restraining herself until he drove away. She could just control herself as he walked from her front door to the car. As he finally reached the door handle, and opened and shut it, she let out a piercing scream and then a loud sob.

Chapter Six

Naomi couldn't sleep. She lay on her bed, her heart alternately numb and aching with heart-breaking pain. Suddenly, Marvin's face unexpectedly appeared before her eyes. She hadn't given him hardly a thought since the Chanukah party. Now she found herself not only thinking about him, but also praying that certain disaster would be averted—that Marvin wouldn't end up hearing about the break-up until the far-off future—like sometime after the long-awaited Messiah appeared.

However, as was the case with other events in Jewish history, deliverance was averted. Within a week, tragedy struck. In an unlikely coincidence, Lisa happened to see Marvin's Aunt Ida at a Brooklyn deli counter. She told her about her father's stroke, and about the break-up between Naomi and Darrin. And then, in an even more devastating blow, Aunt Ida told Marvin as she drove him and his mother in her silver Lexus to the dialysis center. A broad smile exposed Marvin's crooked teeth, which Aunt Ida caught in her omnipresent rear view mirror. She glared at him, and scolded him like a school teacher in a one-room country schoolhouse—with the addition of a four-letter word.

"What the *hell* are you smiling about? You think David Kaplan's stroke is funny?"

Marvin was embarrassed in front of his mother, who was preparing to leave the now-parked car.

"But Aunt Ida…"

Ida was in rare form, partially attributable to a temporary flare-up of her arthritic hip. But she controlled herself and waited until Marvin's mother walked into the dialysis center before she turned to him and let loose.

"Don't 'Aunt Ida' me, Marvin! Wipe that smile off your face. Get Naomi Kaplan out of your mind. Do you hear me? I may have encouraged you two at one time, but you've said and done too many stupid things since then. I shouldn't have opened my mouth and told you about the break-up. And you know what else? If I see Naomi, I'm going to tell her she's crazy for leaving that handsome goy. And she'd be *just* as crazy if she ever gave *you* the time of day again. Oh. And by the way. I should have told the same thing to your mother when she married my meshuggana brother…may he rest in peace."

Marvin stopped smiling when she mentioned his late father. But that didn't stop him from thinking about his renewed chances with Naomi. He had learned how to agree with his aunt, but also how to ignore her advice.

By the next morning, Marvin decided he must act quickly. Naomi was an hour into a fairly busy housewares department Thursday morning when Marvin considered texting her. He knew she wouldn't be able to look at it until her lunch break, but he wanted to be sure it arrived with plenty of time to spare. He knew this text would be more important than any text he had ever sent her. He had to catch her attention at the beginning of her lunch break, and then convince her to drop whatever bag lunch plans she had and meet him at Ben's Deli. That wouldn't be easy—unless he lied. As he donned his green coat and orange sock hat, preparing to leave the house for Manhattan—and Macy's—he wondered if the rabbis ever permitted lying in life-or-death cases like this one. He was sure they must have. After all, wasn't it like them to allow for exceptions, like sick people not fasting on Yom Kippur? And didn't those midwives lie to Pharaoh? At least he thought he remembered it happening that way.

By the time Marvin got on the D train, he concluded that texting wouldn't work—no matter *what* the text said. Instead, he decided on another strategy—a more direct, if possibly riskier, one. He arrived at the 34th Street station at 11:30 a.m., and then walked the short distance to Macy's. As he followed the flow of pedestrian traffic through the Seventh Avenue doors, he pulled his hat off. He had brought his comb especially for this occasion. He hadn't used it in several days. Fortunately, he had discovered it under his bed that morning. He pulled it out of his pocket as he walked through Macy's second set of doors. He hadn't seen Naomi in over a month, and he wanted to make a good impression. He dragged the comb through his stubborn shock of grey hair. Then he unzipped his winter coat, exposing the only clean white shirt he owned, which he had adorned with a thin black tie.

He had pondered three or four lies to quickly catch Naomi's attention before she got away from him—and had rejected the near-death state of his mother and one or two others in favor of a job offer that morning. Surely, if the rabbis permitted the lie of the midwives in the Torah, they would allow for that. Knowing that Naomi now worked on the eighth floor, he proceeded to the bottom of the main escalator and stationed himself next to it.

Naomi was just finishing with a bed sheet sale. The customer was female, Jewish, and well dressed, with a stately appearance and salt-and-pepper hair—and about her age. Feeling numb after the self-imposed loss of Darrin Brock, Naomi rang up the sale and whispered an anemic "thank you." Life no longer seemed worth living, what with her father's serious stroke symptoms and the untimely demise of her romantic relationship. But she knew she had to carry on, like a soldier in a defeated army. The sale of light tan king-size sheets—designed to facilitate the successful marriage of an enviable landsman—was her present painful responsibility. When that was finally accomplished, she alerted the other saleswoman that she was going to lunch, and grabbed her pocketbook and bag containing an egg sandwich and an apple—the kind of lunch her father would sometimes prepare for her when he was well. She headed for the elevator and then began to travel the eight floors to the main level.

Between the sixth and fifth floors, she pulled out her cell phone. Perhaps Lisa had texted her with news of her father's condition. Had it improved or deteriorated? When she flipped the phone open, she saw a text. But it wasn't from Lisa. The first sentence of Aunt Ida's familiar cadence leaped out from the tiny screen. Naomi's heart jumped. She instinctively looked down just as the fifth floor swallowed up the escalator stairs. She jumped off just in time and stepped onto next escalator down. As soon as she got on the next set of stairs, she looked at the screen again, pressing continually as the words came in.

Whats going on Lisa says father sick and Darrin out and u say 0 to me Do we have to have Applebee's talk or what CALL ME! PS Marvin knows

It took the entire trip between the fifth and fourth floors for the text to sink in. Aunt Ida knew. That was okay. Naomi was going to tell her anyway—eventually, although not at the Newark Applebee's where she helped Naomi after Darrin was shot, while Naomi ate kosher kugel in a napkin. But not Marvin! Between the fourth and third floors, she felt like throwing her phone over the escalator rail before a text from Marvin could reach her. Between the third and second floors, she decided she wouldn't answer any text from him. That was settled. As she traveled the last escalator steps to the main floor, she could just see a squat Jewish man in a white shirt and black tie, who looked disturbingly like Marvin. When she arrived on the main floor, her eyes averted his. She began to pass him on the way out of the store—looking forward to a quiet bench lunch on this unusually mild January day.

"Naomi!"

Was that actually Marvin's voice? Of course it was. She had known it was Marvin since ten feet from the bottom of the escalator—in spite of his shirt and tie. She just didn't want to believe it. He began to chase after her as she sped up to get away from him. She could just hear his labored breathing. She hated the fact that he was as out of shape as an amoeba—unlike Darrin Brock. He continued to chase her out of the Seventh Avenue doors.

"Naomi! St…Stop…St…Stop!"

It was no use. She turned on her heels, almost colliding with him as the pedestrian traffic flowed around them.

"Marvin…what do you want?"

"Look…I…look…"

"What, Marvin? What?"

"I got…a…a…job. See?"

He grabbed his tie with his left hand and waved it in her face. "See?"

"Congratulations, Marvin. Now if you don't mind…"

"I can pay for lunch…yours too. They gave me an advance… yesterday…when I got it…the job."

Actually, he barely had enough money for himself, owing to the fact that he didn't really have a job. As usual, he had squeezed just enough out of his fixed-income mother for that. But he figured he could tell Naomi that he wasn't hungry—although he was. She, of course, had her bag lunch. Perhaps he could eat that while he paid for her lunch. Then he could beg her to give him another chance. It was now or never, before she met another handsome goy somewhere. She looked straight at him, the fire in her eyes almost burning his.

"Marvin, I wouldn't go to lunch with you if you took me to the most expensive kosher restaurant in Manhattan! Oh, I don't know…Abigael's on Broadway, for instance! Do you think I don't know you heard Darrin Brock and I…?"

She pressed into him, her nose almost touching his. Surprised, he exhaled involuntarily. She rolled her eyes.

"You've got terrible breath, Marvin. You're disgusting. You don't really have a job, do you? *Do* you! That's just your one shirt and tie that I gave you five years ago when you took me…no, I took *you* to that horrible Broadway show I wasted *my* money on. No job, Marvin! Isn't that right! Isn't that right!"

He hesitated, which told her everything she needed to know. She began to walk away from him. He knew he couldn't let her get away. He went after her and grabbed the sleeve of her winter coat. She wheeled around and slapped him hard in the face with her red-gloved hand. He stopped cold. She could see his eyes moisten as the shock of the slap registered. She pursed her lips in a sign of no regret. He had to say something—and fast.

"Wait! Thank…thank you. My…mother says she should have slapped me silly…a…a long time ago."

"Oh, your mother! Your mother! That's all you ever talk about. And thanks for lying to me. Okay, okay. What do you want? And make it fast. This is taking up half my lunch break."

Now was his chance.

"See...see...you almost converted, but I'll take you back...if you haven't defiled yourself."

She practically swung at him.

"How *dare* you!"

"Wait a minute. I didn't say you...you did. But it's just that when Jews who abandon our holy Torah for *Yeishke*...well, that's what the Christians who go after them expect. So I just wanted to be sure."

Naomi sighed. She remembered her own past ignorance, so she decided to take a different approach.

"Look Marvin, it's not like that. It's not at *all* like that. And *I'm* not like that. I thought you knew that. I guess after all these years, you really don't know me, do you?"

"But you let him *touch* you."

"Yes, Marvin, I let him touch me. But not *that*."

"Well, I just wanted to...to know...before...before we..."

"Before we what?"

"You know. I'm the only one who would take you now...in all of Brooklyn...and I'd have you if you didn't..."

"Well, Marvin, I didn't...and you *won't*!"

"Won't?"

"Won't! That's right Marvin. *Won't!*"

"But...I see them coming out of that messianic place they call a synagogue, holding hands and I don't know what else...taking the bus on Shabbat...eating milk with meat...idolators, *meshumids*....traitors. I'm sure they...they co-habitate. Some people think that you...but I'm glad to know..."

She didn't care about what people thought. But she did have one question to ask him.

"*What* place?"

"They're not Jews. They'll never be Jews again. But I would have you back."

"Marvin..."

"You would make *teshuvah*...repentance...and we would have a kosher home...you...and me. So here I am, Naomi. Right here."

"Marvin..."

"I'll get a job. Look at my shirt and tie…and a ring…I'll get a ring—but not right away, of course."

"Marvin! Stop! Now!"

She took a deep breath, and repeated herself.

"*What* place?"

"Place?"

"Yes. What *place* they call a synagogue?"

"Oh. It's called Beth Yeshua, God forbid."

"Where?"

"I don't know. I've passed it. It's somewhere near Borough Park…but not *that* near, *Baruch HaShem*."

"Okay, thanks Marvin. I was just curious. I never noticed the place. Well look, I have to go. My lunch break is almost over."

"You know, no one who goes in there leaves Jewish. It's like an old horror film, like that snatcher movie we saw on DVD…remember? Anyway, I couldn't have you then. Just so you know."

"Okay. Thank you, Marvin. I know that now."

"Can I text you?"

"No."

"Please?"

"Let's put it this way. You can try, but I won't respond. I've got to go."

She left and walked back into the store. She would have to eat her lunch on the eighth floor in the back room instead of outdoors on her favorite bench, near Macy's. But at least she'd gotten rid of Marvin—for the time being. He walked down the subway steps, still feeling the sting of Naomi's gloved hand slap. Somehow, it felt good—as if, underneath everything, she still cared.

CHAPTER SEVEN

Lester Brock noticed Darrin's depression first. Like an undisciplined tenth grader, he began to oversleep on weekdays, leaving for work at the last possible moment. Consequently, he missed the traditional kiss on his mother's dementia-confused forehead—which deeply concerned his father. A week into Darrin's odd behavior, Velma still continued her regular habit of bowing her head to receive his kiss as he passed. Then, a few days after that, she stopped. A few days beyond that, Lester spoke up.

"I heard you whisper to your mother the other night that you might do something with Homeland Security, Son. Is that why you're acting like this?"

"No sir. And you're not supposed to know that, although I wanted to tell you."

"You know I never share your business, Son. But when you ignore your mother on your way out the door, that is my business. What's the problem?"

"I…I can't say. I can't."

"Well…can't you at least see that she no longer expects your morning kiss? Whatever's bothering you, she misses that from you."

Darrin backtracked like a movie in reverse, and kissed the top of Velma's head where her silver-grey hair was thickest. Then he quickly left the house before his father could ask any more questions. He reserved any weeping for his drive to work. And while tears filled his eyes, he replaced his usual habit of praying for the work day ahead with WINS 1010 AM News Radio—at high volume.

After he parked his car at the southern tip of Manhattan and took the subway to NYPD Manhattan South Precinct station, he slinked up to the second floor and past Inspector Lewis' office—finally barricading himself in his snug little cubicle. He hadn't done any actual work since the evening he visited Naomi. And if he had prayed *anything* at all since then, it was simply that Ralph Lewis wouldn't notice—and in addition, that no new information about any responsibility with Homeland Security would be forthcoming. He put his head on his desk and promptly fell asleep.

When five o'clock finally came, Darrin once again slinked past Inspector Lewis' office and proceeded to leave. He had barely eaten anything all day, due to a deep depression he hadn't begun to address, or even care to address. When he arrived at his Teaneck home an hour later, he passed by Lester and Velma as they sat in their usual chairs in the living room, and went straight up to his own room. Lester realized that things were at a crisis point, and he proceeded up the stairs. After a short hesitation, he finally knocked on Darrin's door.

"Darrin, please help me with dinner. Your mother has been waiting."

Darrin exhibited a teen-like behavior similar to his new oversleeping habit.

"No she hasn't. She hardly knows we're here. It's a joke, and she's a vegetable."

Lester chose to be gracious and not to respond to that remark, although it wounded him. He knew something was going on, and it was time to find out what it was.

"Will you let me in, Son?"

"No. Leave me alone."

Now we're getting somewhere, Lester thought. *At least he's letting me know something big is bothering him.* He decided to take a more aggressive approach, which was unusual for him.

"I'm coming in. If you expect to live in this house, you can't just ignore your mother and me."

In all his years, Darrin had rarely heard that tone from his father.

When he had, it was in response to childhood behaviors like teasing the nerdiest kid in class. He went over to the door and opened it. Lester could see that his eyes were red.

"So what's this all about?"

"What do you *think* it's about, Dad? Use your God-given discernment, for God's sake."

Lester hadn't heard that tone for a long time either.

"We…we…didn't raise you to use God's name that way."

"Fine, Dad. Are we finished now?"

"No…no."

Lester quickly glanced around Darrin's room. He hadn't been in it for a long time—maybe a year or even more. He was taken aback by its sparseness—just a few thick books on his night table and little else. He hazarded a guess.

"Is it that Kaplan girl?"

"Woman, Dad. She's a full grown Jewish woman. Yes sir. It's Naomi Kaplan. That's right. You win the prize. Naomi Kaplan," he repeated slowly. "Naomi beautiful Kaplan. I'm trying to forget her name."

"Well…"

Lester searched for words. He didn't know the details, and he hesitated to say anything he would regret later. He wanted to tell his son that the relationship never had a chance, because their backgrounds and religious perspectives were so different. Darrin knew well his father's *unequal yoking* conviction from Second Corinthians Chapter 6. But Lester could see his son was still in love, so he held himself back from lecturing him. Darrin waited for his father to say more.

"And?"

"And she left you? Or you left her? You had a fight?"

Darrin went over and sat on his bed. He betrayed impatience with the whole conversation, as teenagers often do with prying parents.

"No, Dad. You're way off. Her father had a stroke, and she feels like it was her fault…that it was because of…of…us. So she ended it. Just like that, she ended it. Just like that."

He snapped his fingers. Lester went over and sat next to him.

"Then…then maybe she isn't really in love with you."

Darrin turned to his father and vehemently shook his head, eyes closed.

"No, Dad. You don't get it. You *just* don't get it at all. She's madly in love with me. It's about her love for her father…and how much this hurts him."

Lester put his arm on his son's shoulder.

"I see. Well, you know, this tension is not unexpected. Even in Scripture…"

Darrin threw up his hands in frustration, knocking his father's arm off his shoulder in the process.

"I know, Dad. I know about that. You don't have to remind me of something you've told me since before I could understand what you were even *talking* about. I know. Maybe God is allowing this, because He knows it wouldn't work, *shouldn't* work like this."

His exasperation increased.

"But it's *more* than that. It's years and years of…of frankly, church history, anti-Semitism…which Naomi has brought up with me more than once."

His father understood that he was talking about the Church's superior attitude toward the Jews, and the view that it has replaced them as God's chosen. That was something Lester had made it his business to study.

"Yes, that too. That too. But when you get over your broken heart… and you will…what will you do then?"

"You know what, Dad? I can't think about that now. I can't think of anything….anything but Naomi…unfortunately."

"Don't lose your job over this, Darrin, especially with this latest assignment. That wouldn't be wise."

"Who cares about my job?"

His father became unusually direct.

"This is not a time to lose your job."

There was a pause.

"Do you understand me, Darrin? The timing would be unwise."

"I hear you."

"It will all work out. You'll see. Will you join us for dinner?"

"Yes. I will. I'm not hungry, but I will."

Darrin followed his father out of the room. As the living room came into view, he could see Velma sitting in her chair, her eyes fixed on the opposite wall. Lester went over and took her by the hand. He pulled her up and put his arm around her. Her response to him seemed mechanical, reflexive. As Darrin watched, the words *futile love* came to his mind. *It will never be returned*, his new cynicism informed him—*like my love for Naomi.*

Mechanical and reflexive continued to be the operative words through dinner—not only for Velma, but also for Darrin. And even though he had no natural appetite, his soul remained famished. He slurped his soup like a lazy adolescent, and nibbled on his roast chicken like an anorexic girl. Lester, on the other hand, tried to initiate some normal conversation.

"Did you know that your mother eats more when you're at the table?"

"No Dad, I didn't know that."

"It's true. Love creates an appetite, is what I think. She knows you've arrived home from your detective work, and she's glad to see you're safe. That's because she loves you, Darrin. She would always pray about your detective work when she could still talk. Do you remember?"

Darrin didn't want to talk about prayer, but he forced himself.

"Yes, Dad. I remember."

Darrin wasn't sure his mother felt anything about his safe arrival. In fact, as of recently, he was more and more convinced that she didn't know where Darrin had been before he came home—or even that he was there eating dinner with them. But he chose not to express any more of his cynical thoughts. They would just end up sounding like so many disrespectful remarks, spoken to one he actually deeply respected. Instead, he just continued to slurp and nibble. After dinner, he once again went up to his room to try to sleep through to sunrise. Maybe that way he would at least end up at work on time.

CHAPTER EIGHT

Marc Silver had changed—or at least it seemed like he was in the process of changing. Ever since the underworld boss Prima had been shot and killed by members of the Russian mafia—who had in turn been shot and killed by the police—Marc had become increasingly less selfish and more attentive. This manifested itself not only with his wife Lisa and his children Lindsey and Noah, but also during his workday. He no longer had the mafia corruption-connected privilege of parking his black Mercedes Benz on any street in Manhattan—without concerns about being ticketed—courtesy of powers higher up than Inspector Ralph Lewis. Consequently, he was now regularly taking public transportation. Gone was the sense that he owned the city, as he drove down Broadway in his shiny black Mercedes, steering with one finger like he was floating ten feet off the ground. But that was perfectly fine with him. He was alive, his marriage was stronger than ever, and even though his salary was lower, at least he had a job.

This unusually mild winter Manhattan day was a pleasant exception for Marc. Because he needed to be in the vicinity of Columbia University, around 116th Street and Broadway, he decided to take the car instead of the subway. He didn't like going to food establishments in that part of upper Manhattan—no matter what mode of transportation he took to get there—but he sometimes found it necessary as a part of his new lower-paying job responsibilities. As he drove through midtown Manhattan on this day, he felt more like the city owned him than that he owned the city. It was mid-afternoon, the traffic was unusually thick, and he had time to think. As he passed the vicinity of the New York Public Library, his father-in-law David Kaplan's old friends Stanley and Mahmoud came to mind. The three usually met regularly there Tuesdays and Thursdays. He figured they were probably in the library this Tuesday—in the Dewitt Wallace Periodical Room, to be specific, wasting the afternoon away. Normally, the thought would have vanished as he moved northward. But this was not the normal Marc Silver. This was the increasingly new Marc Silver, and his more thoughtful mind suddenly realized that Stanley and Mahmoud probably didn't know about David Kaplan's stroke. He swung over to the right lane as quickly as possible and double-parked in front of the Orvis store, across the street from the library, as he had typically done just a few months prior. Then he put his flashers on and dodged traffic to cross the street. He ran up the library steps and into the library, veering left toward the periodical room.

As soon as he entered the room, he recognized them—with their respective newspapers in disarray on the table before them. Out of breath, he raced over to them. Stanley looked up, and spoke in his usual loud whisper.

"Well if it isn't the loyal son-in-law of Mr. Disappearing Act. What brings you to this part of town, Silver? Free parking?"

Marc was still trying to catch his breath. He didn't have time for more than just a few words, and he was trying to get them out.

"I just came..."

Mahmoud was about to interrupt him, when he stopped him.

"No...I don't have time. I just came to tell you..."

Stanley jumped in.

"What's your hurry? Stay all day. Take a seat."

"No! I can't! I don't have free parking, and I'm double-parked. I just came to tell you..."

Mahmoud finally got a whispered word in edgewise, something he was unusually good at.

"You're liable to get a ticket. If you don't have an exemption, you'll get one for sure. That's how the police make their money, you know. I've seen it often from my cab window."

"Never mind that! I came to say that…"

He was still catching his breath, which gave Stanley one last chance to whisper loud and clear.

"No more parking big shot, eh? Well, you may not have all day, but neither do we. We have to get back to our newspapers. The world is falling apart, and we need to keep up with it. So if you have something to say…"

Marc lost his patience and his whisper.

"David Kaplan had a stroke. They've sedated him. He's at Maimonides in Brooklyn."

Three or four people shushed him, but he ignored them. Then he headed for the Dewitt Wallace Periodical Room doors, on the way to his car. Stanley shut his newspaper and rose up, pushing his chair back in his usual noisy way.

"Let's go."

"Yes. Our friend needs us," Mahmoud responded. They donned their winter coats and left almost as quickly as Marc Silver had. When Marc arrived at his car, there was a ticket on the windshield and a note along with it. He pulled out the note and read it.

I thought you realized your free ride was over, Silver. This is what a parking ticket looks like. You'd better hurry back to your car before we tow it. Sincerely, your friendly NYPD, Midtown Manhattan South Precinct.

He smiled and got into his Mercedes. Connecting with Stanley and Mahmoud had been the right thing to do. He was glad they knew about David Kaplan. For their part, David Kaplan's two friends left the library just in time to see Marc drive off. Stanley was already worn out, due to the fact that he was big, stout, and more or less limped with both legs.

"My knees are killing me. Kaplan isn't going anywhere. We can go tomorrow."

Mahmoud, on the other hand, was relatively fit—even in his seventies and bald like Gaza Strip sand.

"What are you talking about? By tomorrow, he could no longer be with us. Or they may put him in some home for helpless souls…who knows where. I want to see him now. I want to see him while he's still in the hospital. We should have gone yesterday. We'll take a cab. I will show you something."

He scanned the landscape and focused on the dotted array of yellow cabs. Then he lifted one hand and chose one of the hundreds of Palestinian gestures—a relatively new one called Rabia, first used during the Egyptian revolution of 2013. He pointed four fingers up and tucked his thumb in. Within seconds, a cab cut off three cars to arrive literally at his feet. The driver lowered the passenger window and Mahmoud began a conversation with him in Arabic. It went something like this. *An aged Palestinian he knew was visiting a relative in Brooklyn when he fainted of exhaustion near Maimonides Hospital. He was taken there, la samah Allah, God forbid. He—Mahmoud—who used to drive a cab, needed a favor. Would the driver take him, together with this old Jew—a retired doctor and not a very good one—to convince the other Jewish doctors to let the man go? And would the driver give him a deep discount?*

Mahmoud flashed his cab driver's license. Within seconds the cab whisked them away. The driver knew the story wasn't true. But it was a very good story, and Mahmoud was a fellow Palestinian cab driver—and an aged one at that.

Mahmoud watched the driver apply every trick of the trade to expedite the trip. He did all of the talking as he artfully navigated the Brooklyn Bridge, and Stanley could tell when either he or one of his landsmen was the subject of the monologue. "*Alyahudi,*" the driver declared disdainfully. When they arrived at the Maimonides Medical Center, Mahmoud was presented with the "discounted" bill. After a few minutes of friendly disagreement that Stanley seemed to understand every word of, a figure was arrived at, and the odd couple left the cab and entered the hospital doors.

David Kaplan was propped up in his bed when Stanley and Mahmoud finally walked into his room. Although his speech hadn't returned, except for a few indistinct words here and there, he no longer needed assistance breathing. When he wasn't sleeping, he could respond to commands. However, he happened to be sleeping when his friends approached him. Stanley responded with a finger over his mouth.

"Shhh."

Mahmoud, not to be outdone, whispered in Stanley's ear.

"What do you think, I'm stupid enough to wake him up?"

A nurse came in and walked in front of them. She went over and gently tapped on David Kaplan's shoulder.

"Mr. Kaplan, wake up. I think some friends have come to visit you."

He opened his eyes, and a crooked smile crossed his face. He tried to reach out with his good right arm, and slurred through an unintelligible few words. Stanley searched for his own words. He didn't want to endure the embarrassment of not understanding David.

"I never *could* understand a word you ever said, Kaplan. So you might as well give up. We'll do all the talking."

Mahmoud was trying to obscure his teary eyes with his left hand.

"We didn't know. Your son-in-law told us. We came right here. You are our brother. If we had known…"

David tried to pat his hand, which was resting on the bed. But he missed by a few inches. Mahmoud reached back the short distance and grabbed David Kaplan's hand.

"You are getting better and better, '*in sha'allh*.'"

Stanley agreed with him in Yiddish.

"Yes. *Got greyt*."

Hearing the affirmation in those particular two languages caused tears to fill David's eyes. The response wasn't so much to universal agreement across religious and cultural lines, as it was to these two specific dear friends expressing their love in these two disparate and emotion-drenched tongues.

Stanley did something completely counter to his typical brash and cynical behavior. He grabbed a tissue from the box on the food tray table and dabbed David's eyes with it. Mahmoud began to cry more openly.

"I cannot stand to see you like this, dear brother."

He leaned over and kissed both of David's cheeks, slowly moving from one to the other. After he withdrew, David tried to speak to him, but only mumbled syllables would come out. Stanley knew it was time to leave.

"David, I'm…I'm…not good at…saying things like *I love you*. At least, my son tells me that. So…"

He couldn't bear to continue expressing sentiments that would cause him to lose control, let alone break down.

"So…you'll never hear it from me! Just don't keep avoiding us…and get back to the library…soon."

He affectionately smacked David's hand and left the room, leaving Mahmoud standing there alone.

"He's a big baby. But you know that. I…I…I…love you, my brother."

Tears were streaming down his face.

"We will come back soon and you will be talking."

He left without another word. As he walked over to meet Stanley, it seemed to him for an instant like all the world's problems were solved. Such was the tender compassion that he felt for his Jewish friend. Stanley, on the other hand, seemed anxious as Mahmoud approached him.

"That'll be me someday. Do me a favor and don't visit me."

"What makes you think I would, my brother?" he teased. "I'm going home by the subway. We spent enough on that 'cheap' cab fare."

"I agree with you. I don't trust your Arab cabbie friends…the *gonafs*…thieves."

"They don't trust you either. See you tomorrow."

They went their separate ways. Inside Maimonides Hospital, David lay on his bed and thought about his two friends—and his two daughters. He didn't know whether he would ever get up off his sickbed. But he did know that he wanted to. He longed to surprise his two friends by showing up at the Dewitt Wallace Periodical Room—reminding Stanley to keep it down, and Mahmoud to not be so affectionate. As far as his daughters were concerned, he wanted to be there to remind them of their Jewish heritage in the face of Lisa's secularism and Naomi's romance with a Gentile man. As he inwardly resolved to get better, he once again drifted off to sleep.

CHAPTER NINE

Naomi finally received Marvin's promised text about two weeks after she had seen him during her lunch break. It was obvious that he had no intention of giving up his pursuit. And there seemed to be no way for her to stop him. Even if his aunt Ida could convince him to desist—which Naomi doubted—contacting her for help in the matter was out of the question. Naomi had scrupulously avoided her, ignoring the one text she had sent a few weeks earlier. She knew Aunt Ida would disapprove of her decision to break up with Darrin Brock, and she was in no mood for a lecture from her—especially because she might be persuaded by it. After all, her own heart had been fiercely resisting the break-up ever since she made the decision. But reversing course was out of the question, especially while her beloved father was recovering from his debilitating stroke. When she had entered his hospital room over the past week or so, his attempt at a smile let her know that he was glad to see her. But she also thought she detected a sadness that her subjective mind interpreted as displeasure with her romantic interest. Now more than ever, she wanted him to be pleased with her.

During her lunch break, Naomi looked down at Marvin's text. As usual, his grammar was inappropriately perfect—kosher, as he would say.

Will you meet me tomorrow? I have lunch money for both of us, and almost a job. And I love you. Only going to that Beth Yeishke place would separate us now. Not that you would ever go there, God forbid. I just mention it so you know that nothing will separate us. My mother agrees. Please respond.

Marvin had never before actually told her he loved her, let alone texted it on a phone. Yet it felt to her almost infantile that this socially challenged man would express himself this way—like a five year old wanting to marry his mother. The text was so upsetting that Naomi knew she had to find some way to stop Marvin's obsession with her. But how? She sat on a bench on 34th Street, outside of Macy's, and ate her dry cheese sandwich with her winter-gloved hand. *There must be a way,* she thought.

Suddenly, a brilliant idea emerged. She would inoculate herself. And the vaccine that would eliminate the risk of contracting Marvin's infection would be—of all things—one quick visit to this place called Beth Yeshua. One booster shot of this *House of Jesus*, as the name of the place was translated, and she would be free of Marvin forever! It was a small price to pay for such long-lasting protection.

When Naomi got back to work, she decided she didn't have the patience to wait until she got home to the empty house late that afternoon. She had to have the address and she had to have it *now*. Maybe they had a website. Even the most Orthodox synagogues in Brooklyn had websites these days. Certainly, this place had to have one. Her heart began to race as she glanced around the housewares department. There were a few customers in the aisles. She knew she had a very limited period of time to check the internet. She took a deep breath and began the most forbidden search she'd ever attempted—and at work, yet. It was one thing to check for a name in the store records, as she had the year before when she looked up Darrin Brock's name and address under the merchandise returns database, after he brought back Christmas gifts. It was quite another thing to search for something in the wider internet world. The access existed, because salespeople had to be able to check other dealers' prices, as well as communicate with wholesalers. But Beth Yeshua in Brooklyn wasn't a dealer—or a wholesaler—unless peddling cheap religion counted. She once again looked all around her. Her manager, Mrs. Lazar, was nowhere to be found. She reached for the mouse.

As she had almost a year earlier, Naomi's shaking hand clicked her way through the Google portal and onto the first page titled Beth Yeshua. There it was, at the top. She clicked on the website. It came up, all blue and white bordered graphics—the colors of Israel, God forbid. *Beth Yeshua Messianic Jewish Synagogue, Brooklyn, New York. Jews, as well as non-Jews, who have come to believe that Yeshua (Jesus) is the Messiah of Israel.* Naomi flinched in the face of those stark words. Perhaps she should skip the vaccine after all, and risk Marvin's harassment for the rest of her life—or give up, give in, and marry him. So what if his kisses sometimes stunk of oily sardines mixed with decaying teeth? On the other hand, maybe one visit would be worth it. It would be over and done within an hour or so—or even less—maybe a lot less. After all, who said she had to do more than cross the threshold to be free of Marvin forever?

For the first time, Naomi began to think seriously about actually entering a house dedicated to the one whose name most of her neighbors would not even allow to pass their lips—or, like Marvin, would substitute the Yiddish slang word Yeishke when they spoke it. She knew it would take planning, and even with that, it might still be impossible to accomplish. The synagogue—if it could actually be called that—was located in the Midwood section of Brooklyn, near the Midwood Press, where her father volunteered teaching school children about the Linotype machine he used to work at the *New York Times*. And that was several miles from her house. Why would Marvin have even mentioned the danger of visiting Beth Yeshua for their Shabbat service, when he knew she could never walk that far on the seventh day of the week? He must have thought she had been so defiled by her relationship with Darrin that she was now capable of *anything*—even taking the subway or bus on the Shabbat. But now, as she sat staring at the computer screen, she began pondering the distance dilemma herself. She realized that if her plan was to be executed at all, it had to include a two-step journey. And that, in turn, would require an observant Jewish third party in Midwood, or close to it—which, even if she found a willing host, would require subterfuge—if not outright lying.

There was only one person who might know an observant family in the Midwood section of Brooklyn, and that was Aunt Ida. She had been there for Naomi during her painful crisis several months earlier, after Darrin was shot. But now, since she had received the probing text from her weeks earlier, Naomi had come to wish Aunt Ida didn't know her and she didn't know Aunt Ida. And yet, it dawned on her that Aunt Ida might be the only person who could solve her present dilemma. Indeed, she seemed to know someone in every Brooklyn neighborhood. This was remarkable for a Reform Jew from Long Island. But Aunt Ida wasn't a typical Reform Jew. She was, in fact, extraordinary. She seemed to know *everyone* from *everywhere*, and everyone seemed to know her. Naomi suddenly realized that, whereas seconds before she wished she was one of the few people who *never* knew Aunt Ida, she was now once again thankful that she was one of the many ones who *did*.

Naomi's mind multitasked as she waited on the next customer, an easy Cuisinart food processor sale. Her mind disengaged from the moment, and the customer. She would call Aunt Ida that evening, and ask her if she knew an observant family in Midwood. As she mechanically keyed in the sale, she couldn't help but smile. The customer—another one of those fortunate attractive young brides—smiled back at her, the typical friendly Macy's employee. However, Naomi's smile actually came from somewhere else completely—from the memory of the Applebee's in Newark, where Aunt Ida had come over to her side of the table to comfort her. With the tender memory of that moment, the intentionally buried feelings for her beloved Darrin swept uncontrollably through her for the first time in several days. Her smile turned to a short inappropriate giggle, and then manifested in a small tear falling from her right eye. The customer stared at her as she received the Macy's bag containing the Cuisinart.

"Are you okay?"

"I think so. You'll love the food processor."

"Oh, do you have one?"

"Oh, yes, I love mine," she lied. "It processes amazingly." She would ask God's forgiveness for the sin of bearing false witness later. At least the customer was happy.

"Well, I hope I cry tears of joy for *mine*. I mean, I hope my new husband does, since I'll be cooking his favorite meals. Maybe he'll cry when I chop onions in it." A broad smile crossed her face as well.

Naomi let out another short giggle. She *knew* it! She could always spot the new brides. Perhaps someone would spot her someday. Although at this rate, she doubted it. She waited until the happy customer took her package and receipt and disappeared down the aisle. Then she let out a long exhausted sigh. *I can't wait until I get out of here*, she thought. *The sooner I plan the trip to that place, the better I'll feel. I hope Marvin doesn't bother me again until then.*

As of the subway ride home and her arrival at her silent-as-a-morgue Brooklyn house, Marvin hadn't sent another text. Before heating up her meager meal, consisting of some leftover chicken soup and noodle kugel, she took another deep breath and called Aunt Ida's number. The phone rang twice before she answered.

"Where the *hell* have you been? Why didn't you answer my text?"

Naomi decided to lie again. Was she leaving the Torah and everything it taught her behind, now that David Kaplan was lying helpless at the Maimonides Medical Center?

"I…I…don't believe I got the text, Aunt Ida."

"Really! That's a new one. Well, for your information, I texted you at least once to tell you that you're crazy to end it with that man. Since you didn't respond, I've decided it's your life to ruin. So what is it you want?"

Aunt Ida could be painfully blunt.

"Um…Aunt Ida…can we go to that Applebee's again…the one in Newark? I mean, I want to tell you everything."

"Everything?"

"Well, yes. Everything."

"You mean the unkosher traif Applebee's? The one with cheeseburgers and bloody meat?"

"Yes, that one…in the same booth, if possible."

"I see. Do me a favor. This time, bring your own kugel, instead of depending on me to bring it."

Aunt Ida was referring to the kugel she took from a friend's house and brought to their last outing at Applebee's. Naomi looked at the noodle dish frying in the pan. Was Aunt Ida some sort of prophetess, like Deborah in the book of Judges? She held her cell phone a few inches from her face and glanced at the time on its tiny screen.

"Could we go now?"

"Now? But…it's almost 9:00 p.m. By the time we get there…"

"Well…if they're open, that is."

"They're open, honey. They do that for the *goyim* on the second shift. I'm coming. Give me a half hour."

Before Aunt Ida could hang up, Naomi decided she had to clear her conscience.

"Aunt Ida…just so you know, I wasn't telling the truth about your text."

"I'm not *that* stupid. Do me a favor and tell me the truth, the whole truth, and nothing but the truth when we meet."

With that, she hung up. Naomi spent the next half hour alternately relieved she could tell Aunt Ida everything and regretting the idea of telling her *anything*. But by the time Aunt Ida arrived to pick her up, she felt a bit more relieved than regretful.

During the trip to Newark, Aunt Ida—who was convinced that Naomi's whole purpose in calling her was to discuss Darrin Brock—used her considerable oratorical gifts to remind her that Darrin was her last best chance. Naomi was glad to be sitting in the front seat, where the reflection of Aunt Ida's eyes in the rear view mirror couldn't bore into hers. When they finally parked in the Applebee's lot, Aunt Ida finished her campaign speech just as she pressed the button on the ignition.

"Well, I think I've covered every angle. Now we can eat something while you tell me how much you agree with me. Let's go."

Naomi got out of the car and followed her across the parking lot and into the restaurant. There in the distance was the same booth they sat in the last time—*empty*.

"We'll take that one." Aunt Ida pointed as she collared the hostess. After they sat down and Aunt Ida ordered her usual cheeseburger and flavored iced tea, Naomi unfolded her napkin with the warm kugel inside. Suddenly, she was startled by a sharp cracking sound. She instinctively jumped in her seat and looked up. Was it a gun? No, it was Aunt Ida, slapping the table. Her eyes burned Naomi's.

"Wh…wh…what's the matter?"

"I'm not arranging a marriage for you, honey. You have something to say about the matter. All the way here, you didn't say one damn thing… like a mummy."

"I'm…I'm sorry. The reason I didn't respond to your text…"

"For God's sake, Naomi! It's not about the stupid text! Do you think you're still a little girl, that you can play with hearts like they're toys in a child's playpen? Is that what you think? *Is it*?"

"Aunt Ida…I…I didn't come here to talk about that."

"Well, we're not talking about anything else until we talk about *that*! Is it because your father would disapprove? You know what? You deserve my nephew Marvin. You're Daddy's little girl, just like he's Mommy's little boy."

She leaned in to her and pronounced the next two words quietly but deliberately.

"Grow up!"

Naomi didn't expect this attack. Aunt Ida or not, she jumped to her own defense.

"Not that it's your business, but if you must know, yes. I broke my father's heart, and I had to end it with Darrin. When my beloved Abba fully wakes up, I'll…"

Aunt Ida raised her voice. She didn't care who was around.

"What, is your father your boyfriend, that you call him your beloved? Darrin is your beloved, if anyone is! Your father, on the other hand, is… is…your father. And you're forty-nine, by the way. And guess what. Before this is all over, you'll end up breaking *Abba's* heart *anyway*… when he sees how unhappy you are…which he will when he recovers from the stroke."

She started to mumble to herself, as if sharing the information with Naomi was a waste of time.

"A man who loves you like few men love…a man who did nothing wrong except stir up your misplaced guilt. So now you throw him under the bus?"

Naomi, who heard every word, defended herself.

"I thought about it. I thought about it *a lot!*"

"I *bet* you did. Your father would be ashamed of you. *Ashamed!*"

Naomi sat up and almost shouted.

"Aunt Ida, my father knew that Torah tells us not to marry outside the faith. He would *never* accept that. And now I see that I can't either."

"You don't understand, do you? You *really* don't understand. Yes, your father couldn't bring himself to condone the marriage. I'll give you that. But he *never* would have treated Darrin like you treated him. So okay, don't marry him if you don't want to. It's your life. But I still say, it would have worked out."

"I had no choice."

"Choice! Choice! What do you know about choices?"

Aunt Ida put her hand over her eyes. Naomi found herself beginning to shake, and tried to calm herself down.

Why am I getting so worked up, she thought. *I know I'm right.* She tried to quiet herself.

"Aunt Ida, could we start again? I didn't ask you here to talk about Darrin. I need to talk to you about something else—something that will get your nephew Marvin off my back for good. I think you can help me."

All of a sudden, Aunt Ida's voice sounded submerged, under water, buried in the distant past, beyond Naomi's present dilemma with Marvin.

"Choices. Choices. Ah yes, I know about choices."

"What are you talking about, Aunt Ida?"

"I know *all* about choices. When I was in my twenties, I thought I had no choice. But I was wrong. I was very young, and I was very wrong. Believe me, I had a choice."

"I don't understand."

"There was someone who loved me, Naomi, like Darrin loves you. Just that way. And believe it or not, he was Orthodox, just like you are. My family was Reform, very Reform. My parents didn't think much of Meyer."

She betrayed a thin smile.

"I used to call him Mickey…Mickey Mouse, just to tease him. But oh God, I loved him. I loved that man. He was gorgeous, by the way, with wavy wild black hair under his black kippah, and deep blue eyes. As a single man with a single woman, he wasn't supposed to kiss me, or even touch me. You know all about *that*. But he did, more than once. *Believe* me he did. And was he great at it! I can still taste it. Then he would ask forgiveness. I loved when he did that, because I knew he would be asking forgiveness again for the same sin…and I looked forward to that confession…if you know what I mean."

Naomi blushed. She was familiar with that feeling. Aunt Ida continued.

"And he was more tolerant, more open to different people, more truly compassionate than my Socialist agnostic father was. As a matter of fact, he was more like your father...and like Darrin. He wanted me to make *Teshuva*, become observant. But he didn't force me. He *never* forced me. He was gentle that way. He was willing to wait, to let us consider everything. But my father used to belittle him...behind his back, and sometimes to his face. He hated him and everything he represented."

Aunt Ida's voice lowered even more.

"Then, just like your father, my father got sick. He got lung cancer from smoking two, three packs a day. And I was the oldest daughter. I knew I had to help take care of him. Of course, I loved my dad. As a child, I always wanted his approval, but he never quite gave it to me. He couldn't ever seem to say *I love you* to me. He was just that way. He cared about justice, and I was proud of him for that. But I could never quite bring myself to tell him I was proud of him, when I didn't think he was proud of me."

Aunt Ida leaned in, and looked straight into Naomi's eyes.

"When it seemed like he was declining, I couldn't take the pressure anymore. I just stopped taking calls from Meyer, stopped answering the doorbell, stopped communicating. There were no cell phones back then, no texts or emails. He wrote me several tear-stained letters, but I didn't answer them. I was such an idiot that I did something only the worst kind of coward would do. I had an Orthodox girlfriend of mine tell Meyer I couldn't see him anymore. That was so rotten of me! You see, I wasn't the Aunt Ida you see today. No. *Now* if I have something to say, I say it myself. Then, I was under the shadow of my father's opinion of me...or what I *believed* was his opinion. I wasn't my own person, just like you're not your own person."

Naomi tried to ignore that last comment. Aunt Ida leaned back in the seat and stared at her now-cooling cheeseburger. Naomi waited, and then spoke haltingly.

"So...what happened to...to Meyer?"

"Oh...Meyer. What do you think happened? He married a plain-looking girl who wore one of those *sheitel* wigs and had a zillion children."

"Oh."

"And me...I married Melvin, may he rest in peace. Melvin. I never loved him. *Oy vey.*"

She put her hand to her mouth.

"Don't tell anyone I said that."

For the first time in Naomi's experience, Aunt Ida's eyes moistened. She dabbed them with her Applebee's napkin. Her voice broke up.

"But...I want Mr. Right for *you!* I thought it might be Marvin. But then I realized you were way too good for him. You're forty-nine, Naomi. It's time. It's past time. And as far as Darrin is concerned, I know there are challenges. But can't God do miracles? That's what you believe, isn't it?"

Naomi was so overwhelmed by Aunt Ida's story, and so full of conflicting emotions, that she didn't know how to respond. She just sat perfectly still and allowed Aunt Ida's life-long regrets to expose her own loneliness like the scan of an MRI. Finally, she decided to change the subject to the reason she wanted to see Aunt Ida in the first place. She cautiously began.

"Aunt...Aunt...Ida...can I...can I...change the subject? I need a family...an Orthodox family in Midwood to stay with over a Shabbat. Do you know any?"

Aunt Ida paused for a second, and then snapped out of her reverie.

"Yes, of course. I know several. What for?"

Naomi shared her strategy to inoculate herself from Marvin's interest in her. As she listened, Aunt Ida's mouth began to shape itself into an ever-broadening smile.

"You would actually go to one of those messianic places just to stop him from bothering you?"

"Yes. It means that much to me."

She nodded her head for emphasis.

"This I have to see to believe."

"*Please* don't tell them my reason for staying with them. I'll just tell them I don't feel up to going to synagogue with them, and I'll take a walk to the...to that place."

"I see. More deception."

"I suppose so. But I only have to walk across the threshold and then back out. Maybe I'll catch up with them at their synagogue after that."

"I think I understand."

"Will you help me?"

Aunt Ida thought for a few seconds.

"Why not? Of course. Now that you've entered the house of cheeses and meat, why not enter the house of Jesus and *meshumeds*, traitors, for a few minutes. In both cases, you don't have to actually try anything."

Naomi chuckled softly.

"Thank you, Aunt Ida. Thank you!"

She put her hand over Aunt Ida's. She didn't mind the remnants of cheese and meat that might still be on her fingers. It was a small price to pay to solve her dilemma.

CHAPTER TEN

Darrin Brock's depression hadn't improved. If anything, it had deepened. His acceptance of the fact that Naomi was gone had become his sad new reality. Perhaps his father was right. God had stepped in to put a stop to what was not His will in the first place. In spite of the fact that the Lord seemed to have drawn Naomi to the hospital when Darrin was in the throes of a coma—and then awakened Darrin when he heard her voice—He now seemed to have closed the door on any future contact between Darrin and Naomi. The Lord certainly works in strange ways, came the unoriginal thought.

Darrin rarely ate lunch out. However, on this particular day he decided that he would drown his sorrows with some genuine comfort food, washed down with a Dr. Brown's cream soda. He sat in one of the green booths at Ben's Deli, facing a Reuben sandwich dripping with non-dairy cheese, and packed with corned beef. Ben's was famous for them. It felt strange to be alone at the kosher establishment, but he knew why he had chosen to go there. It wasn't for the fat-laden cuisine. He wanted to be where he and Naomi were, to sit in a booth like the one they sat in when they asked each other all those questions about each other's faith and families. Now he wished that he hadn't chosen Ben's, whatever the reason. His loneliness was only exacerbated by the Yiddish being spoken at various volumes, floating around his straight-as-straw blonde hair like a joyous bride and groom in a Marc Chagall painting. He picked up the thick sandwich and was about to take a big bite, when his cell phone went off. It was Inspector Ralph Lewis—just about the last name Darrin wanted to see on his screen. But he was on the clock, so it was only right to answer. He waited through three rings, so he would appear busy. Then he answered. Lewis' voice boomed through the speaker.

"Where are you? Down the street, or across town?"

He was maybe a ten-minute walk away at most, but he didn't want to rush back.

"I'm sort of near…but not that close."

"Sort of near? What the hell does that mean? I bet you're right around the corner. See you in ten minutes."

How did the inspector know? Darrin was almost tempted to look around for human intelligence or a hidden camera. Just then, his waitress passed by with a suspicious look on her face. Maybe it was her—or maybe she was just busy serving customers.

"Could you box this up?"

"Sure. It looks like you've got somewhere to be."

He repeated what he'd said to Inspector Lewis. "Sort of."

"I'll be right back."

She made good on her word. He grabbed the box, paid his bill, and left, taking all of the ten minutes to get to the precinct station. He climbed the steps to the second floor and proceeded to Lewis' office, doggy bag in hand. The door was open, and he walked in. Inspector Lewis was standing behind his desk.

"Sit down."

He pointed to the chair on the other side of the desk. Darrin didn't want to sit in the low chair, but he had no choice. Besides, he didn't have anything to plead for on this particular day, so the low chair wouldn't be such a big deal. Lewis walked back and forth behind his desk, eying Darrin intermittently.

"Brock, do you know what a person of interest is?"

"Yes, sir. It's someone who isn't necessarily guilty. But he…or she, as the case may be…isn't necessarily innocent either."

"Very clever, Brock. Very clever. Remember when I showed you the map of the landmarks? And you agreed to get involved with the radical threat thing?"

What with 9/11 and every Jihadist attack on the homeland after that, Darrin thought it was a bit odd for Inspector Lewis to use that expression...*the radical threat thing*.

"I do, sir. But I didn't exactly..."

Lewis stopped and leaned over his messy desk, his head bowed and his eyes focused frowningly forward on Darrin—at least to the extent that eyes can frown.

"You did, and don't try to get out of it now, Brock."

Darrin's eyes diverted sideways.

"Yes, sir."

The inspector stood up straight.

"Well...there's been chatter...of course there's always chatter. It doesn't mean a damn thing. But when I was asked by Homeland Security if there are any detectives...and I mean *any* detectives...that I trust... and that know New York like the back of their hand..."

He slapped the back of his hand several times.

"...that are in *my* department, right here in Midtown Manhattan... *my* department, Brock...who do you think I recommended?"

Darrin was squirming in the low chair as Lewis challenged him.

"Are you listening?"

He moved to the front of the desk and towered over Darrin.

"You have two choices, Brock. You could do next to *nothing* in this department, which is what you're doing now, and don't think I don't know it...with the exception of visiting that little Jewish boy...what's his name?"

"Natan."

"Right. Nice name. *Or...*"

He put his hand on Darrin's shoulder.

"*Or*...you could have the thrill ride of your life...like the good old days...chasing the five mobsters in the eighties...remember that? And more exciting than the Russian mob. Are you ready for this, Brock? Are you *ready*?"

Darrin tried to get up, but Lewis held him down with the hand that was on his shoulder.

"Don't get up until you decide."

"Decide what, sir?"

"Decide to stop moping over that plain Jane Jewish girl…what's done is done…and help me here with some *persons of interest*. I mean *really* help me, by going after some real characters…some wild and crazy individuals…real *out there*…fascinating…young…zealots, so to speak."

He spoke of them like he was referring to famous celebrities instead of ruthless radical Muslims. Darrin decided to set the record straight, and then ask a few key questions.

"Her name is Naomi. Naomi Kaplan, and she's not plain. She's extraordinarily beautiful."

"The eyes of the beholder, Brock. And it's time to stop beholding her and move on."

"I'm trying, sir. But she is beautiful. Period. May I ask another question?"

Inspector Lewis closed his eyes and nodded. Darrin had just one question.

"Is it dangerous? Because I just got shot, as you know, and…"

"You're damn right it's dangerous. But don't you see it, Brock? Don't you understand? You *need* dangerous right now. It'll get you out of that shell you're in. Oh, and just in case you're wondering, we'll have your back."

Darrin squinted as he looked up at Lewis, who was haloed in the ceiling fluorescent light.

"Thanks…but…"

"You're welcome. Stay seated."

He walked around to the desk, sat down, and grabbed a piece of paper off the top of a pile.

"Omar Shehadulah…it has a nice ring to it, doesn't it? Omar Shehadulah…from Pakistan…that is, his parents are. We know where he's staying…in Queens, of all places, for God's sake. They think there has been some texting. But then it seems to come to nothing…or maybe not, if you get what I mean. All very *spy versus spy* stuff. I'll have the Homeland Security guys train you next week, and then you'll interview him. Meanwhile, keep your eyes open."

"I don't know. I just got through this whole thing with the Russians…"

Ralph Lewis reached so far over the desk that Darrin felt they would touch noses.

"Now you listen to me, Brock! If you don't get over that whole thing, you'll lose your nerve and disappear into the woodwork. You're my best man…well, *one* of my best. New York City needs you."

Darrin felt like putting in for his resignation right then and there. But just as he was ready to open his mouth, his father's admonition echoed in his inner ear—*Don't lose your job.* Inspector Lewis sat down in his chair and leaned back. Darrin could tell that the conversation was wrapping up. Then, all of a sudden, Lewis saw the bag from Ben's Deli in Darrin's hand.

"What's that? Is that lunch? It smells good. Is it a Reuben?"

"Yes, sir"

"Split what's left with me? I'm starved."

"Well, actually, you can have the whole thing."

"That's even better."

Darrin took his sandwich out of the bag and put it on the napkin it came with, along with the lone pickle. He placed it on Inspector Lewis' desk. The inspector pointed his finger at him.

"All right. Tell someone out there to run and get me a can of Dr. Brown's."

Darrin nodded.

"Okay. Well…enjoy your lunch."

"Believe me, I will. Homeland Security will be in touch. I can guarantee you that."

With that, Darrin left the room and headed for his cubicle. As he passed the rectangular windows looking over 35th Street, his detective sense kicked in. Instinctively, he walked over to one of them, and peered out. Was it paranoia, like his ridiculous notion that he was being spied on by the waitress at Ben's Deli? Or was there someone actually out there, casing the precinct building? Maybe Ralph Lewis was right. Maybe his brush with death at the hands of the Russian mafia had caused unseen damage that was distorting his perceptions and affecting his work. *Just another reason to quit,* he thought. *But then again, maybe I'd just be quitting on life. Is that what I want? Is it what God wants?*

He walked back to his cubicle and sat down. He took a picture out of his drawer that he had only recently taken off his cubicle wall.

Naomi looked up at him, caught in the middle of an infectious giggle. She seemed like a specter from the distant past, a forty-nine-year-old translucent shadow that had passed from his life and into the darkening night—never to return.

Chapter Eleven

On an unusually mild late winter Friday morning in February, as Naomi Kaplan packed her small red plaid suitcase, it suddenly dawned on her that she didn't have to account to her father for her whereabouts for the next few days. Although the reason for that fact was a sad one—her father's stroke and subsequent hospitalization—a slight smile formed on her face, as the thought crossed her mind that for the first time she could actually choose to go anywhere without accounting to anyone. Did it take her a full forty-nine years to finally grow up? *Maybe this is what growing up is all about…along with falling in love*, she mused. Just then, a sharp pain pierced her heart, causing it to skip a beat, and her eyes began to tear involuntarily.

"Stop that!" she commanded herself.

One person she still had to account to in life was Mrs. Lazar, her manager at Macy's. She had asked for the day off, and she'd gotten it. That would allow her to take the bus to the Midwood section of Brooklyn, to the observant home of…*what were their names?*

She reached into the small black pocketbook that sat on her bed next to her suitcase, and pulled out a folded piece of lined paper. She sat on the bed as she unfolded it.

"Avram and Leah Milstein."

She spoke out loud as she stared at the address and phone number.

"I can't believe I'm doing this. I hope I can pull it off. I *have* to pull it off."

Aunt Ida had prepared the way for an arrival by late morning. Naomi wasn't sure just what she had told the Milsteins, but apparently it had worked. They were expecting her. Although she had a phone number in her possession, she had been told that there was no reason to call beforehand.

"Just show up," Aunt Ida had told her. "They're expecting you for lunch…and to celebrate Shabbat with them, including the morning service at their synagogue. You'll have to deal with that part of it. Lie if you have to, and you'll be fine."

Naomi wished Aunt Ida hadn't given her that last piece of advice. She grabbed her red plaid suitcase and winter coat and left the house, headed for the Midwood section of Brooklyn. She road the bus to within a block of the Milstein brownstone, and got off.

"Well, this is a pleasant-enough block," she remarked to herself after she got off the bus.

Midwood was settled by the Dutch in 1652. They named the town after the wooded area it had become known for. They called the village nearest to it Breukelen—known as Brooklyn today. The English acquired both Midwood and Brooklyn in 1664. Midwood remained largely rural and undeveloped until it was annexed to Brooklyn in the early 1890's— about ten years after the Kaplan menorah first sat in their ancestral home in Kiev. A strong Jewish presence developed there in the first part of the twentieth century, and it continues to the present day—although many other cultures poured into Midwood in the 1970's and 1980's.

"Avram and Leah Milstein," Naomi whispered to herself as she climbed the few stone steps to their door. Leah was waiting for her, and opened it before she had a chance to knock. Naomi immediately noticed that Leah was at least ten years her junior. Dressed in a mid-length black skirt and beige long-sleeved blouse, she definitely didn't seem Chassidic—or as conservative looking as Chaya Mendel. She wore no sheitel wig, but instead had a smart curly brown short haircut, which framed a particularly attractive face. And she wore a subtle pink shade of lipstick. She reached out her hand toward Naomi as she confidently greeted her.

"I'm Leah. You must be Naomi. It's very nice to meet you."

Naomi entered the house. She was immediately struck by the tasteful high-end interior decoration. The quality of the furnishings was unquestionable. Everything radiated wealth—even the antique Jewish artifacts enclosed in a large glass hutch, which all seemed to be either solid gold or at least covered with it. As she stood there and gazed around the room, Naomi couldn't help but comment.

"This is a very beautiful room."

"Well…it's my husband Avram. He has the decorator's taste. Can I show you to your room? You can freshen up. And then if you'd like, we can have some lunch. Can I take your bag?"

"Oh…no. I have it."

The further they moved into the interior of the house, the more intimidated Naomi felt. Each room seemed more palatial than the last. Who knew that a Brooklyn brownstone could look like this on the inside? When they finally entered the guest bedroom at the top of the stairs, Naomi involuntarily gasped. The appointments were exquisite, all silk and polished walnut, with a spotless, seemingly brand-new plush beige rug and richly adorned pastel blue and yellow papered walls that seemed worthy of *Home and Gardens*. And the Sleep Number bed was queen size. Just looking at it almost made her doze off.

"My, my…"

"Yes, even this room is my husband's idea. I call him my Renaissance man. He's an oncologist, in addition to being a talmudic scholar of sorts. I think you'll really like him. He'll be home before Shabbat starts, of course."

"Of course."

Leah smiled, and Naomi remarked to herself that it seemed like a lovely smile.

"I…I look forward to meeting him. My…father…may God bless and keep him…is also a rabbinic scholar…a very knowledgeable one."

She wanted to say that David Kaplan was the most knowledgeable rabbinic scholar in the world. But that would have been inappropriate, considering the situation. Besides, she could hardly keep her voice from cracking as she spoke of the one who was even now in a hospital bed at the Maimonides Medical Center, and headed for who knows what kind of care facility after that—that is, if he wasn't yet ready to come home to live with his devoted daughter. Leah, however, didn't notice the emotion in Naomi's voice, and barely noticed the comment about David Kaplan.

After Naomi "freshened up," as Leah had put it, she came down for lunch, which consisted of tuna salad on a bed of lettuce and slices of toasted buttered challah—and after the short blessing before the meal, small talk. Leah grinned as she surveyed Naomi's face. Until now, she had been too preoccupied with greeting her and showing her the guest room to focus on her appearance.

"You're...what...in your late forties?"

Naomi's fork stopped in mid-air.

"Y..y...yes. That's right. I'm...I'm...forty...forty...forty-nine."

Leah's eyes lowered to take in Naomi's bare ring finger.

"You're not all that bad looking. So are you widowed or divorced?"

Naomi was taken aback by Leah's frank, if not stark, assessment.

"Um...neither. I've never been married."

"Oh. Then you're one of those observant...you know..."

"I'm sorry. I don't know. Um...what?"

Leah mouthed the next word without breathing, although there was no one there to overhear them.

"Lesbians."

"What? I don't understand."

Leah spoke out loud.

"Lesbians. Lesbians. There's a whole group of them in Brooklyn. But since I guess you're one of them, you must know that. Personally, I can't see it. But if you are...I mean, Ida is pretty progressive...and you being single at your...well...you know. Personally, I don't approve of it, but... live and let live, as even a few of our more observant rabbis are telling us these days. Not at our synagogue, of course, but..."

Naomi, who had been staring at her, blushed. Her fork, which had been holding onto her loosening grip for dear life, dropped with a crash onto her gold-trimmed plate.

"Oh! I'm so sorry! I hope I didn't damage it."

Leah didn't even blink. Instead, she tried to put Naomi at ease.

"Listen, who am I to judge? My husband, however, may be a different story. As I said, he knows what the Torah teaches on such a subject. So you may not want to mention your sexual preference in his presence…if you don't mind."

Naomi's face now became redder than Passover horseradish. Finally, her tongue followed her grip's example, and loosened enough to allow her to speak.

"No…I would never…It's not Torah…I have…had, that is…I *had* a wonderful boyfriend. Very wonderful, that is. I mean, I am…that is, I *was*…very attracted to him…*very* attracted. He's *very* attractive, that is…to me."

She couldn't believe she had spoken about being attracted to Darrin—and for the first time since David Kaplan's stroke, yet. But considering the circumstances, she felt the need to mention it. Consequently, her suppressed deep-as-a-well love and longing for him began to surface.

Down! Stop! Enough! Stop it!

Again, Leah noticed nothing.

"*Had.* I see. So, at your age you still have no prospects?"

Naomi took a deep breath and shook her head no.

Leah let out an almost imperceptible giggle before she responded.

"I won't ask what happened to your intended. If your ex-boyfriend is alive and well and a good Jew, he should have recognized his responsibility and asked you to marry him. Perhaps he did, and perhaps you declined the offer? I must say, I only hope for you that you don't die an *alta moid*, an old maid…not that it's any of my business."

Now Naomi tried to hold onto her fork for dear life. Then she tried to respond as graciously as she could, although it didn't end up coming out that way.

"Um, no…I guess not. I guess it's not."

"Of course, I wouldn't wish that on *any* Jewish woman."

Leah, who hadn't noticed much that was going on inside of Naomi, did now notice that she was uncomfortable. Actually, she had been too shocked—and frankly offended—to even touch her tuna salad and toasted challah, even though she was so hungry that she normally would have had a second helping by now. Much of her just wanted to call this whole venture a mistake and walk out the front door. Leah, on the other hand, chose to change the direction of the conversation.

"Well, you will love our synagogue. It's the friendliest group of people…sort of modern Orthodox. There's a lot of young couples…my age and younger…and so many eligible men…maybe even a few in their late forties, seeing that your boyfriend has left you…or whatever."

Naomi realized that at least one thing about Leah reminded her of Aunt Ida—the matchmaking part.

"Well, I'm not looking right now, what with my father recovering from a stroke. I don't know if I told you that."

"I think you did. We'll say a *Mi-Shebeirach* prayer for him at synagogue tomorrow."

Realizing that she wouldn't be at the service—at least if things worked out the way she planned—Naomi did a little subject-changing herself.

"We also have a very nice synagogue. It's sort of more traditional Orthodox. I like it that way. It's…it's got more people…my age…and older."

"That's very nice."

The more the lunch continued, the smaller the talk got—until Naomi finally left for her room while Leah finished clearing the table. She lay down on her bed, exhausted. She didn't come downstairs until Leah called her down to meet Avram, just before dinner. When Naomi reached the bottom of the stairs and finally met him, he ended up looking something like she expected—that is, after having met Leah. His beard was trimmed like a fastidious CPA's—one whose intention is to divert attention from it. His dark-brown hair was curly, the analogous opposite to Darrin Brock's straight blonde hair—with every wiry strand in place. He was thin and fit, and wore a black suit that looked more like her brother-in-law Marc Silver's than her father's traditional loosely draped black garb. And his yarmulke was small, tightly knit, and aqua-marine— the sign of the modern Orthodox. Leah introduced him to Naomi.

"My husband Avram, Naomi. Naomi, my husband Avram."

The two shook hands, which, while not acceptable among Chassidic Jews, is among modern Orthodox Jews. Avram escorted Naomi to the living room and invited her to sit on one of two plush luxurious taupe couches. Leah excused herself and went to finish preparing dinner. After the lunch fiasco, Naomi wasn't quite ready to be in Leah's presence again. But part of her wanted Leah there so she didn't have to converse alone with Avram. At first glance, he seemed even more intimidating than

Leah—if that were possible. Avram sat down on the other couch and began his own version of small talk.

"Leah tells me you want to try out our synagogue before you consider moving to Midwood. Believe me, you won't be disappointed."

So that's what Aunt Ida must have told them. Naomi crossed her legs and tensed up.

"Well, that's not exactly..."

She quickly decided that it wouldn't be a good idea to address Aunt Ida's lie just yet.

"...exactly...I haven't fully decided yet...what with my father in a bit of a...a coma."

"A *bit*?"

Naomi suddenly remembered that Avram was a doctor.

"I mean, he *is*. So I...I don't plan...that is, at this time..."

Avram cut in.

"So why are you here?"

Apparently, he was a pretty fast thinker, which forced Naomi to think just as fast.

"I'm...I'm shopping for the future. My father said to me before his stroke...um...he told me..."

Naomi lowered her voice an octave and raised a finger declaratively.

"Naomi, we must move to Midwood so we can find you a husband at the synagogue there."

She switched back to her normal voice.

"You know, like Avraham of blessed memory, asking his servant to find a bride for Isaac among his relatives. That's my father. He...he thinks of everything."

She let out a nervous giggle to conceal her brazen lie. But then she wondered if perhaps the lie was exposed by the giggle instead.

"Then...then he had a stroke...my poor father, that is."

Avram glared into her eyes like an oncologist searching for cancer cells.

"Well...you're honest if you're anything, although it seems like an odd and somewhat quaint plan."

Naomi exhaled to break the tension. It worked. He fell for her story.

"Yes, well...so, here I am."

She smiled like a cat who just ate a mouse, knowing it was anything but kosher. As her face held that expression, Leah came in to say dinner was ready. Avram led the way to the dining room, where he pulled back a chair from the massive polished walnut table. The expensive white bone china and gold flatware made the versions available at Macy's look like paper plates and plastic utensils. Challah similar to the challah at lunch sat next to an elaborate etched crystal cup full of wine. Naomi stared through the smaller kiddush wine cup at her place, wishing she could get drunk on ten glasses of it and just disappear. Leah came out of the kitchen with a steaming brisket, and then went back for baked potatoes and broccoli.

After Leah chanted the blessing over the candles, and Avram chanted the blessing over the wine and bread, the three sat quietly as Leah served the food. The only sound was the clinking of gold serving utensils on silver serving dishes. Then Avram interrupted the clinking with a question.

"So Leah has told you about our synagogue?"

"Yes. Yes, she has."

"It's one of many modern Orthodox synagogues in this area, and in our opinion the best one. You'll see for yourself tomorrow."

With that comment, Avram's eyes seemed to take on the role of an expert lawyer, their piercing gaze cross examining her. She could almost hear them make their case.

I know what you're planning to do. You're planning to skip going to services with us tomorrow so you can go to that evil place. Aren't you! Admit it! But you won't get away with it. I've got my eye on you.

Naomi averted her eyes and looked down. Avram passed her the brisket as he continued.

"So what do you do, Naomi...that is, do you have some sort of occupation?"

Naomi didn't want to talk about herself. But he gave her no choice.

"Yes, well, I work at the housewares department at the Manhattan Macy's."

"That's nice," he responded, with a hint of condescension. "But...I thought you said you were Orthodox. They must not give you Shabbat off. Or do they?"

"Well, yes, they do…like the *New York Times* gave my father every Shabbat off when he worked there as a Linotype operator many years ago. He helped me get this job."

That ended up sounding like Marvin the momma's boy, depending on his mother for everything.

"That is to say, he…my father…was a kind of reference, if you know what I mean. And we…that is, I…sort of insisted on it…getting Shabbat off, that is."

"Well, that's nice of Macy's to have agreed to that."

As Avram passed the potatoes, Leah interjected.

"My parents worked retail. They owned a little kosher delicatessen. I hated it growing up. Hated it! I couldn't wait to get away from it. They used to say, 'If you don't want a life like this, marry a doctor.' So I took their advice."

She quickly nodded to emphasize her victory over retail, which caused Naomi to suddenly feel the need to justify her job.

"Well, it's something to do. So I don't mind it so much. You meet people. I've met some interesting people…from all backgrounds. Of course, *you* do also, Dr. Milstein. So I guess you know what I mean. You meet Jews, Christians…all sorts of people."

Avram nodded his head.

"Yes, and in my line of work, some of them are dying. So you really see what their religions mean to them. I've even had some of the Christians try to proselytize me. If they're dying, I sometimes just let them go on and do it. Of course if they're not, I sometimes stop them. I've even had a Jewish convert to Christianity do that to me once. He was one of the dying ones. He actually called himself a Jew…a m*essianic.* I didn't tell him he was no longer a Jew…which of course, he wasn't. I just let him go on. He's dead now, poor brainwashed guy."

Naomi tried not to choke as she washed down a mouthful of brisket with water from a large crystal goblet. At least that kept her occupied so she wouldn't appear nervous, as if she had something to hide—such as her recently interrupted studies in the New Testament with Darrin Brock. Then she impulsively blurted out something she had been wondering about since she entered the Milstein house. Did they know about Beth Yeshua?

"Isn't...isn't there a place where they worship around here...people like that man who died?"

Leah dropped her fork almost like Naomi had at lunch, though not as loudly.

"Please, don't make me lose my appetite. Thank God we don't have children. Let's change the subject, please."

Naomi couldn't help but ask what Leah meant.

"I don't understand. Children?"

Avram's face reddened. He put down his own fork. Then he sighed.

"I asked that man if he went there, here in Midwood. He said no. He attended somewhere on Long Island. Of course, he probably drove there on Shabbat. If he had said he went to *that* place, I wouldn't have let him try to convert me—even if he was right at death's door."

Naomi couldn't help herself. She had to enquire further. After all, she was secretly planning to cross the threshold of the very place Avram was referring to.

"What do you mean? Just what do they do in there that they don't do on Long Island?"

Avram turned to his wife.

"Sorry, honey. I'll just answer Naomi's question, and then we'll talk about something else."

Then he faced Naomi.

"I don't know about Long Island, but I do know that they steal children here in Midwood...little Jewish children...off the streets...and bring them into that place to *brainwash* them. It's disgusting."

"How little? I mean, how young?"

"I don't know. Young enough."

"Why haven't they gone to jail? That's illegal. It's kidnapping."

Leah spoke up.

"They never get caught. They don't do it *all* the time. Maybe once in a while. But that's enough."

Avram interjected.

"Too much."

Naomi stared through her half-drunk glass of wine.

"That's terrible. Somebody needs to do something about it."

Avram responded.

"People try. But by the time their parents find out, the older children are brainwashed and the younger ones…well, from what I've heard, they're never quite the same. Can we change the subject?"

"Yes, of course," Naomi whispered in response. As she took another bite of her baked potato, she wondered how much Darrin had heard about this kind of thing. And why didn't the police stop it? After all, these were innocent Jewish minors.

The rest of the meal consisted of a rabbinic discussion about the Shabbat. She found herself just about able to hold up her end of the conversation, due to the precious hours she had spent with her beloved father every week after synagogue services. At least this was better than the "small talk" at lunch…and the talk about *that place* during the first part of dinner.

CHAPTER TWELVE

Naomi knew instinctively that she had slept late. And the digital clock on the night table proved her correct. It read 8:30 a.m. She remembered trying out different sleep numbers at about 11:00 p.m. the night before, and for some totally unscientific reason, settling on 85. As soon as she buried her head on the "My Pillow" provided by Avram and Leah, she began to doze off. The only thing that kept her from immediately fading into a deep sleep—besides a hot flash or two—was a nagging question mark about exactly what she would do when morning came. Now that it had arrived, she realized that some problem-solving mechanism during her REM sleep state had offered a solution—which was to pretend she was too sick to attend the Milsteins' synagogue that morning.

She could hear the gentle clink of dishes being placed on the dining room table, and the soft indistinct murmur of two voices. She looked beyond the parted curtains and out the bedroom window. The sky was clear and ethereal blue, and the winter sun was low and radiant. She slipped out of the silken sheets and headed for the bathroom.

When she finished relieving herself of the remainder of last night's Erev Shabbat evening wine and iced tea, she looked at her face in the mirror. What to do with that relatively healthy-looking face? She wouldn't have to make herself look as miserable as she had when she rouged her face in a deep fit of depression months before, over her physical appearance and poor prospects with Darrin. But she needed to look convincingly sick. She rubbed her eyes, saturated them with warm water, and then rubbed them again. Of course, the state of her hair was not directly related to the state of her health, but still the thought crossed her mind that messy hair could send a psychological message that her homeostasis was out of kilter. So she mussed it with both hands. Yet going too far might give her away. So she partially re-combed it. Then she poured hot water on a washcloth and put it on her forehead, just in case Leah or Avram—especially Avram—chose to feel it. She decided that the final touch would be to descend the stairs in her flannel pajamas and light cotton flower-decorated robe. Finally, all was in order—or in this case, out of order. As she left the room, an added thought crossed her mind. *I can't have an appetite. I'll eat later, not now.*

Leah was in the dining room, presiding over bagels, lox, cream cheese, orange juice, and the bittersweet aroma of coffee that had been put through a strainer and poured into a third vessel—which reputable rabbis permit on Shabbat. Naomi was well aware of this method, as her father had sometimes employed it. She wanted to sit down and dig in after the short prayer preceding the meal. But none of that was possible this morning. Leah was already dressed in an expensive yet modest white Shabbat dress. She turned to Naomi and eyed her robe and pajamas—and her mussed-up hair.

"I guess you slept well. It's late. We leave in a half-hour."

It was now or never. She chose a headache and low-grade fever. That would fit her flushed look.

"I think I'm a little sick."

Leah came over and felt her forehead, as Naomi expected.

"You do feel a little warm…well, maybe just a little."

Naomi jumped right in.

"Right. I don't think I need to take my temperature, or get checked out by anyone…Avram, for instance. After all, I'm not dying of a fatal disease and in need of an oncologist."

She tried to giggle and cough at the same time, like a sick person would.

"But do you mind if I stay in this morning? For one thing, I don't think I got enough sleep last night," she lied.

Leah pouted like a Jewish-American princess.

"Oh, I'm so disappointed. Avram will be, too. Are you sure you're not feeling well enough to come? It's just a short walk."

Naomi was glad Avram wasn't in the room. She might not have been able to think as fast if he was.

"Maybe…maybe I can catch up with you later. Do you mind if you leave a key for me to use with the front door? Are you okay with that on Shabbat? My father allows it…that is, he did when he was well. I think I just need a little time to rest."

Leah blinked her eyes a few times, closing them on the last blink as she processed Naomi's request. By that time, Avram had entered the room, dressed in a fine black silk suit and a smart white shirt and red tie. The same yarmulke that he wore the night before sat atop his curly black hair, held in place by a bobby pin. Leah turned to him.

"Naomi seems to feel a bit under the weather… maybe a low fever."

He walked over to Naomi and put his hand on her forehead.

"Mmm…"

Then he asked her to open her mouth wide and say *AHH*. He lowered his head and focused his eyes on her throat.

"I don't see anything. What are you feeling?"

Naomi was trapped. She was standing before a genuine medical doctor—an oncologist, no less—someone she would be glad to get checked out by if she were *really* sick. But she *wasn't* sick, and he was just about to blow her cover. She realized she couldn't just fake symptoms like a school girl with an unfinished report. Still, she had to say something— *anything*.

"I…I just don't feel well. I think it's…well, I know it's…"

Come on! Think fast! Think!

"Um…menopause. I've had some…some menopause symptoms. I just saw my gynecologist. He…I mean she…told me if it gets too bad…I was too embarrassed to tell Leah. Sorry, Leah."

Her eyes averted Avram's. This had to work. After all, he definitely wasn't a woman, and Leah wasn't menopausal. Besides, this wasn't a specialty he was an expert in. Did oncologists diagnose menopausal women—that is, those without cancer? No, Naomi was pretty sure they didn't. He couldn't know exactly how menopause symptoms feel. So how could he judge her for feeling this way! That is, if she really was feeling this way. He nodded slowly.

"I see. Well, if you're not feeling well, you're not feeling well. Perhaps we should stay here with you."

Baruch HaShem...thank God, it worked! Now on to the plan. But their staying can't be a part of it.

"Oh no! I wouldn't think of it. I...I told Leah to leave me a key, and if you let me know exactly where the synagogue is, I'll meet you there if I feel better. I just need a little time to rest and get over these...these hot flashes and headaches."

Avram eyed Naomi's pajamas and robe.

"Very well. The synagogue is this way on this street...three blocks." He pointed.

"I hope you feel better and can join us. Meanwhile, if you're up to it, grab a bagel."

"Maybe later," she responded, opening the way for her to eat a huge breakfast after they left. She headed up to her room, relieved that she had passed the test. But wait a minute! There was one thing left to attend to. She turned to Avram and summoned up all the emotion she could.

"Oh. I...I don't want to come anywhere near that place we talked about last night...especially not on Shabbat. So I hope it's not in the same direction. Is it?"

"No worries. It's on this street, but a few blocks in the opposite direction. So you won't have to run into them, and let those deceivers ruin a perfectly beautiful Shabbat. Feel better. We'll say a *Mi-Shebeirach* for you."

"Thank you. I'm so relieved."

She was actually relieved more than Avram knew. Now she could relax and take her time getting dressed. In a very short time, she would cross the threshold of *that place*, and finally be immune to Marvin's proposals forever!

After downing two cups of warm coffee and a bagel and a half with lox and cream cheese, Naomi put on the plain black dress and cream-colored sweater she had brought for just this occasion—the kind of outfit that people would hopefully look past and not at. She would slip past a few people as she entered the forbidden "synagogue," and then slip out and walk the opposite direction to the *real* synagogue, mission accomplished—hopefully. She left the house ten minutes before the service was supposed to start. After turning the lock, she carefully dropped the key into her small purse. As her black high heels navigated the thankfully dry Midwood sidewalk, she couldn't help but think of all the times she had walked arm-in-arm with the greatest Jew in the world—her father—as they took their Shabbat walk to their warm welcoming synagogue in a similar Brooklyn neighborhood. What would her father think of her destination now? Indeed, what *did* he think of her now-broken romance with a Gentile Christian man? Actually, she *knew* what he thought, and would straighten that situation out as soon as she got the chance. Come to think of it, why hadn't she told him already, even before he recovered? She didn't have an answer to that question. She only knew she *would* tell him soon.

She was so busy thinking about her father, her synagogue, and her forbidden destination, that she almost passed by the goal of her journey. And she would have, if she hadn't turned her head by chance and glanced at the small black letters on white background above the door. *Beth Yeshua,* they plainly read. There was no one entering or exiting, which seemed odd to her. Wasn't this just before the start of the service? Then she glanced once more at the sign. Written in a smaller font underneath the name of the establishment were the times of the service. Shabbat Service, 10:00 a.m. Avram was wrong. The service was in progress. *There is no point in going in now*, she thought to herself. *I might as well just go past the Milstein's house to their synagogue and catch most of the service there.*

She began to walk away, when the voice of her own thoughts stopped her short. *Wait a minute! I didn't come here to attend a whole service. I came to cross the threshold and make myself immune to Marvin's constant nagging about matrimony.* She steeled herself and walked up the few steps to the main door. She spied a *mezuzah*—the small box containing Scripture from Deuteronomy 6—to her right on the door lintel. She chose for the first time in her life not to reach out and touch it. After all, who knew what Scripture was inside *this* mezuzah? She walked through the door and into a small vestibule with another door at the other end. She could just hear familiar chanting through the door. She pulled the door open. She had achieved her goal. She'd crossed the threshold. Wasn't that Marvin's requirement to reject her as his future wife? Now she could just run out, passing that same threshold going the opposite direction.

Just then, a middle-aged man who appeared to be some sort of usher—with a black rayon yarmulke perched on top of his head, and a simple prayer shawl uncomfortably draped over his shoulders—pointed to a seat in the back row.

"Would you like to take a seat in the last row here?"

No, I wouldn't!

The voice inside her head spoke so loudly, she was almost convinced the "door man" could hear her. His hand made a gentle sweeping motion.

"This way."

His gesturing hand created a particularly awkward moment for her. She stood for an instant, until the voice in her head expressed itself again.

It's one thing to be pushed into staying, and another to be unnecessarily rude. I guess it couldn't hurt to stay for just a few minutes.

As she peered at the back of the assembled group's heads, she shivered at the disturbing sight of a gender-mixed service. Three or four dozen men, women, and children stood in front of cheap-looking tubular steel and plastic chairs, with gaps of empty seats here and there, giving the "sanctuary" a not quite half-full appearance. The room was a plain rectangle. with bare fluorescent lights in rows on the ceiling—providing shadowless light to the assembled group—and bare white walls, which gave the whole place an appearance more like a warehouse than a house of worship. How unlike the warm glow of her beloved synagogue! The only indication that this was *supposed* to be a synagogue was the presence of a small wooden cabinet in the front of the room, with the first ten letters of the Hebrew alphabet glued on the front in two vertical rows of stained block wooden letters. This was obviously some kind of excuse for a Torah ark. In addition, Naomi noticed two gold and red embroidered banners to the box's left and right. She couldn't quite make out what they were about.

Naomi hesitated, but then proceeded to a back row seat, being sure to leave on her winter coat. She ended up standing next to a tall burly man with hair as blonde as Darrin Brock's, a very straight long blonde beard, and an off-white prayer shawl just a shade lighter than his beard.

She had arrived just in time for the traditional *Shema* prayer, which she couldn't help but notice was projected on a large screen at the front of the room, in large Hebrew block letters and transliterated English. She quickly turned her eyes away from the glowing image, fully aware that the sight was no more kosher than watching television on Shabbat. Between the mixed seating and the offensive depiction of Judaism's holiest prayer, deep regret began to grip her now-defiled heart. What would her beloved father think of all of this?

As the familiar chant began, she couldn't help but overhear the strange burly man boisterously bellow out a mispronunciation of the word Shema—"Shee-ma"— matching the way Inspector Ralph Lewis and Marc Silver pronounced *Prima*, the name of the late underworld figure that Marc had worked for. A sense of deep disgust overtook her. She quickly surmised that this man was one hundred percent Gentile— *so* Gentile that Darrin Brock seemed like the late Chabad Rebbe from Crown Heights in comparison. His use of Jewish sacramental garb now seemed as dissonant to her as a man wearing women's clothes—or perhaps more like a yellow cat dressed in a tuxedo. She'd had enough!

Just then, a small curly-headed child that looked a bit like Natan raced from the front of the "sanctuary," up the makeshift aisle, and toward the back of the room. She quickly turned around to see the usher grab him and pick him up. The boy defiantly squealed as the usher disappeared through the back door.

"Let me go! Let me go!"

It suddenly dawned on Naomi that this poor child must be one of the kidnapped victims. Her body began to shake involuntarily. She knew she had to leave now or she would throw up all over the cheap seats and the Gentile's prayer shawl. Marvin was right. No one who entered this horrible place deserved to remain within the pale of Jewish community.

She grabbed her purse and was about to walk out, when her eye caught the eye of a man in the front, who was obviously pretending to be some sort of rabbi. He seemed to be in his late forties or early fifties—like her—and he looked vaguely like Avram Milstein, with a well trimmed beard. For sure *he* was Jewish, or at least he *had* been at one time. She could just hear his perfect Hebrew pronunciation over the rest of the group as he chanted the basic liturgy—without the assistance of a cantor, who seemed nowhere to be found. She recognized the "Love the Lord with all your heart" portion from Deuteronomy 6—the *V'Ahavta* verses that are also encased in the doorpost *mezuzah*. She hadn't been able to bring herself to touch that object as she entered this place, and she likewise couldn't continue to listen to the chanting of the holy words now. She had crossed the threshold. It was past time to cross back over it.

She left her seat and walked to the back of the room. She couldn't help but notice that the usher was gone, as was the abducted child. Instead, standing in their place—and almost in her way—was an impeccably dressed seventy-something African-American woman, wearing a light green chiffon hat with a green flower on its narrow brim. The thought involuntarily crossed Naomi's mind that this woman might look more at home in a Brooklyn Baptist church—which added to her conviction that she needed to get out of there.

By this time, the out-of-place visitor's face was beaded with sweat. The "Baptist" woman seemed to notice that, and put her left hand on Naomi's shoulder, as she extended her other hand to shake Naomi's. Naomi wanted in the worst way not to reciprocate. But David Kaplan hadn't raised her to be rude. As she responded, the woman's eyes penetrated hers with an electricity that she knew she'd seen before—in Darrin Brock's electric blue eyes.

"Are you all right?"

"I…I…have to leave."

"You're not feeling well. Here. Take this tissue. Do you mind if I pray for you?"

"Yes…no…I mean…"

What would her father—the man with the wisdom of the sages, who wore a Santa hat to reach out to dying Christian children—do? The one thing Naomi decided to do was to accept the tissue and wipe her forehead. Then she tried to think of something polite to say that would add up to a "thank you" for the tissue and a "no" to the prayer. She knew the woman's prayer would in all likelihood not be the usual *Mi-Shebeirach* healing prayer she was used to. But she wasn't in any mood to find out. She also knew that if she didn't say something fast, the woman would begin praying. And who knows what would happen after that? Any place that was capable of kidnapping children was capable of brainwashing, or pronouncing curses…or *anything*. She opened her mouth again to decline the offer, but it was too late. The top of the woman's light green brimmed hat went parallel to Naomi's eyes, as she bowed her head. When she finally spoke, it was much louder than Naomi expected—especially since the supposed rabbi/cantor was in the middle of leading the congregation in the familiar chanted section of the traditional *Amida* prayer. The woman's hand pressed on Naomi's shoulder as she started in neat and clipped diction.

"Yeshua HaMashiach!"

Naomi involuntarily flinched as cold shivers shot through her. The woman's hand held on to her now slightly shaking shoulder.

"You brought this daughter of Abraham here today."

That was what Darrin told me God called me, came the instant thought. *Is that what they all say?*

"She did not cross this threshold in vain. No she didn't."

That's funny. She's using the term I used. No, lady. I didn't. Now Marvin will stop bugging me. But you wouldn't know that.

"She may have been well when she came here, but she's sick now…or maybe not."

Is this their way of brainwashing their subjects?

The woman lightened the pressure on Naomi's shoulder while keeping it there. She paused, and looked into Naomi's eyes again while keeping her head down.

"Hmmm. Hmmm."

"Okay. But regardless, I pray you'd touch her and heal her…hmmm…"

Then the woman closed her eyes and just stood there, like she was trying to listen to somebody or something. She lifted her head until the bowed brim of her hat faced Naomi, and her deep brown eyes found their mark again.

"…her broken heart. Yes, her broken heart…the one she refuses to acknowledge."

Wait a minute! Stop!

Naomi chose to be rude and pulled the woman's hand off her shoulder. Now she was free to run the fifty-yard dash, and get out of this wicked place as fast as she could. She turned and faced the door. Her feet were just beginning to navigate when she almost ran into the usher, who was once again holding the little curly-headed hostage in his arms.

"I see you've met our key intercessor."

Your what? came the internal response.

"Yes…I suppose I have…whatever that is. I…but, I need to leave."

Suddenly, something like a holy boldness rose up in Naomi, a cry for justice that echoed back to the Jewish patriarchs themselves, who defended the little ones. She loved all children as if they were her own—for example, her niece and nephew, her sister Lisa's children. And now she was about to defend a child at risk. After all, *someone* had to do it. Why not a real Jew? She pointed her finger at the usher.

"Before I go…you should be ashamed of yourself! I don't know whose child that is, and you probably don't either. But you should return him to his rightful owner, somewhere out there in Brooklyn. And now, I will go…never to return. But you can be sure I will contact the authorities."

The welcomer seemed puzzled, but the woman with the green hat wasn't. She turned, and this time totally blocked Naomi's path. She stared at her like a disappointed mother.

"Let me ask one thing before you leave."

"Well?" Naomi responded as she held her head high.

"Would the *Chofetz Chaim* be proud of you?"

Shocked at the mention of one of her father's favorite sages, Naomi's head returned to its normal position.

"I…I…don't understand."

"Just what I said. Would the *Chofetz Chaim* be proud of you?"

How could this African-American "Baptist" woman know about the great nineteenth-century rabbi who railed against gossiping and rumor-mongering—which he called *Lashon Hara*, the evil tongue? The woman continued.

"Well? You heard me."

Naomi saw no reason why the *Chofetz Chaim* would be ashamed of her. She responded in confidence.

"No, ma'am, he wouldn't," she said, using the title Darrin used when wearing his detective's hat.

"He *would be ashamed* of you!"

Naomi froze. The woman didn't miss a beat.

"I see. Then I will take the liberty of asking one more question. Who told you that this child, or any other child here, was kidnapped? An anti-missionary, I suppose?"

A what?

A descending sense of shame began above Naomi's temples and seemed to spread all the way down to her toes. She measured her words as she responded.

"No. No. A…a friend. A reliable friend, if you must know the truth," she shot back, realizing she was using the word *truth* a bit loosely.

"Hmmm. Gossip is always reliable…until it isn't!"

"Listen…I…I…"

"Please be my guest and go. And while you're at it, tell your reliable friend that there are *no* kidnapped children here. That's *his* child" she said, pointing at the usher. "And by the way, I'm Mahalia…Mahalia Morse. No, I'm not Jewish, as you can readily see. But you are, as I *can* see. You're also under a lot of stress, aren't you? But I notice that you don't look as sick as you did a few minutes ago."

Suddenly, her resolute mouth formed into a smile as her eyes continued to track Naomi's, like Aunt Ida's in the rear view mirror of her car. What else about Mahalia Morse reminded her of Marvin's Aunt Ida? Naomi couldn't quite put her finger on it. But something did.

"Listen, would you like to stay and hear the rabbi's message? He's really quite good. His name is Sheldon Goldberg. Have you heard of him?"

"No. Why would I?"

If the edge in that question was hard to miss, the edge in the next few sentences wasn't.

"To tell you the truth, Ms…Ms…Morse…I just came here to…to… cross the threshold over there. So now I think I need to leave and go to my reliable friend's synagogue."

"Mission accomplished?"

What was it with this woman? Was she invading Naomi's mind, so she could put her own thoughts in there—or worse, someone else's thoughts? How could she possibly be using Naomi's very same language, mention one of her father's favorite rabbis, and expose her broken heart…if indeed it *was* broken? Certainly dark forces were at work in this evil place—forces that were out to destroy her. And it seemed that

Mahalia wasn't finished with her handiwork.

"Well, it's been nice meeting you…I didn't get your name…"

Naomi realized that she hadn't been gracious enough to reciprocate when Morse shared her name. Would it hurt to be nice, even to this frightening woman? Her beloved father, who lay incapacitated at the Maimonides Medical Center, would say no. Besides, she didn't have to give her her last name.

"I'm sorry. N…N…"

Suddenly, the word wouldn't come out. What was it that was catching her tongue as she tried to say her name—which she'd pronounced maybe millions of times? Suddenly she realized that perhaps this black woman would think she was using the "N" word, and taunting her. But Mahalia just smiled and put her arm on Naomi's shoulder again.

"It's Naomi, isn't it? Isn't that it, Naomi? The one who said, 'call me Mara—bitter.'"

Naomi wanted to lie to her face and tell her that her name wasn't Naomi. But something told her that this woman who seemed to know so many things might just know that too.

"How…how did you know that?" she gasped involuntarily.

"Never you mind, Naomi. Never you mind, God knows you much better than I do. He is aware of much more than your name. He knows your *heart*…and your heart's *yearning*."

She spoke the word "yearning" with such earnestness that Naomi could almost feel the impact somewhere in her midsection. Mahalia's head motioned for Naomi to stay.

"Perhaps you could just hear the rabbi for a few minutes before you leave. He's got a message on Matthew five. Have you ever read that particular passage? It's pretty famous. Even some Orthodox rabbis know it. It's sometimes called the Sermon on the…"

"Yes, I know."

Naomi flashed back to Darrin's bedside at Mount Sinai Hospital. She could still see the words on the unfamiliar page and hear Darrin say "Like you are" when she told him how beautiful the passage was. *Blessed are the poor.* And she could hear her father as he told her the Sermon on the Mount wasn't her Scripture—or his. Now she was convinced she had to get out of this place. Mahalia betrayed a surprised look—which was unexpected, considering the knowing look she had given so far.

"So you've read it."

Naomi felt her defenses rise.

"What…what makes you think I've read that forbidden book, or that I'd want to hear someone who pretends to be a rabbi speak on it?"

That was too harsh. And on top of that, it was untruthful.

"But yes…I've…I've read just that one portion, if you must know… just that one…in a hospital once…to someone I …I…I…"

"You loved. And someone you still love."

Naomi had had enough.

"What makes you think that? And anyway, it's none of your business."

Then, without warning, the last thing Naomi would ever want to happen inside a congregation dedicated—of all things—to Jesus, happened. Tears began to flow from her eyes, and she began to shiver as if she was standing outside in short sleeves, instead of in the coat she had never taken off. Mahalia Morse pulled her toward herself and very gently embraced her, releasing in Naomi the kind of crying heaves that she hadn't experienced since the Newark trip with Marvin's Aunt Ida, during the time Darrin was in a coma. Mahalia whispered into Naomi's ear, speaking in some kind of strange language that definitely wasn't Hebrew and definitely wasn't Yiddish. *Perhaps it's from somewhere like the Caribbean Islands*, Naomi thought as uncontrollable tears continued to flow. A few people turned around in their seats and stared, including the strange Gentile with the long blond beard. Mahalia looked back at them and shook her head slowly, as if to say, *turn around and mind your own business.*

After Naomi was all cried out, her head remained on Mahalia's shoulder, who then began to squeeze her tightly, like the mother she had lost so many years before. Naomi tried to speak, as her crying slowed to a whimper, like a little baby's would.

"What…what's going on? I…I…don't understand. Why…why do I feel this way?"

"You'll understand by and by, child. You go now. Your friend is waiting."

"But…but…why…"

"Let me give you my card. Call me. You pick the kosher deli and we'll grab lunch…Brooklyn, Manhattan…you name it."

She released Naomi and pulled a card out of her small black purse. Naomi took it. Now, for the first time, she wasn't sure she wanted to leave so fast. But Mahalia nodded and then walked away. Naomi clutched the card and quickly walked out of the building and into the sound of staccato Saturday morning Brooklyn traffic. She faced the Milsteins' synagogue and headed in that direction.

CHAPTER THIRTEEN

2:00 a.m. is a lonely time at any hospital. Sleep at that hour is often interrupted by the nursing staff. No matter the name of the institution, their names are always penned on white boards with red, blue, or green erasable markers. This is so the patient knows who to ask for, and so the staff can appear friendly to the patient. Invariably, their hushed voices blend with the indistinguishable hum emanating from the part of the corridor closest to any given room. And as opposed to the daytime, their words are always few.

Maimonides Medical Center was no different in this regard than any other hospital. And David Kaplan's hospital room was no different than any other room at Maimonides. It was, however, one of the single-bed rooms. So it was generally a bit quieter at 2:00 a.m. than rooms with more than one bed. David lay on his back as he slept, the head of his bed raised up several degrees. Much of his memory and at least part of his speech had returned. But he still needed the assistance of a nurse and a walker to navigate to the bathroom.

With those things had also returned, with the fangs of a vampire, the disturbing Linotype dreams he had experienced periodically in the past. Over the last few weeks, they had visited with perseverating regularity, which may have been at least partially attributable to neurological damage. The clicks and whirs of the Victorian machine were amplified, as was the intense downward flood of silver letter matrices, the creation of hot lead slugs, and the pressure to type ever faster, until hot lead poured all over David Kaplan, scalding his hands and arms.

On this night, there was an unpleasant addition. He could feel not two, but four piercing eyes behind him as he was in the process of losing all control over the sprawling iron monstrosity. Who or what was there? Like Norman Bates greeting his mummified mother in Hitchcock's *Psycho*, he steeled himself, and then turned around. Standing in the nebulous grey space were the pleading eyes of Naomi and Darrin—pulling at him, tearing at him, rending him, splitting him in two with sharp optical daggers. He cried out with indiscernible words.

"Wha doo yoo waan? Wha doo oo wa? Whaa! Whaa! Fom Mee. Wha oo wan fro mee?"

Forty-something veteran RN Mary, dirty-blonde hair pulled back with a 1960's-style red wool hair band, sprinted into the room. She leaned over the now wide-eyed David Kaplan and took his left hand into both of her hands.

"It's Mary, your nurse. It's okay, Mr. Kaplan. It's only a dream."

Only? he thought to himself.

She dabbed his sweating brow with a tissue.

"May God bless you, Mr. Kaplan. It's all a part of the healing process. You're getting better. You really are."

For several seconds he just stared at her, clearly detecting compassion in her gentle hazel eyes. Then, with all the energy he could gather, he forced his resistant head to nod and his stubborn mouth to form a subtle smile.

At that very hour, across the Brooklyn Bridge, on the pre-dawn 3:30 a.m. streets of Midtown Manhattan, Omar Shehadulah stood across the street from the Midtown South precinct building—the same building whose flimsy barricades Naomi had confronted in anger many months earlier, when she showed up to give detective Darrin Brock a piece of her mind. It was just before he kissed her in the Channel Gardens. The barriers she had confronted were not erected to keep the likes of Naomi Kaplan out—or, curiously, even would-be terrorists like Omar Shehadulah. Their original purpose had been to stop, or at least slow down, approaching Black Lives Matter protestors, and the Occupy Wall Street protestors before them.

Shehadulah had recently returned from Pakistan, his parents' country of origin. No one had stopped him at LaGuardia, or anywhere else. While in Pakistan, he had been given only one contact in the New York vicinity, a young Muslim man whose family had emigrated from the UAE when he was two, and whose police record matched many other young men in Queens—with rap sheets that were more about peddling marijuana than perpetrating murders.

There was nothing on Omar's person—either on pieces of paper in his pockets, messages or numbers in his phone, or anywhere else—that anyone could learn anything from. Two names were in his mind. One was an inspector named Ralph Lewis. The other one was an inept detective who had been stupid enough to get shot by the Russian Mafia—and who, according to one source, might at some point be shadowing Muslims like Omar—one Detective Darrin Brock. Shehadulah didn't expect either Lewis or Brock to be in the building at that early hour. They were both too stupid and lazy to even be up, let alone at work. But he did have a reason to be standing across the street from the Midtown Manhattan South Precinct building. He crossed the street and stood directly in front of the wooden barricades for at least three minutes. There, behind the flimsy barrier, was the same middle-aged dirty-blonde female officer who had, months earlier, stopped Naomi during her mission to confront Darrin Brock. She tried to be gun-slinger subtle as she moved her hand to within an inch or so of her service revolver. She had been trained to remain vigilant.

"Sir? Can I help you?"

She spoke the word "sir" the same way she had spoken the word "ma'am" with Naomi the prior year.

"I am on my way to my workplace. I just wanted to thank you for keeping the city safe, Allah willing. In my country, it seems like no one is safe. A few ruin for many.."

This young man seemed to be a nice Muslim, and she was glad to encounter him. The experience could end up as another great example to share with her Islamophobic husband. He was always telling her to keep an eye out for the Islamic terrorists.

"Well, it's a twenty-four hour job, as you can see. So where is it you work?" she asked purely out of common curiosity.

He was ready with a prepared answer.

"A deli restaurant on East 33rd Street. It's owned by Jews…some of my best friends in New York. Very nice Jewish people. I go in very early to set up," he lied.

She smiled and nodded. She couldn't believe what she was hearing. She knew she would be tempted—after he left—to take the rest of the day as a sick day, so she could go home and wake her husband to tell him about this Muslim's nice Jewish friends at the deli where he works.

"Well, I wish we all got along with each other like you do with your friends."

"Thank you."

She was enjoying the conversation, but she knew she had to do her job—and part of her job was to keep traffic in front of the precinct station moving.

"Yes, well, it's so nice to meet you. You made my day. But…we try to keep the area clear. I hope you have a good night."

She made a sweeping motion.

"Yes. I'll be on my way. I hope to come back and visit again soon… maybe during the day."

He meant that literally. She watched him as he drifted down the street and into the dark winter pre-dawn. A slight grin formed on his face.

She's another stupid one. Surely her trust will come in useful someday.

Omar left the precinct building and headed down the short blocks of numbered streets, zigzagging periodically on one of the avenues that cross the streets. The steam of his breath pulsated before him like a locomotive engine pulling cattle cars on a genocidal death mission. He reached Broadway, and followed that to 23rd Street at Fifth Avenue. As he drew near to his destination, the Flatiron Building, he eyed a row of twinkling white lights running down the cutting edge of the soon-to-be-destroyed structure. He had never seen the primitive yet elegant skyscraper in the dark. Thanks to what he believed was a reactionary political correctness in place years after 9/11, he felt as he walked the relatively quiet major avenue like he owned the city. Someday, he would be a blessed martyr here.

Hidden under Shehadulah's L.L. Bean black winter coat was a dummy bomb vest, complete with dummy dynamite sticks. He wanted the vest to be just apparent enough so that someone who was looking carefully might see something suspicious. His whole purpose for this nighttime mission was to test the Homeland Security readiness of Manhattan. And so far, he passed the test while Manhattan failed. Next, he would test this fool Darrin Brock. But that would require daylight.

From across the street, he stood and stared at the blinking Flatiron Building. He prayed silently as the steam continued to escape his nostrils like the fiery breath of a dragon.

Allah, may there be many Jewish and Christian infidels in this wicked structure on the day I martyr myself. May the whole city of New York collapse around it. May your caliphate reach from Harlem to the Battery, when the One World Trade Center falls like the Twin Towers. I ask for a great blessing of death to America, Allah willing. May my small deed make a big impact.

His work this early morning was over. He turned and walked away, heading for the subway—and Queens.

Chapter Fourteen

Naomi lay in her bed and watched the glowing iris of the rising winter sun squint between her venetian blind slats. She hadn't been able to sleep for the last three hours. Over that time, Mahalia Morse had transformed from a mysterious all-knowing and all-wise seer into a frightening Christian witch, leading observant Orthodox Jew Naomi Kaplan down a deceptive path to destruction. She knew she hadn't gotten near enough sleep. Soon she would have to get up and go to work. She adjusted her head on her pillow and played eye-games with the sun, as it played peek-a-boo through the blinds. She needed those shafts of light just now. She had had enough of darkness—including darkness that pretended to be light. As she lay there, she decided that it was high time she tell her father that her sinful crush on the Christian detective Darrin Brock was over. In fact, it was more like *past* time—*way* past time. And she knew why she had delayed telling him, although she hadn't wanted to admit it to herself. The truth was, she had secretly harbored futile feelings of hope. However, considering the fact that it was *she* who had decided to break things off in the first place, she knew that there was no reason not to share the truth with her father as soon as possible. As she lay there stressed and sleepless, she came to a firm decision that she would visit him after work. Realizing that getting more sleep was futile, she flung the covers off, sprung up, and got ready to go to work.

Over the last month, Naomi had noticed that the traffic pattern in the Macy's eighth floor housewares department was different than when it was temporarily in the basement. There was usually some traffic in the basement, even when there wasn't much. That wasn't true for the eighth floor. The department seemed like it was either crowded with purchases and returns, or completely empty. On this day in late January, it was the latter. Naomi had plenty of time to think about what to say to her father, as he lay in his bed at the Maimonides Medical Center. She tried to memorize every word so she wouldn't hesitate.

Abba, I have some really good news. Do you remember that Darrin fellow? I thought you might. Well, I'm no longer involved with him. So you can get better now, because I know I made you sick by liking him.

No, that wasn't right. Even if he knew it was she who made him sick, he would never acknowledge it. She tried again, as she stared at the multicolored casual sturdy dinnerware bowls in the distance, half-consciously regretting not giving her father grandchildren and consequently not having to purchase such "unbreakable" items.

Abba, I just want you to know it's over between me and that Gentile detective.

This time she chose not to mention Darrin's name, because even thinking his name had elicited a yearning deep in her heart that she could definitely do without.

So when you come back home, we can live there in our wonderful Brooklyn house for the rest of our lives…which, God willing, will be a long time…because I'm never getting married…ever. No, Abba, I'm not going to marry Marvin, because I walked into one of those messianic places so he wouldn't ever bother me again.

That wasn't right either. Why would she mention that place? She tried several more times throughout the day, finally ending up with something she felt she could remember and deliver.

Abba, please forgive me for having disobeyed you and strayed from our people and traditions. I've decided I'm not going to marry either that Gentile detective or Marvin. I've told both of them in no uncertain terms that I'm not interested. So please get better so you can come home and I can take care of you. That's all I care about. I miss you. You are the most important person in my life, besides HaShem, and I love you.

As Naomi rehearsed every word over and over, without missing one small article or conjunction, her eyes moistened and her heart warmed. Finally, her affections were focused in the right direction. Now she could completely close the one chapter in her life that she should never have opened in the first place. She was impressed with the maturity and finality of her decision. She was even glad that she had walked into that Beth Yeshua place and met that woman with the *evil eye*—a Jewish term describing witchcraft. It was the only way she could rid herself of Marvin's constant nagging. And she was confident it would work.

By the time six o'clock came, Naomi had pitched what was possibly the only no-hitter in the history of her time at Macy's. Not one customer had entered the housewares department, from the time she opened until the time she closed. The Almighty must have brought that miracle to pass so she could prepare for her time alone with her father—the greatest Jew in the world, and HaShem's obvious candidate for healing—David Kaplan.

On the D train, Naomi repeated her chosen speech. By the time she reached the Maimonides Medical Center forty-five minutes later, her heart was beating rapidly. The chill Brooklyn winter night air greeted her as she arose from the subway and walked the short distance to the center, whose lighted faux brownstone exterior stood out like a dark brown velvet Torah cover surrounded by the black velvet night. She entered the building, and headed for David Kaplan's room, armed with the memorized paragraph.

As she traveled the corridor leading to her father's room, she could hear familiar high-pitched children's voices. She quickened her pace until she stood just outside his partially closed door. The voices were even more recognizable now. When she gently swung the door open, there was the entire Silver family, along with—of all people—Marvin's Aunt Ida. Before Naomi even had a chance to glance at her father, Ida's eyes met hers.

"Look who's here to see her Abba. My God, it's a Kaplan family reunion!"

The sight of Aunt Ida, standing next to the Silver family in David Kaplan's hospital room, seemed so out of place.

"Aunt Ida, what are you doing here?"

Lisa came to her defense.

"I gave her a call last week to ask her…and another party as well…to help our father with something. I mean, *you* haven't been around. Where've you been?"

Naomi had to admit that Lisa's question was a good one. Where *had* she been? The truth was, she had been avoiding her father, rather than following through with the responsibility she knew was hers—to repent and renounce before David Kaplan any and all connection with Darrin Brock. And now that she was there to do just that, the plans had to be shelved temporarily—at least while all these people were packed into his room.

"I…I…I don't know. I saw him recently. Didn't I, Abba? Last week I think. Remember?"

That happened to be almost true. Actually, it was about two weeks before. And she had spent the whole time during that visit knowing what she *should* be telling him and not ending up saying anything about it to him. She turned and, for the first time since she entered the room, looked at him. He lay there, looking thinner and paler than she remembered, his eyes trained somewhere between the two sisters. Then suddenly, he struggled to speak.

"Mmm…mmm…my…dau…dau.…ter"

Everyone's eyes then focused not in David's direction, but in Naomi's. They had heard him speak in that fashion before, and now they were more interested in her response to his slight improvement. She felt unusually self-conscious—as if they all knew why she was there, and what she was prepared to tell him. She already knew what Lisa and Aunt Ida thought of her break-up with Darrin, and they weren't positive about it, to say the least. She wished everyone in the room would just vanish through the white board with the friendly nurses' names—like Alice through the looking glass—so she could tell her father everything and get this whole thing over with. But unlike accounts in Lewis Carroll's novel, wishing wouldn't make it so. So she just stood there at the entrance of the room and gave her father a little wave with her right hand…like a silly teenage girl might.

"Hi Abba."

There was a deafening pause while Lisa gave her an incredulous look.

Finally, it was up to eight-year-old Noah to break in with the latest news.

"They finally got Grandpa into the…"

He paused as he accessed his childish language memory banks.

"…Kings…Kings…brick…"

Marc, who hadn't said a word yet, helped him out.

"Kingsbrook."

Noah nodded enthusiastically.

"Yes…that."

The rest of the information flowed smoothly from Noah's older sister Lindsey's lips.

"The Kingsbrook Jewish Medical Center in Flatbush. Right Daddy?"

"Yes, that's it, honey," her father responded.

Naomi stuttered softly.

"I…I…didn't…I didn't…know that. Why didn't anyone…why didn't anyone…tell me about that?"

She felt totally left out. How did that all happen without her? Was she that distracted by the whole mess with Darrin? She walked over to David Kaplan, and held his right hand in hers. A tear escaped from his left eye, which was able to focus more clearly on Naomi from this closer vantage point. His mouth struggled to make a crooked smile. A corresponding tear escaped from her right eye.

"Abba…I…"

She knew she couldn't say what she had planned to. So what *could* she say with all these people there? The only thing that would come out was, "Abba…I love you. I love you so much."

Then she added, almost involuntarily, "And I'm sorry that I…"

Lisa quickly broke in.

"Naomi, I don't know if you're aware of this, but there is no hospital… even a hospital as great as the Maimonides Medical Center…that would ever keep Dad for more than a few weeks at most. Everyone knows that hospitals try to move patients to the next step."

She tried not to sound too irritated, considering the reconciliation between her and Naomi that had occurred just a few months before. Then she took a tense breath before continuing.

"So…so…we had to find a very good care center where he could get the help he needs. And…"

She took another tense breath before her next words.

"And…"

Naomi was getting impatient.

"And?"

Lisa quickened the pace of her words.

"Darrin Brock, *wonderful* Darrin Brock, who by the way has visited Dad a few times over the last…I don't know…whatever…he, as an NYPD police department detective with a lot of contacts…along with the social services department here…and Marvin's Aunt Ida, who…as I'm sure you are aware, knows *everyone*…just yesterday…got him into…and it wasn't easy, mind you…the Kingsbrook Medical Center in Flatbush… tomorrow. He goes there tomorrow."

Naomi felt her face redden. At first, words wouldn't come out—only thoughts. *How dare Darrin visit my father! How dare these people work with him…and behind my back!*

"Wh…What!"

She began to feel faint, and the only thought that crossed her mind was that she didn't want to hit her head on the hard linoleum floor. She let go of her father's hand and clutched the bed sheet to secure her balance. Aunt Ida, oblivious to Naomi's condition, enthusiastically jumped in.

"You should see the eye contact between the two of them. He loves Darrin. Don't you, David? And Darrin loves him."

She nodded, and looked David Kaplan's way. He responded with a somewhat indefinable look in his eyes—one which Naomi, who caught it out of the corner of her eye, interpreted as a lukewarm "eh." Yet she also had to admit it contained a small measure of benign kindness, or perhaps resigned acceptance. Or was it something else? Still, they had interfered with her plans, and gone behind her back. She steadied herself.

"Well…I don't know what to say. I…I came here to tell Abba something. But I'm not going to tell him with all of *you* here. And Darrin…Darrin…"

She wished she didn't have to say his name in front of them.

"Obviously, Darrin broke his word to me by visiting Abba…behind my back, yet. You all know I'm…I'm not seeing him anymore. You all knew that. This is just not right."

She turned once again to her father.

Abba…I was going to tell you…"

Aunt Ida quickly turned and lit into her.

"Excuse my French, Naomi, but who the hell do you think you are? You can't just stand there and run everyone else's life for them! They have their own minds, their own relationships."

Then something occurred that Naomi hadn't counted on. Lindsey, who was just entering an adolescent's attendant habit of independent thinking, interrupted all of them. She placed her hands on her hips and addressed her aunt as a peer of sorts for the first time in her life.

"Yeh, Aunt Naomi. What's wrong with Darrin visiting Grandpa? I love Darrin, and I love Grandpa. So what's wrong with them loving each other? Just because Darrin's not *Jewwwiiish?*"

She drew the word out as she spoke it—or rather, sang it. And then she stayed on her soapbox for a few more sentences.

"That's what's wrong with the world today. Why can't everyone just forget all that stuff and be friends?"

Finally, she raised her voice to an *I Hate Everyone* teenage girl's shrill complaint.

"I *hate* it when people act that way!"

Lisa walked over and put her arm around her daughter, affirming her.

"Spoken like a sage, Lindsey. Like a sage."

"I agree!" Noah chimed in as he stamped his foot.

Naomi hadn't counted on the children bonding so closely with Darrin, even though she had witnessed its origin during Chanukah, when he bought gifts for them. Everything was becoming so complicated. She intentionally ignored Lindsey, although much of her wanted to respond to her niece. But right now, it was more important to straighten out this whole mess, especially with her father. She turned back to him.

"Abba…Abba…"

He gently reached out with his shaky hand and signaled something again quite undefinable—giving him the mysterious appearance of a mystical Jewish saint. Then he gave her another "eh" look—or maybe it was that resigned acceptance look—and added a silent word or two with his lips that may have been, "It's okay"—or maybe not.

Naomi experienced a disturbing feeling she had never experienced before. It had always been *Lisa* that had felt left out, second best, jealous of her older sister's close relationship with their father. Now it was *Naomi* that felt left behind, disconnected from all that had been taking place concerning her father over the last few days—and perhaps before. And as for *Darrin*, he was one of the people, God forbid, who had replaced her in her father's life—and very possibly without David Kaplan's expressed permission! It was all too much to take in. Now, she just wanted to disappear.

"Well…I'm leaving now. I'll see you soon, Abba, in the new place. I love you."

She reached out and kissed him on the forehead.

"Then I'll have something to tell you…when we're alone."

She took a deep breath, and walked out of the hospital room door without saying goodbye to anyone else, even her niece and nephew. As she was leaving the room, she could just hear Aunt Ida's intentionally loud sarcastic voice.

"I wonder what *that* will be about. I love that stubborn girl, but she's just wrong."

Naomi fought as hard as she could to hold back tears as she walked down the hospital corridor, her emotions in confused disarray and her head still spinning.

CHAPTER FIFTEEN

Omar Shehadulah's closely cropped black hair had been growing out for the last few months, since he last took a razor to it. By the last week in February, it was curly and school-boyish—making him look a few years younger than his twenty-three years. His growing hair was not meant to camouflage his identity, Middle Eastern or otherwise. He just liked it that way, and had decided to wear it at that length when he blew up the Flatiron Building. The changing length of his hair also didn't confuse the Homeland Security surveillance team that had been tracking him since late December. All that time, they had been debating among themselves about the possible danger he posed. And every week or two, they checked on his whereabouts.

When a text from Homeland Security ended up on Inspector Ralph Lewis' secure phone, Omar was in the midst of a leisurely walk through Grand Central Station at 42nd Street and Park Avenue. A few moments before, he had looked around him at the cavernous interior main concourse of the vast "terminal," as Grand Central Station was called before the name *station* stuck. The walls glowed with a golden hue, periodically interrupted by rectangular advertisement signs and a long row, on one side, of the white letters on black train departure marquees. The large American flag, which hung vertically from the front of the hall, threatened to make him physically ill. The bright navy green ceiling with the detailed astronomical design work made him want to blow the roof off so *real* stars could reflect off dead bodies. But that would have to await another soldier of Allah.

The ceiling was designed in 1912 by French portrait artist Paul César Helleu. That was forty-one years after the original terminal, funded by railroad tycoon Cornelius Vanderbilt, was built. Much about it had changed since 1871, but not the symbol of American imperial decadence it represented to Omar. Just the constant stream of soldiers who had passed through its gates and halls in all the wars against all the people of Allah was reason enough to despise every granite inch of it.

Omar was headed straight for Mendy's Kosher Deli. He had only one thing on his mind, and that was his second taste of a pastrami on rye. He had read about the world-record-breaking 958-foot line of Nathan's hot dogs that was used to promote their Grand Central Station operation, and he craved one of them. But he hesitated, not sure if he trusted Nathan's boast that they were all-beef. It was essential that they contained no pork, and were therefore *halal*, or appropriate for Muslims. So he chose the pastrami on rye instead.

He had just arrived at the deli counter when Inspector Lewis, who was swiveling at his desk to work off stress, received the text.

Short notice. Can you get your detective to GCS Mendy's Deli to check out terror suspect OS with our agent?

He shot back a text.

What am I? A magician? My guy could be anywhere.

HS shot back.

Don't know his intentions. We'll use a GPS and track OS. Hurry.

Okay, Okay. What's your guy wearing?

Grey suit, black tie. black hair, thick mustache.

"Figures," Lewis mumbled to himself. "Blues Brothers. All that's missing is the black suitcase."

He called Darrin Brock, who picked up after three rings. He stopped swiveling and sat up.

"Where are you? *New York Times* Building? Ground floor? Good. Well, get over to GCS in a cab, to that Mendy's Deli place. There's an HS contact there. Grey suit, black tie, black hair, mustache. Now! It's five minutes away. I know you haven't received any training from them yet. You'll be fine. Just flash your damn badge at the cab and hurry up. I know about your limp, and that ridiculous cane. Five minutes. Tell him to step on it. Apparently, our Omar may have some plans. Just go!"

Darrin Brock didn't want to see a Homeland Security agent. He didn't want to interrogate a potential terrorist. The fact was, he was less interested in chasing terrorists than he had been in chasing Mafia dons. But he was also, like every other New Yorker old enough to remember, a victim of terrorism on 9/11—and every hostile act since then. And like everyone else in the NYPD, he knew cops who had lost their lives in the towers, and others who had succumbed to lung ailments years later. He happened to be in Harlem at the time the towers fell, but that made no difference. He had suffered alongside his fellow city servants. And like all NYPD personnel, he was duty bound to keep the city safe—at all costs. Using his badge, he grabbed a cab within a minute, and five minutes later he was standing within the boisterous bowels of Grand Central Station—a bit out of breath from his limp, and right outside Mendy's Kosher Deli. The agent with the grey suit and black tie was clearly identifiable from twenty feet away, as he, Darrin Brock, was to the agent. He walked up to him and flashed his detective's badge. The agent rolled his eyes.

"What took you so long?"

Darrin wondered whether he was kidding. The agent introduced himself with deadpan directness, and without shaking Darrin's hand.

"Lawrence Schmidt."

"Brock, Darrin, NYPD detective."

Schmidt leaned in and half whispered, his round, almost Hemingway-like face so close that Darrin could almost smell the tobacco brand.

"Well, maybe we're onto something, Brock, or maybe we're not. I don't make final determinations about those things myself…even when they're about to slaughter innocents, if you know what I mean. If I did, I'd probably get fired. My superiors decide. But that's another story."

He pointed up, as if his superiors were somewhere in the sky, beyond the main concourse ceiling with the constellations. Then he pointed inside the deli.

"He's in there. Omar Shehadulah."

He let it roll off his tongue, like a hip hop artist would.

"They tell me he's never threatened anything to anyone that they know of. And from what I understand, there's no known connection to anything organized. So we're probably wasting our time, which I've been doing a lot of lately. You're packing heat, I hope."

"Yeh. Yeh. Sure."

"Good. Just in case."

Darrin tried not to appear nervous. He was paid not to be nervous, but he had also never participated in this particular kind of activity before. Nervous or not, he had to admit that his heart wasn't in it. Years ago, it may have excited him to be dealing with the Islamic radical terrorist threat. But not now—not at his age, and not after having lost Naomi.

"So...so...what do we do?"

Schmidt closed his eyes momentarily, signaling that he was in no mood to train anyone about anything.

"Just keep your mouth shut and follow my lead."

They walked into the restaurant just as Omar was about to take a seat with his pastrami on rye. Schmidt walked up to him, with Darrin so close behind that he was almost stepping on his shoes and hitting the back of his legs with his cane.

"Mind if we sit with you while you eat?"

He referred to Darrin without turning around.

"Brock, you want anything?"

Darrin didn't know if he should say yes or no. What was the protocol when interviewing possible terrorists? He guessed.

"No, I ate already."

Omar shrugged, trying to appear relaxed, while he deliberated whether he should pull his knife out. Schmidt took the shrug to mean yes.

"Okay, well, this is Darrin, and I'm Lawrence. I might get something myself in a few minutes. Please, be seated."

Omar realized he was standing right next to the same Detective Darrin Brock whom he thought about killing only recently. Was this Allah's doing? And who was this other guy? FBI? The sharp switchblade knife was in his right pocket. He could use it now, and kill both of these infidels with a few quick slashes. He had been trained for such opportunities. But that would interrupt his plans for a *bigger* prize— even if it was smaller than a prize like the Empire State Building. Still, it was definitely bigger than this prize. Anyway, he wanted to know what this was about before acting. Maybe they had seen him outside the precinct building, or maybe in front of the Flatiron Building. But if they had anything on him, why would they ask to see him here, out in the open, right in the middle of—of all places—Grand Central Station? He decided to play along. He slowly placed his tray on the table and sat down. Brock and Schmidt sat down across from him. Schmidt began.

"Look, I'll shoot straight with you. I'm a detective of sorts, and he… well, he's a detective with the NYPD. We just have a few questions, if you're up for it."

Omar shrugged again and looked down at his sandwich.

"Sure. You mind if I eat?"

"Of course not. It looks good. I've heard they have good food here."

"It's my first time."

"Is that so?" Schmidt asked as a thorough HS agent would.

Omar took a bite of the sandwich. He hadn't purchased a drink. He never drank and ate at the same time, and couldn't understand why Americans always insisted on drinking while they ate—like pigs in a sty. He turned to Schmidt, and faked friendliness.

"You want some?"

"That's okay."

He looked over at Darrin Brock. Just the sight of his Western Christian blonde hair made him want to pull his knife out. He offered his sandwich instead.

"You want some?"

"No. Like I said, I ate already."

"Oh. Right. So how can I help you two?"

Schmidt leaned in.

"My…my superiors have some…some concerns. Let's say just a few. Maybe just one. So I'll shoot straight with you, like I said…because personally, I think you're a fine upstanding guy, and I think they do too. But they just wanted me to ask about that last trip to Pakistan…just for the record. Do you mind telling us about it…just for the record?"

Darrin was looking at Omar's eyes as Lawrence was speaking. It seemed to him that something not quite right was lurking behind them—something he only faintly detected, and only in the part of him that *knew* that it *knew*—somewhere in the recesses of his spirit. But Omar was prepared for occasions like this. He had a truthful cover.

"I visited family in Pakistan. You can ask my parents. It was my aunt and uncle on my mother's side, and very close to my mother. I hope you take my word for it, because I love this country, the US. It is the country of my birth, and I love this city of New York, and you know…well, sometimes…sometimes, unfortunately, devout Muslims like myself, and my family are…are…what's the word?"

He knew the word.

"Oh, yes. Profiled. Some of my friends have had to contact CAIR. You know what CAIR is, I'm sure. The Council on American Islamic Relations."

Darrin spoke for the first time, as Lawrence held his breath.

"Yes, we're familiar with it. You know, I used to deal with some of the biggest underworld figures in the world…in the 1980's. They were a murderous lot."

Schmidt thought to himself, *Where's he taking this? Who cares about the mobsters in the 1980's?*

Darrin continued.

"The guilty ones always reminded me of their legal rights. Not that it was wrong to do that, mind you. But…it's just how it was."

He kept his eyes fixed on Omar, who eventually turned his eyes toward Schmidt.

"What's with him? Is he saying I'm guilty of something?"

Schmidt shook his head.

"What are you driving at, Brock?"

"I don't know," Brock responded as if in a trance of some sort. Then he took a deep breath and threw up his hands.

"Nothing. Nothing. I'm not saying anything."

Schmidt got up and extended his hand to Omar, who responded in kind.

"Yeh, well, we just had some concerns. But you've answered them. Everything looks okay here."

Omar feigned a desire for them to stay.

"I thought you were going to stay a while and grab something to eat."
Schmidt glanced instinctively at the counter.

"Too many people waiting. Let's go, Brock."

They left Omar to finish his sandwich. *That couldn't have gone better*, he thought as he started to devour the second half of his tasty Jewish sandwich. *I can hear the future news broadcast now. They interviewed him at Mendy's Kosher Deli, before he blew himself up at the Flatiron Building. He slipped through their fingers.* He chuckled as he took another bite.

As the two law enforcement officials walked through Grand Central Station, Darrin turned to Schmidt.

"Something's not quite right."

Schmidt didn't miss a beat as he continued to look forward.

"What in the world are you talking about? I've been doing this a long time, Brock. He didn't stab anyone in the deli. He didn't blow anything up or pull a gun out. He didn't run. He had perfectly believable answers. That's my report. If we went any further, it would be seen as profiling. Well, thanks for the time."

He separated from Darrin like a train headed down a different track after a switch had been thrown.

Darrin headed back to the precinct building. The winter weather was still unseasonably mild, so he decided to slowly walk toward 35th Street at Ninth Avenue instead of taking a cab. The "physical therapy" would do him good. As he made his way from one street and avenue to another, he went over the Grand Central Station rendezvous in his mind. Although he couldn't quite put his finger on it, something in his intuitive heart detected a dark spot of some sort behind Omar Shehadulah's eyes— something almost opaque, and subtly sinister. And he determined to mention it to Inspector Ralph Lewis as soon as he saw him.

When Darrin finally arrived at the second floor of the precinct building, he began to make his way toward Lewis' office. Seemingly out of nowhere, Margaret cut right in front of him. Then she suddenly turned 180 degrees and stood directly in front of his face. He could smell her sweet breath as their lips practically touched, as well as their eyelashes. As close as their faces were, he could just detect that her chestnut-brown hair wasn't pulled back as usual, but instead formed a youthful-looking parenthesis around her middle-aged yet well kept smooth face. Startled, he tried to back up. But she moved forward. He could smell her exotic perfume. He had to say something.

"Excuse me, Margaret, but…"

They were so close, he could even feel the shape of her figure. This was getting embarrassing. He moved to the side. She let him, but grabbed his hand as she looked into his eyes.

"Guess what, Darrin Brock?"

"I…I don't have a clue, Margaret. But…I'm kind of in a hurry. I came to see Inspect…"

"He's not here, Darrin. He's out. So…guess what?"

"I don't know. But can I sit down in my cubicle…please?"

She looked around and saw a few officers staring.

"Of course…of course."

She took him by the hand and led him to his own desk. He put the cane in the corner and collapsed into his chair.

"Now what is it, Margaret? I'm busy."

Without asking, she sat on his desk. Even in her police uniform, he could see how attractively built she was—and how fit and trim. He looked up at her as he leaned back in his chair. He spoke quietly, so no one around them would hear.

"What's *with* you today?"

She whispered as loudly as she could.

"Can't you tell?"

"No, I can't. I mean, your new hairstyle looks very nice. I'm sure your boyfriend likes it. But that can't be what you want to tell me."

"I broke up with him. I threw him out. We're no longer living…in sin…together. He wasn't very good for me…too young and…worldly."

"Okay."

"Can't you guess now?"

"Well…it certainly can't be *that*. I mean, your boyfriends and living arrangements are your own private business. They're certainly not *my* business."

"But…I just gave you a clue," she pouted, sticking out her lower lip.

He wanted to get this conversation over with.

"Okay. Look, I'm busy."

She jumped off the desk and got down on her knees, taking both his hands in hers. He froze. No woman had ever been this physical with him except his mother...and Naomi. She held his hands tight. He tensed up, and spoke as firmly as he could.

"This is not appropriate, Margaret. It's against regulations to fraternize like you're doing, and you know it. I could report you...not...not...that I necessarily would. But still..."

She let go of his hands.

"Well, you still haven't guessed."

"No, I haven't. Okay, you can tell me, and then leave."

"I got saved, Darrin! At Times Square Church. Sandy, from Midtown North Precinct station on West 54th Street, asked me to go last Sunday. Did you know that the senior pastor, Pastor Conlon, used to be in law enforcement?"

"No, I...I didn't know that. That's a pretty large church, isn't it? That's very nice that you went there. My church is smaller."

Darrin tried to appear excited. After all, this was good news. Margaret had always seemed so lost. Now, she was obviously found. She grabbed his hands again, and squeezed them even more tightly.

"Eight thousand people, Darrin. Can you imagine that? Eight thousand! Anyway, he gave a message about God's love, and I went forward. And...so much has changed since then. I'm reading my Bible... wait..."

She sprung up and ran to her cubicle, and then ran back. In her hand was a small dark-red faux leather Bible. She got down on her knees again and held his hands and the Bible at the same time—as if she was about to take an oath...or a vow.

"I've been praying, Darrin, praying a lot. And I think...I think...that God wants me to tell you that I've always loved you...and that we should be together...sometime..."

She began to blush, as if it suddenly dawned on her that she was making a fool of herself, or at least risking it.

"Oh God, I don't mean *now!* But...someday...like a prophecy...for the future. Oh God, Darrin Brock, I love you. The life I lived before... that was just sinful me, choosing...choosing what's his name...my old boyfriend. This is the real me, and the real me *always* loved you."

Darrin had to say something or her words would stand.

"First of all, Margaret…I don't use God's name that way, in vain like that…and that's just the *first* thing."

"I'm learning. I'll never use His name that way again…ever. I swear."

"I don't swear either."

"I'm so sorry. I promise not to do that either."

"Second, Margaret, I told you…you shouldn't talk to me like that at work. It's *wrong*. You could be accused of harassment. And besides all that, you're just a baby…spiritually speaking, of course. You shouldn't be thinking about romantic relationships right now. Not only have you just left a serious relationship, but in order to hear what God is saying to you in these areas, you must gain some maturity in your relationship with Him. Give those things a little time."

The last thing Darrin expected to be doing this day in late winter was to be spiritually instructing anyone—especially Margaret. But if he was going to spiritually instruct, he might as well be direct about it.

"And can I ask you to do something for me? And I hope you're not offended when I tell you."

"Yes. I want to hear everything you say…and grow."

"Good. Could you please remove your hands? They're practically on my lap, and that's uncomfortable for me."

She quickly removed her hands again, along with the Bible, and placed her right hand and the Bible on his desk. He looked into her eyes, which he'd never even once noticed before. He instantly noted that they weren't like Naomi's. But they *were* full of hazel-green fire, and extraordinarily beautiful—in a sweetly seductive sort of way. He realized for the first time that Margaret was a very beautiful woman. Why hadn't he noticed that before? And he also realized that he had to lay down the law with this woman, and he had to do it now.

"Margaret…I don't feel comfortable…getting that close…touching… even like that, like you just did…even if we weren't at work. You see… you will have to…to…give up for a while…I mean…you've been living in a different way. You can't go around…with men…now…with what you now know…that is, *Who* you know. You see, I don't…and I never have…never…even once. Do you understand?"

He couldn't bring himself to be more specific than that. She got the point.

"I'll wait. God has given me self control. I'll wait for as long as it takes. I'll wait for you, Darrin. I'll wait. But I want you to know that I do want to fall in love with the One who forgave all my sins…of which there were many in my life…*believe me*. And I want to learn. I want to grow. I do feel like a newborn baby. You're right about that. I do."

A strange mix of heart-warning conviction and heart-warming compassion began to fill his vulnerable heart. He realized that something genuine had most likely happened in the life of this formerly love-deprived woman, and he wanted to encourage that. But he also knew that he needed to back her off when it came to any hint of an expectation that he was the one. And yet, an identifiable fraction of his beating heart had to admit that he was indeed attracted to this wide-eyed spiritually hungry—and frankly, quite sensual and sexy—woman. And in the absence of his beloved Naomi, that felt emotionally, as well as physically, stimulating.

He ended the cubicle discussion by rising and taking her hand, but only so he could help her up from a kneeling position. Then he looked directly into her eyes.

"Margaret…I'm going to be praying for you. I'm so happy for you. I do care about you…as a sister in the Lord. And I will continue to care about you. I will mention your feelings about me to no one. And we won't discuss them with each other."

He let go of her hand.

"Now, I need to get hold of Inspector Lewis about something important. So I have to go and give him a call."

She reached over and kissed his cheek lightly. Even with that peck, he could feel how soft and moist her lips were. She smiled.

"That was like a sister, right?"

"Okay. Okay."

She walked out of his cubicle and toward hers. He sighed quietly and collapsed back in his chair. Suddenly, he remembered how urgent the need to speak to the inspector was. He pulled out his phone and called him. Ralph Lewis picked it up immediately and started in without so much as a beat.

"Brock, I talked to Schmidt. He told me the Pakistani kid is fine. So you'll be glad to hear you're off the hook."

Darrin knew he had less than a second to insert a word about his sense that something about Omar Shehadulah felt wrong. And that second passed by in a flash of indecision. Lewis continued, his voice betraying more than a hint of impatience.

"Of course, soon I'll have another one for you and Schmidt to check out. There's always more of them...like locusts."

"Yes, sir. But I thought you might want to know that..."

The inspector interrupted.

"I gotta go, Brock. I'm at one of those police community relations training things. Aren't you supposed to be here? No, I guess not."

"Yes, but I just wanted to bring something up about it..."

"What? The Mandy Mendel thing again? Stick with the script, Brock. Let the past go. Prima is dead. That Russian Igor in dead. Case closed, or it will be soon, hopefully. I'm waiting for the final report. Just concentrate on this HS thing, and be ready for the next interview. That's an order! "

"I wasn't going to mention the Mendel thing. But since you have, I *have* been thinking about it, and..."

Darrin instantly regretted saying that. He should have been disciplined and stayed away from the temptation to mention the Mandy Mendel murder. Lewis was right in this case. Stick to the script, and just mention his reservations about Omar Shehadulah.

There was a pause as he detected an unusual silence on the other end. As he took a short breath before speaking, he wondered if Inspector Lewis had already hung up before he had a chance to give his take on the Shehadulah meeting. That wouldn't be good. He spoke up.

"Inspector, I thought I'd give my take on the aforesaid...encounter... with the young...the subject of our...investigation...which you asked me to...investigate. In my opinion...in my view...I have some concerns... it's only a hunch, but...hello? Hello?"

He realized he was talking to dead air. He pressed disconnect on his cell phone and collapsed back in his chair.

THE
SECOND SPRING

Chapter Sixteen

Naomi had been to Kingsbrook Jewish Medical Center in Flatbush just once since David Kaplan had moved there. As it turned out, the campus was massive, and included several modern buildings that took up a full city block. One of those facilities was called the Kingsbrook Rehabilitation Institute, which specialized in patients with strokes. It was one of the finest facilities of its kind in the country. It had occurred to Naomi upon arrival that Lisa, and Aunt Ida—and yes, Darrin, not that any of this was his business— had chosen well. Another building housed a well run nursing home. For the time being, Naomi's father was in the Rehabilitation Institute. Whether he would end up at the nursing home or his own home was dependent on his progress.

During Naomi's first Sunday afternoon visit to Kingsbrook, the early spring light had shone through strategically placed windows in the physical therapy room, creating a cheerful motivation for healing. It had taken an extra ten minutes before Naomi finally found the spacious room, which had been full of recovering stroke patients. David had been in the middle of an intense therapy workout. She had been surprised and pleased to see her father sitting in a wheelchair, attempting a still slightly crooked smile, and holding a colorful beach ball. A young, pleasant, and obviously well trained Ethiopian physical therapist named Abrihet had greeted her. Her facial features were similar to a particular group of other young Ethiopian women—specifically, those from the Beta Israel community—stunning, with a small straight nose and a flawless coffee-with-cream complexion.

David had been able to talk a bit more clearly than at the Maimonides Medical Center. While Abrihet had kept her watchful eyes on him, she had explained the progress he was making with the beach ball. That had been followed by a demonstration, which emphasized his day by day improvement. Then, with some difficulty, David had explained to Naomi that Abrihet means "She brings light." Indeed, something about Abrihet did light up the room. Naomi had understood all of her father's words. Everything about the visit had been pleasant. However, as in the past, there had been no opportunity for her to share about her break-up with Darrin.

Now, she sat on her unmade bed in the approaching dusk of that same Sunday. When David Kaplan was in the house, she had never failed to fastidiously make up her bed—as well as her father's. But she had pretty much neglected that task since then—as if to remind herself of his absence through something akin to a flag at half-mast.

She got up and went downstairs to look for something to eat. If she felt ambivalent about anything during her first visit to the Kingsbrook Jewish Medical Center, she hadn't yet processed it. Now, as she grabbed a cup of yogurt from the refrigerator and a slice of challah from the cupboard, she began to do just that. On the positive side, she was very pleased with the Rehabilitation Institute, the staff—particularly the physical therapist whose name she had already forgotten, except that it started with an "a" and then a "b"—and the improvement in her beloved father's health. On the negative side, she regretted not having any time alone with him, and not telling him things were over with Darrin. As she thought the name *Darrin*, her heart fluttered slightly, followed by the thought, *Oh my God in Heaven, I thought I would be over him by now. Help me with the evil inclination, the Yetzer Hara.*

Just as she sat down at the dining room table that held so many Shabbat afternoon memories, she heard an aggressive rap at the front door. It reminded her of Marvin's incessant and insensitive knock, but it *couldn't* be him. And if it wasn't him, who else could be there on this spring Brooklyn dusk? She cautiously approached the door, and shouted nervously.

"Who is it?"

"Marvin," came the loud and disappointing response. She rolled her eyes.

"Go home!"

"Naomi, I came all the way here…by subway."

"So? Don't bother me. I want to be alone," she borrowed from Greta Garbo. "Go away! Go away!"

"No! Let me in…or I'll tell my mother."

"So tell her!"

"And she'll tell Aunt Ida, and she'll be mad at you."

"O, I'm scared," she mocked. "Just leave! I'm going to bed."

Naomi proceeded to go upstairs. When she got to her bedroom, she flopped down on her unmade-up mattress. Surely, Marvin had gotten the message. As she lay there, she was surprised and pleased that she felt no guilt about treating him the way she did. The dysfunctional relationship was over. No more carrying Marvin emotionally, and even financially. She was thankful to HaShem, to the God who had steeled her resolve. She had walked into that disturbing messianic place, through a door she never thought she'd darken. That was over and done with. Now she had just shut the door in Marvin's face, so to speak. That was like bolting an already locked door. Their *friendship*—if it could be called that—was finally over. No more of his constant begging for her worn-out hand. Over and done. Period! He must have gotten the message and left. Time to eat dinner, before the yogurt sours—well, sours more than it should.

She slowly closed her eyes, just to fade to black like the finality of a bad movie. But a dreadful sound like a howling mutt triggered an involuntary fade up. What was it? There was a pause. Then it repeated.

"Naaay-oh-mee! I Love Yoooou!"

Of course, it was Marvin's obnoxious way of serenading her under her window. And he kept at it. He would not be denied.

"Naaay-oh-meee! Naaay-oh-meee!"

She had no choice. He was disturbing the entire neighborhood. She ran to her window and pulled it up. The crisp air of an early spring night stirred her to action.

"Marvin. Stop that! It's over. Go home and go to bed!"

"I can't!"

He looked like his usual Marvin self, not even dressed as well as the last time she saw him at Macy's. He had his usual orange hat on. She wondered if he'd left it on day and night since mid-winter. He wore his hideous lightweight green jacket—the one she despised. It was time to tell him off for the last time, and shut the window. Delighted to see her, he spoke first.

"You see, I know you went to the Yeishke place. My Aunt Ida told me. I think she wants me to stop asking you to marry me. But it didn't work. HaShem is wiser. When I went to synagogue last Shabbat, He helped me understand that I should give you one more chance. I'm ready to forgive."

"Are you? I don't need your forgiveness! And Aunt Ida is right!"

As was often the case, Marvin ignored her comment.

"My mother forgives you too. She told me to say that."

Naomi's plan had failed. She should have known that Marvin would break his own word and continue to pursue her even after she crossed the Beth Yeshua threshold. Now, a more aggressive strategy was necessary. But what form would it take? She wasn't quite sure, even as she skipped downstairs and opened the front door. She walked onto the front step and half shut it after her so Marvin wouldn't get any ideas about being welcome at the Kaplan house. She glared at him, and as she did so, her strategy came to her. She would be like David, who lied to the king of the Philistines about his sanity. As she looked into Marvin's pathetically eager eyes, she feigned a revelatory look.

"Marvin…I didn't want to tell you. But you've forced me, by coming here without notice, interrupting my quiet evening with your rude barking."

Marvin, instead of listening, was focusing his full attention beyond Naomi, on the half-shut door. His obsessive mind concluded that if he pushed it hard enough, he could end up inside the Kaplan house. Once there, he could refuse to leave until Naomi agreed to marry him—or at least agreed to begin the process by offering him some milk and a kosher Mi-Del cookie. Naomi continued with her strategy, endeavoring to sound like one of *them*. She borrowed an affectation from a television evangelist she had once stumbled upon—before apologizing to HaShem and quickly changing the channel.

"Yes, I entered the sanctuary of the Lord Gawd Almighty, the Miracle Temple of…of…Yeishke, whom they…affectionately call…"

She shut her eyes tightly.

"…*Jee*-sus. I saw miracles. Miracles of…Gawd."

"Why are you talking like that? My mother told me…"

She stopped him cold.

"I met a woman named…named…"

She suddenly and inexplicably remembered the woman's name.

"…um…Mahalia…Mahalia Morse, to be exact…she's a Holy Roller of the…the first degree, as they call it…very high up there, and a prophetess in her own right…like Deborah in the Book of Judges… *Shoftim*."

"They've…they've brainwashed you…"

"Yes, they have. They have definitely convinced me. As I was… testifying…that's the word they use…she prophesied to me and said, 'You shall not marry Marvin.' She knew your name. 'You shall be a virgin nun dedicated to *Jee*-sus."

Marvin gasped.

"It's witchcraft! She's a witch! Stay away from her, or I'll…I'll…"

Once again he hesitated, unable to bear losing her.

"Well, as long as you…as you don't go back, I think it will wear off… if you go to synagogue and…and…make *teshuva*…repentance."

She widened her eyes to appear as if she'd been hypnotized, and drew close—like she'd seen thick-mascaraed actresses do in old silent black-and-white Bela Lugosi films.

"But I've been back…two, three times already," she declared in a monotone.

He stumbled back.

"The evil eye! The evil eye!"

Then she silently asked God's forgiveness for lying before she grabbed his hand and shared the clincher.

"I've accepted *Jee*-sus. Would you like to accept Him too? Let's pray right now!"

He yanked his hand away and turned around. His clumsy body lumbered down the street. She hadn't meant to scare him quite that much, but she knew she had to do something drastic. After all, she couldn't allow all the effort she had put into visiting the messianic place go to waste. She walked back into the house and shut the door. As she returned to her yogurt and challah, she determined to skip work the next day and once and for all tell her father everything.

CHAPTER SEVENTEEN

The next morning, Naomi awoke from a restless night, determined to resort to her lying tongue once again. She knew that Monday was an item return day, and that the morning could be particularly busy. But there was usually another employee there on Mondays to assist. She decided that this was the best time to follow through with her responsibility to tell her father about her decision to break things off with Darrin, and to apologize for the sin of ever having gotten involved with him in the first place.

After stumbling through a quick call to her supervisor, Mrs. Lazar, and getting the all clear to "recover from a twenty-four-hour virus," she dressed quickly and left the house for the Kingsbrook Rehabilitation Institute. As she shut her heavy eyes on the subway bench seat, the steely rhythm of the rails seemed to whisper, *you know you're guilty, you know you're guilty, you know you're guilty.* One sin had piled high on another— her *affair* with a *goy*, perhaps the way she ended things with that same kind and loving Gentile, her lie to Marvin, her lie to her boss. As the train approached Utica Avenue and the first bus transfer, a tear formed inside her still closed eyes. She knew she was guilty as charged. And that made it all the more important to follow through with her mission. By the time she arrived at the door to David Kaplan's room, she was focused and ready to confess all of her guilt to him—along with her firm decision to end things with Darrin.

She heard elevated voices in the room before David reached her line of sight. When she entered the room and could finally see who was speaking, she immediately recognized the Ethiopian woman Abrihet—who was standing with two large men, one African American and one Caucasian. She realized by their light-blue outfits that they were some sort of aides. The three were hovering around her father, whose eyes were fixed on the trained physical therapist. The three were obviously intent on moving him off the bed and into a wheelchair. The atmosphere seemed tense. Was something wrong? Had he suffered another stroke? Alarmed, Naomi approached and interrupted them.

"Where are you taking him? Is he…?"

Abrihet responded in a soothing voice, which Naomi immediately questioned. Was it simply professional and therapeutic, like the young woman's trained hands?

"I'm so glad you're here, Ms. Kaplan. Your father is a blessed man. I'm honored to call him a friend. Isn't that true, Mr. Kaplan?"

With some effort, his improving mouth formed a smile, as his eyes turned to Naomi and then back to Abrihet.

"God loves your father."

Where had Naomi heard those kind words before? The woman's whole affect sounded somewhere between Darrin Brock and Mahalia Morse. Was she one of *them*? Naomi felt at once both terrified and inexplicably comforted by that thought. She instinctively realized that her mixed-up feelings were a symptom of just how truly mixed up she was about *everything* in her life right now. Old questions about whether Darrin worshipped the same God as she and her father did suddenly rose to her consciousness. And they were just as suddenly suppressed by her need to know just what was happening to David Kaplan in this moment.

"I know that. Of course He does," she responded more defensively than she knew was appropriate for the occasion. "Just tell me. Is he okay?"

She turned to her father.

"Are you okay, Abba? Where are they taking you?"

David reached his hand out toward her.

"I'm okay, my daughter. They'rrre…they…they are taking me somewhere…sp… special. I'd…love…"

He took a vocal-cord-relaxing breath.

"…love for you to…to come."

"Where?"

Naomi looked directly into Abrihet's earnest eyes. She responded with a grin.

"We're going on an outing to Midwood Press to use the Linotype machine and teach the children about it."

"But…but…that happens on Thursdays, doesn't it? And this is a Monday."

Abrihet nodded.

"Yes, but our God had other plans. Ben, who works there, arranged for the children to come today."

Our God? Was this Ethiopian woman one of those Ethiopian Jews, like the ones who were air-lifted to Israel many years before? Of course. Why hadn't she thought of that? Perhaps HaShem had arranged for a Jewish woman to help her father. That made sense, considering the fact that the Rehabilitation Institute was a part of the Kingsbrook Jewish Medical Center.

Abrihet's sweet voice continued, her lilting Ethiopian accent just adding to the sweetness.

"Maybe you'll come with us, as your father asks? In my world, there are no coincidences. You're here, and we're ready to go. I think it would be good for you to be there. Don't you? For such a time as this, as Mordecai said."

That sounds more like Mahalia Morse than a good Orthodox Jew from Brooklyn. But perhaps all the Jews from Ethiopia sound that way.

Tired of thinking, Naomi said the next thing that came to her mind.

"Sure. Why not? Let's go, Abba. I can't wait to see you use the Linotype machine!"

Naomi was suddenly much more glad than regretful that she had lied to Mrs. Lazar. Now she had the whole day off, and she could take as much time as she needed to go with her father wherever he was going, for as long as that took. And maybe she could finally get to talk to him… alone. She made a conscious effort to calm herself and go with the flow—

something she wasn't usually very good at, except for the few times the year before when she had impulsively followed Darrin Brock.

She joined Abrihet and the aides, as they wheeled David Kaplan through the halls of the Kingsbrook Rehabilitation Institute, down the elevator, and out of the facility. There, waiting for them, was a well polished red and white emergency vehicle. A platform slowly lowered from the center of the van. The aides assisted David's chair onto the platform, which rose and retreated into the vehicle, taking David Kaplan with it like the gangplank of an alien spaceship. The aides entered through the back and proceeded to anchor the chair and strap David in for the ride. They invited Naomi to enter and take a small pull-down seat next to her father. Abrihet and the aides entered the emergency van through the front doors, taking seats provided just behind the driver and passenger seats. Once the three helpers were strapped in, they took off down the street toward Midwood.

As the streets became more familiar, Naomi thought about her evening at Avram and Leah Milstein's house. It seemed longer ago than just a few weeks. She was wondering if they would actually pass their house, when she suddenly recognized the inauspicious door to Beth Yeshua as it whizzed by. She almost ducked, irrationally expecting one of the members—perhaps even Mahalia Morse—to blow her cover and yell at the passing van, "Hey Naomi, glad you visited Beth Yeshua!"

Finally, the vehicle arrived at the Midwood Press. One by one, everyone piled out, ending with David in the wheelchair as he was slowly lowered onto the sidewalk. Naomi looked up at the five-or-six-story traditional Brooklyn brick office structure. She had heard so much about the Midwood Press, and her father's frequent visits there. But she had never visited there herself. With a typically inviting smile, Abrihet extended her hand as she led the way into the building and then into a somewhat claustrophobic industrial elevator. She pressed the round black button with the number 2, and the elevator lurched upward. When they finally arrived at the second floor and accompanied David Kaplan into the Midwood Press facility, Ben looked up from the massive Linotype machine. A huge smile lit up his face, competing with his beacon of blonde hair which protruded from his grey baseball cap. He rose and ran over to David, reaching down to hug him in his wheelchair.

"David Kaplan, the great *New York Times* Linotype operator! It's been so long. We've missed you around here. And I *know* the kids have missed you."

David craned his head back in his wheelchair and addressed Naomi.

"Naomi...this...this is the B...Ben I was telling...telling you about."

Naomi stretched out her hand to greet Ben.

"Thank you for giving my father a chance to teach the children today, Ben. He lights up whenever he even thinks about this place."

David turned back to Ben.

"And this is...Ab...Abrihet, my...my physical the...therap...you know. And also Mark and Greyson, my...my aides. All friends of mine. The driver didn't...didn't come in."

Naomi wasn't surprised that her father would introduce everyone who came with him—and even those who didn't. She had missed his thoughtfulness for everyone created in God's image, and was deeply affected to see the father she knew so well act more and more like his old self. Her lips curled in pride and her eyes glistened. Her personal tender moment was interrupted by a loud clap of Ben's hands.

"Well, let's get started. The children will be here soon. David, I thought we could wheel you up to the Linotype machine, and you could explain everything while I type."

Abrihet moved forward toward the iron and steel machine and spoke up, her voice starting quiet with her initial sentence, and then rising incrementally with every word.

"Ben...I'd like to humbly ask a question, if I may. Do you think we might help Mr. Kaplan sit at the machine and try some typing himself? You see, this is one reason why we brought him. I believe he can operate the machine, and perhaps his daughter could teach the children. He has come a long way over the last few months, and so I believe...with the help of God...he is ready. We've talked about this, haven't we, Mr. Kaplan?"

Ben could tell by the ambivalent bow of David Kaplan's head that he wasn't quite convinced. Nevertheless, he embraced the idea. Ben agreed.

"Good idea. Okay, let's do this! They're almost here."

Abrihet gave Ben one of her infectious smiles, and then stooped in front of David.

"Okay, Mr. Kaplan. Let's get out of this chair and walk over to the machine. Mark? Greyson?"

She motioned to the aides, who took their place at David's side. Then, with a glance at each other and a "one, two, three," they each took hold of an arm and lifted him out of his chair. David valiantly struggled to put one foot in front of the other, until he arrived at the seat facing the Linotype machine. He nodded, and the men moved him forward and placed him on the chair. With another nod, David motioned to Greyson, whose hands were still holding his.

"Please put my hand on the k...key...board."

Naomi stepped forward and took his other hand.

"Abba, are you feeling up to this? You seemed a little uncomfortable when Abrihet suggested..."

"You're right. You cert...cert...ain...ainly...are my daughter. You notice. But if you help....help...I can...I can do...this."

"How can I help, Abba? How can I...?"

"You see the keyboard. I know it's different. But...I will type with my...my...good hand. And you...reach the other keys. We won't go...go...ff...fast. But they will see it...work. And you explain it like you re...member...like I taught...taught you...when you were...were...young."

"That was a long time ago, Abba. But you've certainly shared with me about it since then."

Ben smiled.

"That'll work."

By the time the elementary school children arrived with their bag lunches, each filled with cheese, tuna, egg salad, or other sandwiches, and Capri Sun drinks, David and Naomi Kaplan had practiced together for perhaps a half hour. They sat next to each other, he on the designated chair, and she on another chair just to his left. David rested his right hand—his good hand—on the right side and middle of the Linotype machine's strange-looking keyboard. Naomi rested her right hand on the left side. She would do most of the typing, as David's portion of the keyboard only included capital letters and punctuation. She had all the lower-case letters. He had told her to keep her touch light so as not to release any matrices from the distributor mechanism and down the channels by mistake. But he was well aware that, due to the tendency for even his good hand to tremor, the challenge to keep a light touch would now be more his than hers.

The plan was for Naomi to tell the children about her father and his Linotype experience, as they sat on the concrete floor in one large group. Then the two would type something together. After a last-minute quick study of the seemingly random letters before her, Naomi turned from the machine and faced perhaps thirty or forty noisy second and third graders, as diverse as the streets of greater New York City. Mrs. Johnson—a dedicated and compassionate disciplinarian in her early thirties, who had been raised in the same black neighborhood a few of the children lived in—clapped her hands several times, which had the effect of a cracked whip on the roar of the excited class.

"Pay attention, please, to Ms...."

"Ms. Kaplan...Naomi Kaplan. And this is my father David."

Naomi realized that she had just told everyone in the shop, including Ben and this teacher, that she was middle-aged and single. What they didn't know was that there had been prospects. But no more. *Oh well. You'd think I'd be used to all that by now*, she mused. Ms. Johnson turned to her.

"I'm Mrs. Johnson. These are young people from three different schools. They were chosen because of their good grades and good attendance."

She's married. What else should I expect? Almost everyone is but me. Stop it, stupid thoughts!

The children turned their eyes toward Naomi.

"This looks like such a wonderful group of young people, Mrs. Johnson. Good morning, everyone."

Here goes.

"Does anyone know what this machine is called?"

Hands reached out toward her, followed by guesses that ranged from "a printing press" to the comedic "a caveman's computer." Then she began in earnest, while her father sat silent, his eyes focused on his shoes.

"Thank you all for your creative guesses. Well...as a matter of fact, this is called a Linotype machine. They don't make them any more. Computers took their place. So that one answer about it being like an old computer wasn't that far off."

She glanced at the beautiful Latino boy who came up with the caveman's computer answer. He had extraordinary inquisitive eyes and adorable rings of curly brown hair. He smiled and giggled, and the girl next to him blushed with infatuation. He was obviously the popular class clown. Naomi continued.

"My father, David Kaplan, operated one of these many years ago, when he worked at the *New York Times*. He was one of the greatest Linotype operators that…that ever lived. And one of the most wonderful human beings, too."

David Kaplan looked up at his daughter, surprised by her effusive statement.

"Linotype operators decided what the pages of the newspaper would look like by typing on this machine. They were real artists, and everyone respected them. When they typed, metal letters flew down these chutes, these channels, and ended up here."

She pointed to the tray at the bottom part of the machine.

"Then comes the amazing part. Hot liquid metal came from over here, and molded sentences out of those letters. They then put the sentences together to make the newspaper page."

Naomi noticed that the children's eyes began to wander, and a few of them stretched and yawned. She realized she needed to move on. But before she did, she had one more thing to say.

"I just want to say that…my father, who I call *Abba*…"

A few children giggled. They'd never heard a father called that.

"…he hasn't been feeling too well. He had what's called a stroke. But he's getting better. I couldn't have asked for a better father. I love him so much."

David Kaplan's eyes began to moisten, perhaps partly because the stroke had removed restraint. His heart overflowed with affection for his daughter. Embarrassed, he turned toward the familiar Linotype machine as Naomi wrapped up this part of their demonstration with a final comment.

"I'm sure you all feel that way about your fathers."

Without a beat, the young comedian shouted out, "I don't have a father. I never had a father. I just showed up."

A few children giggled nervously. Naomi searched for words.

"Oh, I…I mean, you *had* one. I mean…well…I'm so sorry."

How could I be so stupid! Of course some of these children are fatherless! I wish I could just disappear!

"Well, I know that God loves all of you…like a father. That I know. You're all special."

The children weren't used to hearing a teacher talk about God. Now they were embarrassed too. Naomi closed her eyes and rolled them invisibly.

Why did I say that? That sounds Christian, like Darrin…certainly not like me.

It was time to move on. She turned to the machine and spoke to the children behind her.

"Now we will type a sentence. Watch what happens while we do that. Letters will fly down the channels, liquid metal will pour into molds, and sentences will be created. Then the letters will go back up to the distributor bar for later use. Ready?"

The children all said "Yeah!" at once. She turned to David Kaplan.

"Ready, Abba?"

He nodded his head. They had decided on a sentence beforehand.

It's so good to meet such wonderful children. I hope you like the Linotype machine.

She told the children the two sentences, and then she and David began to type, beginning with her father's capital I. Very slowly, the words began to form. She took her time finding the letters, not wanting to make even one mistake. David pressed the few keys he was responsible for, like apostrophes and periods, with one shaky finger. To Naomi, it felt like a special father-and-daughter piano duet, resulting in melodic clicks, grinds, and clinks. She giggled with delight as they worked together. To David, this was even more meaningful than when he "hung the bucket" at this same machine months before, racing at high speed to suck the liquid lead out of the overflow container. It felt like the high point of his Linotype experience. But he only betrayed his feelings with a slight crooked grin.

After the demonstration, the class filed in and out of the bathrooms and then ate their bag lunches on the concrete floor. Ben approached Naomi and her father as they rose from their seats.

"This was good. This was very good. You two make a great team. Can I count on you both again sometime soon?"

David nodded as Naomi spoke.

"Yes, absolutely. Why not? Of course. We'd love to, wouldn't we, Abba?"

Her eye caught Abrihet, who was several feet away. She was down on her knees in front of the boy with the caveman's computer comment, and no father. Her lips were just inches from his ear, and she was whispering something. He stood with his intent eyes focused just beyond Naomi. She could clearly see the effect Abrihet's whispers were having on those extraordinary eyes. Then he turned and whispered in Abrihet's ear. Naomi couldn't take her eyes off either of them. The girl who had sat next to him earlier was also watching from just a few feet away. Naomi turned away and back to her father. But the the image of Abrihet whispering in the "comedian's" ear remained like the after-image of the blinding sun.

After a minute or two, Abrihet brought Mark and Greyson, and they brought the wheelchair around for David. With some effort, he more or less fell into it. As they were walking out to the emergency vehicle, Naomi turned to Abrihet.

"Did you know that little boy?"

Abrihet responded without missing a beat.

"Javier? I was *getting* to know him."

"Oh. I felt so bad about what I said about...fathers...my father, and..."

Abrihet turned to her.

"Please. Don't feel bad, Naomi. He'll be fine. I know you will see Javier again. I'm sure of it."

"How do you know..."

Abrihet moved on to evaluate the day.

"It was a very successful outing for this perfectly beautiful spring day, don't you think? You and your father were wonderful. Many were touched."

Abrihet's comment at least partially comforted her. She hadn't thought about anyone being touched by the demonstration of the Linotype machine—other than her beloved father. When they all climbed into the vehicle, Naomi sat next to her father again. Now, finally, was her chance to tell her father what she had wanted to tell him for the last few weeks. She gathered her thoughts and silently practiced her memorized speech. Then she started.

"Abba, please forgive me for having disobeyed you, and strayed from our people, and our...our traditions. I've decided I'm not going to marry...either that Gentile detective or Marvin. I've told both of them in *no uncertain terms* that I'm *not interested*. So please get better so you can come home, and I can take care of you. That's all I care about. I miss you. You are the most important person in my life, besides HaShem... and I love you."

She was proud that she had remembered the whole speech, and had shared it so clearly. David, safely strapped in as they drove toward the Kingsbrook Rehabilitation Institute, looked as directly at her as he could—considering the fact that they were in a moving vehicle, and his constraints made him vulnerable to bumps, and narrow turns.

"My daughter, it is...goo...good that you have...have...placed Darrin Brock on the...al...altar of...of sacrifice, as Abraham did Is... Is...aac. This man is indeed a good man, as...as Isaac was. Still, it is good that you have done that...just, as I say, our fa...th...ther Abra...ham did. It is indeed a...a mitz...vah. And I must say, too, that I...I loo... look forward to living with...you in our...house, and in my own bed too...G...God willing."

Naomi's face took on a quizzical look.

"But Abba...didn't Avraham get Yitz-chak back?"

Her father nodded his head twice—or perhaps once, the second time being the result of a pothole.

"Yes, that's true...but that only...only...happ...happens... sometimes."

Chapter Eighteen

Darrin Brock couldn't sleep. Too many diverse individuals were clamoring for his attention. Margaret had the greatest sensual impact on him. He couldn't shake the feeling of her hands resting on his lap, their warmth radiating through his grey detective's suit pants. She was definitely sending a signal that he received in the way she intended it—either consciously or unconsciously—and he spent an inordinate amount of time in the middle of the night trying to keep his mind from going where her mind had obviously already been. *It's not her fault*, he told himself. *She's brand new at living a different kind of life than she had been living, and this was just her way of telling me that she likes me...a lot. But boy! Part of me just wants to give in and take her in my arms...and you know what! The lonely part, unfortunately. I have to admit, she is quite a beautiful woman...in her police uniform, and I'm sure out of it.*

Then there was Naomi. She had basically ripped his heart out, and left him as devastated as a jilted lover in a depressing country song—and as foolish as some of those lyrics. If he couldn't shake Margaret's hands, he definitely couldn't shake Naomi's eyes, and her sweet innocent lips. But when he thought of her that night, all he ended up experiencing was a dull ache—a phantom pain where his amputated heart had been.

Next, there was Chaya Mendel, and the unsolved case of her husband's murder. Inspector Lewis had shut Darrin down—twice. But that couldn't possibly be the end of it. Someday, little Natan would want to know what had happened to his father Mandy, and who was responsible. Darrin wanted to be able to tell him, whether as a result of another investigator's work, or his own.

Finally, there was Omar. What was there about him that kept Darrin up that night? What elicited, not sensuality, as with Margaret—or love lost's ache, as with Naomi—or questions about a deceased father, as with Natan—but fear? Whatever it was, he couldn't say at this point that his detective's skills were trustworthy. After all, he hadn't been following up on almost any lead since he had recovered from being shot—and then from being dumped by Naomi. He was basically out of commission, gone fishing, way out of practice. That night, he was particularly beating himself up over his promise to the widow Chaya Mendel—and to himself—to pursue her husband's murderer. Inspector Lewis had told him others were investigating the Mendel murder, and he should stay out of it and stick to cases given to him. And he had obeyed. He had never asked Chaya Mendel about her husband's life—or death. Nevertheless, he suspected that Mendel was probably in the diamond trade, as he had been killed in the Diamond District. But that was just a guess. And he was so rusty at his own trade that he had come to even second guess all of his guesses. Now, how could he trust such lousy instincts about Omar Shehadulah? And yet, those same instincts told him this wasn't just some nice bright young Muslim man with a desire for the good life in America—or maybe he was, after all.

By morning, after about four hours sleep total, Darrin decided he would at least address one of the individuals who haunted his night. He would strike out on his own to pursue the Shehadulah investigation. And he would start by asking the advice of a Muslim he could trust.

He left his house in Teaneck, and headed for the tip of Manhattan, and from there by train to the heart of Manhattan and the New York Public Library. Once inside the massive off-white literary cathedral, he turned left and headed for the Dewitt Wallace Periodical Room. When he arrived, he stood at the entrance and scanned the room, searching for Mahmoud and Stanley, David Kaplan's New York Public Library buddies. He had last seen them at David Kaplan's home during Chanukah. That seemed so long ago—and so painfully tender in his memory—like an oozing open bedsore too stubborn to heal. But it was recent enough to remember the faces of the two men he was looking for. And it was obvious they weren't there.

As he left the library, the thin-as-silk-sleeves Manhattan spring air barely brushing his cheek, he sought to call on his detective powers to locate Mahmoud—with or without Stanley. But like Superman in kryptonite's presence, those powers were weak. And the memory of Naomi was the rare mineral. He stood on the sidewalk, numb and feeling useless. Omar was the only person of interest given to him by the inspector that he was in any way motivated to follow up on—even though Inspector Lewis now seemed satisfied there was nothing to it. Like his whole life, even something as simple as a talk with Mahmoud was turning out to be a dead end.

All these thoughts were the result of a consistent depression that had enveloped Darrin for the last few months. But he wasn't objective enough to perceive that—let alone notice the young man with a taupe Mets ball cap, businesslike silver wire glasses, fake carefully applied mustache, blue Mets T-shirt, and pressed jeans—that had been tailing him since he had arisen from the subway station at 42nd Street/Bryant Park, like a ghost in a graveyard. The man with the Mets hat had followed him in and out of the library, and was now standing across 5th Avenue waiting for his next move.

Darrin looked around him, as was his habit, but saw nothing unusual. He tried to focus. That was particularly difficult, since he hadn't eaten or drunk anything since the night before, even a cup of coffee. He had been too consumed with the four persons who had haunted his night— Margaret, Naomi, Chaya Mendel, and Omar Shehadulah. He decided to hit Ben's Deli on 38th Street, on the way to the Midtown Manhattan South Precinct station, and his little cubicle.

Ben opened his original deli in Baldwin, New York in 1972, with $5000.00 capital. It wasn't until 1996, after opening six more locations, that he was able to conquer Manhattan by acquiring Lou G. Siegel's venerable deli on 38th Street. And conquer it he did, with the likes of Jackie Mason and Ed Koch frequenting the establishment often.

Darrin Brock's feet began to slowly navigate 5th Avenue, and headed south toward 41st Street. Despite a decreasing and yet still pronounced limp, and the sometime use of his cane, he was glad to be walking instead of traveling by car or subway. He breathed deeply until he felt a slight residual pain from his still-healing chest wound. But he was glad to be able to inhale the Manhattan air, and repeated the process a few times. As he walked on, the young "Mets fan" used the always crowded sidewalk to obscure himself.

After nearly a half hour of leisurely walking, Darrin finally reached the deli. As he entered the restaurant, he suppressed memories of conversations he'd had there with Naomi Kaplan. He didn't bother to check out anyone around him, as he usually might. He was too focused on his choice of matzoh ball soup—and on himself—to bother with his detective's habit. He took a seat in one of the booths. After he ordered soup and began the job of carving up the huge matzoh ball, he heard a loud familiar voice in the booth behind him.

"I used to tell the manager here, 'If you really knew what the hell you were doing, you wouldn't put so much salt in the matzoh ball soup.' But did he listen? No. Still too much salt."

Darrin Brock never forgot a voice, just like he never forgot a face. And out of practice as he was, he realized whose voice had just spoken that inaccurate opinion—considering the fact that he was presently eating a perfectly good bowl of soup. He quickly picked up his soup and walked the few feet to the adjacent booth. Sure enough, the voice belonged to Stanley, the former deli counter man and good friend of David Kaplan. And there across from him was former taxi driver and other good friend of David Kaplan, Mahmoud. What were the odds that he would find them here, having just looked for them at their usual hang out, the Dewitt Wallace Periodical Room several blocks away? Perhaps the God Darrin had taken a semi-conscious vacation from was nevertheless guiding his steps. He sat down uninvited next to Stanley and across from Mahmoud.

"I can't believe this! I just looked for both of you at the library."

Mahmoud smiled.

"My friend and boyfriend of David Kaplan's daughter! It's so good to see you. Allah must have led you to us."

Stanley wasn't as thrilled, but was nevertheless surprised.

"Allah had zilch to do with it, let alone *Adonai*. You were hungry. We were hungry. And Ben's Deli has way too salty and overrated matzoh ball soup. That's what happened. So how's your future father-in-law? We haven't gotten over to visit him at that Kingsbrook place yet."

Darrin Brock instantly determined not to mention the break-up.

"He's getting better, little by little. I think he'll be going home soon."

Mahmoud took a bite of his hummus and pita bread.

"That will be good for him and his daughter. And he will undoubtedly be visiting us again soon at the periodical room."

Stanley scoffingly raised his voice.

"Since when has he visited us in the last six months...no...more?"

Mahmoud struck a more conciliatory tone.

"Remember, my friend, David Kaplan has had a stroke."

Stanley couldn't let that comment stand.

"I don't mean that, Mahmoud. I mean before that. He stopped coming to the library long before that. Why do you think it took so long for us to find out about the stroke?"

"Yes, and maybe he wasn't feeling well even then? Did you think of that, my good friend?"

Stanley raised his voice another notch. Indeed, that was possible at Ben's, as opposed to the Dewitt Wallace Periodical Room.

"He was well enough to go to that broken-down printer place and let them take advantage! They paid him bupkis to teach the children, and he showed up there! Some friend!"

"Well...I'm sure he had a reason. However, now we must visit him. He can't come to us."

Stanley softened.

"Good point. Do unto others, as the Torah says."

Mahmoud smiled broadly, exposing a few moderately crooked teeth. Darrin realized that he had to interrupt, or they would continue their friendly arguing all day. He, on the other hand, had a limited period of time to get down to business with these two whose full-time job was retirement.

"If I may, I was hoping one of you could give me some advice."

Mahmoud was still in the teasing mood.

"Stanley is full of advice. He's always giving advice to everyone."

"Well actually, Mahmoud, I think you can help me in this case."

Stanley made an exception and didn't respond. He, like Mahmoud, was curious to know what this was about. Mahmoud turned to Darrin.

"How may I help you, friend of David Kaplan's daughter?"

Suddenly, Darrin Brock felt awkward. But he had come this far. And wasn't there something almost miraculous about this chance encounter at Ben's Deli?

"Well...Mahmoud...I was asked to question a young Pakistani man. I...I know you're not Pakistani. But...he is of the Islamic faith... and...not to be stereotyping, or profiling, or anything like that...but, to get to the point, my boss...he felt after I talked to this young man informally...that is, with a Homeland Security guy...because evidently, there was some chatter...he, that is my boss...he felt that there was no problem with this...this Pakistani...person...that is, after discussing it with the HS guy. I should add that the meeting with the young man was somewhat informal...at the Mendy's Deli Grand Central Station...for what it's worth."

Stanley couldn't let that reference pass.

"Worthless! A worse deli you couldn't have gone to! The McDonalds of delis. The worst!"

"Yes well, that may be true. At any rate, unlike my boss, who has never actually met this Pakistani...and unlike the Homeland Security expert...who *has*...something about this kid bothers me. I've been an NYPD detective for a long time. And although I may be a little out of practice for reasons not necessary to mention, I've got a hunch something's up with this...this Pakistani person. I've dealt with well-intentioned Muslims from the Middle East before. This feels different. What should I be looking for, Mahmoud? I thought you might know."

Mahmoud paused and then nodded.

"This is a serious question. And because I trust you as a man and as a police detective, I myself will ask you just one question. Do you sense anger...I mean, underneath? I mean underneath in this young man?"

Darrin felt as if someone had just given him the last bit of information necessary to cure cancer. It was an *of course, how could I have missed it* moment.

"Yes. Yes. That's right. *Way* underneath. But yes, beneath the nonchalant answers to basic questions...and professed love of all things

New York and American…something wasn't right."

Mahmoud lightly tapped his right hand on the table.

"I trust you. I trust your skills. If you say something isn't right about this man from Pakistan, then follow your hunch. I will tell you that these murderers are my enemies, and the enemies of the Islam I practice. Do you see this man here?"

He pointed to Stanley.

"His friendship…this Jewish man's friendship, is an example of the religion I practice. No other religion's teaching. *No other.* Not even the teaching of some who teach a distorted form of Islam. You see, I can even be politically incorrect, as some call it. It is bad Islam, not good Islam. Myself, I am Mahmoud, the Palestinian Muslim…Mahmoud the former New York taxi driver…and I may say, a very good New York taxi driver."

Stanley put his hand on Mahmoud's shoulder.

"Brock, I think Mahmoud would agree that whatever he knows about religious things started with the ancient Jews. *That's* why he's my best friend, better than some of my landsmen big shot *macher* so-called friends who treated me like a nothing at the deli counter. They give Jews a bad name. But Mahmoud, on the other hand, treats me like a *something.*"

Then he turned to Mahmoud and spoke pointedly.

"Mahmoud, you are the most Jewish Muslim in New York." Stanley spoke these words with affection. And indeed, Mahmoud had long ago learned to take comments like these as the highest form of compliments— when other Muslims might not. In the spirit of the moment, Darrin could have shared how his Christianity was totally informed by Torah and all other things Jewish. But he restrained himself, as that would have taken the conversation in another direction, and he was trying to stay as focused as possible.

As the amiable conversation continued, the "Mets fan" sat at the opposite adjacent booth to the one Darrin initially occupied. Darrin would have taken note of him if his detective's skills hadn't been so rusty. But he hadn't paid attention, and missed him altogether. The young man sat in his booth, his deep anger boiling over through clenched teeth. He wasn't angry at Darrin, or Stanley. After all, Darrin was only acting like a suspicious detective, a stupid suspicious detective. He could be mollified later—or eliminated. And Stanley was only an old Jewish fool, the kind of fool that was apt to vaporize in a well-timed explosion—in Allah's good time. Actually, it was Mahmoud he was furious with—Mahmoud the traitorous so-called Muslim. In fact, the "Mets fan" that turned out to be Omar was furious to the extent of murder, a very imminent murder. Making sure Darrin's back was to him, he quickly left for Ben's men's room, where he pulled off his mustache and hat and threw them in the trash. Then he just as quickly left the restaurant. Once on the street, he was just another foreign face in the crowd.

Omar found himself heading down 38th Street toward Eighth Avenue, and then back again past Ben's to Seventh Avenue, and then back again, like he was pacing in a claustrophobic room. Every time he passed Ben's Deli, he glanced in the window to make sure his prey was still inside. He didn't even care if Darrin Brock saw him. He was too filled with rage now to concern himself with camouflage and covers. After four passes, he watched from a few hundred feet away while Darrin walked out of the restaurant and headed toward Eighth Avenue, until he disappeared from sight. He was obviously headed toward the NYPD Midtown South Precinct station. Combining the lucid strategy of a good soldier of Allah with the impulsivity of his recent rage, he considered his next step.

I will not let this traitorous so-called Muslim out of my sight. And I will not rest until the sword of Allah strikes him, Inshallah—God willing.

With those few words, he concluded his block-long pacing and waited for Mahmoud and Stanley to emerge from the deli. He had to wait for another hour, while the two continued to tell each other lies—that is, as far as he was concerned—over potato pancakes and Dr. Brown's soda. Finally, after they paid their bill and walked out, they gave each other a what he could only describe as a repulsive hug, and went their separate ways. Omar followed Mahmoud at a distance, tailing him down several streets and avenues. While Mahmoud walked into a McDonald's and entered the bathroom, Omar ordered one of their cheap ice cream cones. He didn't take his eyes off the bathroom door.

You empty your gut now. I will rip it out soon. Infidel!

When Mahmoud entered the subway during rush hour and took the number 7 train, Omar squeezed through the closing doors just in time.

When Mahmoud transferred, Omar was right behind him. Before long, he realized that Mahmoud, like him, lived in Queens—albeit a different part of Queens. *How convenient.*

Finally, Omar tailed an oblivious Mahmoud into a Queens neighborhood halal market/restaurant.

Does this guy go anywhere else besides restaurants? He must be near his home, or he wouldn't choose such a place to purchase food. I must act soon. But it must be darker.

Omar felt the small closed switchblade knife in his right pocket.

He only wished that it was longer, so he could insure an immediate death with no inconvenient writhing or squirming. But a longer blade might incur a risk as he walked the streets of what he sometimes called the *decadent city.*

Mahmoud spent the next half hour inside the store, while Omar stood guard outside. When Mahmoud finally emerged, he was carrying an overstuffed bag with both hands—several small bags of fresh pita bread balanced on top of all that was beneath them, with cans, boxes, and other items filling out the bottom of the grocery bag. As he headed toward what Omar presumed was home, he navigated past one brick apartment building after another, whistling some sort of minor key melody that evaded Omar. By the time he had walked two or three blocks, the sun was beginning to sink in the western horizon, which was located approximately in the center of the road. Omar had to think fast, as the sporadic appearance of one person here and another one there dotted the sidewalk.

Not yet. Not yet.

Then, without warning, Mahmoud made a sharp left into what appeared to be a tiny alley. He was obviously nearing his destination. Now was Omar's chance. He glanced all around him. There didn't seem to be anyone in sight. His heart instantly began to spurt blood through the adjacent vessels in an involuntary eruption that caused all of his limbs to shudder and shake. He stuffed his hands in his pockets to regain control, and consequently felt the knife. He was now perhaps ten feet behind Mahmoud. He couldn't make even a tiny mistake, and thereby get caught—not when he still had the destruction of the Flatiron Building in his future. This was a small act compared to that. He couldn't ruin his chance to bring honor to Allah later.

He closed in until he could just reach out and touch the light grey jacket Mahmoud was wearing. Finally, Mahmoud detected him and made an about face, so that Omar came just short of running into him. The shock of the encounter caused Mahmoud to lose control of the bag and it tipped over, ripping and spilling its contents onto the alleyway.

He still suspected nothing, as there were many young men who looked similar to Omar in this Queens neighborhood.

"I'm so sorry. I did not notice you. I suppose I've lost my balance and dropped my bag."

Mahmoud bent down to pick up the contents. Omar knew what he had to do. He leaned over him, knife out now and exposed, with his head just behind Mahmoud's neck. Then he whispered so that only he, Mahmoud, and Allah could hear his pre-planned words.

"Death to the traitor to Islam…Allahu Akbar."

Mahmoud tried to rise up, beginning to turn his head in the process. Omar raised his right hand and then plunged the knife into Mahmoud's neck with all his might, until it blocked the airway and just protruded from the front of his neck. Mahmoud fell forward flat on his face, gurgling softly. Then Omar quickly pulled the knife out and plunged it into Mahmoud's back in the vicinity of his heart, instantly killing him. Mahmoud lay still, lifeless. Omar wasn't sure what his next move would be, but he knew he had to act fast. He looked around him, and began to quietly give praise. Just inches away was a manhole cover. It wasn't the kind that was impossible to move. There was what appeared to be some kind of handle. He put the knife down on Mahmoud's jacket-clad back and walked the few feet to the cover. Adrenaline rushed through him as he grabbed the small hook that protruded from two holes and lifted the cover slightly, finally pushing it to the side enough to just fit the body. He picked up the knife and folded it closed. Then he dragged Mahmoud over and dumped him into the opening, head first. It took a split second for Mahmoud's head to make a cracking sound, like a walnut, perhaps ten feet or more below the street.

Omar looked back to the spot where Mahmoud's body had been. There was some blood on the street, but not too much. In fact, the scattered groceries might passably give the appearance that someone merely fell and hurt themselves. He knew he had to clean the mess up. But he also knew that if someone approached, he wouldn't need to appear overly suspicious. He could even pretend that it was *his* blood.

After all, as might be expected, some of it had ended up on him. So he took his time at a corner store purchasing several gallons of water in three or four bags, and then cleaning up the blood on the street, and on his knife. He then put the groceries in a few of the bags and exited the alley. He headed toward the subway and his Queens neighborhood, thinking about his good deed.

I have killed my first infidel. Allah is pleased. There will be many more...many.

CHAPTER NINETEEN

Naomi Kaplan woke up on the last Sunday in April with the spring sun projecting brilliant white patches on her light brown sheets. She couldn't remember experiencing stronger sun rays that spring. She realized—because bright sunshine was the number one natural trigger— that the cherry blossoms must be in full bloom at the Brooklyn Botanical Gardens' Cherry Esplanade.

As unusual as it was for her to cry upon first arising in the morning, she found herself doing just that when the Esplanade came to her mind. This would be the first spring in years that she and her beloved father would miss their yearly walk through the Esplanade, under the pink cherry blossoms that awakened for only a few weeks a year in April. Some of their most intimate conversations had taken place during that walk. Would this year be different, just because David Kaplan was recovering from a serious stroke? It didn't have to be, she mused. After all, he had recovered to the point where he could navigate his way down the halls of the Kingsbrook facility using a walker. And if he could do that, why couldn't he slowly stroll through at least part of the Esplanade, arm in arm with his devoted daughter?

It suddenly occurred to Naomi that if she was going to plan an imminent visit with her father, she needed to "spy out the land." And now meant *now*. She quickly ate and dressed, and then left the house for Prospect Park, and the ceiling of extraordinary blossoms. When she finally arrived in late morning, her expectations were immediately confirmed. Indeed, it seemed like the expectations of all of Brooklyn were confirmed along with hers. Old and young, families with children and lovers holding hands, populated the lush gardens. And among the Sunday strolling Brooklynites were—of all people—Avram and Leah Milstein. As soon as she saw them standing several yards away, Naomi felt involuntary shame and guilt for hiding from them her clandestine visit to the messianic place. Her overnight with them a few months before seemed so long ago.

Naomi noticed that Leah still sported attractive pink lipstick, as if she hadn't removed it since the winter. And her black slacks and short-sleeved flowered blouse were as tasteful as her winter outfit had been. Avram sported a different knitted kippah, one more befitting spring, bright blue with yellow trim. His suit was replaced by a stylish light-blue polo shirt and dark-blue shorts that matched his head covering. He turned and saw Naomi before Leah did, and tapped his wife's shoulder. Leah smiled and waved as she approached Naomi, who just wanted to walk away. But it was too late.

"Hello, Leah. How are you and Avram doing?"

Leah smiled slyly.

"The question is, how are *you* doing with that man you almost let slip between your fingers, Miss forty-nine?"

Naomi was trapped. She wanted to turn to Avram and ask him to shut his wife up. But she knew he wouldn't comply. She had to say something. But what?

"No…I…he…we don't…anyway…listen, I've got to go. Thank you for having me…at your house. I've got to…"

Avram stepped in.

"Leah can be a bit blunt. That's what I love about her. Hey, I seem to remember that your father had a stroke. Is he still with us, or perhaps his name is for a blessed memory? I've seen so many pass from those. But hopefully, he's one of the fortunate ones. God willing, the percentages are getting higher…and also, God willing, with my terminal cancer patients."

After the good oncologist's clinical assessment, Naomi knew she had to set the record straight.

"Well...*Baruch HaShem*...praise God....he is recovering at the Kingsbrook Rehabilitation Institute. I actually hope to bring him here soon, before the blossoms disappear. That's why I came today, to see if they're in full bloom. He loves the Cherry Esplanade. We come every year. So I thought I'd just walk through it myself on this beautiful spring day."

Leah took Avram's hand and squeezed it. Then she interjected in a singsongy intonation, "Well, it's also great to walk through it with a boyfriend, intended...or like me, a husband."

Naomi nodded slightly, a precursor to her bowing out.

"Well...I'll have to try that someday."

"Before it's too late."

"As you say. Well, I guess I'll just...walk through it now...alone."

She gave each of them a quick glance and then backed away as if she were leaving remote royalty. Then she turned and headed toward the shimmering ceiling of cherry blossoms. As she approached the heavenly canopy, she couldn't help but compare this confidently successful professional observant Jewish couple to the greatest living sage she ever knew or would ever know—one, unlike them, whose Solomonic wisdom was matched by his Mosaic humility—her beloved father, David Kaplan. How she wished he was with her on this day! She was almost tempted to take the necessary buses and subways to Kingsbrook right then and there, and bring him back. But, of course, that would be impossible. She would have to check him out of the Institute, and that Abrihet woman, or some other helper, would have to get him ready. Then he would have to slowly navigate all the way back to Prospect Park, using his walker between modes of transportation. Or he would need an emergency vehicle. By the time they would arrive, the moon and stars would be drizzling a small pinch of silver mist on the blossoms, which would be barely visible.

Just as Naomi was ready to reject this line of thinking as useless, a most extraordinary coincidence took place. The very person that had just crossed her mind—her father's helper—was standing beneath the first blush of blossoms, not twenty feet from her. It couldn't be. Yet it seemed to be. Yes, it was! It was unmistakably Abrihet, the attractive young Ethiopian physical therapist. Close to Abrihet's side, and holding her hand, was the unmistakable figure of Javier, the precocious fatherless child Naomi had met at the Midwood Press. And standing next to both of them was a familiar-looking seventy-something black woman, one that Naomi knew she'd met somewhere before. But where? As she drew near to the Cherry Esplanade, a bolt of fear struck her—and with it, the terrifying thought that this coincidence was more than extraordinary. It was, perhaps, even diabolical. There, standing next to her father's physical therapist, was the Christian witch herself—Mahalia Morse, wearing a green turban of some sort that almost completely covered her hair. It was definitely her! Abrihet smiled broadly as Naomi approached.

"Naomi Kaplan! My wonderful patient David Kaplan's oldest daughter! What a miracle it is that we meet at Prospect Park on this most beautiful of Sundays. Do you remember Javier?"

On top of the initial shock of seeing these two women together—and of the implications the "coincidence" brought with it—came the shame of remembering her father-comment at the Midwood Press, along with Javier's response.

"Yes, of course I remember Javier. I remember him very well."

Driven by her deep love for children—her niece Lindsey, nephew Noah, fatherless Javier, and all children—a sudden compulsion to erase the Midwood fiasco and start afresh with Javier overwhelmed Naomi before she could even mentally process it. She dropped to her knees in front of him, their faces ending up so close to each other that their noses almost touched. Javier stiffened in a way he obviously hadn't with Abrihet at the Midwood Press, as Naomi's arms enveloped him. She instantly felt the awkwardness of a rebuffed embrace, and she backed off and stood up.

"Well, it's…it's good to see you again, Javier."

He answered with his usual tinged humor, as he squeezed Abrihet's hand tightly.

"Sure. I remember. She's the one who felt bad that she had a father and I didn't."

Naomi laughed stiffly.

"Yes, I suppose you're right. That's very observant of you, Javier."

Abrihet realized that she needed to introduce her friend Mahalia

Morse to Naomi.

"Naomi, this is my best friend Mahalia."

Best friend? I'm sure someone sent her to convert my beloved father! Such a shonda, a shame in the eyes of God! Such evil!

Abrihet put her hand on Mahalia's arm. Mahalia nodded as her eyes locked onto Naomi's.

"Yes, I've had the extraordinary pleasure of meeting Ms. Kaplan. We met at Beth Yeshua, didn't we?"

Abrihet reached out her other arm and took Naomi's—against her will.

"I cannot believe that this is happening. It is truly a miracle from the heavens! You were at Beth Yeshua? You were actually there? I *must* ask out of curiosity, what brought you there, Miss Kaplan…if I may be so bold?"

That was not a question Naomi had any intention of answering honestly, especially when these two were obviously being less than honest themselves—not to mention the fact that her strategy to stop Marvin's proposals was none of their business. But she knew she had to say *something*. So she responded with the first thing that came to her mind.

"I…I was visiting friends near there, and I…I just…well, I just wandered in. And I…I didn't like it…that is, I felt uncomfortable with…"

She turned and directly faced Mahalia.

"Well, with you, as a matter of fact. I was uncomfortable with…with you. You…you tried to…I mean, I felt like…like you were…you were… well, pushy. I don't think I'll ever go back there again. I mean, I definitely won't."

She turned the intensity up.

"You turned me *completely* off."

Her words stung Mahalia, which Naomi noticed. *Good.* She was glad they had that effect. That's just what she wanted them to do. She wanted to get her back for something beyond anything she had personally said or done. She perceived what appeared to be the pain of rejection in Mahalia's eyes. Her words had hit their mark. Then suddenly, she remembered Shakespeare's Jew Shylock from her college years.

If you prick us, will we not bleed?

Shakespeare's Jew was human in the best sense. But in this case, a different notion crossed her mind, one that reflected poorly on Mahalia. *So she is human after all…just a weak religious fanatic looking for approval…just a wicked Christian missionary looking to steal souls…a fake. I thought so. I thought so.*

Mahalia was indeed stung by Naomi's words. It hurt in a very old and still tender place. And there was no way she could hide it, as much as she wanted to. She decided that she should probably apologize in some way—and then hopefully change the subject. She tried to keep her wounded eyes fixed on Naomi's, which was a difficult task.

"I'm so sorry. I'm sorry I…offended you. I'm so sorry. But…anyway… well…I'm glad you've met my friend Abrihet. She attends Beth Yeshua whenever she can. She is a very special person. I would love you to hear her story sometime. She suffered much in her country."

Special person! Special indeed! This Ethiopian aide—or physical therapist, or whatever she is—turns out to be just the long arm of this Beth Yeshua cult trying to proselytize my father. No wonder she reminded me of this Mahalia Morse woman.

Not that there was any danger of David Kaplan being vulnerable to Abrihet's deceptions. He may not have answered all of Naomi's questions about Darrin Brock's God, and whether he was the same God as her God. But he certainly knew how to answer a missionary to the Jews! Naomi knew that much. She was actually more concerned about how all of this might stress him, just as he was recovering from the stroke. If these two witches ever ended up causing him any harm…God forbid!

Abrihet felt the need to respond to Mahalia's comments.

"I do not think of those days so much. Yes, it's true that in my country, we had many enemies. Those that called themselves by the name "Christian" often hated us and blamed us for everything bad that happened to them. We were sometimes seen as a curse. At times they even murdered us."

Naomi had no desire to hear anything about Abrihet's past. But her curiosity got the best of her. She couldn't help but ask her why people who believed what she did wanted to kill her.

"I don't really want to ask…I mean, I don't…have time to…but, since you brought it up, why would Christians want to hurt you, since you yourself must believe, going to that place? What I mean is…"

"It is not easy to explain. You see, we were those in Gondar that were descendants of Jews. And some of us…some of us, believed in…were… they called us *Falash Mura*…bad words. We were…part of *Beta Israel*, the house of Israel, but…well…the Muslims too, they hated us. And the Chassidic Jews in Israel, even when we were starving…which happened to us much of the time…wouldn't let us go to Israel unless we…we denied believing as we do…in Yeshua, you see. So they wouldn't…"

Naomi had heard enough. Maybe she agreed—at least just a little bit—with Marvin's disdain for Brooklyn Chassidic *Chabadniks*, what with their peculiar messianic focus on the late Rabbi Menachem Schneerson. But she wasn't about to listen to this missionary's accusation that they would be responsible for the starvation of any fellow Jews. Anyway, who was this woman to talk about persecution, when so many Jews from Naomi's ancestral home of Kiev were mercilessly slaughtered by Christians like these two Messianics?

"Look, I don't want to hear anymore. It's obvious that one of you sent the other to…to…to proselytize my father. So I'm going to have you fired, Abri…Abri…whatever your name is! And don't tell me about persecution. My family lost everyone who stayed in Kiev."

Javier squeezed Abrihet's hand even harder and anxiously turned his eyes up toward Naomi.

"You certainly are mean to my friend Abrihet, lady."

Tears began to fill Abrihet's eyes as she answered him.

"She doesn't mean it, She just cares about her father, Javier. She loves him, and she wants the best for him."

"Yeh, she told everyone that already."

Mahalia took a deep breath, and then thundered out a response in defense of her friend.

"Naomi…Naomi Kaplan…I think you owe Abrihet an apology. You heard me! An apology!. For your information, I didn't know she was helping your father until just a few minutes ago. In fact, I didn't even know you *knew* her."

Naomi wasn't finished defending herself.

"Maybe that's true. *Maybe*. But how can I know for sure?"

"It's as true as what I told you at Beth Yeshua about the child kidnapping lie. Listen, woman, everyone here knows suffering…me, you, her."

She pointed at Abrihet.

"And him."

She was referring to Javier.

"I know the Holocaust was specific to itself. But nevertheless, my ancestors were slaves who suffered the loss of family and dignity. They found their Moses in the Messiah's suffering. He suffered what they suffered, and granted them hope in this life and beyond. They followed His Spirit north on the Underground Railroad, and their children taught me to love Him, and His people…the Jews. Maybe I came on too strong at Beth Yeshua, but God laid you on my heart and gave me a word for you. That's just the way it is. *Just the way it is.* Take it or leave it."

Naomi had never heard the words *God gave me a word for you* before. She figured that Mahalia was referring to the uncanny remarks that seemed to her like witchcraft because they fit her situation with Darrin so well. She looked over at Abrihet, who was drying her tears. Guilt overtook her. Her beloved father would not have acted this way. She closed her eyes momentarily, and then found words she knew she had to share or she wouldn't be able to sleep that night.

"Okay. Look…I'm…sorry. I promise, I won't have you fired. But… please don't say anything about…Beth Yeshua to my father. I think it might upset him, and I want him to get better…as I'm sure you do. Again, I'm sorry for accusing you."

Abrihet smiled a thin smile that released a few more tears.

"I will say nothing…unless perhaps I'm asked. It is a miracle that we all know each other, I think. Miracles are all around us. No?"

Naomi ignored the last statement.

"Well…I guess if he asks where you attend. But…look, I know you do well with him. I saw. For that I'm thankful. Well, I've got to go now."

Mahalia took Naomi's hand.

"We will see you again. That I know."

There were those kind of words again.

"If you say so. Goodbye. Goodbye, Javier."

He gave her a kind of childish salute. She wasn't sure whether he was being serious, or sarcastic.

Everyone else waved goodbye. Naomi moved on to the beginning of the Cherry Esplanade. She tried to shake the whole encounter with the two women and the young boy, and focus on practicing the promenade through the Esplanade, in preparation for a walk with David Kaplan. She began to slowly move forward, taking his arm in her imagination. As she took one step after another, it seemed in her imagination that her father let go of her arm and replaced it with Darrin Brock's—as if he were giving her away in a bridal processional. Against her better judgment, she imagined Darrin's strong sure arm leading her underneath the *chuppah*, or canopy, of pink blossoms. She could just hear the music of Solomon's *Song of Songs*, and the chanted words *Dodee lee v'anee lo, I am my beloved's, and he is mine*. Before she could get a chance to reject the daydream, the arm slipped from her and was again replaced by another arm. Unbearable overwhelming compassion accompanied the new arm. Whose was it? Suddenly, she heard a voice like calm waters speak words she hadn't forgotten since the day she had read them months before in Darrin's hospital room—*Blessed are the merciful, for they shall receive mercy*. She quickly shook the imaginary arm off and ran through the rest of the Esplanade like she was fleeing a house on fire. She longed to go and cleanse herself in the traditional *mikvah* bath, even though she was not in that part of her quickly vanishing monthly cycle. As she ran, she mouthed a prayer.

"Oh God, keep me from Mahalia's evil magic! It's one thing to learn about Darrin's faith. It's another to be led astray into…idolatry. Please forgive me! Forgive me! Forgive me!"

CHAPTER TWENTY

Inspector Ralph Lewis had been observing Darrin Brock's performance for the last few months. During the prior year, he had talked Brock out of leaving and going into some kind of work with at-risk youth. That seemed like decades ago, before his brush with death at the hands of the Russian mafia, and his later break-up with Naomi Kaplan. The present Darrin wasn't bringing up leaving. In fact, he hardly brought up anything at all—except, perhaps once or twice, his opinion about Omar Shehadulah. Inspector Lewis realized that Darrin was in a deep depression. He also realized that Margaret was aggressively going after him, and that Darrin seemed to be giving in—or at least not totally resisting her. Workplace harassment-related or not, Lewis didn't care about that situation one way or another. He was just looking forward to a bounce-back to the old Darrin, whom he knew was capable of top-quality detective work. The one thing he still insisted on was a monthly visit with now five-year-old Natan, the youngest son of the widow Chaya Mendel, whose husband Mandy had been killed in Manhattan's Diamond District February a year ago. Lewis realized that this connection was important for Darrin. To put it scientifically, it was therapeutic. But these days, Darrin needed to be reminded to visit Natan—unlike before the break-up with Naomi Kaplan.

By the time the day to visit Natan finally came, he had been reminded twice. Ralph Lewis hadn't been quite sure he was listening the first time. But he had heard the reminders both times. On the morning of the visit, he grabbed a quick breakfast while his father Lester was in the bedroom helping his mother Velma get dressed. Darrin knew all the details, from the chore of lifting her out of the wheelchair, to placing her on the toilet (on the good days), to putting her pant legs on one by one—all while she stared ahead. He was always ready to help with his mother any way he could, but he left this part to his father. After his quick bowl of raisin bran and a weak cup of coffee, he threw on his light jacket and left the house.

While riding the subway toward his destination, he marveled that he still looked forward to seeing little Natan—that is, compared to every other thing in his life. He'd always heard how depressed people see everything in drab colors, even when those colors might in reality be quite vibrant. *Well, that's me now,* he mused. And it didn't help that the interior of the subway car actually *was* drab looking, even in the apex of a sunny spring morning.

When he arrived at the Mendel house in Brooklyn, he was greeted by Chaya, who was dressed in her finest ankle-length thin black spring dress and long-sleeved white blouse. She looked particularly young and attractive to him this day, with her stylish short spring Chassidic *sheitel* wig. In another universe, he could even imagine falling for her Eastern European beauty. He spied the usual milk and Mi-Del kosher cookies waiting for him and Natan on the dining room table. Strangely, the child was not yet in the room. Chaya pointed to the pristine white couch.

"Please, sit for a few minutes. I want to speak with you."

Darrin was surprised. She didn't usually initiate any serious discussion before playtime with Natan.

"Is there something wrong?" he inquired as they sat down, with Chaya the usual few feet from him, so they would not even get close to touching.

"No, there's nothing wrong...at least not with me. But, if you don't mind my asking, you don't seem happy lately. I'm concerned about you."

Darrin didn't want to talk about what Chaya Mendel already knew— that he and Naomi were no longer seeing each other. He figured she *must* know that this was what was affecting him. So why was she asking?

He glanced down and sat silent for several seconds. She took the lead.

"Okay. I know it's because of Naomi Kaplan. That's what I want to talk to you about. I've watched you month after month since she broke up with you, listless and depressed, and it pains me to see you like this. You brought sunshine into this home after the death of my husband, may his memory be for a blessing. We were under death's cloud, and you helped lift it, for Natan especially. Now it seems that *you're* the one that is under the cloud. No?"

Darrin looked over at her.

"Yes, I suppose so. So perhaps I should leave. But…selfish as it may sound, seeing Natan helps. I look forward to that…and little else, to tell you the truth."

She moved perhaps an inch closer, but no more.

"Darrin, would you say that you and I are both religious?"

He was caught off guard by her question.

"Well…yes. I might put it a bit differently, but…of course…yes…we both believe in God."

"That's right. *And* a God who knows what's best. You believe that, don't you? And perhaps He knew that things would not have worked out between you and Naomi. We both know that there were great differences. Even *you* are taught about that. Isn't that right? That is, that if you are married, you should believe the same thing about God…and about… about…well, *you* know."

He knew she meant Jesus, but wasn't free to speak the name out loud—according to her Chabad tradition. And she would never be so disrespectful as to use Marvin's substitute word. Darrin nodded.

"I understand."

He also understood that Chaya Mendel's living room was just about the last place to complain about the loss he was still grieving over. After all, she had a greater reason to grieve, having lost not only her husband, but also her children's father. But in Darrin's observation, she didn't seem to be suffering from depression, at least not anymore. Of course, she was right about what he and other Christians referred to as unequal yoking, from the book of First Corinthians. But that was definitely not something he wanted to talk about. So all he could do was say he understood. She nodded in response.

"I'm glad you understand. No, I don't want you to stop visiting Natan. I just want you to begin to feel better. Take it from me. There's a time to move on with your life. In due time you'll find someone else."

That too was something Darrin *definitely* didn't want to discuss—especially if that someone was Margaret. Chaya stood up.

"I'll get Natan."

She left the room and came back seconds later with a bouncy Natan, who was so full of energy that you would think he had been released from a crate or cage of some sort. He jumped up into Darrin's arms and clung to him for what seemed like minutes. After that, Chaya spread out his puzzles and books on the rug, and then got the milk and cookies. The usual playtime was going well, with Darrin clapping every time Natan properly fit a puzzle part of the great Rebbe Menachem Schneerson's face in place. He had just clapped twice enthusiastically when suddenly a much larger louder crack thundered throughout the room. That was followed by the crash of front window glass and two or three whizzing sounds. One appeared to come from perhaps an inch above Natan's head. Then, the wall mirror behind them shattered. Darrin dived on top of Natan.

"Chaya, get down and stay down!"

She quickly crawled under the dining room table.

"Is he okay? Oh my God! Is he…"

Darrin could hear Natan whimpering beneath him, and felt his rapid heartbeat. But he felt no warm blood.

"Are you okay, Natan?"

"Yes, Abba. I'm scared. Who broke the mirror, Abba?"

"I don't know, Natan. But you're safe with me. You're safe."

Chaya had the same question.

"Who would do this? Who?"

Darrin tried to choose his words carefully, what with Natan beneath him listening.

"I think whoever…whoever got…you know…your spouse…and…and me, maybe. Russians, I think. Maybe. I thought the police got every one of them. But…I guess not."

He reached into his pocket for his phone and called the station.

"It's Brock. Backup at my present location. No injuries here, but several shots. Shooter or shooters still active."

Within two minutes, sirens could be heard. The police arrived in their cruisers, as he crawled to the door with Natan still protected under him. When they knocked on the door and shouted "Police," he quickly shouted back, "Darrin Brock, NYPD detective. No shooters here." Then he unlocked the door from a kneeling position. Three cops rushed in, guns cocked. When they saw him on the floor, they lowered their guns.

He pulled Natan into his arms and stood up. Chaya crawled out from under the table and approached Darrin, taking Natan from him. Darrin caught his breath.

"Nice work getting here so quickly. They shot through the win dow. We're okay."

One of the policemen began examining the mirror behind them, and the rug beneath the mirror. One of the other policemen took a pad out.

"I think your inspector over there in Manhattan is on his way."

Darrin shook his head.

"Tell him to forget it. Even with sirens on, he won't be here for at least a half hour."

"Let it go. He's halfway here."

Natan, who had been in a state of shock, began to sob into his mother's shirt. She turned to go upstairs.

"Darrin, I'm going to spend some time with Natan. Call me if you need me."

"Of course. Thank God we're all okay."

"Yes. Baruch HaShem."

He turned back to the three NYPD policemen.

"Her husband was the one who was killed in the Diamond District a little over a year ago. And you know about me. I think they were trying to kill me here…to send a message."

"Right. Well, I guess the investigation starts here and now."

"Frankly, it should have progressed long before now. Then it wouldn't have gotten to this place…and almost killed little Natan. I'm telling you, they were trying to finish the job with me, and send a statement to Mendel's widow. They must think I'm here as a part of the original investigation. I wish I were."

After another ten minutes, an unmarked car arrived. Chaya came downstairs.

"Well, miracles from HaShem never cease. It was almost his nap time, and he actually fell asleep. It's because you're here, Darrin. It comforts him just to know you're here. He asked if you would still be here when he wakes up."

"I hope so. I'll find out when Inspector Lewis arrives…whenever that is."

Two men in plain clothes stepped out of an unmarked car that had just pulled up. They were both thin and in their thirties, and both dressed in black suits, black ties, and white shirts, like the Blues Brothers might wear, but with beards and kippot—Jewish head coverings—and traditional fringes below their suit jackets. They stepped up to the door, and quickly flashed badges of some sort. Darrin noticed that Chaya smiled when she saw them.

"Do you know these guys?"

She reassured him.

"Not exactly. But they're obviously from our community. This is how we do things here. We have our own…protection, for want of a better word."

Darrin nodded.

"Oh. I see."

One of the men introduced both of them. He had a distinct Brooklyn-Yiddish accent.

"We're from Crown Heights. We just want to check some things out."

She immediately acquiesced.

"Of course. Thank you for coming."

She noticed an unsettled look on Darrin's face.

"It's okay. I've seen this many times. It's okay."

They walked into the house and walked back toward the kitchen for a moment, and then up the steps to the second level. A few minutes later, Inspector Lewis pulled up half onto the sidewalk, sirens blazing. He exited his vehicle on one side, and Margaret exited on the other. By this time, a small crowd of curious Chassidic Jews had assembled across the street. Lewis paid no attention to them, as he escorted Margaret—who was dressed in her police uniform, complete with her cap, which half-covered her now blonde hair—up the walk and into the house. Darrin sighed upon seeing Margaret. He addressed Ralph Lewis.

"You know, you didn't have to come down here."

Lewis was clearly impatient.

"You alright?"

Darrin answered like a teenager being grilled by his father.

"You can see I'm fine."

"Yeh? Well, some things just can't be seen. You're damn lucky to be alive…you and everyone else in this house."

He spied Chaya Mendel out of the corner of his eye.

"Hello, Ms. Mendel. Nice to see you again, despite the circumstances. It's been a long time."

"Likewise, Inspector Lewis."

"Now back to you, Brock. If you think this was the work of that goofball Omar Sheh-what's-his-name, you're wrong."

"I didn't say it was."

"Yeh? Well, you'd better wake up and screw your head back on straight, Brock, because someone still wants you dead…no offense, Ms. Mendel. And Brock, don't think we haven't been investigating and covering your backside, because we *have*. Nothing is closed. But of course, I admit we didn't exactly predict this. However, we'll get these guys. You can be sure of that!"

His eyes found and met Chaya's.

"*All* these guys, whoever did *whatever*. We're on it."

Darrin mumbled as he turned away from the inspector.

"You could have fooled me…fooled me to death."

Lewis, of course, didn't miss a word.

"Oh yeah? What you don't know is a hell of a lot. I'll tell you *that*. Say hi to your friend Margaret, by the way. You like her new blonde hair? I've assigned her to stick to you like glue. She's taking the cruiser I brought. I'll get a ride with one of these guys from this precinct. And who's this guy?"

He was referring to one of the two thin men in black, who had just come downstairs. The other one was still on the second floor. Chaya sought to put the inspector's mind at ease.

"He's from Crown Heights. He's just here to check on us."

"The Crown Heights brigade. Yeh yeh. Just don't contaminate anything."

"No, sir, officer," he intoned in a thick Brooklyn accent. "We are about to leave."

"Good."

Darrin desperately wished that Inspector Lewis hadn't brought Margaret to "protect" him. He wanted to just leave and take the subway for the long trip back to the police parking lot at the tip of Manhattan. But he knew he couldn't do that until the work here was finished. Margaret drew close and put her hand on his shoulder. He could feel the heat even through his light jacket and shirt.

"Are you okay, Darrin...Inspector Brock? I've been...been... worrying about you since the report came in. And I've been...been praying that no one...no one would be hurt. Where is this little Natan I've heard about?"

Chaya stepped up to her.

"Hi. I'm his mother. He's napping, safe and sound. Thanks for coming, officer. I'm glad you will be teamed up with my friend Darrin. I'm *sure* if the inspector chose you, you'll keep him safe."

Can Chaya possibly sense that this lady is after me? Darrin couldn't help thinking. *What, is she trying to pair us up so I'll forget Naomi? Maybe she's working behind the scenes with Ralph Lewis. Maybe even the shots were a plot to push me Margaret's way!*

Darrin realized his thoughts were getting more irrational by the second. He moved away from Margaret and stood next to Inspector Lewis, addressing her from there.

"I'm okay, Margaret. Except I'm somewhat drained. If I'm not needed here, I would like to go. I guess you're supposed to take me home so I don't have to take the subway."

He turned to the inspector.

"If that's the case, can we leave soon? That is, if you don't need me, sir."

Inspector Lewis looked at his watch. He thought for a few seconds and then nodded.

"Yes, believe it or not, you can leave now. She'll drive you to Teaneck. We'll post a guard around the house tonight. I'll see you tomorrow morning, Brock. Margaret will pick you up in Teaneck and park the cruiser in one of the spaces behind the precinct building. We'll have your car there. And we'll debrief then."

"Fine. Chaya, I'm sorry I can't stay until Natan wakes up. Please say goodbye to him for me. I'll be back as soon as possible."

Chaya smiled.

"I will. May HaShem keep us all safe."

Without another word, Darrin left, followed by Margaret. They got in the cruiser, with Margaret in the driver's seat, and drove off through the streets of Brooklyn. Darrin closed his eyes and leaned back on the head rest. He was in no mood to talk. But she seemed like she was.

"You look tired. You know, these new cruisers have reclining front seats, even with the cage behind them. Lean your seat back."

"But I don't…"

"Just do it. You need the rest. I'm so glad you're okay. You don't know how worried I was. I don't know what I would have done if anything happened to you. I'll keep you safe, Darrin. I promise. Me…and Jesus."

He didn't want to recline next to her. But then again, he figured, he wouldn't have to converse with her if he did that. He found the lever on his right side, and the seat moved back to a reclining position. He kept his eyes closed. Sure enough, they drove the rest of the trip in silence—save for the sound of ebbing and flowing traffic through closed windows, like distant waves on a concrete shore line. He could tell when they reached the hollow buzzing sound of the George Washington Bridge. After that, he actually began to fall asleep, which was almost as miraculous as Natan's recent nap had been—that is, since he was riding in the front seat of a police cruiser, next to Margaret.

As the car reached his street in Teaneck, he was roused from a now sound sleep by the sound of the parking brake. Before his eyes opened, he felt the heat of Margaret's well conditioned lips pressing on his. Suddenly, he felt her left hand unbutton one shirt button on his white business shirt, and slip it underneath. She began to caress his chest, then moving down toward his belly and then back again, in a sensual circular motion. He opened his eyes fully as his mind registered what was going on. Just then Margaret began kissing his neck with intentionally wet lips.

"Do you like my hair?"

"Margaret."

"Oh, Darrin, I've dreamed of this moment every night. Please love me…please…love me back," she breathed between the kisses and soft licks of her tongue that reached behind his ear lobes, as her well cut newly blonde hair teasingly tickled his cheek. Stark temptation and urgent resistance fought an immense battle. He knew he needed to pull away, but didn't want to knock her face with a stray arm or elbow in the process. She continued to plead.

"I love you. I *want* you. Please. I know a secluded spot around here where we can park. It's in a wooded area. God will forgive us. He wants us to marry anyway. I *know* it."

It felt like they were teenagers making out in his father's car. Only they weren't. They were mature adults in mid-life. The whole thing seemed like it was taking place in an altered time and place. He turned his face until their lips were almost touching again. He had been quiet since they had gotten in the car, but knew he had to say something *now*.

"Margaret. This is very tempting. You are a truly beautiful woman. There's no question about that. But…I can't. And I'm not ready for marriage now…to anyone. Maybe later. Not now. Give me time."

She quickly sat up.

"Do you *mean* that? Do you *really* mean that?" she squealed with glee. "There's hope? I've been praying for hope. I really have…but…there really *is* hope?"

In the dull light of an adjacent street lamp, he looked directly into her astonishing hazel eyes. In his logical mind, he believed he should shut all hope down. But some secret part of him wondered if this hungry responsive woman would actually be an antidote for his lonely aching heart. Perhaps he could find some kind of happiness with her. After all, she was a new believer and a churchgoer. He could teach her all about God's ways. But this was no time to make that decision. He had to respond to her last comment.

"I'm sure you've been praying. And God has His answer. But this is all too fast for me. I…I…don't work that way. Please…I need to go now. I'll see you tomorrow."

She tried to calm her trembling heart.

"Okay. Okay. Okay. May I kiss you one more time…a short one…

please?"

He remembered Naomi's impulsive last kiss in the Channel Gardens the year before. Did all women act like this? Before he could answer, she quickly licked her lips and turned to him as he sat up, locking them onto his and then pressing them softly for about ten seconds. There was a sweet experienced sensuality about the kiss that was different from Naomi's. Not better—and maybe not worse after all—but different. Without another word, he exited the vehicle for his house. He knew he had to shift gears immediately. As he walked toward the front door, Margaret rolled down her window and shouted.

"I'll pick you up at 6:00 a.m. Inspector Lewis' orders."

Then she drove off. He unlocked the front door and walked through it. Lester and Velma were sitting in their chairs, as if they were waiting for him. But he knew that couldn't be, because he was actually arriving home early. His father looked up at him.

"You're home early, Son."

"Yes I am."

"Do you still have your job?"

Darrin didn't expect that question. He knew his father had given him advice to hold onto his job, but his mind was in a completely different place.

"Yes, Dad, I do."

"Where is your car? Why did you come through the front door instead of the garage?"

"It's a long story. This fellow police officer…Margaret…have I ever mentioned her? She's very nice."

"No, you haven't, Son."

Velma's eyes fleetingly met Darrin's, before staring ahead once again. Darrin barely noticed. All he could think about was that he didn't want to talk about the attempt on his life that day, at least not now.

"Well, she took me home. Inspector Lewis asked her to. Can we talk about it later? It feels like it's been a very long day, short as it may have actually been."

"If you say so. So who is this Margaret?"

Darrin blushed so obviously that he was sure his father noticed.

"She's…nobody, Dad. Just a fellow officer…and…a friend."

"And she's nice?"

"What?"

"You said she was very nice."

"Yes, Dad. She's nice. I'd like to get some rest before dinner. Maybe we can talk then.."

"I'd like that."

Darrin left for the second floor—and his bedroom.

CHAPTER TWENTY-ONE

Omar Shehadulah felt like he'd arrived. He was a true soldier of Allah now. If he could take the life of one apostate Muslim, he could surely destroy a multitude of infidels. And there were more of those in New York than in most American cities. He walked tall through the streets of Manhattan on this moist and misty spring day. He liked those days better than the sunny ones. They reminded him of the moist blood on the bodies of his victims.

What would my contacts in Pakistan think of me now? he mused. *The Flatiron Building is before me...and with it, paradise.*

Omar descended the steps to the subway. He was headed to the Dewitt Wallace Periodical Room in the New York Public Library. He wanted to see the look on that dirty Jew Stanley's face, as he—Omar—pretended to be a relative of Mahmoud's, wondering where he might be. Of course, Stanley was so supremely stupid that he wouldn't know the difference between a Pakistani and a Palestinian. To him, they were all Arabs. Typical American Jew!

Omar stood on the platform and waited for the D train. When it arrived, he pressed in with the throng. All at once his feet left the ground, as both of his arms felt the pain of heartless hands squeezing them like a boa constrictor. He was no longer moving under his own power. Forces much stronger than him dragged him back and away from the train doors. Just as he tried to look to one side and then the other to see who was holding him, he noticed that someone was also directly in front of him. Then, another person behind him pulled something over his head. Everything went dark. Four men in synchronization moved him this way and that, like a pawn on a chessboard—one at each side, and one in front and one in back of him. He felt his feet being dragged up what were obviously the same subway steps he had come down. Soon he was out on the street. He felt himself being pulled into a vehicle of some sort. The two at his sides were still holding him. One spoke to the other in Russian, a language he had never bothered to learn. He wanted to shout out, "What are you doing? Where am I?" But he realized it was useless.

After about ten minutes, he was roughly pulled out of the car and dragged into a damp cavernous place of some sort—at least by the sound of it. Then he was thrown down onto a concrete surface. Someone pulled off whatever had been pulled over his head. He looked up and saw a tall square-faced man with a dark brush mustache standing over him, holding a sharp machete. He tried to get up, but someone behind him kicked his shins hard, and he fell back down on the grimy wet concrete floor, in excruciating pain. The man who towered over him spoke in typical Russian-influenced English.

"Hello Omar. I am Leonid. I like how you kill the other day. Good. But…I hate you. I hate you *terrorists*. If anyone causes terror, it will be me. I could chop your head with machete. Like you chop heads of Russians. No? But…I will not."

He leaned over until his beady black eyes came close to Omar's.

"Instead, you work for me now. Not for Pakistani friends. My dead friend Igor didn't end up killing this man Brock last year. A stupid blunder. And an incompetent idiot among us missed him the other day. So now he's dead too. And I…I am impatient."

Omar was still wincing in pain. But he was also listening, and his ears perked up at Leonid's next words.

"You did good job on Mahmoud the taxi driver…I admit."

Omar froze in the first hint of fear he had felt since this whole bizarre situation began. Would they turn him in? He hated American jails, with their corruption and their Muslim-hating Christians. Leonid continued.

"Don't worry. We have body you stupidly left in sewer. You're a better killer than hider of bodies."

He laughed as Russians tend to laugh at bad jokes.

"So we took care of him."

He laughed again, this time in a short extended grunt.

"Our eyes are on you now. You will forget terror plans, or we will kill you before you kill others for your Allah. You will kill Darrin Brock, but only when we tell you…and no one else until that. You are never out of our sight."

Leonid walked over and kicked Omar in his stomach with his sharp pointed shoes.

"We own you."

Omar barely got the chance to reinforce in his mind his intent to blow up the Flatiron Building, when he fainted from the unbearable pain. He lay on the concrete floor for an undetermined time, unconscious. Even if he were conscious, he wouldn't have understood Leonid, as he spoke to his soldiers in Russian.

"Good. Now this son of a Pakistani whore, with a pig's heart like a Chechnian, will do what you and all of the others didn't do. He will kill Darrin Brock the detective at the Jewish widow's house. Only this time we will find the diamonds. We will kill two birds, as the stupid Americans say. Our man will find them, and right under their noses. Get him out of here." The two soldiers lifted Omar's body and walked it out of the empty warehouse.

When Omar finally woke up, he was in his own bed in Queens. Part of him wondered whether the whole episode had been a dream. But he quickly realized it wasn't—especially when he felt the extremely painful bruises in various places on his body.

Chapter Twenty-Two

Sunday was always the first day of the week in Naomi Kaplan's life—as it was for all traditional Orthodox Jews. And it being the first day of the week, momentous events sometimes took place on that day. Perhaps it was because the Shabbat the day before acted as a kind of restful preparation—like a baseball pitcher's stretch—before the fastballs and curveballs that sometimes took place starting Sunday. At any rate, such were various Sundays over the past year—for example, the day Aunt Ida took her nephew Marvin and Naomi to Teaneck as a part of Naomi's deceptive plan to see her secret crush Darrin Brock—or the emotionally wrenching day months later when Naomi visited a critically ill Darrin Brock at the Mount Sinai Medical Center.

On this warm still spring Sunday, Naomi was waiting for her sister Lisa Silver, who was coming over to discuss plans with her. The first dramatic event had already taken place early that morning. In a post-Shabbat call, the Kingsbrook Rehabilitation Institute had apprised her of the imminent return of David Kaplan. He was to be released within the next week, back to the house he shared with Naomi. Lisa had also received a call from the center, and she was on her way from Englewood, New Jersey to Brooklyn in her shiny black Cadillac Escalade. Marc Silver stayed home with their children Lindsey and Noah. There were a lot of things to discuss, and having her husband and children there would be a distraction.

Naomi sat at the kitchen table, nervously tapping a pencil on a blank legal pad that Lisa insisted she have available when the planning began. That request was reason enough to be nervous. It didn't seem like there was any need to write things down. Yet apparently, Lisa didn't feel that way. On the phone, she had seemed quite insistent about the pad. Was that a precursor to some sort of drama? *Please HaShem, I hope not*, Naomi prayed silently. While she was tapping and pondering, the doorbell rang. Naomi dropped the pencil and went to open the door. Lisa, in a pink sleeveless shirt and tight white pants, walked in as if in mid-stride. As much as Naomi had been making every effort to dress more stylishly, she couldn't compete with Lisa's simple ensemble, perfect figure, and knockout black short curly haircut. But Naomi wasn't as self-conscious about those things as she used to be—before Darrin opened her eyes to her own beauty. That was the one positive thing that came out of their ended "affair." Lisa went over to the dining room table, grabbed a chair, and started right in.

"Take this down. No, on second thought, I will."

As she picked up the pencil. Naomi came over and sat down next to her, grabbing hold of the pencil, and Lisa's hand.

"Can we just talk?"

"I don't know, Naomi. *Can* we? I mean, I know I'm your little sister, but…for instance, you didn't listen to me about Darrin, and that really frustrated me. It *really* did. Now Dad is coming home. I wanted to take him in, in Englewood. After all, I don't work. I mean, it could work out… temporarily…that is, until Marc has had enough of it. But…of course, Dad said *no*. He'd rather be here, with the Orthodox, and his synagogue that he walks to…and of course, you."

She had barely breathed between sentences, until now. She paused. Naomi picked up on the skipped beat.

"Well, I'm leaving my job. We'll make out somehow."

"No, you're *not*. You're absolutely *not* leaving your job."

"Lisa…"

"See, Naomi? That's why I came all the way from nice quiet spacious Englewood to good old squeezed-together Brooklyn on this beautiful spring Sunday—because I want to help you not make any stupid mistakes. You helped me when Marc was depressed after his boss Prima was killed, and now…now, I'm helping you."

"But Lisa, I'm not asking for help. Abba and I will be just fine."

"No, Abba and you will *not* be just fine!" Lisa practically shouted. "And I'll tell you why. Dad needs to learn independence. He doesn't need you here twenty-four hours every day, waiting on him hand and foot… excuse the cliche´. We've talked to the social worker. Dad's ready for this. There will be home health care visits daily. Marc will check in on him, and…Darrin said he will keep in touch too."

Naomi's eyes widened.

"Darrin! Oh, *please!*"

"Yes, Naomi. Darrin. He gets along quite well with Dad."

Naomi tried to hide the new feelings of jealousy she had only just begun to experience since the time she ran into the Silvers and Aunt Ida at her father's Maimonides Medical Center bedside weeks before— feelings of being left out of her father's care, feelings of other family members, and even Darrin, coming between her and her beloved Abba— and frankly, feelings of her sister Lisa being closer to David Kaplan than she, for the first time in her memory. But as hard as she tried to hide these feelings, sarcasm bled through her hidden wound in unavoidable crimson droplets.

"Well, then maybe *you* should plan his care without me. You wasted your time coming here. You missed a wonderful Sunday morning with your lovely family in Englewood."

"So you're jealous that I'm helping out with decisions on his care? Is that it? I guess now you know how it feels to be left out."

"I am *not* jealous."

Beyond those four lying words, Naomi was left speechless, her eyes focused on the unswept greenish rug beneath them. How did things get to this place? Was it because her anchor, her father David Kaplan, was no longer present to guide her with sage-like wisdom? Or was it something else? Whatever it was, the reconciliation with her sister that had materialized during the previous Chanukah, like a miracle from heaven, was disintegrating now. And she was sure that she was at least partly to blame. Several seconds had gone by. She had to say *something*. Her eyes remained focused on the rug.

"Okay. Look, Lisa. I'm...I'm sorry. I'll keep my job. I'll...I'll work with you, and Marc...and even Darrin...although I don't want to see him, if you don't mind."

"Why? Is it because you still love him?"

Naomi's eyes focused back on Lisa's. She had been exposed, and she had no choice except to speak the truth. She quietly and calmly spoke words that surprised even her.

"Yes. Of course, Lisa. What do you think?"

Lisa bit her lip so hard, she wondered if it would start bleeding. Her eyes teared up. After an awkward pause, she responded as quietly as Naomi had—even more quietly, in a whisper.

"Oh, Naomi. Naomi. My poor precious sister Naomi."

Naomi couldn't allow the conversation to continue in this vein.

"Look, I'm going to see Daddy this afternoon. I'll talk with him about coming home...here."

Without another word, she walked out of the room and up the stairs. Lisa looked at the blank legal pad. She thought about taking the pencil and writing "I love you," but for some reason she decided against it. She grabbed her pocketbook and walked out the front door, locking it behind her with the key she always carried with her.

Naomi watched from her bedroom window as Lisa walked through the front gate of the Kaplan brownstone house and got into her Cadillac Escalade. She stood still at the window until the car drove away, the Sunday morning late-spring sun reflecting off its gleaming black surface. As soon as the vehicle disappeared around the corner two blocks up, Naomi realized that she didn't have to wait until the afternoon. A strange impulse gripped her. She would leave the house as soon as she could, and be at Kingsbrook by late morning.

About an hour after Naomi made up her mind, David Kaplan was using his walker to navigate the sidewalk outside of the Kingsbrook Rehabilitation Institute, with Abrihet by his side. She was in a particularly good mood. This very Sunday morning, the rabbi from Beth Yeshua, Sheldon Goldberg, would be visiting a recovering stroke victim, and member of their synagogue. After that, he was planning to grab a bagel in the Institute deli with Abrihet, where she could share the latest news about her family back in Ethiopia. Her mother had recently suffered a stroke not unlike David Kaplan's, and they could take this opportunity to pray for her. Deep within her heart, she also wished that Rabbi Goldberg could pray for David Kaplan's health while he was at the Institute. But she was hesitant to suggest that. She didn't even have the courage to pray over David Kaplan herself. After all, she knew it was against standard protocol for the nurses and other staff. But she did do the one thing she knew she could do, and that she loved doing. She encouraged him.

"Mr. Kaplan, you are doing so very well. I am so pleased with how hard you are working...for your daughter, and your other daughter with the two little ones. Soon you will be leaving us. I hope you will remember me, and that I will see you again."

David smiled with the increasing facility of a stroke victim in the latter stages of recovery. His voice was clearer as well.

"Of course, I want you to..to..."

Words still sometimes got stuck for a few seconds somewhere in his cerebral cortex, before being released into the rest of a sentence. But the frequency of the occurrences was decreasing.

"...to, to vis-sit me. You have been very kind. Our...our book the... the Pirkei Avot speaks of *g'milut chasadim*, acts of lovingkindness, as being equal with Torah, which is what we call our Jewish law...and *avodah*, service to God in Hebrew. These two things. You are very... very...kind, Abrihet. *Very* kind."

As his speech issues decreased, his rabbinic references were increasing to their former place in his conversation. And his conversation overall was becoming more complex as his memory continued to improve.

Of course, Abrihet knew that the Jewish law was called the Torah. But David Kaplan didn't know that Abrihet knew that, even though he understood that her family believed they had some sort of Jewish connection in Ethiopia. They had talked about her family back home— particularly her mother and father—but had never discussed anything beyond their health and basic welfare. Now she felt compelled to respond to his comment with more information about her present life. She prayed for wisdom, and then spoke up.

"Yes, I...my...rabbi...I have a rabbi, and he will visit me here today... he speaks about those things."

Just as David's interest was piqued, he felt a distinct sharp pain in his forehead. He wanted to continue with the conversation. Did she actually see herself as a practicing Jew? Why had he never asked her about that possibility? Who was her rabbi? Did he know him? Where did she attend synagogue? Was it a synagogue for Ethiopians? He knew that such places existed in Israel, where some like her were brought by Chabad Chassidic Jews. But even though he was interested, he felt that something wasn't right in his head. Suddenly, his thoughts wouldn't come out as words. Somehow, he had to tell her something was wrong, and they had to go back inside. He squeezed her hand.

"Abrihet, can we go…back…could we…"

"Are you alright, Mr. Kaplan?"

"Not …really…go back…"

"Of course. We are now right at the entrance. It has been enough today. We will talk later. Let us go slowly back."

They walked up to and through the entrance. Abrihet saw an attendant, and asked for a wheelchair. After placing David in the chair, she hurriedly wheeled him to the elevator. He held his head in his left hand.

"I'm feeling very…tired."

Abrihet was worried, but said nothing except, "You will be fine, Mr. Kaplan. God will take care of you."

At that exact moment, Rabbi Sheldon Goldberg from Beth Yeshua entered Kingsbrook Rehabilitation Institute, visiting eighty-two-year-old Harold Stein, whose room was just a few doors down from David Kaplan's. The rabbi had arrived about a half hour before, and was seated in a wheelchair opposite Harold, who was relaxing in his bed in his crimson bathrobe and worn leather slippers. Harold had joined the synagogue two years earlier, after a life of problems stemming from fierce action in the Korean War, and more fierce action through three failed marriages. He had straight silver hair, a balding crown, and a large levitical nose. His newfound Messianic faith and new Messianic friends were just about all he now possessed. But to him they were enough. The rabbi, dressed in a light white short-sleeved dress shirt, black trousers, and a black rayon yarmulke, was slowly rolling the wheelchair back and forth with his feet, as he laughed with Harold, who had just described the food at Kingsbrook as kosher cardboard. For Harold, it felt good to laugh. He had almost died two weeks earlier, so laughter was a definite reaffirmation of life. And it was reflected in the improvement in his speech and gait. In fact, he had been recovering more quickly than David Kaplan. Of course, every stroke patient is different in that respect. After the laughter died down, Harold's voice took on a sober tone.

"Rabbi…Sheldon…if I never leave this place…that is, by the front door…I just want to say that the last few years have been the happiest in my whole life. I was born in Brooklyn. And…I've lived here all my life. As I've told you many times before, Rabbi, I've always believed in God. I've had a good Jewish upbringing, went to *chader*…Jewish day school, to synagogue. But I've never had this…this…"

Words escaped him.

"…and after I've made so many mistakes…*so* many. Tell them *that*… my children, our friends, everyone…at my funeral. Tell them."

This is what Sheldon Goldberg lived for—spending time at an Orthodox Jewish-run care center with an eighty-two-year-old member of his synagogue whose life had been transformed by the same One that had transformed his life twenty-five years earlier—when he was a young college student at NYU, empty and needing to be filled with something other than beer. He was never sure exactly what to say when a congregant like Harold Stein spoke this way. There had been other Harold Steins who had spoken similar things before—and it was always the same.

"Harold…I…I have lots of challenges around me. Good challenges, difficult challenges…sometimes difficult people."

He realized that for all of the challenges over Harold Stein's long life, he probably wouldn't be able to imagine the challenges a Brooklyn Messianic Jewish rabbi might face. And there was no need for him to. The rabbi continued.

"You, however, are not a challenge. You are nothing but a blessing and a joy, and the reason God sent me to do what I do."

Just then, there was a commotion outside the door. Before Rabbi Goldberg could wonder what it was, Abrihet poked her head in the room.

"Rabbi…Rabbi…It's the Jewish man that I work with!"

He could see the tears streaming down her face, even at the distance between Harold's bedside and the hallway. Abrihet had no time to weigh the consequences of what she chose to do next. She saw Harold lying in bed, and then looked straight in Rabbi Goldberg's eyes

"Hi, Harold. Excuse us."

Sheldon got up from the wheelchair and followed her. They walked into David Kaplan's room, where a staff doctor and two nurses were surrounding him—shining lights in his eyes, checking his pulse, constantly talking to him. Abrihet grabbed the rabbi's hand and led him up to the bed. Then she took the hand in hers and reached out to touch David's arm. She began to pray.

"Oh God, please help my friend. My rabbi and I are praying. Please bring him out of this…this…whatever it is…maybe…another stroke."

Rabbi Goldberg began with the first line of the traditional Mi-Shebeirach prayer in Hebrew and English.

"May He who blessed our ancestors rescue from any distress…"

If the intensely focused doctor and nurses noticed Abrihet and Sheldon, they didn't react. They were too busy trying to assist their patient.

Then, Sheldon Goldberg gingerly and quietly prayed an extemporaneous prayer, just as Naomi Kaplan rounded the corner from the elevator and walked into David's room.

"God of Israel…please bring your healing now to this…"

Naomi quickly surveyed the overall situation.

"What's happening? Abba! Abba! What's going on?"

The doctor looked up and spoke over the other voices.

"Your father seems to have had an episode. We've got to get him to the hospital. The attendants are on the way."

Naomi put her hand to her mouth. Was she too late? Then, for the first time, she noticed Abrihet, and the unforgettable face of the Beth Yeshua "rabbi" standing next to her.

"Abrihet! What's *he* doing here?"

Abrihet's heart began to speed up.

"I…I…I've asked this wonderful man to come and pray for your father. This is Rabbi Goldberg. Rabbi Goldberg, this is…"

"I *know* who he is, Abrihet. What's he *doing* here? You tell me…now! *Answer* me! What's he doing here?"

The hostility in Naomi's voice intimidated Abrihet. She wanted to explain that Rabbi Goldberg was visiting a congregant a few doors down. But her tongue froze, which in turn left more room for Naomi to fill in the blank spaces. She turned to Goldberg.

"You…get out! You have no business here. And *she* had no business asking you to come. Do you understand me?"

He tried to explain himself.

"I was just visiting…"

Naomi lost all decorum, which she knew was unlike her—and unlike her father.

"You shut up, phony rabbi! I don't even want to hear you say a word in this place!"

By this time, the aides had come into the room with a gurney, and were quickly preparing David to transfer to it. Naomi realized she needed to refocus, but not until she was finished with Abrihet and her *rabbi* friend. She grabbed one of the younger nurses.

"Make sure these two are taken to the director's office. They tried to convert my father," Naomi blurted out, totally forgetting that she had promised at the Cherry Esplanade never to recommend that Abrihet be fired.

The nurse put her hand to her mouth and spoke through it, as if to mute the shock. She had been trained thoroughly about the inappropriateness of such behavior.

"How *horrible!*"

She glanced at Abrihet disdainfully. Then she reached out her hand and took Naomi's in an act of empathy that didn't escape Abrihet's notice—or Sheldon's.

"We'll get an aide to assist with that…right away."

She left the room. Tears were now flowing from Abrihet's eyes, but Naomi was too worked up to notice—and wouldn't have cared if she did. She turned to her father. He appeared unresponsive as he was fitted with an oxygen mask and wheeled out of the room. Naomi followed closely behind him, out into the hall and toward the service elevator. The nurse came back with two large security guards, complete with some sort of intimidating officer-type caps.

"Take these two down to the front office. I'll call ahead and explain the situation. Believe me, the management won't like it."

Abrihet was still weeping as she and the rabbi were summarily escorted out of the room and taken the opposite direction, to the staff elevator. The two guards stood silently, heads bowed and eyes awkwardly focused on the ground. As they arrived at the first floor, Sheldon quietly tried to comfort Abrihet.

"Well...your heart was in the right place. So be encouraged."

Abrihet exhaled a sigh, trying to release tension and quiet her breathing. Besides a cordial smile in the corridors of the institution, she hadn't connected with the director since she was in a meeting with several other employees over a patient rights issue. That was about six months before. The other time was about two years before that, in a one-on-one meeting when she was hired. He seemed pleasant then. He told her that her chances of being hired were good, and it turned out they were. He must have liked her, and she hoped that was still the case. She mentally recalled his name. *Levitz...Mr....or was it Dr...no, Mr...Mr. Levitz.*

The four stepped off the elevator. The guards took their place at each of the accused's sides as they walked to the director's office and knocked on the door. A voice spoke from inside.

"Come in."

One of the guards opened the door and escorted Abrihet and Rabbi Goldberg into the room. Abrihet had tried to dry her eyes with a tissue. The sixty-two-year-old director was seated behind his meticulously clean mahogany desk. He had a full head of salt-and-pepper hair, and wore a white dress shirt with red suspenders and a little red bowtie— and no jacket. There were two wooden chairs in front of the desk. He dismissed the two guards.

"You can go. Thank you."

They nodded in unison and left, their caps still firmly fixed on their heads.

"So...Abrihet."

She cleared her throat and tried to speak up.

"Hello, Mr. Levitz."

"Dr. Levitz."

"I'm so sorry. Dr....Levitz."

He leaned back in his chair.

"Yes…well, I understand you've gotten yourself into some trouble."

"Well…"

"And who is this?"

Sheldon responded, trying to look directly into the director's eyes in an attempt to make a statement about his own integrity.

"Yes, I'm Sheldon Goldberg…Rabbi Sheldon Goldberg."

"And what synagogue are you affiliated with?"

"Beth Yeshua, Midwood…Brooklyn."

"I see. Well, I'd ask you two to sit down. But unfortunately I don't have much time, as I have another meeting. So this will have to be short, I'm sorry to say. First of all…Sheldon. We have a rule here. Congregational leaders may only visit patients from their own…congregations… churches…whatever. Our patients come from diverse backgrounds… besides Judaism. We are very proud of that. And we expect our staff to respect each patient's faith traditions. For instance, we know that Harold Stein affiliates with your synagogue. So, of course, you can visit him. However, other patients from other faith traditions will be visited by their own clergy…and of course, our chaplains. Is that clear?"

"Yes, sir. I was, in fact, visiting Harold when…"

Dr. Levitz interrupted.

"Fine. Now to you, Abrihet. From what I understand, you have been a fine worker…until now. So, I will just ask you. Did you solicit Sheldon's help to pray for Mr.….Mr. Kaplan, who was having a medical crisis?"

"Yes sir, I did. I was very concerned for Mr. Kaplan, and…"

"I see. And by any chance, do you affiliate with this man's house of worship? I just have to ask, if you don't mind."

"Well….yes…"

"I see. It was just a guess, but apparently it turns out to be true."

He picked up a pencil that was on his desk and tapped it a few times. Then he put it down. Abrihet took a breath and began to make an attempt at defending herself.

"I'm so sorry, but…you see, Rabbi Goldberg was a few doors down with Harold Stein. We were to have a cup of coffee after he visited him… Rabbi Goldberg and I. And then…I was so upset…that something would happen to Mr. Kaplan…I…I wasn't trying to persuade him to believe, like his daughter said. I was just…concerned…"

181

"I see. I understand your good motives."

He leaned forward.

"But, Abrihet…you know the training every nurse receives about praying with patients. And what's more, Mr. Kaplan's daughter Naomi expects our staff to abide by those guidelines. They trust our policies and procedures. They depend on us to uphold them. And when they are not followed…they expect…well…"

Abrihet put her hand to her mouth as tears once again began to flow.

"Oh, please, Dr. Levitz. I don't know what I'd do if…where would I go? I have nowhere. Please. I promise…please."

Dr. Levitz stood up and walked to the front side of the desk.

"I feel terrible about this. I really do. But I have no choice. You will get a month's severance pay. Please see HR. I promise you, we will give you a good reference. I'm sure you will find something else. You are a good worker. That's all. I really must go now. I'm late for an important meeting."

Abrihet found breathing difficult. But she tried to inhale and exhale in order to keep from fainting. Dr. Levitz reached his hand out and shook both of their hands, starting with Abrihet's.

"Good luck, Abrihet. And it was good to meet you, Sheldon."

Dr. Levitz left first. And then, Rabbi Goldberg and Abrihet left, with his arm on her shoulder for support.

Chapter Twenty-Three

MRI's are slow procedures. They can be almost as uncomfortable for family members in the waiting room as they are for the patient in the narrow tube. Sometimes, as was the case with David Kaplan, they are *more* uncomfortable for the loved ones. David wasn't conscious enough to be claustrophobic. But his beloved daughter was wide awake to the extreme danger her father was in. She had hoped to never have to visit the patient floors and waiting rooms of Maimonides Medical Center—let alone the Mount Sinai Hospital, where Darrin had lain between life and death—ever again. And yet, here she was.

As she sat in steadfast stillness, staring at an inane abstract painting that was supposed to, in some way or other, depict Jerusalem at dusk or dawn, sibling competition once again crept into the empty crevices of her heart. This time, a barely conscious synapse in her memory pointed to the death of her mother many years earlier, in her comparative youth. But that had metastasized since, into a sometimes dormant dysfunction in the family dynamic that awakened again after her father's first stroke—and her sister's newfound connection to him. The first slight twinge was triggered by the original text from Lisa months earlier, received while Naomi was working at the housewares department at the Manhattan Macy's. Why did Lisa find out about the original stroke before Naomi did? Naomi was supposed to know things about David before Lisa. Now, she had a chance to *return the favor*, so to speak, and get the jump on Lisa.

Naomi was well aware that this competitive drive stemmed from the kind of evil inclination that David Kaplan so passionately opposed. But that didn't stop her from acting on it—especially on this day. The fact was, Naomi hadn't yet processed the heartless way she had treated Abrihet after seeing her and her rabbi in David Kaplan's room. She was still in the self-justificational phase. Therefore, she wasn't in what one might call a *good place*, as she sat waiting for news of her father's condition.

Dad has had an episode, maybe another stroke. I was with him. At Maimonides now, she texted. She might as well have texted *I was with him and you weren't.*

Lisa had arrived home hours earlier, after having visited Naomi that morning. She was sitting on the deck in her black two-piece bathing suit, with her large circular white plastic-rimmed Audrey Hepburn-style sunglasses darkening the brilliant spring sunlight. Marc was taking a nap, and the children were watching some sort of superhero action movie on HBO, when the text caused her iPhone to ding.

Dad has had an episode, maybe another stroke. I was with him. At Maimonides now.

Lisa stared at the text, not wanting to believe its contents. It did not communicate Naomi's neurotically driven attitude. It simply startled her, and caused her heart to skip a beat. She'd heard about second strokes before. And they always seemed to end in death. She got up from the patio chair and opened the sliding door, heading for the bedroom. When she got there, she saw Marc—asleep in black shorts and an old white tee shirt, lying diagonally across the bed, prone on his back, and with his mouth open like a codfish. Her neurotic response was reserved—not for Naomi's text—but for him. Every lack of willingness or ability on Marc's part to communicate with her—either during last year's crisis when he worked for what turned out to be mafia don Prima, or in present situations—coldly smacked her in the face like the codfish he unconsciously mimicked. He hated being woken up, but that was unavoidable in this case. She slapped his leg.

"Get up!"

His mouth closed as a quickly as a codfish's would, and his eyes opened.

"What the…"

"Dad had another stroke. He'll probably die. They always do. Do you want to come down to Maimonides with me? That's where he is. We'd have to take the kids. Maybe they should see him one last time anyway."

He rose to a sitting position, sighed, and leaned on his elbow. He was still waking up.

"Um…no. You go."

"But he may die."

"I guess he probably will. But he never liked me anyway."

Lisa raised her voice.

"*What*? I can't believe you're saying that!"

With the uninhibited response of one lost in a recent dream state, he let loose.

"Come on. He likes that goy Darrin more than he likes his own son-in-law."

"That's ridiculous!"

He let every wall of self-consciousness collapse.

"Yeh? You know what? *You* like him better than me too. I see how you look at him, with his cute little waspy nose and those goyishe blue eyes. It's lust, is what it is. *I* should get some of that, Miss sexy black bikini and stupid sunglasses! But you always have a headache."

Lisa put her hands on her hips.

"I can't believe this! First of all, I'm constantly pushing for Naomi to stop her foolishness and marry Darrin Brock."

Marc started to say something, but Lisa talked over him.

"Second, I spent all last year listening to your insanity about me trying to kill you, and having an affair behind your back with the very man you're talking about. And on top of *that*, you thought *he* was also trying to kill you. You didn't even know he was a detective. You thought he was a hitman of some sort! What a joke. I should have divorced you after that. But guess what? I didn't. And now you're back to that mishigas again? Get your ass out of that bed, and get some clothes on. You're coming with me to Maimonides. I'll tell the kids."

CHAPTER TWENTY-FOUR

At that very moment, the subject of the Silvers' argument—Darrin Brock— had no idea that David Kaplan had had another stroke and was even now struggling to survive. The information hadn't been withheld from Darrin Brock purposefully. It was just too fresh. And Naomi would never have thought to contact him anyway—no matter when it had occurred. She had been opposed to any contact between her father and Darrin from the moment she broke up with him.

Monday morning, as Darrin Brock sat in Inspector Ralph Lewis' cluttered office, he still knew nothing about Kaplan's latest stroke. As usual, Darrin's chair was lower than Lewis'. However, their heads were at the same level, owing to the fact that Lewis was leaning back in his chair, with his feet up on his desk. His eyes were closed as he spoke Darrin's last name to the ceiling.

"Brock, I'm taking you off the terrorism task force thing. I want you to follow up with the Mendel case. We've reopened it."

"I thought you never closed it."

Inspector Lewis could easily detect the edge in Darrin's voice. There was a time when Darrin's voice never had that edge. But that was before the new cynicism he had acquired over the last several months. Since then, Lewis had picked it up several times. He pulled his legs off the table, and sat up in response to the new hardness he still hadn't gotten used to.

"Oh, come on, Brock. Don't take me so damn literally. You *know* it's still ongoing…until it's solved. What I meant was, we're putting fresh resources in that direction, thanks to you almost getting your head blown off in the deceased's house. And those fresh resources include you."

"Okay. So what do you want me to do?"

"I want to know if this was the same Russian syndicate that Igor was running last year, before we killed him just as he was about to shoot Marc Silver. We don't have much on-the-ground intelligence. Too much going on in community relations and homeland security, etc. But…that's where you come in. Start with these contacts."

He slapped several sheets down on top of an existing haphazard pile of papers on Darrin's side of his desk. Darrin reached over and picked them up. As he began to peruse them, Lewis stopped him.

"Brock, look at me."

Darrin looked up.

"One more little thing. It's very possible that the Kremlin is somehow involved with this. I don't know how I know this. Maybe it's thirty years with the force. Maybe it's the news cycle. The same powers that messed with our elections…and a lot of other country's elections…may have some connection. So watch your back…including your emails and text communications."

"What? I mean, how do I do that?"

"Just take it for granted that someone is watching and reading everything you put out there, even police encoded stuff."

"Are you kidding?"

Ralph Lewis slapped his hand on his unkempt desk. Darrin jumped slightly, as Lewis leaned forward.

"No! It's a new world out there."

Darrin sighed. And as if on cue, there was a knock on the door, and then another. The inspector shouted.

"Come in."

Margaret popped her head in. Darrin turned around and then turned back and bowed his head, as if Inspector Lewis could see every passionate second of his last encounter with her.

"An old Jewish man named Stanley came to report a missing person—tall, with a kind of pocked face. He said he wants to see you."

Something in Darrin wondered whether this was the deli man David Kaplan knew. But then, he thought, there must be a thousand tall old Jewish men in Manhattan named Stanley, with bad skin. He turned to Inspector Lewis.

"I know a Stanley, but…"

Ralph Lewis impatiently waved his hand at Margaret.

"Okay, okay. Hurry up and bring him in."

As soon as she left the room, *the* Stanley entered. He walked hunched over, like a giant trying to avoid doorways—although there was a clearance of a few inches. He slinked over to the guest side of Inspector Lewis' desk, and then glanced down at Darrin, who was sitting in his low seat.

"Detective Brock, I…I hope you're feeling better."

"Thank you, Stanley. I am…physically."

Inspector Lewis stood up and extended his hand over the desk toward Stanley, with the intention of speeding things up so he could get back to his conversation with Darrin.

"I guess you *do* know him, Brock. How can I help you, Stanley?"

Darrin could detect a furrowed brow on Stanley's face.

"I…I…wanted to report a missing friend. A close friend."

"I see. There's an office on the first floor where they expedite…"

"No. I wanted to see the top man. You see, this is a very close friend. It's not like him to just disappear and not show up at the library for several weeks …and not answer his cell phone. He has no family here…"

"I see."

Darrin sat up as much as he could in his low seat.

"It's not Mahmoud, is it?"

"Yes, Detective Brock. I hate to have to tell you that it is. Detective, I remember you came and asked about that young…man. Remember?"

Darrin hadn't told the inspector about his visit with Stanley and Mahmoud to inquire about Omar, and he didn't want to explain it now. He tried to get off that subject.

"Of course. When did you see Mahmoud last?"

"I don't know. I guess not long after we saw you at Ben's Deli."

The detective part of the inspector wouldn't let the subject go.

"What man?"

Darrin attempted to switch subjects again. He knew that Inspector Lewis asked him to drop any suspicion about Omar.

"It's nothing."

Now Stanley wanted to play detective. He held his hand up like a wise old rabbi.

"I don't know that it's nothing. Maybe it's not nothing. You didn't think it was nothing then. I'm a good reader of faces. And your face said this man was guilty of something. God knows what."

Lewis was losing patience.

"*What* man?"

Stanley continued before Darrin could stop him.

"Omar something, I think. See, I remember names like faces."

Ralph Lewis pounded on his desk.

"Damn it, Brock! I told you to back off after you interviewed him. You better hope this wasn't after that. Well? Was it?"

"No sir...I mean, yes sir. But...I just wanted Mahmoud's take."

"And who the hell is Mahmoud?"

"That's...that's Stanley's missing friend."

"I didn't mean that. I meant, who is he that you should ask him... especially when I told you to stop investigating Omar."

Inspector Lewis turned to Stanley.

"Oh, forget it. Stanley, this has zero to do with that kid Omar. Everybody's ready to jump on these young Muslims. This friend of yours is probably okay. Maybe he got sick, or I don't know what. Mahmoud, right? Where's he from?"

"The West Bank. Around there somewhere. He's maybe my age. A retired taxi driver...and the nicest man, Inspector. The nicest man. I worked the deli counter. I met a lot of big shots I could have done without...including my own landsmen, if you understand. This is a mensch. A real gentleman."

"I mean here, not in the Mideast. Do you know where he lives?"

"I wish I did. Somewhere in Queens. I don't even know his last name. He's just Mahmoud to me...all these years...many years."

"Well...you go down to room 118 and give them a description. Tell them I sent you. I'll follow up."

"Thank you. Thank you."

He turned to Darrin, who was still sitting in the low seat.

"It's nice to see you. Is Mr. Kaplan doing well? His daughter, your... your..."

Darrin realized that Stanley didn't know about the break-up, and didn't want to go there.

"They're doing well."

"That's good. Well, I should visit David soon, and tell him Mahmoud is missing. I won't bother you two anymore. Thank you."

With that, he promptly left and closed the door. For the first time, Darrin stood. Ralph drew close to him.

"I'll deal with you about all this later. Just stop with the Omar thing. Stick with the Russians, and the Mendel case. You'll live longer. I've got to get somewhere now. I'll get you some leads...through Margaret."

Inspector Lewis walked out of his own office, leaving Darrin to flop back down in the low chair.

Chapter Twenty-Five

Kaplan's boss at the Manhattan Macy's housewares department put a high priority on Mondays—especially since, from the start, she had given Naomi every Saturday off to observe the Shabbat. So, with few exceptions, there was no choice but to be at work, and to be there on time.

With each floor reached by the escalator, from main to eighth, she repeated the *Mi-Shebeirach* prayer for healing. The latest news was that David Kaplan was stable, although not conscious. The RN promised that any preliminary test results or status changes would be texted to Naomi's phone, and Mrs. Lazar had graciously given her permission to monitor the texts.

Once on the eighth floor, Naomi opened up and prepared for the first customer. She wondered if it would be a return. Early Monday morning customers often were. Suddenly, as that thought crossed her mind, Darrin Brock's electric blue eyes appeared before her. They sparkled like the key attributes of an angelic apparition. She recalled first looking into them a year and a half before, on December 26th, when he came to her department to return gift items. That memory triggered the present "vision," as it had triggered so many obsessive daydreams the year before. A warm spring-fever breeze wafted through her whole being. Longing welled up within her, and tears began to appear. It happened to be June, which only added to the pressure of her suppressed love, as it began to seep into the lonely spaces that had been sealed off through the winter and early spring. She mouthed words she didn't dare whisper.

"Darrin, I love you. I love you, Darrin Brock. I love you."

As she moistened her lips in preparation for a virtual kiss, she heard what sounded like high-pitched squeals coming from the direction of the escalator. At first, she barely paid attention. She had opened her heart to a few seconds of uncensored feelings, and those feelings had her complete attention. But as the sounds grew louder, she couldn't ignore them. It turned out they emanated from two children—two pre-teen boys, to be precise. They were loudly laughing over one another. As they walked toward her counter, she couldn't tell which was older and which was younger. But she guessed that they were brothers. However, she couldn't tell that from their body types, because one was stocky—even chubby—and the other was slightly taller (neither could be called tall) and thin. Together, they resembled a hamburger and a hot dog, like the old cartoon that depicted starving Laurel and Hardy-like characters in the desert. No, it was in their faces—their cheekbones, and something about their eyes. They were definitely brothers. As they approached Naomi, they seemed to periodically bounce into each other, like magnets alternatively attracting and repelling. She quickly wiped her eyes with her fingers, as it was too late to access a tissue.

"Can I help you boys?"

The thinner one spoke up. His voice was as high as it had sounded on the escalator. Apparently, neither of them had quite reached puberty.

"Um…we have…um…"

The rounder boy cupped his hand and pressed it against the skinny boy's ear. When he was done whispering, the other boy said, "…almost twenty dollars."

Then the whispering one decided to speak. He was louder and higher-pitched than the one Naomi supposed was his older brother.

"Okay, so we want a really sharp set of knives. Almost twenty dollars worth…but…maybe not quite that much. Really sharp."

"Like *kill* sharp."

Was that a threat? These boys looked innocent enough. But these days…maybe they weren't as innocent as they seemed. *Maybe* they were child jihadists of some sort. Or perhaps they were members of some sort of street gang, like MS 13. Crazier things had happened in New York. One thing was for sure. Naomi wasn't about to show them any knives. She just hoped they weren't about to show her any either.

"Knives? I…I don't think so. Why aren't you boys in school on a Monday morning?"

The thin one laughed in his high-pitched tone, his dark brown wavy hair almost vibrating in unison with the pitch.

"That's funny. School's out, Lady."

She realized she had been too nervous to think clearly.

"Right. Still…you should be in some kind of…of summer program."

"It's still spring. They haven't started yet. And anyway, me and my brother Josh are home-schooled. I'm Jeremy, and we live in Teaneck, New Jersey. And we're *very* independent."

She tried not to appear surprised that they came from the same town as Darrin Brock. The chubbier one piped up.

"*Very.*"

He made a safe sign with his hands, like an umpire. His shorter lighter-brown hair peeked out from under a Mets ball cap, accentuating his baby-fat face.

"*Very* independent. And *very* responsible. He's a year older, but we're just as responsible as each other."

"Yes, I'm sure you both are. But not with knives. Not today."

She was beginning to relax. Whatever these two brothers were, they didn't seem to be terrorists or gang members. Joshua's voice claimed new heights as he began to beg.

"Please. You don't understand, lady. It's almost Father's Day, and my dad always cuts the ham."

Jeremy's voice harmonized a step lower.

"*Always.* And he always messes it up."

"Not *always.*"

"Okay, not *always.* But a lot. And we want to surprise him."

"I see. I didn't know ham was so hard to cut. But then I've never…"

Jeremy raised his pitch another half step.

"You're *Jewish!*"

Naomi instinctively looked around.

"Y…Yes. And?"

Jeremy stamped his right foot twice.

"Listen to this, lady!"

"No, let me do it!"

"No. Me!" Joshua squealed.

"Together!" Jeremy protested.

Then, as if they were auditioning on *America's Got Talent*, they began to sing the watchword of Israel from Deuteronomy 6:4, together—although slightly off pitch.

"Shema, Yisrael, Adonai Elohay-nu, Adonai Echad"

Naomi was speechless. Were they actually Jewish? Non-observant Jews might eat bacon, God forbid, but a whole ham?

"I…I don't understand."

Joshua changed the subject.

"Hey, lady, are you gonna sell us the knives or not? We could go to Target. But that's junk."

"*Junk!*" Jeremy vocalized. Joshua repeated his umpire safe sign.

Naomi was too curious to let go of the last subject.

"Wait a minute. How did you know that…that prayer?"

"Church," Joshua said matter-of-factly.

"Church?" Naomi echoed. "You sing that in…church?"

"Yeh, church, lady," Jeremy repeated.

"I…I don't understand. What church does that? That…that prayer belongs to us…us Jews. That's *ours*."

Jeremy sighed with frustration.

"No. We don't sing it in church, like a hymn…like *This is the Air That I Breathe*. That would be silly. No one would know what the words mean."

Naomi had never heard of *This is the Air That I Breathe*, or any other Christian hymn outside of Christmas carols.

Jeremy used his own sign, which was more like a Chassidic Jewish shrug.

"See…we learn Jewish things at home. Our dad…the one with the dull knives…he teaches us about Israel, and everything."

"Oh. So he taught you how to sing that?"

"No, no, no," Joshua remonstrated, each no ascending to a higher note. "He doesn't know that one."

"We learned *that* from our Sunday school teacher. Our *favorite* teacher."

"We *love* him," Jeremy screeched with his lower voice.

"Yeh," Joshua intoned, lowering his frequency out of respect. "He taught us that…and Shalom, and the prayer before eating too. The Mo…"

"The *Motzi*," the older boy reminded his brother.

"Yeh. The Motzi."

"He learned them when he was going with a Jewish lady."

"A lady like you, I guess."

"Yeh, like you. Maybe."

Joshua looked Naomi up and down, and released a high-pitched giggle. Jeremy leaned in closer to her than he had to his brother, and whispered in his own lower high pitch.

"She dumped him."

Jeremy continued, not bothering to whisper.

"Kaput. Dumped him real good. *Real* good. For a while he wasn't such a great teacher. And before that, he was the best teacher we *ever* had."

"The *best*. She did that to him."

"But he's better now."

"Yeh. Better. 'Cause of Margaret."

"Yeh. Margaret. She came to church last week, and he introduced us to her. He's better now. Our friend Mark told us he saw them kissing in a car outside his house last week. So he's all better."

Joshua giggled as only a boy of eight or nine could.

"Yeh. *All* better. Now that he's kissing Margaret a lot. So I guess we told you all the Hebrew we know. See? We're very responsible home-schooled students. *Very* responsible. So what about the knives? Can we buy them?"

"You okay, lady?"

Naomi's ears had begun to turn red somewhere between the words *dumped* and *Margaret*. And the redness had quickly spread to her face. But lest her elevated heart rate and blood pressure be for naught, she *had* to know for sure. How could she ask without letting on? She gravitated back to the knives.

"Okay. Okay. I shouldn't, but…what kind of knives do you want?"

Playing the role of the older brother, Jeremy spoke up.

"A little less than twenty dollars worth. Whatever that buys. Just so they cut ham…or steak…or whatever."

"Whatever."

"Okay. I'll see what there is."

Naomi walked down one of the aisles while they stayed at the counter. When she returned, she had a long thin light-brown box in her hand. She placed it on the counter and opened it. Inside were three gleaming steak knives of different sizes and edges, with well crafted polished wooden handles.

"Now, I'm *not* removing them. And I don't want you to either. I'll wrap them right here."

She didn't have real wrapping paper on hand, but she did have some white tissue wrap. That would suffice to cover the box so no one would question her—or them—about two pre-teen boys purchasing sharp knives. The gift came to $24.99 plus tax. As she wrapped it, the brothers each emptied their pockets of wrinkled one-dollar bills and clusters of stray change. They spilled all of it on the counter as if they were spilling the contents of a buried treasure. It took significant self control for Naomi to not laugh out loud. After the box was wrapped, Naomi had no choice but to count all of the change—which took at least five minutes. Fortunately, no other customers were waiting. The amount came to $18.79.

"Well, there's not quite enough here, boys."

She looked at them. They looked at each other. Disappointed, Jeremy spoke up.

"Oh. Is there something cheaper?"

"I'm afraid not…I mean in a *nice* set like this. I can sell you one knife, but it won't be boxed like this—maybe in a bubble card."

The boys looked at each other again. This time Joshua sighed, and then spoke up.

"Well, it's off to Target."

As they began to scoop up their money, Naomi stopped them.

"Look, you boys are very nice boys. I'll cover it."

They looked at each other a third time. Jeremy asked a question any home schooler might.

"What would Dad say?"

"What would *Mom* say?"

Then they both read each other's minds and squeaked at once.

"What would Mr. Brock say?"

So it *was* him. That was all Naomi needed to hear. She smiled from ear to ear.

"For some reason, I think I know what he'd say."

She grabbed her purse and made up the difference in bills and change. Then she walked to the other side of the counter and put a hand on each of their shoulders.

"Jeremy, Josh, promise me you won't take this paper off until you give this to your father on Father's Day."

Joshua made his umpire hand sign, almost striking her.

"We *won't!* Thank you! Thank you! You're an answer to prayer!"

"Yeh. A big prayer."

They grabbed the box. As they walked away, Joshua shouted in the highest note yet, "Thanks again, lady!"

After they left, Naomi exhaled and spoke to all the housewares around her.

"That was *crazy*. Darrin Brock is their Sunday school teacher. What are the chances of that?"

Then, she more or less half-prayed.

"Was that you, HaShem…or the evil one?"

Then she added in a whispered sneer, "*Margaret. Margaret.* Kissing my Darrin. Well I guess that's the end of it. It's over for sure."

The rest of the morning consisted of three returns and four small purchases. And then, just before her lunch break came another surprise. Naomi was still in a kind of serendipity shock—consisting of alternating feelings of overwhelming awe over the uncanny Darrin Brock connections she had just been witness to, and unavoidable sadness over his new affections for a sinful seductress whom she suspected was a much better kisser than she was—and related things as well.

Just as her conflicting emotions were reaching a crescendo, a strangely familiar light-green chiffon hat—complete with a green flower brim—appeared from the escalator like a fancy pastry rising in an oven in time-lapse photography. Under it was a stern-faced Mahalia Morse. After she stopped rising, she lifted off from the escalator like a jet from an aircraft carrier, and headed right for Naomi.

"You're the one I want to talk to!"

Naomi put on her professional Macy's demeanor, the one she had used the year before to maintain distance between Darrin Brock and her dream-inspired attraction to him. She concluded right there on the spot that it would be best to pretend they had never met—which was a stretch, since they had in fact met twice.

"Yes, can I help you, ma'am? We've just gotten some *lovely* dishes in."

Mahalia raised her hand in the air like it was Moses' rod.

"I'll dish *you*, girl! You said you wouldn't have Abrihet fired. And there you go, sending her down to the administrator's office, knowing…I said, *knowing*…they would let her go! Like *Jezebel* and Naboth's vineyard, *that's* what it is!"

Naomi was peripherally familiar with the Naboth's Vineyard story in the Biblical book of I Kings. King Ahab had tried to make a deal with Naboth, so that he would sell his vineyard to him or trade it for another. But Naboth had refused, because it was part of his family's inheritance. So Ahab's wife Jezebel used two accusers to frame Naboth, and he was taken away and executed. Then she told Ahab he could take possession of the vineyard. But what did that have to do with Naomi? She'd never stolen anything from anyone. However, she didn't want to discuss the matter with this Christian witch, or whatever she was. So she figured if she got as angry at this woman as her father had when he first met Darrin Brock the year before, maybe she would just go away and leave her alone. Consequently, she chose an approach that would have been out of character even for David Kaplan.

"Listen you…you…how *dare* you! Abrihet broke the rules. And believe me, *I* knew what she was up to. So if you don't have a purchase to make, I'll just contact the authorities, just like I contacted the administrator at Kingsbrook Rehabilitation Institute…unless you leave *right now*. So just…just…go…just…"

She petered out a bit at the end, which Mahalia noticed. After one last quieter "go," Mahalia Morse suddenly burst into a thunderous peal of laughter. She started upright, blasting howls like a fog horn, and then doubled over. She lost her breath for a few seconds before taking a second laughing lap, until she was pretty much laughed out. She had just ceased when Naomi, obviously confused, just said "Stop. It's not funny." Mahalia finally straightened out, and looked Naomi in the eye.

"No? You know what's funny? God's got it all under control. That's what's funny. Even if you meant it for evil…which you *did*…God meant it for good."

Naomi had had enough of the Biblical references pitched at her like curve balls by Christians who, as her beloved and wise father had told her, take the Bible out of context.

"Please! Go. Just…go."

"I will. Believe me, I will. But with you. Isn't it lunchtime? And I've got a kosher lunch for two. Hmm Hmm. Not just kosher *style*, mind you. But real kosher. Ben's Deli. Do you know of it?"

Naomi rolled her eyes.

"Of *course* I do."

She wanted to say, "You knew I did, by the *evil eye*." But she figured you should never give a witch too much credit. Mahalia, in turn, betrayed a smile as big as her laugh.

"Well now, then…"

"Tell me, just why would I go out to lunch with you? I don't know you. And guess what. I don't think I *want* to know you."

"Sure you do. And anyway, I want to get to know *you*, because I like you. I really do. And you should want to get to know me too. I think you'd like me. Anyway, Abrihet meant well. She really did. She just wanted your father to get better. She's still searching for another job. But enough of that. I mean well, too."

"Well, even if you do…I don't think so…"

"Now what am I going to do with this knish and matzoh ball soup? Come on. I'm not going to hurt you."

Naomi was about to say no again when something unexpected occurred—an unexplainable thing. Naomi noted that Mahalia's eyes were dark brown. Darrin's were bright blue. But as Naomi looked into Mahalia's, she definitely felt like she was looking right into Darrin's instead. The shock of this discovery had the immediate effect of disarming her.

"Well…anyway, someone has to take over before I leave. And they're not here…won't…be here for a while. So…"

"Honey, I'll wait. Anyway, they're almost here right now. Right?"

"No. They're not."

Mahalia came to the other side of the counter before Naomi could stop her and intertwined her arm with Naomi's like they were buddies, old friends, even sisters. Naomi was ready to pull away and demand that she retreat to the customer side of the counter, a rule clearly stated in the Macy's rules handbook. Just then, and somewhat early, the help arrived in the person of bleached-blonde Chelsea—who was young, brand new, and knew one thing for sure about her work so far—to be there in time for Naomi to go to lunch. She arose to the top of the escalator like a bright yellow sun rising from the sea. Naomi had only gotten a chance to utter three words—"Chelsea, you're early"—when Mahalia's arm escorted her away from the counter and down that same escalator. Chelsea watched as her associate's head disappeared below the surface of the eighth floor like a toy figure retreating into a jack-in-the-box—along with some old African-American woman wearing a light-green chiffon hat with a green flower brim.

Mahalia's arm detached itself from Naomi's, as they headed out of the store and over to Seventh Avenue. The June sun was particularly bright as it reflected off the tall glass-and-steel structures, and the breaks in those structures revealed a cloudless blue sky. Mahalia speeded up, as if she was deriving locomotive energy from the hot pavement. Naomi tried to keep up with the odd senior citizen, questioning as she did whether she should just turn around and head back to the store. But then she remembered those eyes.

"Will you please let me know just…just *where* we're going."

"Do you like red roses? Lots of bold big bright red roses?" she asked, relishing the alliteration.

Not there, Naomi thought to herself. *Anywhere but there.*

She hoped it wasn't the Channel Gardens at Rockefeller Center, where she and Darrin had shared an intimate kiss…twice. But somehow she knew it was. Sure enough, they walked in silence until she could see hundreds of bright red roses, made brighter by sunshine, on either side of a rectangular pool she had seen the prior spring. One thing that was thankfully missing was the huge Easter bunny constructed out of flowers, which had so distracted her then. But that omission just made a pagan statue of Prometheus stand out more. He was blowing what seemed to Naomi like a blasphemous version of a shofar, or traditional ram's horn blown on the High Holy Day of Rosh Hashanah—and made even more blasphemous by his nakedness and grotesque fishtail.

Mahalia Morse proceeded to walk a few steps ahead of Naomi and plop down on a section of the bench astride the pool. She slapped the open spot next to her, indicating for Naomi to sit down.

Well, she missed sitting on the part of the bench Darrin and I sat on. I guess she's not much of a witch, Naomi observed. Mahalia pulled two generous containers of Ben's Deli soup out of the bag like Mary Poppins pulling her magic umbrella out of her carpet bag. Next came two knishes.

Well, her word was good there.

"Eat while I talk, Naomi."

Naomi couldn't tell whether Mahalia was doting like a Jewish mother, or demanding like a cult leader. She settled on the former simply because she was hungry and had a limited amount of time before she had to get back to work. She began with a plastic spoon and the matzoh ball soup— which was lukewarm by this time. Mahalia began with a sweep of her hand.

"You know what all these red roses remind me of?"

She didn't wait for Naomi—who was navigating her way around one large matzoh ball—to respond.

"They remind me of *this*—"

She froze and paused for three to four seconds, and then pulled a small pocket Bible out of an unknown place in her dress, leafing through it for about ten seconds.

"Oh, yes. 'Let him kiss me with the kisses of his mouth.'"

Song of Songs. More verses pushed at me by Gentiles, Naomi couldn't help thinking.

Mahalia froze for two more seconds, before she explained herself.

"*That's* what it reminds me of. You see, this is where I experienced what felt like *pleasant* kisses…like these roses. *Pleasant* ones, mind you."

She looked straight at Naomi for the first time since they sat on the bench.

"...now mind you, not all kisses in my life were pleasant. Picture this. A little nine-year-old child, precocious and if I may say, adorable...but poor, with prejudice all around...oh yes, right here in New York...more specifically East Brooklyn—oh yes, racism was *alive*...oh *yes*."

She seemed to bring it to life just by saying it that way.

"I've been called the 'N' word many more times than once...*many more. But...*"

Another dramatic pause.

"...but in this case it was my father's best friend...not a white racist in this particular case, mind you...but like me, you know...his *best* friend...who went to church with us every week, like a good Christian man. Like *he* was...who at times stayed with us Saturday night, and always got drunk...oh, *yes*."

She stopped to digress.

"It could have been seven nights a week, but all I knew was Saturday nights. That's all this little girl knew."

She refocused on Naomi.

"Yes. And sometimes, when he and my father got in late at night, stinking of stale beer and stinging whiskey...mind you, everyone was asleep, my mother, my three older sisters and my two younger brothers, all of them asleep, and then my father, asleep...he would come into my room and pull me out of bed before I could take a quick breath, and carry me down to a little closet off the kitchen, like a bat out of you know where..."

Naomi had heard enough. She didn't have to endure this sordid account. She took a quick bite of the matzoh ball and a sip of the quickly cooling soup. Then she responded, mouth half full.

"Mahalia...I don't want to hear anymore. I want to go back to work."

She began to rise, uneaten knish in hand, when Mahalia pulled her down with her right hand.

"Now just you wait. I'm almost finished. It's not polite to interrupt me by just getting up and leaving. Let me finish."

"Okay, so when does Jesus come in? That's what you want to tell me about, isn't it?"

"Oh honey, He already came in," she more giggled than spoke. "But you knew that."

"Is that supposed to be funny?"

"Now just you listen. I want to get to the part where I tell you about the kisses...the *good* kisses. But I digress. Well, that drunk old man kissed me with *bad* kisses right on the mouth every time, with his scratchy beard...*bad* ones, right there in the broom closet. And he did everything he could do, short of...well, those were the kind of kisses that got me to drinking like he did, but later on...when I was old enough to understand more about what a man like him could do...what he *wanted* to do, and what he *did* end up doing to me and others. My my. And there were a lot of men in *those* days, a lot of *bad* kisses. I tell you, not one of those kisses were like the kisses in this book here. I know that now. And when I first read the book, I didn't see *nothing* good in *no* kisses...not from any men, anyway."

Naomi closed her eyes so she couldn't see Mahalia's.

"I'm...I'm sorry. I really am. But why did you bring me out to this... this...to the Channel Gardens, just to tell me this? I've got to get back to work before I'm disciplined for being late."

"Because...on that bench over there, that part of a bench...right there..."

Naomi opened her eyes and followed Mahalia's finger. It pointed directly to the very bench, in fact the very part of the bench, where Darrin Brock had kissed her passionately under his big black umbrella. She turned back to Mahalia, who withdrew her hand.

"...yep. Right there. On that bench..."

Now she had Naomi's attention. Had she been watching...snooping was a better word...at least one of the two times Darrin and she kissed there...or maybe both times? That couldn't be. Mahalia didn't even know her then...or did she, in some wicked way? What was going on here?

"On that bench *what*?"

"That's what I was getting to...if you'll let me. Right there, on that bench. I was alone, praying. Divorced, broken, and alone, as I said. And my Yeshua...*my* Yeshua...He was insensitive enough to remind me of kisses I had been trying to forget...He can be so insensitive sometimes... to me it seemed that way at first, anyway..."

Naomi was too engrossed in Mahalia's story to flinch when she heard the name "Yeshua," or to even realize that she didn't flinch.

"…and the touching…and the hurting. Like I was back there, in that sweaty broom closet, and he was pressing against me…my father's friend, that is. And then…and then…and I'll let you get back to work… and then…"

She paused. Now she *really* had Naomi's attention.

"Well?"

"Yes, well, *He* said…He said, 'Those weren't the kisses of the mouth from Song of Songs. Those weren't the kisses of My love for you, my daughter Mahalia, my precious child.' Just like that, just those words. You don't forget words like that. And then…*then*…then, I felt his gentle Father's kiss on my cheek and brushing past my mouth…and then right on my closed eyes, which began to pour tears…just like that. And then that was it."

"That was *what?*"

"What do you think? The memory of the bad kisses was gone, completely gone…the pain part…the unclean part…and even the whiskey part. That left me too. That was before I married my Mr. Morse, mind you…the poor side of the Morse shoe people. Yes, he was Jewish. He's passed away now. But that's another story, for later."

She drew near to Naomi.

"Thank God you only know the *good* kisses, Naomi. Those kisses you had were *good* kisses. I think you can tell what good kisses are. I'm sure you can. Oh, and what else was I going to tell you?"

Naomi was speechless. She froze, unable to move a muscle, even though she knew she would probably be late getting back to work. Mahalia thought for a second, and then looked straight at her.

"Oh yes. You should think about Abrihet, and I know you will."

Then she slapped her thigh with the little Bible.

"Okay, we're done here. Let's go. If you're late, don't you go blaming me."

Mahalia unceremoniously jumped up and walked off in a different direction from the one they came in. By later that afternoon, Naomi couldn't remember anything about the walk back to work. All she could remember were Mahalia's eyes.

Chapter Twenty-Six

Late that afternoon, Naomi sat in her kitchen and stared at a shaft of late spring light, rendered visible by dust particles she had neglected to address since her father's original stroke. She turned to the window and squinted at the sun responsible for the dust's exposure. Then she shut her eyes tightly. A strange thought gripped her. *What inner dust in her own heart would shafts of HaShem's light reveal?*

Her closed eyes teared up, which was the last thing she was in the mood for. She arose and walked over to the cupboard. She wasn't the least bit hungry. But she preferred eating to thinking about Mahalia's words…and consequently about Abrihet. She grabbed the well used metal cooking pot, which she more or less threw on the stove. It dropped on the burner with a hollow clanking sound. Then she went to the refrigerator and took out an old gefilte fish jar half-filled with matzoh ball soup from the week before. She dumped the soup and one immense matzoh ball into the pot. A few cold drops of soup splashed on her hand, exacerbating her raw feelings.

The soup took too long to heat up, and then took too long to consume. As she sipped the last tablespoon of soup and consumed the last bite of the immense matzoh ball, she glanced at the books in her father's library. The wisdom of the sages seeped through the leaves and binders, reaching her through the dying shafts of light. She couldn't catch their specific words, and David Kaplan wasn't there to teach them to her, as he had during their Shabbat times together. But she knew what the sages would say about her responsibility for Abrihet's firing. And she didn't want to hear it. She threw the dirty dishes in the sink that was reserved for meat meals like chicken-based matzoh ball soup, and headed up to her room.

As she lay in her bed on her back, the sedative effects of the immense matzoh ball began to take effect. As she began to drift into a light semi-consciousness, she realized that before she ate she hadn't been any more sleepy than she had been hungry. But the weight of her guilt, combined with the starch in the matzoh ball and the hot broth of the chicken soup, quickly took effect. She dozed for perhaps five minutes. During that short period, she could swear she could reach out and touch her father's face, and feel his chicken soup breath on her cheeks. She heard his lilting Brooklyn accent coming, oddly enough, from a deep place in his eyes. She knew it wasn't coming from his mouth, which was closed.

Why do you treat the other differently than you would treat your own?

David Kaplan had often emphasized his respect for those coming from other backgrounds. Naomi tried to speak to him about it as she dozed. She had *so many* questions to ask him—especially about the "stranger's" prayer Abrihet had prayed over him—and she desperately wanted her father to answer them. What did he think of Abrihet doing such a thing? How did he feel about Abrihet's possible—though unproven—motive to convert him? But Naomi couldn't speak the words out. Her mouth remained as shut as her father's. And yet, somehow his eyes seemed to have the answer.

Suddenly, as if the soup contained a hidden stimulant, she shot up in bed. She immediately found her voice and exclaimed out loud, "Oy vey! I've sinned. Without evidence, I had that poor Abrihet fired. I know how much she loved Abba…how much she cared about him and cared *for* him. Oh my goodness! Oh my! What do I do? How can I make things right, Abba? How?"

That short five minutes ended up being the only period of sleep she got all night. She ended up pacing and weeping, weeping and pacing, from the time the sun went down in the west until it rose in the east—as if it had traveled all the way from Jerusalem with a rabbinical response to Naomi's burdened heart. When the first rays struck the opposite side of the house, she knew what she must do. She would visit that messianic place one last time. There was no other way to contact Abrihet. Even if she wasn't there, Mahalia *would* be. And she would know how to reach Abrihet. There was just one hesitancy. Naomi had no desire to spend another night at the Milsteins. They were intimidating, and asked too many questions—about Darrin, her single status, and any number of other things that were none of their business. So there was no way of going to Beth Yeshua, in the Midwood section of Brooklyn, short of breaking the Shabbat—God forbid. And she had no intention of asking Aunt Ida for another contact. So solving the problem of contacting Abrihet would have to wait until later. There was a more pressing concern. How was she going to get through the day at the Macy's housewares department without falling asleep behind the counter?

The sun was rising that morning on other areas of New York as well. It had shone on the borough of Queens at approximately the same time as it had in the borough of Brooklyn. As Omar Shehadulah rose from his bed, a sharp pang greeted him. An anxious fear gripped him. Why hadn't the thought occurred to him earlier? His opportunity to honor Allah was bound to be extremely short lived. He didn't care about the inevitability of his death, especially in the service of the great cause. That meant nothing to him. But he hadn't considered that it was only a matter of time—and probably not much time—before he would be questioned in the death of Mahmoud the taxi driver. No matter what the Russians ended up doing with Mahmoud's body, he would be listed as missing. And considering the fact that he—Omar—was already in Darrin Brock's and Lawrence Schmidt's sights, there was a real possibility that they could interrogate him now about Mahmoud's whereabouts. If that happened, his ability to destroy the Flatiron Building—or any other Manhattan structure—would be greatly diminished. He would either end up rotting in a decadent American jail, or be extradited to Pakistan. And what good would that do? His destiny was *here*, in New York, where a dozen other plots against the infidels had been foiled in the last year alone. He, and he alone, was now in a position to actually carry out a successful operation. The stupid NYPD had let him slip through their investigation process. *Now* was the time. And *now* meant *now*, this very morning.

How foolish he had been to kill the traitor Mahmoud, and reduce his chances to fulfill his mission! But it was too late to regret that decision. If he acted now, no Russian mafia could stop him, no American Christian infidel could oppose him, no filthy Jew could catch him.

Omar took what he knew would be his last trip to the bathroom. He was extremely impatient about dispensing with his body's time-wasting needs. As he sat on the toilet, the thought occurred to him that his bowels and kidneys were like demanding infants who insisted on immediate attention—as did his grumbling stomach. But he wouldn't satisfy *that* selfish cry this morning. He would merely grab a few almonds to keep his energy high and his mind sharp—like other soldiers of Allah had.

After his body was impatiently attended to, he strapped the live bomb belt on, as he had the unarmed version. Although he'd never strapped it on live, he barely gave it a second thought. He was not prone to second guessing or regret. He worked industriously, without any fiddling or unnecessary steps. He had promised a quick encrypted text to his Pakistani contact. He would wait to do that until he rose from the 23rd Street subway station like a sword rising over the neck of the infidel. He felt no anxiety save the panic of being too late.

After he donned a black trench coat that he realized was somewhat unusual for a sunny late-spring day, he left the house and headed for the subway—and Manhattan. There, he fit in with his trench coat, in one of the subterranean cars, sitting on the sideways bench seat like a homeless vagrant. He closed his eyes and pretended to doze. He focused his mind on the welcome fact that within a half hour, hundreds would be facing the wrath of Allah while *he* entered paradise—inshallah—God willing.

He left the subway car at the 23rd Street station. The sense of urgency left him as he slowly climbed the drab steps and exited the station into the grayish-blue light of a partly cloudy morning. There before him in all of its Victorian imperialistic corruption was the goal of his mission—the Flatiron Building. He had researched the site meticulously. Although he realized that the explosives strapped to his recently rested and almond-fed body wouldn't have the power to effect 9/11 style devastation, he had long ago settled for the complete destruction of the first two floors—inshallah. He stood in a small alcove across the street from the structure and pulled out his phone. He was one quick text away from the death of the infidel—and paradise. He pulled up his Pakistani contact and typed a few words without hesitation or error. He knew that within two minutes, his contact would receive the results of his handiwork, along with the rest of the world. He didn't expect a response, and he didn't require one. That would present an unnecessary risk for the contact, and a waste of the little time he had left. But about thirty seconds later, a text came in. However, this one was from an unknown party. It was without abbreviations, totally "longhand," just like Marvin's old emails to Naomi.

We see you. Two guns trained on you right now. Don't waste bomb belt, and your worthless life. If we hacked world leaders in the past we can hack you. We know all texts you send. Disarm or we kill you instantly and waste your martyrdom, killing no one or maybe one or two there on street. Do only what we tell you. Martyrdom later, when we say.

Omar had no idea about hacking world leaders, which was an accurate bragging flourish communicated by the texter, as he stood next to two Russian marksmen peering through the scopes of two powerful rifles. Omar concluded that the strange threat was empty. He had a job to do. He prepared to cross the street, when suddenly he heard and even felt a bullet whizz close to his ears. It pierced a large store window right next to him. He turned and saw the clean small hole that, if it had traveled an inch closer to his head, would have entered it and caused brain matter mess all over the sidewalk where he was standing. He slowly raised his hands and then lowered one and inserted it into his trench coat pocket. He pulled out a small device of some sort and pressed it. Then he pulled out his phone with his other hand and texted back.

Disarmed

The response was immediate.

Good. Go home now. We will instruct you further.

He walked back into the 23rd Street station and disappeared into the cavern below.

CHAPTER TWENTY-SEVEN

Inspector Ralph Lewis had recently observed a restored work interest in Darrin Brock. Along with the quickly vanishing limp from his gunshot wound the year before, a renewed bounce in his healing step resulted in a restored willingness to do whatever Lewis asked—including continued investigation of the Russian mafia. And the inspector noticed something else as well. Margaret and Darrin were doing a lot of hand touching, shoulder tapping, and quick hugging, along with long-distance smiling from across the room. When Lewis noticed this, he found himself thinking to himself, *The hell with work protocol. He's happy, and over that Kaplan woman. And if he's happy, I'm happy. If no one else gives a damn, neither do I.*

The inspector was observing just the bare indications of a quickly developing mutually growing physical passion between Darrin and Margaret—stoked mostly by highly experienced Margaret—and increasingly responded to by totally inexperienced Darrin. It always took place in the front seat of Darrin's car—in the shotgun seat, to be specific—and was now taking place almost weekly. Margaret would typically end up on Darrin's lap, eventually turning around and pressing her lips against his. By the time he would finally convince her to leave, he would experience actual pain from the sexual tension. She finally accepted the fact that he was unwaveringly adamant about remaining a virgin until marriage, so she decided to live with that—for now. He, on the other hand, struggled with a constant "low-grade infection" of guilt. He decided he could live with that, considering the fact that he had by now concluded he would end up marrying this admittedly beautiful woman. At least she professed to believe in Jesus, and went to church every week.

Inspector Lewis hadn't been planning to discuss Margaret with Darrin. But as was often the case with him, he found himself doing it anyway, in the course of a debriefing, while Darrin was in the low seat. He had just finished going over the latest report on the deteriorating yet still dangerous state of the Italian Mafia, when he blurted out, "You ought to marry Margaret before you end up...I mean, she ends up..."

Darrin couldn't hide the shock that contorted his face.

"But I'm not...we're not...we don't..."

"Right. Always the pure one. Well, *something's* going on. Just because I'm not putting a stop to the workplace fraternizing doesn't mean I don't see it, Brock...along with everyone else. I'm just giving you a little friendly advice."

"Well...yes...*something* is. I'll grant you that. But not..."

"Has she met Lester and Velma?"

"My...my...parents?"

"Nobody else's."

"No, she hasn't."

The thought of introducing Margaret to them had never crossed Darrin's now compartmentalized mind. He had just simply mentioned to his keenly observant father that she was a friend. At that time, he didn't even consider asking her to come in from the car to meet him—especially after they had just finished "making out."

After an awkward pause of two or three seconds, Darrin decided he wanted to change the subject back to remnants of the Italian Mafia, which he did—but not before the thought of inviting Margaret over to meet his parents ended up filed somewhere in his now slowly de-compartmentalizing mind.

By that evening's car rendezvous, Darrin had decided to ask Margaret in to meet his parents. He drove her across the George Washington Bridge toward Teaneck.

"I want to take you somewhere special."

"Great. I'm starved."

"I mean *after* dinner."

"Oh. Okay. Well…surprise me."

She took out her lipstick and pulled the mirror down. As she applied the glossy pink substance, he took the opportunity to share thoughts that were never far from his mind.

"Margaret, why are you applying lipstick when you know it will get all over my face…and my neck?"

"Well…it's not permanent. Don't you like how I look in it?"

"That's not the point, Margaret. We can't keep doing this…acting like hormone-saturated teenagers, doing things Paul tells us are wrong in the…the Bible…like in 1 Thessalonians chapter 4. We're *defrauding* one another," he squeaked out like a boy whose voice was changing, emphasizing the English translation of a Greek word that could also be translated using the two words *taking advantage*.

Over the last few months, mentioning verses from Scripture had come to feel strange. They had begun their relationship with short Bible studies and verses of the day. Now, their passion for sharing each other's lips had overtaken a passion for sharing Bible verses from those same lips. Darrin began to blush, even if Margaret didn't. He shut his eyes and spoke as resolutely as he knew how, although it came out not much louder than a whisper.

"I…I…not tonight."

"Oh, come on Darrin. We never actually *do* anything. So what's wrong with a little romance between two mature adults, anyway?"

Darrin turned to her and looked into her limpid eyes.

"You don't understand, Margaret. Listen, if we can't slow down, we should stop seeing each other altogether."

Margaret tried to hide her startled response, but her body language betrayed it. She sat up in her seat.

"I thought you *liked* it."

"You *know* that's part of the problem, Margaret."

"Okay. Okay. I'll be good. I promise. Maybe we can study that verse. You can teach me."

She gently patted his hand as it rested on the steering wheel. Then she turned on the radio and punched the 99.1 button—Christian contemporary music. Darrin found the music to be uninspiring, but at least it filled an awkward space in time.

After they ate pastrami sandwiches at the Noah's Ark Kosher Restaurant, he steered the car toward the Brock house on West Forest Avenue. They parked outside. Every tense fiber inside Margaret's body wanted to repeat the weekly pattern they had fallen into, which generally started with a wet kiss on the cheek, accompanied by the easily detectable reverberation of her pounding heart. She always told herself that this time—finally—it wouldn't end in frustration. Maybe they would take a hotel room. Or maybe they would drive all the way back to her apartment in Brooklyn. But of course, Darrin never allowed things to go quite that far, and she knew it was futile even to approach the subject. At any rate, what she *really* wanted deep down was to marry this exceptionally good and good-looking man, and to spend the rest of her life satisfying him spiritually, emotionally, and physically—although not necessarily in that order.

As they parked in front of the Brock house, Margaret found herself wondering why they were there, when Darrin told her he was taking her somewhere special. As he opened the car door, a symphony of pre-summer crickets greeted their ears.

"I want you to meet my parents."

His suggestion triggered Margaret's heart again, although motivated by a different stimulus altogether.

"You…you do?"

"Yes. It's time you met them."

"Oh. Oh. I'd be honored to. Do you think they'll approve of me, Darrin? How silly of me. Of course they will. After all, I love their son."

Darrin had told her all about his deeply spiritual father and devoted and sweet—although quickly fading—mother. Instinctively, Margaret pulled the lighted mirror down again and fixed her blonde hair with her hands the best she could, although it hadn't been mussed this time by their passionate kissing. She checked her lips, as if pressing them together and dabbing them with a tissue would render them more modest looking. Then she made sure her blouse was well buttoned to the top. She was glad she had chosen fairly conservative pants to change into from her police uniform, and not one of her above-the-knee skirts that she sometimes chose in order to tease him.

"How do I look?"

"Stunning, as usual. But…I think they would be glad to meet you even if you weren't."

"I didn't mean that. I meant…oh, never mind."

She took a deep breath.

"Okay, I'm ready."

Darrin walked over to the passenger side of the car and opened it. Then he took Margaret's hand. As she got out of the car, he held onto it. He shut the door with his other hand, and they faced the house together, hand in hand. He squeezed hers, and then they walked to the front door. Then he took a deep breath himself, and knocked on the door. He knew his father would most likely be in the living room, sitting on one chair while Darrin's mother was sitting in the other. They would either be watching an old black-and-white or early color TV sitcom, or some gospel music DVD. Velma always liked Bill Gaither gospel quartets.

Darrin knocked again. He heard familiar shuffling and rustling behind the door. When Lester opened it, there were Darrin and Margaret, hand in hand. Lester's eyes took in the hands and then rose up to the level of Margaret's face. Then they moved to Darrin's eyes.

"Son?"

Darrin cleared his throat.

"Dad…this is Margaret."

"How do you do, Margaret? I'm Lester. Well…come in."

He gestured with his hand and they entered as their hands parted. Then he led them to the living room. There was Velma, staring at the Andy Griffith Show. Lester went over and turned the TV off. Velma's eyes remained transfixed on the black screen. Lester turned to Margaret.

"Darrin spoke of you to us, didn't he, Velma? Velma, this is Margaret."

Margaret found her voice.

"Darrin…has spoken so well of you, Mr. Brock. It's such an honor to finally meet you…and Velma."

Lester chose a formal response.

"The honor is mine."

Velma's eyes left the screen, but didn't quite make it to Margaret or

Darrin's face. But she did seem to smile ever so subtly. Or maybe it was just an autonomous nervous reaction.

"Velma doesn't say much, but she knows. She can sense. She has always had a keen spiritual sense. And that hasn't left her, has it, Darrin?"

"I suppose not, Dad. Speaking of spiritual things, Margaret has just recently…well, not too long ago…"

Darrin blushed again, this time imperceptibly. He sensed out of the corner of his eye that his father was discerning something. After years of being around him, Darrin tended to pick up on those things. Whenever Lester's face took on that kind of preoccupied look, Darrin would stumble over his thoughts and words. Margaret took up the slack.

"Um…Darrin, perhaps your father would like to know that…that…I found Jesus. And now, I…I believe just what Darrin does."

She let out an involuntary nervous giggle, and then an even more nervous tight little smile. Lester responded with as enthusiastic a reply as his vocal chords could proclaim—although he realized right away that it must have sounded a bit more forced than he wanted it to.

"Well…praise the *Lord*!"

Darrin jumped in.

"Yes Dad. She really did. Now she goes to church and everything. And we've been…been seeing each other."

Velma's eyes came closer to focusing on Darrin and Margaret, and her smile turned into more of a straight thin line. Lester continued with his effusive expression.

"Well, that's *wonderful*!"

The expressions didn't deter Lester's continuous discernment, which was entering his spirit and reflecting onto his mind like the magnetic resonance of an MRI scan. Impressions were coming quickly, in descriptive words…desperation, insecurity—including insecurity-related sensuality, related to a desperate need to be loved—which is everyone's need, but not with this desperation. Someday, Jesus would meet that need in her the only way it can be fully met—that is, hopefully.

Whatever distorted discernment Margaret possessed was pretty well convinced that Lester didn't approve of her. But of course, she wasn't sure God approved of her either. Consequently, she was in the process of convincing Him that that she deserved to have Darrin. That being the

218

case, Lester was just another father to convince—and she was working hard at it.

"Well…Darrin teaches me so much. He's a great Bible teacher."

She realized she was leaving out what she was teaching Darrin. Lester tried to be as reassuring as he could be, considering that he lacked assurance about this attractive police officer. But none of that was an excuse against Christian hospitality.

"Yes, he certainly does know his Bible. Would you two like to be seated in the dining room? I can bring Velma over in her wheelchair. Darrin can assist me with her. We've eaten dinner, but I think we've got some apple pie, and maybe even some ice cream…and some coffee. I think that would be nice. and I believe Velma would like it. Wouldn't you, Velma?"

Velma's eyes navigated slightly in Lester's direction, as her lips remained in a thin line. That was sign enough to Lester. But the outreached hand didn't allay Margaret's nervousness, which by this time was influencing her bladder.

"I'd love that. Wouldn't you, Darrin? We never did get to dessert when we ate out. But first, may I use the washroom, Mr. Brock?"

"Yes, of course. It's just down that hall, on the left."

"Thank you. I'll be back in a minute."

As soon as she disappeared into the bathroom, Lester turned to Darrin. Velma sat slightly behind and yet between them, creating the compositional appearance of a Renaissance painting, complete with dramatic one-source shadowed lighting emanating from the kitchen.

"Darrin," Lester spoke just above a whisper, "She's awfully young."

"Dad," Darrin whispered back, "She's just a few years younger than I am."

"I didn't mean that. Young as a believer. Be careful. I believe I discern…"

"I know what you discern, Dad. You discerned it all through my high school years…fifteen, sixteen, seventeen. And I was so nervous with all the girls I dated, I couldn't wait to get off their porches when I dropped them off. Well, I'm forty-nine now, Dad. And I'll be fine. I'm a big boy."

Lester drew closer, almost touching Velma, who didn't know quite where to stare.

"I understand how you feel about those years, Son. I know it was a difficult time for you. And I'm so sorry you felt that way. But this is different. I *know* you're a mature adult. She just seems like she's not sure what's appropriate and what isn't. And she wants to *please* so much. I don't know. I mean, if you're really serious…"

"I think I am, Dad."

Darrin's recent angry depressive side began to bleed through—the side that emerged after the break-up with Naomi.

"I mean, after all, this woman believes in Jesus, Dad. Naomi didn't. And you never complained about *her.*"

Lester's expression changed. He grinned slightly.

"Well…there was something about her. I will admit that. A love capacity that was ready to receive…and give. But I understand it's over. And I'm not comparing. In fact, you're right. She doesn't believe… presently."

"It's over, Dad. And it wasn't my choice. So now I've…I'm…I'm moving on. And I think…I think I've found the woman I'm going to marry. I plan to ask her very soon."

As Darrin said that, his hand gently brushed against Velma as hers rested on the arm of the easy chair. Or did her hand brush against his? He couldn't tell which had occurred. Lester nodded as both could hear the toilet flush and the sink faucet turn on.

"Well," he spoke even more softly. "Congratulations then, Son."

He took Darrin's hand and shook it firmly. Margaret opened the bathroom door and walked back up the hallway.

"I'm in the mood for that dessert. And some coffee would be good."

Darrin and Lester each took their places beside Velma and prepared to move her to her wheelchair. After they wheeled her to the dining room table, Lester headed for the kitchen to prepare the dessert.

"I'll just be a few minutes."

Darrin sat next to Margaret and Margaret sat next to Velma. She took Darrin's hand in one of her hands and Velma's in the other. Darrin and Margaret smiled at each other, and Velma's lips formed a smile as well—at least it seemed that way.

THE
SECOND SUMMER

CHAPTER TWENTY-EIGHT

Naomi stood at her usual station behind the register at the Macy's eighth-floor housewares department. The only way to tell that it was the first week of summer and not the first week of winter was by the short sleeves and t-shirts, the blouses and tank tops, the shorts of various lengths, and bare feet clad in sandals. There was no more a view of Thirty-Fourth Street or Broadway than there had been in the temporary basement location. She had to travel all those escalator rides up all those floors every day, and all she could see from this high up was shadowless fluorescence reflecting off the aisles of mixers and mugs—and walls of pots and pans.

It was in this sterile environment—together with a department void of customers on this particular Friday morning—that Naomi's guilty conscience endeavored once again to right its wrongs against the Ethiopian Abrihet.

"I would confess my transgression and make whatever restitution necessary. I definitely *would*...if I could. But I don't even know her last name. And I wouldn't even *try* to contact that...that...*Morse* woman, even if I could...not even to get Abrihet's contact information, let alone for any other reason. She always mixes in my business. That's what she does. She probably even put these thoughts in my head in the first place...and made me feel all this guilt. I don't think I even did anything wrong. That Abrihet probably *was* trying to convert Abba. She totally deserved getting fired. She can go back to Ethiopia, for all I care."

At that point, she had to force herself to stop her useless run-on thinking, and face the truth. So she stopped thinking and started speaking out loud.

"No! That's wrong! I shouldn't have done what I did."

She submerged her words and began strategizing how she might right the wrong. For that, she knew she would have to see Abrihet in person. And she knew the only place to do that would be at Beth Yeshua. But… going back there would be uncomfortable enough. Sleeping over at the Milsteins on Friday night would just make it all the more difficult. That Leah was as nosey as Mahalia Morse…a little different but just as nosey nonetheless. And Avram was a close third. She had already decided that was out. But without them, how could she stay over on Friday night so she wouldn't have to take public transportation to get back home…on Shabbat?

Then, in a flash, she suddenly realized that there was one difference between this visit and the last one in February. It was summer now, and the sun wouldn't go down until 9:00 p.m. or later. Just possibly, Beth Yeshua had a Friday night service. And if it did, she could make contact there and then go home before darkness fell. Abrihet might not be there, but then again she might be. Or someone there could give her Abrihet's contact information—hopefully, someone else beside Mahalia Morse. It was risky, but worth a try.

As Naomi keyed in her password on the computer, she smiled. She couldn't help but remember the time she used a similar computer to find Darrin Brock's contact information, when the housewares department was temporarily in the basement level. But enough of that. There was important business to attend to, and very little time to attend to it. She typed the words *Beth Yeshua Brooklyn* into Google search.

Without having to click on the actual website, the service times came up. Good. There it was. *Friday evening, 7:30 p.m., Saturday morning, 11:00 a.m.* That might work. She could arrive a bit early, maybe 7:00 p.m., after getting off work at 6:00 p.m.—part of her summer hours that enabled her to observe Shabbat. In the winter, she was able to get off earlier, before 5:00 p.m. In the summer, 6:00 p.m. was the perfect time to get off and get home to Brooklyn. But in this case, she wouldn't be going home, but instead to Midwood. She could grab a small take-out kosher dinner, and get to Brooklyn by 7:00 p.m. Then she could leave Beth Yeshua before 8:00 p.m. and be safe and sound at home way before 9:00 p.m. It was settled. This was the only way to clear her conscience. And she was sure that if David Kaplan was able to communicate, he would support it as a mitzvah—a truly good work.

Naomi left Macy's at exactly 6:00 p.m. She knew she had to grab something before the kosher delis closed. She ended up running up to the familiar Ben's on 38th Street, and purchased one large potato-filled knish pastry. She ate that on an inside seat of the packed D train, courtesy of a polite young gentleman in a grey business suit. With nothing to wash the savory pastry down—save the oil in the flaky crust—she put up with a dry mouth and rested her head on the train car window, eyes closed. When she finally arrived in the Midwood section of Brooklyn almost an hour later, the car was almost empty. Her heart was beating rapidly in dread anticipation of her second exposure to Beth Yeshua— and a possible meeting with Abrihet. She left the subway and arose to the street level.

When she finally arrived at the house of worship—that is, according to some people's definition—she was relieved to see a mostly empty sanctuary. The first person she noticed was the tall burly blonde bearded Gentile, now wearing a black cone-head-shaped rayon kippah. She remembered sitting next to him during her only other visit. A smirk formed on her face—one that she hoped the few people present noticed. She proceeded to roll her eyes as thoughts crossed her mind.

Look at this crazy goy parading himself as a Jew. I'm sure this place is just loaded with Christian freaks and losers like this guy...including Mahalia, no matter what she told me about her late Jewish husband. As soon as I apologize to that Abrihet, I'm out of here and back to Jewish civilization, thank God.

Just then, a rotund man walked through the front door, with a flat round face not much different than Marvin's. He was obviously Jewish, and obviously every bit the loser that Marvin was. Otherwise, why would he be there? They were *all* losers, and religious charlatans.

From the opposite direction, a door along the other side of the room opened, and out came a fifty-something woman that Naomi couldn't identify as either Jewish or Gentile. She was attractive—perhaps unnervingly so. She was slim, in a knee-length grey close-fitting business dress and white blouse, an outfit Naomi's sister might wear. And she had well styled shoulder-length thick—yet straight—chestnut hair. Naomi continued with her judgments.

She probably knows about as much about true Judaism as Lisa does. So where is Abrihet, anyway?

It was clear that this worldly woman was headed straight for Naomi, and there was no time to get out of the way. She ended up within two feet of her. Then, without hesitation, she smiled and extended her hand. Naomi didn't reciprocate. Nevertheless, the woman still reached out to her with a greeting.

"Shabbat Shalom. Is this your first time with us?"

Naomi couldn't hide the edge in her voice.

"As a matter of fact, I've been here once before. And I can't stay long. I just need to speak with someone named Abrihet. Then I'm going to leave…I have to leave…right away. So, is she here?"

The woman in the knee-length close-fitting grey skirt and white blouse tried to respond calmly and un-defensively.

"First, let me introduce myself. My name is Jody Goldberg. I'm the rabbi's wife."

Figures.

"I don't believe Abrihet is here at this time. Is there something I can help you with, something I can relay to her?"

"No. No. I'll wait, but then I have to leave soon…for home."

Naomi's mouth twisted, as Jody Goldberg nodded her head slightly.

"I see. Why don't I get Rabbi Sheldon for you? Have you met him?"

"Well, you could…you could say…"

Jody interrupted her.

"Look, I'll get him for you. He can answer your questions."

She walked away before Naomi could tell her she had met her husband at the Kingsbrook Rehabilitation Institute. But considering how that episode ended, maybe it was for the best. Within a minute, Sheldon Goldberg walked out of yet another door on the other side of the room and headed her way, dressed in a grey suit, and with his well trimmed beard, a beard not unlike Avram Milstein's. It was obvious that he recognized her right away. Try as hard as he could to appear relaxed and inviting, the unpleasant memory of their Kingsbrook encounter seeped through.

"Hello. I remember meeting you at the Kingsbook Rehabilitation Institute, if I'm not mistaken. Can I help you?"

He had already been told by his wife that Naomi was looking for Abrihet, the young Ethiopian nursing aide whose firing she had caused. And he had determined in his heart not to give her any information about the young woman. As for Naomi, she quickly decided to teach this false rabbi a thing or two, by schooling him on the subject of Jewish repentance and humility—through her *own* repentance and humility. After all, she was sure she knew far more about these things than he did—or any other de facto Christian—save perhaps Darrin Brock. But he was obviously the exception.

"Yes…well…Rrr."

The venerated term *rabbi* wouldn't pass her lips.

"Mr…um…Goldberg…you see…I need to…to see…this Abrihet…I don't know her last name. But at any rate, our Jewish tradition…which I happen to be very familiar with, and which my beloved father taught me…in detail…teaches us to not only *talk* about repentance…as with many other religions, who speak of things like going to confession…not that I'm as familiar as you are with those things…"

As Rabbi Goldberg tried to patiently wait for Naomi to finish, she endeavored to return from the weeds where she had foolishly wandered.

"Well…what I mean say is, *our* religion teaches us to apologize when we're wrong. So anyway, I'm sorry I sent you and Abrihet down to the director's office. And now that I've done that, I need to apologize to Abrihet. Then I must leave sufficiently before sundown."

He tried to take in her quickly spoken, seemingly rehearsed and somewhat robotic words.

"I see. Okay. Well, I appreciate your intention, but she's not here, and she won't be here this evening. She comes in the morning…when she comes, which is most of the time. Sometimes she works, and can't get off. That is, she *worked*. She's out of a job just now. So I suppose she'll be here."

"Oh..."

"Perhaps you might help with that situation. You *might* try to get her job back for her. She could meet you at Kingsbrook. After all, I don't feel sinned against by you. You did what you felt was right in terms of my visit. Abrihet, on the other hand..."

Naomi blanched, and then continued her lecture.

"Yes, the rabbis teach us that, as *Jews*, we are not just to say we're sorry, as in *some* religions, but also to make restitution where possible. Our rabbi used to tell us *that's* what makes us different."

Naomi knew that her father David Kaplan would probably disagree with their rabbi's sometimes condescending attitude about other religions. At any rate, her little lecture was definitely getting to Sheldon.

"Well, good for you. How else may I be of assistance?"

Naomi was surprised that this supposed believer in turning the other cheek could be so rude. But she still needed to see Abrihet, and was planning to hopefully not be this standoffish with her. After all, Goldberg was a leader. Abrihet was merely a follower.

"Well, I just need Abrihet's contact information, if you don't mind. I will make any arrangements with her."

Naomi noticed out of the corner of her eye that congregants were beginning to file in in greater numbers. Just then, Jody Goldberg stepped up. Sheldon put his hand on his wife's shoulder and addressed Naomi.

"Naomi...that's your name, right?"

"Yes. That is my name."

"Well, why don't the three of us step into my office for a few minutes? We can continue the conversation there."

Naomi hesitated for just a few seconds, and then realized that the request was reasonable and might result in reaching her goal, which was to get in touch with Abrihet.

"Okay. I have a few minutes."

Naomi followed Rabbi Goldberg and his wife through the heart of the sanctuary, and then through the same door the rabbi had emerged from minutes earlier. Upon entering, the first thing her eyes landed on was some sort of framed certificate behind a desk, a desk she immediately judged as too ostentatious—over large, with a too polished superficial walnut veneer. From a distance, the certificate seemed to be an ordination of some sort. She didn't remember ever seeing a certificate in her rabbi's office. Was that a Christian tradition?

There were a few paintings and drawings on the office walls that seemed to reflect her world more than his. Rabbis in black praying at the Western Wall, children wearing black kippot on their curly heads, reading from *siddurs*, or prayer books, and one fairly large full color picture of an attractive young female soldier—obviously Israeli—smiling at the camera, an Uzi strapped to her shoulder. That seemed very out of place, very un-rabbinic.

Sheldon Goldberg pulled a dark-red leather-upholstered wooden chair from the side of the room and over to the front of the big desk, where two other matching chairs were waiting. He gestured for Naomi to sit in one chair, while he and Jody Goldberg sat in the other two. After they were settled, Goldberg started right in.

"Naomi. I'm sorry, but we can't give information about Abrihet out. I'd be glad to give her your contact information, and tell her of your intentions."

The disappointed look on Naomi's face was clearly discernible to Jody, who seemed somewhat protective of her husband, and a bit rushed. She touched Naomi's hand lightly.

"Dear, I think Rabbi Goldberg's idea is a reasonable course of action. We are preparing for a service. And you mentioned that you have to leave."

Naomi had no intention of relaying her apology to Abrihet through this couple. She got up and prepared to leave while there was still enough light to get home. Jody's eyes met her husband's. Then she too stood up and faced Naomi.

"I have an idea. I really believe Abrihet would want to see you. She told me of the ordeal at Kingsbrook. I realize now that you are the one who…"

Naomi subtly rolled her eyes, although any actual possibility of true subtlety in eye rolling is debatable. So Jody Goldberg couldn't help but notice. However, she didn't let it deter her.

"Listen. This isn't as crazy as it might sound. Don't go. Every minute that goes by decreases your chances of getting home before sundown. We live in walking distance to the shul."

Naomi tried not to register surprise at Jody's use of the Yiddish word for synagogue.

"Why don't you stay, attend this evening's service, stay over with us, and stay the day with us tomorrow? You could leave after a nice *Havdalah* service at our house tomorrow evening."

She was referring to the short service at the end of the Sabbath, facilitated by the use of a several-wick candle.

"We have paper plates you can use, and *parve* food if you'd like… neither dairy nor meat. There's a very nice room which belongs to our daughter, who is living in Israel right now."

Naomi was too startled by such a questionable invitation to realize that their daughter was the soldier with the Uzi staring at her from the wall behind Jody. She began to shake her head, which Jody had expected.

"*Come on*! This way you can see Abrihet in the morning. I'm sure she'll be here. And you can spend Shabbat resting at our house. We'll treat you like a queen, I guarantee."

Suddenly, without any forethought on her part or expectation on Naomi's, Jody reached out and gave Naomi a deep, warm, long mother-like embrace. Even Sheldon was surprised. Despite the fact that Naomi was only perhaps four or five years younger than Jody, the gentle warm mother's touch elicited an involuntary response, triggered by a longing for her *own* mother, who had died so many years before. She wanted to pull away and run out of the office door, but some kind of emotional glue held her there. She closed her eyes in an effort to trap tears that were forming, and hide her emotions. She tried to focus. How would her beloved father advise her in this bizarre situation? Would he tell her to be gracious and stay? Or to pull away and run? And how did she feel about Jody's offer? She didn't want to take the lonely subway home. The curious part of her wanted to stay, keep her walls up the best she could, and experience this family firsthand. She decided to go to the bathroom, which was calling her anyway, and try to sort it all out there.

While still in Jody's arms, she whispered, "Let me…think about it. I need to go to the bathroom. Could you tell me where it is?"

"It's that third door near the desk," Sheldon spoke up. "Um…take your time making your mind up. We'll be in the sanctuary setting up. You can come get us."

Naomi walked to the bathroom and stepped inside while it was still pitch black. She wished she could just stand there in the dark and transport herself back home with a wish, like Dorothy in *The Wizard of Oz*. That notion vanished when she felt for the light switch and found it. The lit bathroom revealed a painting above the toilet, bordered with a thin gold frame. The watercolor was obviously an artist's rendering of the Western or Wailing Wall. And that depiction was itself a frame for several lines of verse printed in the color violet, and written in some kind of cursive font.

Naomi hesitated to read the words written on the painting, considering them as off-limits as the Bible tracts that had been offered her on Manhattan street corners. But surprisingly, her eyes happened to fall on familiar words—words she had read to Darrin Brock a year earlier just after he awoke from a coma at Mount Sinai Hospital.

Blessed are the poor in spirit, for theirs is the kingdom of heaven.
Blessed are they who mourn, for they will be comforted.
Blessed are the meek, for they will inherit the earth.
Blessed are those who hunger and thirst for righteousness, for they will be satisfied.
Blessed are the merciful, for they will receive mercy.
Blessed are the pure in heart, for they shall see God.
Blessed are the peacemakers, for they shall be called the sons of God.

She wanted to just read a few words and then turn her eyes away to begin considering whether she should just leave the bathroom and walk out of the building. But she couldn't stop reading the whole Matthew text. After she reached the end, she surprised herself with a smile, as memories of reading those startling words to—and then *with*—the only man she had ever loved—or probably would *ever* love—washed over and through her like a warm surfer's wave in a tropical ocean. Whatever advice David Kaplan would give was drowned out by that wave, and the resulting acceptance of staying where she was, and consequently accepting the offer to observe this *apostate* couple firsthand. Besides, wasn't the line about the merciful receiving mercy a perfect description of her beloved father? Even if he hadn't seen this Scripture as *their* Scripture, he had never argued with the content during their discussion many months before. It was settled. She would stay, trusting Jody's promise that she could observe a kosher Shabbat at their house.

She used the facilities, and then washed both her hands and face. After she checked her eyes to make sure they showed no signs of prior crying, she looked squarely into them. Did she still see the extraordinarily pretty woman Darrin Brock had seen? Or did she see instead the grotesque image she had defaced the year before with gobs of rouge, while she looked in the mirror of her own bathroom? She remembered "hanging herself" by her hair and sticking her tongue out, like a dangling gagging corpse. As she continued to penetrate her own eyes in the Beth Yeshua bathroom, she thought she vaguely recognized the *new* Naomi—Darrin's Naomi. Perhaps that was the most precious gift he had given her. She dried her face once more and walked out of the bathroom, and into the sanctuary. There were now perhaps twenty-five people clustered around the back. Sheldon and Jody Goldberg were in conversation with a short elderly Jewish-looking woman—perhaps seventy-five or eighty—with a levitical nose, a bent back, and wearing a wrinkled grey dress. *Only poor Jews would go for such a place*, she decided to herself. *She's probably emotionally disturbed, too.*

It was obvious to Naomi that Sheldon eyed her and began to wrap up the conversation with the *old loser* lady. He took her hand in his and smiled the smile of resolution. Then he took Jody's hand and turned toward Naomi, who approached cautiously. Jody asked the one-word question.

"Well?"

Naomi wanted to decline, retaining her observant Jewish dignity and honor, and then rush to the subway in the approaching Brooklyn summer dusk. Instead, she answered with a one-word answer.

"Yes."

Jody, knowing the risk of the decision for Naomi, answered with subdued assurance.

"We'll take care of all your needs, Naomi. We'll talk after the service. Okay?"

Naomi couldn't help but nod and smile subtly in the face of those few kind words. They actually gave her an odd sense of safety in an otherwise unsafe place. She walked away and took a seat in the back, the same seat she occupied the last time she was there. The service being smaller than on Saturday morning, she was the only one who occupied that row—which she was thankful for. At precisely 7:30 p.m., the service began. Goldberg started with a short extemporaneous prayer in English. She stood with everyone else until that was finished. The informal nature of it was so surprising that she didn't even pay attention to the words—except for the name Yeshua, which was tagged on at the very end like an afterthought—although she knew it wasn't. After that was the lighting of a pair of Shabbat candles by a fairly normal-looking attractive woman who reminded her of her sister Lisa, complete with black curly hair and a tight above-the-knee scarlet dress—except that her accent betrayed her as an Israeli. To Naomi, lighting the candles on Friday evening at synagogue seemed so abnormal.

Why are they doing that here? It should be over the Erev Shabbat meal at home. Do none of them have homes?

She held onto her chair with both hands when she heard the Hebrew name of Jesus—*Yeshua*—which the attractive Israeli woman threw into the Hebrew prayer, like lox and cream cheese with a buttermilk biscuit. She might have left right there and then, if she could have. But she knew that would be impossible. The sun would set in the west while she was still on the subway, when she was less than halfway home, trapping her in the black hole of a Shabbat-breaking universe. So she stayed right where she was through Sheldon's recitation of the *Sh'ma* "Hear O Israel" prayer from Deuteronomy 6—although she stood for that. She couldn't help it. Sitting through that would be like an elementary school student sitting through the Pledge of Allegiance. Fortunately, the chant retained the original words—thank God!

After that, things got increasingly difficult for Naomi's conscience. She tried to hide the horror in her expression as six or seven men and women of various ages took to the bema and began grabbing instruments and microphones. That was the first time Naomi noticed a set of "night club" looking drums in the corner of the stage—all in audacious pinks and reds, like an alcoholic's cocktail. To her deep distress, one of the "players" found his way to that "secular" instrument, and on Shabbat yet! Playing musical instruments is considered a form of work in Orthodox Judaism. They are not to be touched, let alone *played!* When one of the singers asked everyone to stand, and even dance, Naomi popped up and headed for the exit. Jody, looking momentarily back from a seat in the second row, just eyed her. As Naomi neared the door leading to the wider Brooklyn world, Jody quietly slipped to the back, head down, trying not to call attention to herself. By the time she caught up with Naomi at the door, their eyes connected. Jody could see that Naomi's were moist.

"I have to leave."

"Where?"

"The street, I guess."

"Can I come with you?"

"No...no. This was a mistake. I can't listen to the...to the..."

Naomi paused, and Jody tried to figure out what Naomi could't listen to.

"Is it...that name...*His* name?"

Naomi responded instantly.

"No. No. My...old boyfriend used it...in Hebrew. I can take that."

"Then what? Oh. It's the...the...instruments. Is that what it is?"

Naomi registered surprise on her face. If Jody Goldberg knew that, why did she ask her to stay? Whatever this place was, it was obviously not a place meant for her. On the other hand, Jody did seem familiar with observant Jewish ways. At least she realized how uncomfortable this had to be for an Orthodox Jew—*any* Orthodox Jew. As Naomi stepped out of the building, Jody stopped her.

"Naomi...I don't think staying would be against Torah."

She became more assertive.

"It wouldn't be. Even your father would agree with me. I know it."

Naomi screamed inside herself, *Don't mention my beloved father!* But like a skilled ventriloquist, not a muscle on her face moved. Jody pressed her point.

"Look. You hear musical instruments all the time on Shabbat...from taxis on the street, and open apartment windows...in hospital corridors and open restaurant doors. What's the difference in our building? You don't have to *play* one of the instruments. And you don't have to sing along. Please come back...please. You don't need to stand out here on the street. I'd feel bad if you did. After all, I'm the one who invited you to stay overnight, and promised you a kosher home. *Please.*"

That last sentence convinced Naomi that her father would approve of her going back in. Staying overnight and attending services at this…this whatever this was…was now a matter of showing respect to *the other*. And if Jody just happened to be *the other* in this case, who accepted musical instruments in a Shabbat service, then Naomi could stay there with a clear conscience. Whatever Jody's reasons for asking Naomi to stay, she was right about that. Naomi sighed a shallow sigh, and then walked back in and took her seat. As she did, she purposed not to stand for the rest of the service, no matter what anyone else did. That way she would be a true Shabbat-keeping outsider.

After the "rock band and dancing," nothing surprised Naomi. She tried to be unengaged during the singing of familiar and unfamiliar melodies, the seemingly out-of-place Israeli-style dancing in the front, the traditional standing Amida prayer—during which she sat —and the "preachy" sermon by Sheldon Goldberg—which she tried so hard not to hear that she heard every word. The message was about not judging other people's hearts and motives—something she was very aware she'd been doing since she entered Beth Yeshua earlier that evening—from the crazy goy with the prayer shawl, to Jody in her close-fitting grey business dress, to Goldberg's sermon on not judging. And to add to her stress, Darrin Brock's handsome perfect Gentile face kept appearing in her mind's eye, his sky-blue eyes entreating her with unspoken words, *Listen to what he's saying. Listen to what he's saying.*

Why can't I stop that! she berated herself. *Stop it! Stop it!*

After the service, which ended with a vocal rendition of the Aaronic Benediction from Numbers 6:24-26 that Naomi couldn't help but judge as mediocre, she avoided the thirty or so people in the building by walking out—which was also a convenient way to avoid the table in the back with food that she expected would be offered to her. Even if the bagels and cream cheese were technically kosher, the knives that cut them and the plates they were displayed on probably weren't. She was glad to see that Jody and Sheldon were near the front of the sanctuary occupied talking to others. Thankfully, they would leave her alone. She stood on the sidewalk in front of the building, in the warm pleasant summer Friday night, and then walked a hundred or so feet down the block so she wouldn't meet up with anyone leaving the service.

The walk to the Goldberg's house was more pleasant than Naomi expected. Just the act of walking home late on Friday night felt somewhat like a traditional Shabbat experience, even though the place they had been was anything but traditional. And the added fact that the Goldbergs didn't try to strike up a conversation made it even more pleasant. After about ten minutes, Jody turned to Naomi, who continued to stare straight ahead.

"Naomi, we will take care of everything. You can think of us as your *Shabbos goys*, even if we're Jewish."

She was referring to the practice of asking—or hiring—Gentiles to perform certain tasks that are forbidden to Orthodox Jews on the Sabbath.

"Actually, we're just Jews that observe the Shabbat, but not as strictly as you do. Do you understand?"

"Of course I understand. I also live in New York, and I know many Jews who live like you. As you said tonight…Mr.…."

Although she had no desire to be disrespectful, she still couldn't quite bring herself to call this clergyman a rabbi.

"Um…Goldberg…judging can be…well…it's not…helpful. Yes. Let's just say, not helpful."

Sheldon stayed silent. He let Jody continue.

"Yes, I'm glad you agree with what he spoke. So…here's how it will work. And you tell me if any of it is a problem…for you. I will turn on downstairs lights as we enter the house. I will then go upstairs and turn on a night light in your room, as well as the bathroom light. I will also, by the way, make sure there is a fresh toothbrush and toothpaste in there, and towels. I will lay out pajamas for you as well. We will take care of things you can't do, like turning on lights, as it would constitute the prohibition of lighting a fire for you, of course."

"Of course."

Naomi had no idea why Jody had to add that. Perhaps it was to show how much she knew. However, if she had to explain to her—an Orthodox observant Jew—the reason for not using light switches, it just revealed how *little* she knew. After that statement, a now weary Naomi was increasingly regretting she had decided to stay overnight. Jody and Sheldon slowed down and then stopped in front of a brownstone that, even in the dark, Naomi recognized as uncannily similar to the one she shared with her now hospitalized father. As they walked beyond the black iron gate to the front door, Jody continued.

"I will also tear the toilet paper in your bathroom, and in the one off the kitchen."

Naomi immediately jumped in, impatient to respond to that remark.

"That won't be necessary. My father doesn't believe that constitutes work. And neither do I."

"Well, I just thought. I mean, some traditional Orthodox…"

"Not me. Not us. Not my father and me. And he's the most knowledgeable Jew in the world…to me."

"I see. But…about tea…and coffee…and breakfast…"

"If you don't mind…I would prefer a cold breakfast…kosher, of course…and of course on disposable plates and cups, with disposable silverware…not to put you out. And…no coffee or tea, please."

Jody nodded, as Sheldon spoke his first words since they left the congregational facility.

"Honey. I'm sure Naomi appreciates the preparations. You did mention earlier that we would work to provide a traditional kosher experience for her, even though our house doesn't normally meet those standards. But I'm sure she's tired now, and just wants to settle in for the night. Am I right, Naomi?"

"Yes, that would be lovely. Thank you."

Naomi reached up and touched the traditional mezuzah on the doorpost. As she kissed her hand, Sheldon opened the door, and Jody switched on the small ceiling frosted globed light, revealing an unassuming front hall leading to a still darkened dining room. When a chandelier comprised of six lights shaped like candle flames—and in the shape of a star of David—broke the Shabbat injunction in its own turn, a charming room was revealed. Taupe wallpaper was interrupted by a few matching paintings of rabbis that looked a lot like many of the Chassids Naomi passed on the street every day. Two brightly colored matching enamel and silver menorahs stood like squat sentries above a clean swept fireplace. And on the dining room table stood two brass candlesticks with the obvious remnant of burnt-down candles. *So they had lit the candles before some sort of Erev Shabbat meal, just before the service. The lighting at the congregation took place on top of that. Interesting.*

Thankfully, any pictures of Jesus or Mary were conspicuously missing. Naomi had hoped neither of them would be staring down at her. Still, studious rabbis and menorahs were of little comfort. Jody turned to her, while Sheldon headed into the kitchen and started the fluorescent fire of that particular light.

"Would you like something…a glass of milk, or perhaps some orange juice?"

"I don't think so. I think I'd just like to get some sleep. Your husband was right. I'm tired."

"I can understand that. I'll show you to your room, and I'll take care of the lights…as I said."

Jody led Naomi upstairs, and down the hall to a closed door.

"We usually keep this door closed. I really can't exactly say why. It belongs to our daughter Devorah, who is in Israel, as I mentioned in Rabbi Goldbergs' office. I guess we just look forward to opening it whenever she comes home to visit…kind of like the shut Golden Gate in Jerusalem waiting for the coming of Messiah…I guess."

She grinned. The comment just confused Naomi, who also tried hard not to flinch when she heard the word "Messiah" coming from the wife of the messianic congregational leader. She realized she wouldn't have had any problem with flinching if Darrin Brock had said it. It would, in fact, have given her a warm peaceful feeling. No one else besides Darrin and her father could have used a term like that and given her such a warm feeling. But Jody Goldberg, as gracious as Naomi had to admit she was, was another story.

Jody opened the door to Devorah's room. As is often the case with absent children's rooms, everything looked ready for the next visit. Naomi didn't get a chance to look around the room until after Jody prepared the lights and placed towels in the bathroom, as promised. When she finally did leave, Naomi drew close to the walls in the nightlight- dim copper glow which was provided for her. She could make out titles on the bookshelf—Chaim Potok's *The Chosen*, a set of C.S. Lewis' *The Chronicles of Narnia*, The same *Tree of Life Version* Bible translation that she had read to Darrin in the hospital, Gilbert's thick book *The Holocaust*.

Then there were the photographs, tacked to two large cork boards. In the darkened room, Naomi had to draw especially close to take them in. They were obviously of Devorah in different stages of childhood development—playing with, laughing with, and otherwise posing with what appeared to be different family members and friends. A much younger Jody and Sheldon were clearly discernible with toddler Devorah. There were birthday parties with elementary-school-age children, and pictures on laps of what appeared to be grandparents. *What did those obviously Jewish grandparents think of her faith in Jesus?* It seemed she was an only child, as the solitary picture in the office would confirm. She was certainly an adorable child, and a stunning adult—a dark flawless brunette—as pictures with her more recent friends in something called the Young Messianic Jewish Alliance of America clearly showed. Naomi wondered why she left for Israel, becoming in the process what all Israeli young people became—a soldier in the Israel Defense Forces, the IDF.

Devorah's bed turned out to be even more comfortable than Naomi's own bed. And the pajamas Jody provided for her fit comfortably as well. Perhaps because of the exhausting, emotionally draining day, as well as the comfortable surroundings, she slept well.

CHAPTER TWENTY-NINE

Naomi had no idea what time it was when she awoke, and she was surprised when her eyes finally fell on a small digital clock on a desk across the room.

8:00 a.m. It's late.

After she washed and put on the same drab grey dress as the evening before, she came downstairs to see Jody and Sheldon, who were dressed in their Shabbat clothes and sitting at the kitchen table. Her place was set. A bowl of bran flakes had already been poured into a styrofoam bowl, with a plastic spoon on top. The cereal box in front of her was clearly marked "K" for kosher. The cardboard orange juice carton also prominently displayed the "K". About six ounces of juice sat in a clear plastic cup. And a paper napkin finished off the picnic-style decor. The same cereal and juice and the same cutlery was in front of Sheldon and Jody. Naomi had been silent, but now felt the need to express appreciation.

"Thank you for your kind hospitality."

Sheldon played the gracious host.

"Is this okay?"

"Yes, perfect," she nodded, as she bowed her head in an obvious silent *Motzi*, the Jewish prayer before meals.

Jody felt the need to interrupt.

"Can we pray together?"

Naomi hesitated. What if they thanked Jesus? Jody began, reciting the traditional thanks to God for bringing bread from the earth.

"Baruch Atah Adonai, Elohay-nu Melech Ha-olam, Ha-Motzi Lechem Meen Ha-Aretz.

Relieved, Naomi responded with a "hmm" and a slightly nervous grin. Then she ate as quietly as she could, considering the crunch of the flakes. After the short meal, Sheldon surprised her with a recitation from memory of the full melodic grace after meals, the *Bir-kat Ha-Mazon*. But before he started, he displayed a bit of surprising transparency, which had the intended effect of disarming Naomi.

"To be honest with you, we don't usually do this at breakfast, or most of our meals at home…except on Friday evening. But because you're here with us as our honored guest…"

That's when he led the prayer. And Naomi joined right in. It helped her feel just a little bit at home, even though she knew she was actually in the home of a…a…God forbid, *missionary to the Jews*. Still, her beloved father would certainly approve of this traditional prayer thanking God for the bran flakes, and the juice—in the *surely* kosher styrofoam bowl, clear plastic cup, and with a white plastic spoon.

By 9:30 a.m., the three Midwood Shabbat sojourners left the house and walked to what would have to pass for a *shul*, or synagogue—Beth Yeshua Congregation. After all, she wasn't there to worship. She was there to see Abrihet, and perform her mitzvah of repentance.

Naomi sat through the service that morning, realizing that at this point less would surprise her than the night before. And less did—not the halting hesitant reading of the Torah scroll by two women who would be watching from the balcony in her father's synagogue, the large group of attenders hopping around as they danced Israeli folk steps to pounding drums and droning guitars, or the strange raising of hands—as if several people were simultaneously asking the rabbi to be excused so they could go to the bathroom. And then there was Sheldon Goldberg, giving the same exact message as the night before, only more enthusiastically. This time, she had a nagging feeling he was speaking just to her and no one else in the room. If her hunch was true, why didn't he just accuse her to her face of judging? After all, he had all night to tell her off. And just about all he said to her all that time was, "You look tired" and "Is your cereal okay?"

What a Phony! What a Hypocrite! My rabbi wouldn't single me out like that.

The number of attenders was much larger than the night before, and more like during her first visit, but even larger—perhaps as many as one hundred fifty, or even two hundred. Naomi had decided that she didn't want to make eye contact with anyone during the service. She stared straight forward or down at her shoes. Consequently, she hadn't noticed when Abrihet and Mahalia entered. They were seated several chairs to her right, and immediately saw her. As soon as the service ended with the chanting of the familiar Aaronic Benediction, Abrihet grabbed Mahalia's right hand with her left hand, and her Bible with her other hand, intending to lead Mahalia out of the building as quickly as possible. Mahalia just stood fast, as her hand was being yanked—just as Abrihet expected she would. She protested loud enough for those next to her to glance her way.

"No, Abrihet! You tell her how much she hurt you. But you don't run away. It's only those who have something to hide who flee when no one is pursuing."

Abrihet whispered as quietly as she could, knowing that her Ethiopian accent might travel above the post-service social din and reach Naomi's ears.

"I don't want to talk on Shabbat. Another time."

"Shabbat is the time, Abrihet. You go up to her and greet her. Find out what she wants. I'm a busybody, like it or not, and I want to know. Go on. Go on. I'll wait for you."

Abrihet stamped her foot and whispered louder.

"You will come with me, or I will not go."

Abrihet's insistence was pointless. Naomi spotted them and headed their way. Abrihet shut her eyes and whispered yet louder.

"Oh my God! Here she comes."

Mahalia's eyes widened, as she also resorted to a whisper.

"Don't you use His name that way, young woman. I don't care *what* trials you endured in Africa. You *know* your parents taught you different. Come on. Start smiling."

243

Abrihet smiled as obediently as a forced smile would allow. Within three seconds, Naomi reached them and got right down to business.

"I have to talk to you…*you*, Abrihet."

She looked at Mahalia, who got the hint.

"All right. I'll be in the back."

Abrihet shook her head.

"No. I would like her to stay."

Naomi hesitated and then gave in.

"Okay. But…but this is between me…and you."

That comment made Abrihet defensive, and her voice and folded arms betrayed it.

"I have done nothing wrong. You will not accuse me again. I will not let you. You have done *enough*. My good and loyal friend Mahalia and I are leaving. So… we say…goodbye!"

Naomi blocked her path.

"No. Wait. I came to make *Teshuvah*."

"Oh…to ask forgiveness?"

"Yes. To say I'm sorry."

Mahalia nodded.

"Hmm hmm."

Naomi tried to ignore her.

"Look…I…realize…that you…weren't trying to…trying to…"

Mahalia interrupted.

"Proselytize. Is that the word you're looking for?"

Naomi again tried to ignore her.

"I realize that you…that my father…that he liked you. And you… you liked him and wanted him to get better. So you…and this man Goldberg…"

Mahalia continued her contrapuntal exercise.

"The rabbi."

Naomi ignored that comment too.

"You prayed for him. Which is not in itself a sin. Not in itself. My father would not consider it a sin, even when those of other religious persuasions offer it. So I ask your forgiveness…as the rabbis…the *sages*…require. That's what we Jews do. We acknowledge fault…which I have…just now."

While Abrihet's eyes began to tear in reaction to such a direct apology, Mahalia's patience gave out.

"Uh huh. We do too, Naomi Kaplan. And you *know* that. But that ain't all we do…or all the rabbis tell you to do. Isn't that right? This girl lost her *job*. Now what are you gonna do about it?"

Naomi finally acknowledged her.

"I appreciate your advice, Mahalia Morse. But I was getting to that, if you'd just give me a chance."

"Go ahead. I'm listening."

"I'm talking to Abrihet, Mahalia."

"I'm not stopping you."

Naomi broke the tension with a quiet laugh.

"Okay, Abrihet. I would like to go to the Kingsbrook Rehabilitation Institute with you…to see Dr. Levitz…about your job…to ask him to hire you back."

The fire in Abrihet's indignant voice was replaced by a high-pitched childish-sounding whimper.

"You…you would?"

Naomi's practiced answer was firm.

"Next Sunday. 2:00 p.m. I'll contact them in the morning. And since my father just came back to the center from the hospital, I'll…I'll visit him with you after that…if you would like."

"Yes, I would like that…very much."

"Well, Mahalia, what do you think of that idea? Does that meet with your approval?"

Mahalia's eyes were focused elsewhere as she let out an enthusiastic "Amen." Then she focused them back on Naomi.

"I think someone's trying to catch your attention…over there."

Naomi followed Mahalia's finger. There, about twenty feet behind her was, of all people, Darrin Brock—with Margaret yet! But who were those two young boys with them? Where had she seen them before? She didn't have time to recall, before all four of them headed straight for her. And she barely had time to process this whole new challenge when Darrin came within five feet of her.

"Naomi Kaplan! What are *you* doing here?"

Naomi's body language reacted as if Darrin was asking her where she was on the night of a murder. She turned her side to him and raised the nearest shoulder like she was defending herself against a glancing blow.

"Where *else* would you want me to be? And what are *you* doing here?"

After that ridiculous defensive response, she felt a desperate desire to run away and hide. But her mind knew she wasn't a little girl anymore, so that wasn't an option. Margaret made things more awkward. She snickered defensively and then greeted her coldly.

"Hello, Naomi Kaplan."

It was up to Jeremy and Joshua to rescue the remnants of a disastrous encounter. Younger rounder Joshua started.

"Hey, it's the knife lady from Macy's! *You* know Mr. Brock? That is *such* a coincidence! Mr. Brock, this lady sold us a knife set for our dad."

Jeremy jumped in.

"He loved it, Mrs…Mrs…Kaplan. He really did."

Josh whispered within everyone's hearing.

"She may not be married, stupid. You're supposed to say, 'Ms.'"

"Sorry. Isn't this a cool place, um…Ms…Kaplan? We get to say the Shema, and 'Shabbat Shalom,' and *everything*."

"Just like Mr. Brock taught us."

If Naomi's face was turning red, it reddened even more when she saw an engagement ring on Margaret's finger. And Margaret must have noticed, because she clearly displayed it in response. Naomi had to say something.

"Oh…oh…um…congratulations."

Margaret gloated.

"I couldn't have found a better man. But then…you would know that, wouldn't you?"

Darrin knew he had to step in if he were to preserve two sets of feline eyes.

"Naomi…seriously, I'm just wondering how you found this place… it being all the way in Midwood…you know, on Shabbat."

Naomi didn't want to answer, but she couldn't think fast enough to lie.

"I'm staying with Sheldon and Jody Goldberg…down the street."

Darrin betrayed a *what!* look.

"The rabbi?"

Jeremy interjected.

"Cool!"

Naomi clarified.

"Yes…Sheldon…Sheldon Goldberg. I had some business with one of the members, and I had no other way of accessing…this…this…person. So I came last night, and planned to leave in time to get home before sundown. That's the…the only reason I came. The only reason. But it didn't work out. That is, they weren't here last night. And it got a bit late. So the…the…not to use a cliche´, but…the long and short of it is, they were gracious enough to…let me stay there. So here I am."

"Oh. And where do you go from here, this being Shabbat?"

"Back there, until sundown."

"Oh. I see. Well…"

Just then, Naomi made the mistake of looking into Darrin's eyes for a very short second. That brought on a five-second paralysis.

If I hadn't broken up with you, you wouldn't be marrying this harlot. And you would kiss me like in the Channel Gardens under your big black umbrella. You couldn't possibly kiss this…this…whatever…like you kissed me. Oh, I wish you would…I wish you could again!

All Naomi could do after the pause was repeat Darrin's word.

"Well…"

Darrin could feel Naomi's longing—and his own. So could Margaret. She wanted this sparse conversation to end immediately.

"Come on, Darrin…boys. It's time to go. I'm hungry."

Darrin reached out his hand toward Naomi. She responded, taking his. He spoke two words as his goodbye.

"Be well."

Naomi couldn't speak. She nodded as their hands separated. Jeremy and Joshua loudly spoke goodbyes over each other. Jeremy, as the older, taller, and slightly more mature one, had just realized that Naomi was the other woman Darrin had mentioned in the past—and the one they had mentioned to Naomi in the Macy's housewares department. He couldn't wait to inform Joshua, and in fact began to do that directly into his ear as they walked clumsily away. Darrin and Margaret joined them as the distance between them and Naomi grew farther and farther, like the film language of a motion picture camera pulling back to accentuate Naomi's loneliness. She wished she had never entertained the foolish idea of visiting this uncomfortable place on Shabbat. Perhaps God had expressed His displeasure by orchestrating this torturous encounter. She determined to never visit Beth Yeshua again. But first, she had to spend the afternoon at the home of Sheldon and Jody Goldberg. She had no choice, lest she break the Shabbat by taking public transportation home.

The walk to their house was, if possible, quieter than the night before. Naomi tried to hide the tears that kept threatening to burst forth and pour down her already perspiring cheeks. Hiding those tears in the brilliant summer sunshine wasn't easy. She faced the sidewalk in front of her and just kept walking. This was the opposite of those joyous post-Shabbat service walks home with her father. But she knew they were gone forever, having evaporated with David Kaplan's health like she wished the sweat on her forehead would.

In spite of the decent night's sleep the night before, Naomi felt exhausted as she touched the mezuzah by the front door, and followed Sheldon and Jody into the house. The central air conditioning felt good, but didn't help with the exhaustion. Jody walked into the kitchen.

"You want anything particular for lunch, Naomi?"

Naomi wanted to go upstairs to Devorah's room, but she had to admit that her digestive juices longed for a meal like she was used to sharing with her beloved father.

"Well…if you don't mind…my father and I used to have simple cheese sandwiches and tea that was kept warm from before the Shabbat…"

"That'll be easy. But I'm afraid I'll have to warm the tea. I can be your Shabbos Goy again. Would you mind that?"

Naomi couldn't help but laugh at the disarming way Jody asked to serve her.

"No…no…that's okay. Thank you. I suppose it's kind of like the musical instrument players at Beth Yeshua."

"Exactly."

"I…I don't want to put you out."

"You're not putting us out. Sheldon and I are hungry too. We work up an appetite after a morning service."

Preparations only took the length of time it took to boil water and steep tea bags. After the traditional blessing before the meal, Sheldon, who had more or less been in the background since the evening before, turned to Naomi mid-bite. He realized that his hesitancy was based on suspicions about this middle-aged observant Orthodox Jewish woman whose intervention had gotten Abrihet fired. But then it suddenly struck him that he was doing the same pre-judging he had just spoken against—twice. He swallowed a bite of his plain cheese sandwich and then spoke.

"So I'm curious. What did you think of the message?"

This wasn't exactly like the Shabbat Torah discussions that she was used to having with her father—complete with the wisdom of the sages. But perhaps if she brought one or two of those wise men into the discussion, it could almost be. And perhaps this so-called rabbi could learn something.

"Well…I'm reminded of the great Chofetz Chaim, who spoke of *Lashon Hara*, the evil tongue. I guess we judge whenever we gossip. Isn't that right, Mr…"

She had trapped herself. It would be rude not to call Sheldon Goldberg *Rabbi*, now that she was an overnight guest in his home.

"…um…Rabbi."

She became animated as she continued, having dispensed with using his occupational title…at least one time.

"My father loves the Chofetz Chaim, and the respect he had for women. Do you know, he actually advocated for an all-girls' school when other rabbis were opposed to it…in the 1800s. That's what I love about my father. He patiently taught me…um, teaches me about the Torah, and the sages."

Sheldon was glad that, for the first time, Naomi seemed to feel somewhat comfortable in his presence.

"I can see how much he's taught you. I think…that the Chofetz Chaim was right. As Proverbs tells us, 'Where there is no gossip, strife ceases.' So how did you like the service?"

The question made her uncomfortable. She wondered if she should be gracious—or honest. Maybe she could split the difference.

"I can't say. I mean, I don't exactly know. It was…different. I've read portions of the New Testament…for instance the portion you have posted in your office bathroom. But as my father said, it's not my…my

Bible."

"Oh. The *Sermon on the Mount.*"

"Yes. That."

"How did you come across that before?"

Naomi tried not to turn red. She hesitated, and then responded.

"Well…someone I was…close to…very close…someone who…who I…cared about…I read it to him when he was…was…very very sick. But…he's better now, *Baruch HaShem*, praise God."

Sheldon smiled.

"Maybe that helped?"

Naomi suddenly felt a definite lump grow in her throat, like the ones novelists write about. Her face finally turned red and the tears from the walk tried to reintroduce themselves.

All she could say was, "hmm…hmm." Then she shrugged her shoulders and took a sip of tea. Jody realized that Naomi seemed uncomfortable, and thought it might be best to change the subject.

"Naomi…I happened to see you talking to one of our new attenders…a Gentile man, I believe by the name of Darrin. Rabbi Sheldon is better at last names than I am."

She looked Goldberg's direction.

"Do you remember his last name, honey?"

He thought for a few seconds, and then responded.

"I don't know. B something."

Jody continued.

"Well anyway. He's come out a few times with his fiancée and two young boys from his church. Do you know each other from somewhere? Not that it's my business, but I'm just curious. Sometimes it can be such a small world, even in a big city."

Naomi froze. She tried to smile, as she prepared to say Darrin's last name in a matter-of-fact way. Then she planned to mention casually that she met him in the housewares department at Macy's. She was hoping that after that, they could move on to something else, and then after that she could take a nice Shabbat afternoon nap. After all, it was a day of rest. But instead of forming the word "Brock," her lips started quivering like the inside of a volcano under pressure. Then the tears that she had held back since the walk began to flow like hot lava. Shame swept over her, as uncontrollable weeping began in suffocating heaves. She stood up so quickly that the chair she was sitting on crashed back onto the kitchen floor. She put her hand over her mouth as she headed for the stairs and flew up them to Devorah's room. Sheldon raised his hands in the air.

"Do you have any idea what that was about?"

"Of course."

"Well maybe you can let me in on it, because to me it was just crazy."

"You know, Sheldon, you're good at reading people in general. But sometimes you really don't have a clue…especially with women."

"Okay. So I admit you have women's intuition sometimes…about women, at least."

"I have a woman's *heart*."

"Okay. So if I don't have a clue, maybe you could give me one. Because right now, it just looks to me like she's had some sort of breakdown right here in our house. And I just hope she gets over it before she has to go home tonight."

"Well…"

Jody took a deep breath.

"That handsome Gentile man?"

"Don't keep me in suspense."

"I'm not. She's obviously in love with him. And not only that. I also sort of suspect that he just *might* be the one she read the *Sermon on the Mount* to."

"What hat did you pull that from?"

"She's lonely, and unmarried at like fifty. And I saw how she responded when you asked if the *Sermon on the Mount* helped him."

"Okay. So she planned to run into him here?"

"I don't know. I don't think so. He's engaged to that other woman… Margaret, I think. I'm going upstairs to see how she is."

Jody left the table and walked up the stairs, ending up at the closed door to Devorah's room. She knocked. After about twenty seconds she knocked again, and then again. Finally, feeling the weight of responsibility concerning the welfare of someone under her roof, she slowly opened the door and walked in. There was Naomi curled up on the bed, against the wall. Jody went over and sat down next to her. Naomi's eyes were half closed. Her breathing was still a bit labored.

"Sorry for the scene," she spoke sheepishly. "I think I'd rather sleep than explain, if that's okay."

"Let me make it as easy as I can. I'll play three guesses. Okay?"

"I don't know. I think I would just like…"

"Give me a chance. Number one, you love this man…this Darrin B something."

Naomi whispered.

"Brock."

"Brock. Darrin Brock. Am I in the ballpark?"

Naomi nodded from her fetal position.

"Number two. You didn't know you were going to run into him and his fiancée at Beth Yeshua."

Naomi nodded again.

"I didn't even know he was engaged yet…until I saw the ring."

"How am I doing?"

Naomi responded with a sheepish "good."

"Two out of three. Okay. Ready? He's the one who was sick, who you read Matthew five to."

Naomi sat up, red but wide-eyed.

"How did you know?"

"I could tell."

Naomi knew that Jody wasn't that much older than her—maybe five years. But something in her soft empathy and understanding heart reminded Naomi *so much* of her long gone mother. As soon as Jody touched her arm, she reached out involuntarily and hugged her hard, as tears flowed from her face onto Jody's. Years without a mother's affection fed her hunger, and she held Jody in her arms even more than Jody held her in her arms. Jody opened Naomi's heart with three words.

"Tell me everything."

"I loved him *so much!* We met during the returns deluge on December 26th a year and a half ago. He came with a return item…no, maybe two. I don't remember. He let me go to the bathroom while he waited, with that whole crowd pressing in on me. I saw him later on the subway, and then later again. And that was my doing, making my friend's aunt drive me to his house in Teaneck just so I could get a glimpse of him. I knew he was a Gentile, but not like any Gentile I'd ever met. He was a man of faith…a Christian, but with the wisdom of my father, and a deep love for Israel and all things Jewish."

She breathed in and out, and then picked up the pace as she continued.

"Well, anyway, to make a long story very short, eventually he fell in love with me like I loved him…and we fell in love with each other, and kissed in the Channel Gardens. The first man I ever kissed…me, at forty-eight years old. And what a kiss! And then a longer one later, in the rain, under his umbrella. Oh my! But we knew it wouldn't work."

She was unconsciously picking up the pace again.

"Because I didn't believe like him, and vice versa. And I hadn't really told my father about him. But then…then…see, he's a detective. And the Russian mafia was out to get him. Oh, it's a long story…"

"The one in the train station…in the newspaper, last year."

"Yes! That's when I told my father. And that's when I visited him at the hospital when he was in a coma. And that's when I read that Bible his father had been reading to him. And that's when he woke up. And that's when we *really* fell in love."

Naomi started freshly crying in quiet jags, hugging Jody even harder.

"I….I….feel….feel…like….like…you're   like   my….my…late…. mother…my…"

Jody just held onto Naomi—tears, and mucus and all.

"Shhh…shhh…you don't have to say more now."

Naomi hadn't spilled the deepest pain in her heart since the Northern New Jersey Applebee's meeting with Marvin's Aunt Ida the year before, and she wasn't ready to stop yet.

"No. I…I…want to. I want to. I have to tell you something more. Later…when my father had a stroke…I knew…I *knew* it was my fault. So I had to break up with him. My sister Lisa begged me not to, but…but I felt guilty…so…well, we had been studying the Mishna and Midrashim, and…even the New Covenant with each other. Well, that all stopped when I…when I…broke up with him. *I* ended up doing that. That was totally me. Maybe I shouldn't have, but I did…and…and…now, he's engaged to that…that *floozie* police woman that I *know* he doesn't love. And it's *my* fault! *My* fault!"

Jody began rocking Naomi like a mother would her child.

"It's okay. It'll be all right. God will work everything out. He will. I promise."

In spite of the obvious *Person* Jody was believing would work everything out, a wave of comforting restful peace rolled over Naomi like the sun emerging from dark clouds, and she yawned three times. Jody held her for another minute or two, and then released her to a lying position. She pulled several tissues from a Kleenex box on the night stand and actually dabbed Naomi's cheeks with one, before putting them all in her hands. Then she stretched a sheet over her and kissed her on the forehead.

"It'll all work out, Naomi. You'll see. You'll see. You get some rest now. And then we'll have *Havdalah*. Okay?"

Naomi nodded as she lay there. After Jody walked out of the room and closed the door, Naomi took less than five minutes to fall into a deep sleep, and she slept for over four hours.

When she awoke and then finally came downstairs, it was 8:00 p.m., and the sun was lowering in the sky. A light dinner of bagels and lox was waiting. Sheldon had left to visit a sick congregant, so Jody spent the dinner hour reading several psalms out loud to Naomi, and speaking the same kind of encouraging words she had in the bedroom. Not long after that, Sheldon returned, and the three of them participated in the traditional candle lighting *Havdalah* service to close the Shabbat. That lasted about ten minutes. And after one more long hug with Jody and a cordial goodbye with Sheldon, Naomi finally left and headed for the subway.

Seated in one of the seats in the half empty car, she wondered whether the last two days were part of a good work of repentance, or the grave transgression of idolatry. She decided on the former. At least her conscience toward Abrihet was somewhat clear. And she had to admit, the vulnerable time she had spent with Jody Goldberg didn't seem to hurt either. Like the musical instruments at Beth Yeshua, it didn't mean she had to participate in Jody's faith. Now she needed to focus for the first time on exactly how she would approach Dr. Levitz on Abrihet's behalf. She knew she had one chance to straighten out the mess she was now convinced she caused.

I guess it's in God's hands, she mused to herself. *At least I performed the mitzvah of seeking forgiveness from one I sinned against.*

CHAPTER THIRTY

The late July Sunday morning Brooklyn sun sported a hazy halo of liquid saturation, fixed in place by the air's dead stillness, like the yellowed edges of an old newspaper. At 9:00 a.m., the temperature was already in the low seventies, and the weather predicted a high in the upper eighties. The humidity was evidenced by that halo. Everyone in Brooklyn except the black-coated Chassidic men, and long-skirted and sleeved Chassidic women, chose short-sleeved shirts and shorts.

Things weren't all that different in Teaneck, New Jersey, although perhaps a few scant degrees lower, as Darrin Brock transferred his mother Velma from her wheelchair into the back seat of his car. Although she couldn't communicate with words, she did let out a short breathy blast, as if to say, "Boy, it's hot out here." He opened the front passenger door for his father Lester. They were headed for the independent non-denominational church that the family had belonged to for as long as Darrin could remember. They rarely skipped a week, and this week was no different—in spite of the fact that Darrin had already been to a service the day before, at Beth Yeshua in the Midwood section of Brooklyn. But one thing about this week *was* different. It would be the first time Margaret visited Darrin's church, the Teaneck Community Church. She planned to meet them there at 9:30 a.m. for the study on the New Testament book of Romans that he had been teaching for at least three months. And of course, Jeremy and Joshua would be there as well. They had only missed a few of Darrin's studies since they had started coming to the church with their parents a few years earlier. Usually, that was the result of illness or vacation—and one double grounding due to a fight they had both gotten into that week with the school bully and his best friend.

At 9:30 a.m. sharp, Darrin assisted his mother and father into the seventy-year old stone structure whose interior had been rehabbed at least twice—the first time, thankfully, with central air conditioning. After settling Velma into the stair elevator and carrying her wheelchair down the stairs, Darrin wheeled her into the Bible study room. Some forty-odd people, mostly Darrin's age and older, were already seated. There were, however, a few young marrieds and singles, and a sprinkling of teens and pre-teens. And there, front and center, were eager-and-on-time Jeremy and Joshua. Their parents had chosen a different study, among the three offered every Sunday.

Darrin glanced at his watch. Margaret had a habit of being five to ten minutes late. But he had told her to please be on time so he wouldn't be interrupted once he began, and so she wouldn't miss anything. By the time he took to the old oak podium with his Bible, it was 9:43 a.m., and Margaret hadn't arrived. He realized he had to start to get through the material before the 10:40 a.m. twenty-minute coffee break, which occurred just before the main service. He acknowledged Joshua, whose chubby little hand was waving at his handsome Hebraic roots hero and second father figure. It was time. Darrin had no choice but to begin.

"We are now at one of my favorite passages in the sixteen-chapter book of Romans, the third of three chapters dedicated to the subject of the Jewish people."

An excited Joshua proclaimed an enthusiastic "yes," as he pumped his fist in the air. He couldn't see a sixteen-year-old boy behind him shake his head. Some of the older boys hadn't caught from Darrin the same excitement about all things Israel that Jeremy and Joshua had.

"Romans 11, verses one and two, pose just about the clearest rhetorical question in the whole Bible."

Darrin paused for a few seconds and looked up, hoping to see Margaret walking into the room from the hallway leading to the staircase. But it was now 9:45 a.m., and she wasn't there. If he could have slowed down time, he would have. He so wanted her to hear his teaching from the beginning. Although he had brought her out to Beth Yeshua in the Midwood section of Brooklyn more than once, he had never had a serious conversation with her about his strong interest in the nation Israel, and the Jewish people in particular. He had tried to once or twice, but it always seemed like she yawned, and then changed the subject—usually to something related to the Biblical sacrament of marriage, and divinely sanctioned wedded bliss.

Realizing that everyone, including Jeremy and Joshua, was waiting for him to continue, he looked down at his Bible and began to read Paul's words.

"I say then, has God cast away His people? Certainly not! For I also am an Israelite, of the seed of Abraham, of the tribe of Benjamin. God has not cast away His people whom He foreknew."

From these few verses, he began to build a case for God's ongoing remembrance of Israel, using other verses from Romans 11, as well as other verses in the Bible. In the process, he used a few Hebrew words, like *Brit,* meaning covenant, and *Avraham, Yitz-chak, v, Ya-a-kov,* meaning of course, Abraham, Isaac, and Jacob. It was at that very second, while Joshua began nudging Jeremy—as he always did when Darrin spoke Hebrew—that Margaret walked in. Darrin was able to multitask successfully enough to notice that she looked somewhat put out. She took a seat in the back and folded her arms. They stayed folded for the rest of the teaching, all the way through the question and answer session.

It didn't take Darrin Brock's detectives skills to discover the reason for Margaret's negative body language during the study. Coffee in one hand and jelly donut in the other, she walked up to him and gestured with her head, indicating she wanted to go somewhere to talk to him alone. Then she walked away, taking it for granted that he would follow her. They ended up in a small corridor outside the bathrooms. She began her own interrogation.

"What's the story?"

Darrin tried to keep his voice as low as possible, hoping she would follow suit, just as he had followed her into the hallway.

"What story?"

"Oh, come on," she shot back, her voice at typical room level. "All that Jewish stuff is fine at that other place you've been taking me to. I mean, it's educational. But the fact that you would *gush* about all things Israel in a Christian church like this one says only *one* thing to me. No! *Two* things. One is Naomi, and the other is Kaplan!"

The word *Kaplan* came out explosive, as if from an air rifle. He recoiled in response.

"Didn't you hear what I was saying? I was teaching theology, not… not…*bi*-ology. It's what I believe, Margaret."

"Is that so?" she remonstrated flatly.

His voice rose to somewhere between his prior volume and hers.

"Margaret, understanding Israel is the key to understanding God's nature. I've been meaning to discuss my views on this, but you won't… you won't let me. You…you…"

She lowered her voice to try to sound reasonable, although she was really in no mood for reason.

"Okay, I heard that. I did. And thank you for your Bible teaching. You know I'm new at this. But…but…wasn't there at least a little feeling for her in it? Just a *little*?"

He responded without hesitation.

"No. None whatsoever."

He impulsively drew her to himself and kissed her right in the church corridor, almost spilling her coffee in the process.

"It's over. *You* are the one I think about," he tried to convince her. "Don't you think you should drink your coffee before it gets cold, and eat your donut before it gets stale? The service is almost starting."

"I'm sorry, honey," she spoke in a baby-like tone. "I promise I won't interrupt next time when you try and teach me."

Having done everything she could to patch things up after the last hour of barely controlled jealousy, she threw her coffee and jelly donut into the nearest trash can. Then they walked hand in hand into the sanctuary, followed by a giggling Jeremy and Joshua.

CHAPTER THIRTY-ONE

Over the next week, Naomi spent one of the more anxious seven days of her almost fifty year life. After she had protested so strongly in front of Dr. Levitz for Abrihet's removal, she now had to stand before this same man and plead for her to get her job back. She knew that, as the good Jew her beloved father raised her to be, it was her job to not just apologize, but to make whatever restitution was required. And what was required in this case was Abrihet's restored employment at the Kingsbrook Rehabilitation Institute.

She hoped that two phone calls to both Dr. Levitz's office and Abrihet would result in a Sunday appointment in that same office, and the peace of knowing things were moving forward. But after she made the calls Monday morning before work, the anxiety remained. Whether she was at the housewares department selling overpriced Lenox dinnerware place settings, or at home eating her humble kosher dinner on disposable plasticware, the dull ache somewhere between her small and large intestines remained—along with the attendant diarrhea.

When Shabbat arrived, she sat alone in the women's balcony of her and her father's synagogue. He wasn't there to glance back at her from the bema while he read the Torah—something that she had treasured every week. The shafts of summer light that revealed particles of silver dust through the large windows might as well have been dark shadows.

After the service, she walked home alone, trying to think of the majestic words that came from David Kaplan's sagely-wise lips during those after-Shabbat service leisurely strolls. But all she could think of were the words Dr. Levitz would probably say to her the next day.

You're the one who accused her of proselytizing. Now you want to plead for her to get her job back? Did she try to convert you too? Both of you, get out of my office! Now!

She spent the afternoon wishing the evening would come. When it finally arrived, she tried to calm herself, but ended up in the bathroom doubled over on the toilet. Her initial anxiety had morphed into an irrational panic attack that defied reason.

When the sun finally set at about 8:45 p.m., she brought out the several-strand candle, incense box, and cup of wine, to observe the closing of the Shabbat—the *Havdalah* service. She sat alone in the shadows created by the candle, looking at her fingernails in its light—as tradition dictates—feeling extreme loneliness, in contrast to the joy of sharing the ritual with her father. She felt like she was at a birthday party for one rapidly aging old woman. As she recited the traditional *Eliahu Hanavi* chant—Elijah the prophet—tears ran uncontrollably down her face.

Bimhey-rah V'Yameynu Yavo Eleynu Im Mashiach Ben Dah-vid, Im Mashiach Ben Dah-vid. Quickly in our days. Come with the Messiah the son of David.

"At least I'm singing about our Messiah, and not *their* Messiah," she blurted out loud, as if she wanted to reassure God about which Messiah she meant. After she observed the traditional extinguishing of the several-strand candle in the cup of wine, she went to the bathroom once more. Then she extinguished every light in the house and went to bed, hoping to fall asleep quickly so she could forget about the next day.

Instead, she spent the night waking up several times from several troubling dreams in surrealistic succession, all somehow connected to the anxiety located between her small and large intestines. When her fitful sleep finally ran into the rising summer sun, she threw off the covers and visited the bathroom again. A quick glance at herself in the mirror startled her. Where was Darrin's beautiful and mysterious Eastern European princess? She searched for her, staring at her eyes intently.

Was she examining the face of the "old" Naomi, the one who rouged up her face and "hanged herself" by her own hair the night before Darrin first passionately kissed her in the Channel Gardens? Where was the "new" Naomi, the one with the spark? She washed her face, put on a bit of make-up and pale pink lipstick, and got dressed in the flowery dress that Darrin told her he loved—not that she expected to see him. But she did want to look her confident best for the meeting.

The appointment at Kingsbrook Rehabilitation Institute was set for 11:00 a.m. Naomi entered the subway by 10:00 a.m. She sat on the window side of an empty seat and closed her eyes, her stomach still slightly rumbling. Her carefully groomed curly hair, well applied eye-shadow, judiciously and subtly placed rouge, and bright flowery dress acted as honey to a hungry bee. Even before she opened her eyes, she knew someone was staring at her. When she finally opened them, she looked directly into the eyes of what appeared to be a handsome and dignified middle-aged modern Orthodox Jewish man, standing perhaps ten feet from her. He had lots of wavy grey hair, like Leonard Bernstein, and a remarkably sensitive-looking face. He was dressed in an impeccable black suit. After ten seconds or so, she turned away in embarrassment. He took the opportunity to walk over—or perhaps more stagger over, due to the rocking train car—and sit down right next to her. She tried to press toward the window side. He stared at her again.

"No wedding ring?"

She folded her hands, trying to hide them from him. He didn't receive the message.

"May I introduce myself?"

"Um...no," she defensively responded. After all, he could be anybody, and up to anything. She knew Orthodox predators existed. He could be one of them, stalking lonely plain-looking old Jewish women on the subway, looking for a quick sexual favor. He continued, notwithstanding her response.

"I assure you, I am a true mensch...a retired dentist with only the purest intentions. But I couldn't help but notice what a *shayna punim*... what a beautiful face, you have...so like my late wife, may she rest in peace. You remind me so much of her. Perhaps you are widowed, as I am. My beloved wife passed just six months ago, after forty years of marriage. Cancer. I'm sure someone must have loved you once, just as she loved me. Perhaps your finger wore a ring then, as mine did. Tell me, are you *frum*, observant, as I am?"

Naomi looked straight forward, her face growing redder than the rouge. He asked again.

"Couldn't you just be so kind as to answer me, please? I won't bite. I'm a retired professional, as I said. I could refer you to any number of friends in Brooklyn…all nine men who pray with me in the morning, for instance, and their wives too…who could vouch for my reputation."

She spoke just above a whisper, as she continued to look forward.

"Yes, of course I am."

"That's better. I knew you were observant. I knew it. I must tell you, I've never done this before. My friends will tell you that. But after one or the other of us gets off this train, it will be too late. In fact, my stop is next."

Naomi couldn't help but think of the time she followed Darrin out the door of a similar train traveling under downtown Manhattan, the second time she saw him, after meeting him at the Macy's housewares returns counter. She nodded and whispered again.

"Well…so be it."

He drew slightly closer.

"And you are *so* beautiful. You're so…I'm sure your husband told you. You're *so*…"

His voice cracked. She turned to him for the first time. He gasped as their eyes met again.

"So beautiful…your deep brown eyes, your magnificent mouth."

No one had spoken that way about her since Darrin. There were tears in his eyes. She had to say something.

"I've never been married…In love, yes…married, no. I don't know why I'm telling you this. This situation is highly unusual, and very uncomfortable. But, as you say, when you walk through that door…"

He pulled a card out of his suit pocket, and pressed it into her hand.

"You can call me at this number. Think about it. Perhaps this is *beshert*, meant to be. I would treat you like the princess you truly are."

With that, he got up and moved to the door, along with the slowing train. And then, in an instant, he was gone. For just a few minutes, while they talked, the butterflies in her stomach had disappeared. She looked down at the card. *Martin Cohen, DDS.* She wondered if she should just rip it up and throw it away. But she didn't. She couldn't—not after seeing those tears. And he certainly was handsome. She put it in her pocketbook, hoping she would forget it in time.

During the few block walk to the Kingsbrook Rehabilitation Center, she decided to pray the *She-heche-yanu* prayer, thanking God for keeping her in life and bringing her to this season. Whatever happened during the next hour or so, she decided she had to be thankful, and yield control of the whole thing to God—kind of like her own personal Jewish twelve-step program. Certainly, the sages must have recommended this technique somewhere. Her father would know. But unfortunately, she couldn't ask him while he was in a comatose state. Yet certainly, if it worked and took away the stomachache that had by now returned, her father would be happy for her. She quietly recited the prayer.

"Baruch Atah Adonai, Eloheynu Melech Ha-olam, she-heche-yanu, v-kee-imanu, v'higi-yanu, laz-man ha-zeh."

"Blessed are you Lord our God, King of the universe, who has kept us in life, sustained us, and caused us to reach this season."

She checked her stomach. The ache was still there.

Well, I just won't pay attention to it. I've apologized, I'm going to advocate for her job. Whatever happens after that isn't my responsibility. So why am I upset? Just stop it, stupid stomach!

She arrived at the Institute just before the meeting, and stopped at the bathroom for a last bowel-emptying few minutes. When she got to the waiting room outside Dr. Levitz's office, Abrihet was already there. She was hoping she wouldn't have to talk to her before the meeting, but that was one of those things that her "higher power"—Adonai—obviously chose for her. *Oh well.*

"Hello, Abrihet."

Abrihet clasped her hands.

"I'm *so* nervous, Miss Kaplan. What if he gets angry at me this time, and asks me to leave? Maybe I'm remembering all the mean people in Ethiopia, who called me names…told us Jews have devils. I must admit, ma'am, that my stomach hurts right now."

Naomi was taken aback by Abrihet's matching ache. Should she tell her of her own ache? Perhaps that would comfort her. In fact, maybe that should be a part of her mitzvah. She took both of Abrihet's hands in hers.

"Abrihet…I have that ache too. I'm truly sorry for all the bad memories I stirred up. Let's just go in there and whatever happens happens. Okay?"

Then Naomi squeezed Abrihet's hands, going beyond her required obedience to a place of genuine compassion that surprised even her.

"He was nice to you the last time we were here. Remember? And if he does get angry, I'll stand between you and him. I'll protect you."

Abrihet held her breath, and then exhaled as she asked one last request.

"May I pray?"

Naomi hesitated.

"Well…I suppose."

"It will be short."

"Well, we don't have much time anyway."

"Right."

She closed her eyes and squeezed Naomi's hands harder than Naomi had hers.

"My Lord and my God. Whatever happens, I will thank you. And I forgive this your daughter."

She opened her eyes.

"I am now ready."

"Well…"

Just as Naomi spoke that word, a tall young blonde woman approached them and invited them to enter Dr. Levitz's office. When they walked in, Levitz was at his desk. He gestured for them to sit in the two chairs in front of his desk.

"Well, how can I help you two today?"

After a short pause, Naomi knew she needed to speak first.

"Yes, well…when we were in this office, and I insisted that…that… this woman…here…Abrihet…be….be…terminated…"

She had always hated that term. It seemed to imply an execution, an abrupt end to a life. But she didn't know a shorter way to remind him.

"Remember?"

"Of course I remember. We had to let Abrihet go. She broke the protocol. Those are the rules."

From his response, it didn't seem like things were going to end well for Abrihet.

"Yes, well, I…I was wrong…back then…when I accused her of…I mean, she had good intentions, just wanting my father to get better, so…"

He leaned back in his swiveling chair.

"I'm listening. So?"

"So…so…"

"So please get to the point."

Abrihet had learned in Ethiopia to pray inside while appearing on the outside not to pray. It came in handy when guns were being pointed at her and her loved ones. She was doing that now. Naomi was busy just trying to settle her stomach down.

"Well…could she have her job back?"

"Just like that? It's not that simple. There's a record on her, you know."

Naomi had to think fast.

"Yes, and such things exist in Heaven, also. But on Yom Kippur they are erased by HaShem."

"Right. But… I'm afraid this isn't Heaven, and it isn't Yom Kippur either. She broke our rules by proselytizing."

"But she didn't! That's what I'm saying, Dr. Levitz."

He leaned forward over the desk and stared at Abrihet.

"And what do you think, Abrihet? Do you think you broke the rules?"

Abrihet stopped praying to herself and started talking.

"Oh, *no* sir. I broke no rules. I just…I just wanted Mr. Kaplan to get better, so I prayed…to God…just between me and Him. Not for others. You see, I love Mr. Kaplan. I cared *for* him….and *about* him."

"So you prayed. To Whom did you pray?"

"To God, sir."

Naomi knew she had to step in and press her point, or they might as well just walk out. She stood up and raised her voice. An unexpected boldness came.

"Dr. Levitz, I started this, and I'm going to end it…and end it well, for my part. Abrihet is good for my father…very good. And I want her working for him again, right here at Kingsbrook. That's the long and short of it. I will vouch for her, work with her, and keep an eye on her. I take full responsibility. I trust her, Dr. Levitz. So...will you rehire her?"

He leaned back in his chair, swiveled it, and then put his right hand on his brow. He stayed that way for at least twenty seconds. Abrihet resumed her clandestine praying. Suddenly, he leaned forward again.

"Okay, Abrihet. No praying for any patients. Can you keep that guideline?"

Naomi jumped in.

"Except my father. I mean, if she says, 'Oh God, help him,' I will not have a problem. You see, I want her to be a friend to him...because that's what she was...*is*. And he loves her. You see, they're good for each other."

She wasn't sure why she had to say that, except perhaps because she was trying to help Abrihet be as comfortable with David Kaplan as she had been before all this started. Dr. Levitz put his face in his hands for few seconds, and then looked up at Abrihet.

"Okay. No prayer except whatever Ms. Kaplan allows you to do with her father. That's her business, not mine. But...you're on probation, Abrihet. Do you understand that?"

"Oh, yes sir. *Yes* sir. *Thank* you sir!"

"Okay. That's all. Report to my office tomorrow. And I'll...well, I'll get rid of the records. After all, it *is* almost Yom Kippur, isn't it? In a few months. Now I've got an appointment, so if you two don't mind..."

Naomi grinned.

"Thank you, sir...so much. We'll leave now."

She turned around. Abrihet stood up and then backed out, like she was Esther and Levitz was the Persian King Ahasverus. He stayed seated.

"You can turn around, Abrihet. And could you please close the door on your way out?"

After they closed the door, before they even left the waiting room, Abrihet wasted no time giving Naomi a tight hug, exclaiming, "Oh, thank you! Thank you! Thank you!"

After the secretarial staff had a chance to experience Abrihet's warm Ethiopian display of affection, Naomi took both of her hands again.

"Okay. I'm going to visit my father now. Would you like to come with me?"

"Oh yes, I would. I *so* miss him."

"You're not working yet, you know. So if you want to go home and just come in tomorrow…"

"No. I want to see him now."

The tall blonde woman became impatient.

"The office door is that way."

Abrihet agreed.

"Yes, we will go now. Praise God for my job. Oh, excuse me, but…oh, praise Him. We will go now."

Naomi shook her head.

"Is your stomachache gone?"

"Yes it is gone, Praise…excuse me, yes, it is."

"Okay. Let's go."

Naomi let Abrihet precede her, as they went up to David Kaplan's room. Naomi was about to see her father for the first time since he arrived back from the Maimonides Medical Center, and there was no time to adjust before setting her eyes on his unconscious face. Abrihet stood silently next to her in the elevator—although her inner prayer life was anything but silent. She was also unprepared to see Mr. Kaplan, as she was used to calling him. But in her case, that was compounded by the probational arrangement she was now committed to.

As Naomi and Abrihet approached David Kaplan's room, both of their hearts quickened. Naomi slowed her pace, followed by Abrihet. Coming up behind them and then outpacing them was Rabbi Sheldon Goldberg, who had just arrived for his Sunday morning visit with eighty-two-year-old congregant Harold Stein. Abrihet called to him.

"Rabbi! Rabbi!"

He stopped and turned.

"I *thought* it looked like you two. It's nice to see you together. Did you see Dr. Levitz?"

Abrihet's voice brightened.

"Yes, and he hired me back! I'm on pro…pro…bation. But it's okay. We're going to visit Mr. Kaplan together. It would be good if he recognized us. But they say he won't."

She turned to Naomi.

"Maybe Rabbi Goldberg could come with us just to see him…for just a minute? Not to pray, or *anything* like that. Just to…"

Before Naomi could consider the request, Sheldon stepped in.

"Well...I happen to be late for my visit. So, maybe I'll catch up with you later."

Naomi tried not to reveal her relief. She felt like it would just make things more complicated to have him in the room with her father.

"Yes, maybe we'll do that. Later. Thank you so much for your kind hospitality last week. And please send my best to Mrs. Goldberg...Jody."

"It was our pleasure. Well...this is Harold Stein's room. Shalom."

They both responded "Shalom" at the same time as he walked into Stein's room. Then they walked down the hall and into David Kaplan's room. There, lying on his back, with his eyes closed and his hands at his side—like a peaceful corpse—was Naomi's beloved father, and Abrihet's dear friend. His grey face blended with the black rayon yarmulke that had been awkwardly placed on top of his balding head. Naomi was relieved that there were no tubes protruding from his mouth or throat. Nutrition and hydration were obviously received intravenously, resulting in the weight loss she could clearly see. She went over and kissed him on the cheek and then forehead, and then back to his cheek again. Her eyes moistened as she called his name into his ear, while Abrihet took his left hand.

"Abba...Abba...it's me...Naomi, Abba. I miss you so much. I love you, and can't wait for you to come home to your own bed...which is waiting for you, all made up and clean."

She looked up at Abrihet, whose eyes were also moist.

"Abrihet is here too, Abba."

"Yes, I am here, and so glad to see you, Mr. Kaplan."

She looked over at Naomi for approval. Naomi grabbed a chair and sat on the right of her father. She reached out and stroked his few hairs, adjusting his yarmulke. Abrihet went out for a small styrofoam cup of ice water and a small pink sponge on a stick. She came back and stood next to David Kaplan, wetting his lips gently and lovingly. Naomi stood up and shared the latest news directly into his ear.

"Abba, I just want you to know that I'm doing well. I go to our synagogue every Shabbat, without fail."

Abrihet knew that wasn't completely true, since she had seen Naomi at Beth Yeshua only a few weeks before. But she also knew there would be no point in bringing up that exception. Naomi continued.

268

"Every week, I read the Torah portion before I go to synagogue. And sometimes…I read the sages from our shelf. I'm…I'm…"

She wanted to tell him that she had returned to being one hundred percent Jewish, yet without mentioning Darrin's name. She never wanted to mention his name to her father again. She had hurt him enough.

"I'm still your observant Jewish daughter, and I'm praying the Mi-Shebeirach for you every day…no, all the time…many times a day. And I love you, love you, *love* you. I hope you can hear that, because it's true."

She kissed him on the forehead several times, as Abrihet dabbed his lips again. Then she sat down.

"You sit down too, Abrihet. Please…pull up a chair. Please."

Abrihet took another chair from the corner and pulled it over near David. They both sat and stared at him in silence for what must have been about twenty minutes, as they each held one of his hands. Then unexpectedly, an uncanny sensation of holy sweetness seemed to travel from Abrihet, through David, to Naomi, and then back again—and then *over* them all like a canopy of faint glowing glory between the three figures and the harsh fluorescent lighting above it, creating a kind of painterly portrait.

The reverie was broken by Sheldon Goldberg, who entered the room to witness the Renaissance scene.

"Sorry. I hope I'm not interrupting, but I just thought I'd stop by for a minute before I left."

Naomi barely acknowledged him, turning her gaze to Abrihet, who was tightly squeezing David Kaplan's hand.

"Abrihet, I told my father I'm praying the Mi-Shebeirach prayer. And I am. I promised you that you could pray for my father too…and just for him, out of all the people in this institution. And Dr. Levitz told us that would be okay. So you may, if you would like, pray…just a few words, the way *you* pray. And then…we'll leave."

Abrihet's heart began fluttering strangely. That had never occurred before when she planned to pray. Was that because her job depended on her not offending, or was it something else?

"Okay. I will pray a very short prayer…my way—from my heart. And then, we will leave."

She took a deep breath, and then decided to take the full plunge, trusting that Naomi's promise was true. She could pray *her* way.

She opened her mouth and spoke one word—or rather, breathed it like one would breathe a soap bubble into existence.

"Ye-shu-aaa."

She intended to take a deep breath and then continue her short prayer. But suddenly, her hand felt a subtle return squeeze. At the same time, Naomi looked up, eyes wide, which Abrihet instantly realized must mean that she had felt the same thing. Then David Kaplan's head almost imperceptibly moved right and left—but so imperceptibly that Sheldon didn't notice it. Everyone but David stopped breathing. But when he opened his eyes, everyone but him gasped. Then, he spoke in a weak but clear voice, with no hesitancy, and no stuttering.

"Abrihet, Naomi…how long have I been sleeping?"

Naomi laughed her answer.

"Um…a long time, Daddy. A *long* time."

Then she mouthed silently to Abrihet, "Thank you."

David's eyes fell next on Sheldon.

"What are *you* doing here?" he spoke as clearly as an elocutionist.

Naomi's face instantly reddened. *He must somehow know who Goldberg is, and what he does for a living. Oh my God, he could have another stroke!*

"I can explain it *all* Daddy. He's just here visiting one of his…his… friends. He's not here with us. Not with us. Is he, Abrihet?"

David didn't pay attention to Abrihet's hesitancy. Instead, he stayed focused on Sheldon Goldberg.

"You're Irving Goldberg's son, aren't you? May he rest in peace. Your face hasn't changed a bit since you were just a boy…or I should say, a very young man."

Sheldon's unchanged-since-childhood face revealed complete confusion.

"Do I…do I…know you?"

"Of *course* you do. Your father was a CPA who did contract work for the *New York Times*. He used to bring you down to the Linotype room."

Sheldon gasped again.

"Of course! You're Kaplan! You used to show me how you hung the bucket…how you typed so fast, that you drained the liquid lead out of the overflow bucket. You were the greatest Linotype operator of all the great Linotype operators at the *Old Grey Lady*! Oh man, I so loved watching you work!"

"Yes. That's me. And *you're* Irving's son Sheldon. How are you doing, and how did you get to meet my very lovely daughter?"

He might as well have asked him if he was single and open to marry his daughter. Naomi had more than one reason to step in.

"Um…Abba…we just happen to be acquaintances with Sheldon… and his *very lovely* wife…that he is happily married to. And I'm very glad to hear that he watched the world's greatest Linotype operator at work. But Abba…you've been in a coma, and *baruch HaShem*, thanks to God, you just woke up. So I'm getting the nurse right now, so she can check you out. Come with me, Abrihet. It was good seeing you, Mr. Goldberg. I think my father needs to get some rest. It's been a long day…I mean, a long coma."

Naomi more or less pushed everyone out of the room, and went down the hall to get the Director of Nursing. The rest of the visit was taken up with one health care worker after another coming to see what had happened to David Kaplan. There was laughter, and tears, and vital sign testing—and a call to the primary care physician. And when all of that was done, Naomi spent another half hour with her beloved healed father, and then hugged and kissed him, said a heartfelt goodbye to Abrihet, and left in a state of disbelief. She headed down the hall, down the elevator, out to the street, and finally to the inside seat of the subway, to ponder for the first time the possibility of a genuine miracle.

CHAPTER THIRTY-TWO

By the time Naomi got back to the Kaplan brownstone, she knew what she had to do first. She sat down on the same sofa where she had nursed her father back to health when he had a serious case of the flu over a year before. And she flipped open and dialed her simple phone. Lisa answered her i-Phone.

"Hello?"

"Lisa? I have something to tell you."

There was a pause. Naomi could hear Noah and Lindsey whining in the background, followed by the sound of Marc's frustrated voice. Finally, Lisa responded in a tentative tone—after she addressed the noise.

"Quiet everyone! Yes? What is it, Naomi?"

Naomi didn't quite know where to start.

"Um…Lisa…something's happened."

A still tentative pause. Then, finally, a response in a hushed tone.

"To Dad?"

"Yes, yes…to Dad."

"Oh my God. Oh my God."

Another pause, and more background voices.

"Marc, *please*…take the children into the kitchen."

More indiscernible frustrating sounds from Marc. And even more audible frustration from Lisa.

"Just…just…anywhere…upstairs, outside…I don't care. Just… now!"

Another shorter pause.

"Okay. Just let me have it. Is he…did he…?"

"Lisa…no…are you sitting down?"

"Oh my God."

"Please, Lisa, don't use the name of HaShem that way, in English or Hebrew."

"Oh my God. It's that bad."

"No…no…I didn't say that. I mean…actually, he's better."

"What?"

"What I just said. He's better."

"What do you mean, he's better?"

"I mean…somehow, HaShem healed him…I mean, He made him all better. Someone prayed…and he's all better. I just wanted you to know."

"That's *crazy*, Naomi. Look. Just make sense. Don't give me your Orthodox superstitions, okay? Where are you?"

"I'm home, Lisa. In Brooklyn. And I'm not being crazy…or superstitious. I just got home from Kingsbrook."

Lisa hadn't sat down when Naomi asked her to. Now she saw no need to. She walked into the kitchen and opened the refrigerator door. The conversation had taken such a bizarre turn that she had to grab a small Greek strawberry yogurt just to ground herself. She took it out of the refrigerator, grabbed a spoon and peeled the top off—all the while squeezing the phone between her shoulder and her left ear.

"Now tell me the truth. What's going on? And no offense, Naomi, but don't give me any of that *Mi-Shebeirach* crap. Just let me know exactly… and I mean *exactly*…how he's doing…with no exaggeration. Do you think you can do that?"

She dipped her spoon in the yogurt and took a mouthful. Naomi stood up and walked from the sofa to the book shelf. She stared at the great book of wisdom, the *Pirkei Avot, The Sayings of the Fathers.*

I could certainly use some of their wisdom now.

"Lisa…I thought we agreed to get along. I don't appreciate your tone, or your accusations."

"Okay. I'm sorry. Now please, tell me…how is Dad really doing?"

"Well…he talks perfectly. He walks perfectly."

"Oh, come *on*."

"Go to the Kingsbrook Rehabilitation Institute and see for yourself."

"Okay, so could you please tell me what really happened?"

"I'm telling you. Someone….not a rabbi, I'll say that much…used a Hebrew word…a word that means God…HaShem…saves…so, HaShem saved him from sickness. He heard our *Mi-Shebeirach* prayer. That's all."

Naomi was even now developing her own interpretation for what had occurred—an interpretation that she could accept as within the Jewish pale, and without the word Yeshua referring to *that* person—an interpretation agreeable to her father, her father's rabbi, herself, and hopefully her sister.

"*So*…HaShem performed a miracle…and there you have it. I didn't see any stroke symptoms. And I don't believe the doctor did either."

"*Whatever.*"

Lisa threw the yogurt in the trash, and the spoon in the sink.

"Well, it must have been a temporary stroke. Still, that's very good news. I'll get over there tomorrow. Maybe I'll bring the kids."

Naomi knew what her eyes had seen and ears had heard. And she knew that what she had seen and heard was more than a spontaneous recovery from a temporary stroke. But there was no purpose in convincing Lisa of that. She had done her job. She had reported on her father's condition. That part of the conversation was over. But she couldn't hang up just yet. She needed to end their time on the phone in a positive way.

"Listen, let's get together soon. Maybe we can take a Sunday, when I'm not working, and go somewhere with Noah and Lindsey."

Lisa took a deep breath.

"Agreed. Text me and we'll look at a time. I'll talk to Marc."

Naomi was pleased that, even if those plans ended up faltering, the call ended up on a positive note. She capped it off with a "Love you," and hung up. Then she went off to take a nap. After all, it had been an unusually active Sunday.

One person with whom Naomi had no intention of sharing the news about her beloved father's healing was Darrin Brock. He had just visited David Kaplan the day before, on Saturday. He was a committed Israel-loving Christian, and not a Shabbat-keeping observant Jew, so traveling on the Sabbath wasn't an issue for him.

When he saw David Kaplan, he was still in a comatose state. Darrin had stayed for two hours, reading psalms to David out of the Jewish Bible. And on this day, Sunday, he was making his second visit to Chaya Mendel's house since the bullets crashed through her front window. Her older children were home on this particular day. But it was Natan he came to see, for their regular time of reading picture books and putting together puzzles. Reaching out to Natan was one the few good ideas Inspector Lewis had come up with to encourage Darrin to stay in the department. The father-son-like bond between Darrin and Natan had grown since they first met, after Natan's father Mandy was murdered the prior year. But there had been disruptions to those plans. The first had occurred during Darrin's recovery from his own gunshot wound. That recovery only served to encourage them to draw closer. The second disruption occurred after what appeared to be a second attempt on Darrin's life, while visiting Natan. Consequently, Inspector Lewis felt the need for increased security during all future visits to the house, and it had taken some time to plan for that. When it was finally arranged, two or more officers were assigned to an armed security detail in front of the Mendel house. On this day, one was a young recruit affectionately known as Mack, due to his truck-like build. And the other was Margaret, who insisted on protecting her future husband.

The visit began with a short conversation between Darrin and Natan's mother Chaya. When Darrin arrived at the screen door, it was open. Darrin Brock walked in, more or less ignoring the police detail—including Margaret. They were "on the job," and he wasn't. He greeted Chaya without touching her, which is the tradition among Chassidic Jews. She closed the door, and he went over and sat on the pristine white couch. They had long before decided to dispense with refreshments—at least for Darrin—and get down to business. Natan was different. Sometimes he would have a Mi-Del kosher vanilla cookie.

Today, Chaya decided to mention something she had forgotten to mention before. It wouldn't take long, and then she would go get Natan, who was quietly playing upstairs while he waited for Darrin's arrival. Before going further, Darrin wanted to assure Chaya about the safety precaution.

"I know your religious community police are looking out for you. The NYPD is staying on the lookout too, as we continue to investigate the unfortunate occurrence a few months ago. But also, as you've been apprised and have observed, a detail of two or more officers are outside when I visit...just in case."

"That's good. Please thank the inspector for me. He and the department in Manhattan and here in Brooklyn have been very good to us this year and a half since my husband's death. Also, HaShem is watching over this house."

"Yes. I believe that."

She seemed anxious to change the subject.

"I don't have to tell you how excited Natan is about your coming. As you know, he still calls you Abba. I just can't bring myself to break him of the habit, even though the older children keep telling me to. I'm sure they have their own reasons, but...anyway. I've been meaning to ask you. Do you remember those two thin Orthodox young men who were here after the shooting that broke the mirror...when you protected Natan?"

"Yes, yes, of course. I believe you mentioned they were from Crown Heights."

"Yes. I guess I did. Anyway...I don't believe I ever told you. They really tore up our bedroom. I mean, they turned everything upside down...threw all the clothes out of the drawers...left things in such a total mess that it took me a few hours to put everything back the way it was. I just thought you should know that. I was surprised the way they left it. They must not be very good *Chabadniks* to not put things back in their place...to say the least."

Darrin had never heard the endearing term Chabadnik used to refer to a Chabad Chassidic Orthodox Jew. He grinned ever so slightly, and then began pondering Chaya's words.

"That's interesting."

He put his thumb and forefinger on his chin and paused, before responding in a subdued tone.

"It probably doesn't mean anything, except maybe they were sloppy Chabadniks, if such individuals exist. Still..."

Just then, Natan scampered down the steps, his soft cloth bedroom slippers slide-skipping down the taupe plush rug steps as he squealed like a kosher piglet.

"*Da*-rrin! *Da*-rrin!"

He ran across the room and jumped up onto Darrin's lap.

"Ima, you didn't tell me Darrin was here! I love you, Abba! I love you!"

He threw his arms around Darrin's neck like a pendant, as he'd done so many times before. Darrin kissed him on the cheek, just under his long Orthodox side-locks. Then the two tumbled onto the rug, as Chaya brought out the usual books and puzzles, along with a cookie on a plate for Natan. He broke a piece off and gave it to Darrin.

"Thank you, Natan. That's so kind of you. How have you been?"

"I've been *great*, baruch HaShem! It's good to give *tzedakah*."

Tzedakah means righteousness, and refers to generosity when spoken with the word "give." Natan was using more and more Biblical and rabbinic words and concepts, which Darrin loved.

"You're so right," he responded, while he picked the picture book on Abraham. "Sharing your cookie with me is a special mitzvah."

He wished he could have quoted the One who had put the love for all things Jewish—past, present, and future—into his heart.

It is better to give than to receive.

But even just quoting the New Testament verse, as appropriate as it would be in its own right, could be interpreted as proselytizing. A hug, a kiss, and an echoed *baruch HaShem*, bless the Lord in Hebrew, would suffice—along with reading a full color book containing Abraham's lesson to his idol-making father, using an idol in whose hand Abraham had placed a hammer after toppling another idol. The point he was making was that the idol couldn't break another idol or anything else, because it wasn't alive and it wasn't God. This extra-Biblical rabbinic legend with a lesson was a favorite of Natan's, who always giggled as Darrin read it. Consequently, it was a favorite of Darrin's as well.

After about an hour of play, it was time to leave. Amidst protestations, Natan bid Darrin a tearful goodbye as Chaya was taking him upstairs for a nap. Darrin waited for her to come back downstairs. He could just hear the older children in one of their rooms as he waited by the banister for Chaya to return. When she finally did, he could tell she had something on her mind. He wasn't sure whether she wanted to share more about the two men who'd ransacked the room, or if it was something else. She walked with him towards the front door.

"How is your girlfriend Margaret?"

He was surprised that she brought Margaret up, and somehow it bothered him. He had intentionally avoided telling her that she was not twenty feet from them right now, just outside the door. After all, Margaret was "on the job." But he figured he should probably tell her the latest news, considering the fact that if he didn't, she would probably end up hearing it from someone else. He intentionally kept his voice down, so Margaret wouldn't hear her own name.

"We're engaged…Margaret and I are."

Chaya's face brightened. She was so elated, she almost touched him.

"That's wonderful! May you have many good years together! I'm sure she'll make a great wife and partner."

Darrin felt instinctively that Chaya's joy was not based so much on her opinion of Margaret, as it was based on her relief that he, a Christian, wasn't planning to marry traditional Jewish Naomi Kaplan. But that wasn't something he could express openly. At any rate, maybe she was right about Margaret. And he was sure she would want to get to know her. Yet he knew there was a reason, besides Margaret being "on the job," for intentionally keeping his relationship with Chaya separate from his relationship with Margaret. He just couldn't quite figure out exactly what that reason was—or he didn't want to figure it out.

After a few parting words, Darrin left the house while Chaya stayed inside. After shutting the door, he silently waved at Margaret and Mack simultaneously, and then walked down the street and toward the subway—without looking back. His training in hawk-eye observation had never fully left him, try as hard as he sometimes did to relax the habit. His eyes scanned to his left and right. As he was about to descend the steps to the subway, he just caught someone who looked like Omar walking slowly down the street about a block from the Mendel house. Darrin tried to appear as if he hadn't seen anything unusual. He merely stood at the top of the steps and cautiously glanced in the young man's direction. It was definitely him. What was he doing here, so close to Chaya Mendel's house, and right in the middle of one of the most Jewish sections of Brooklyn? Maybe Ralph Lewis and Lawrence Schmidt were right about Omar. Maybe Darrin was unnecessarily suspicious, or perhaps even outright racist, toward a perfectly respectable Muslim young man. After all, didn't Omar Shehadulah have a perfect right to walk down any street of any borough in the city of New York? And yet…

Darrin continued to stand still as a stone statue, as Omar slowly passed the house Darrin had just visited, clinging close to the house side of the sidewalk. He didn't seem to look in the house's direction—or did he? He definitely slowed down in front of it—or maybe he didn't. Within a minute or two, Omar had walked perhaps fifty to a hundred yards beyond the house, and then disappeared from Darrin's view.

I must be getting paranoid for sure. But if that's not a strange coincidence, I don't know what is. It's unusual for sure. But he didn't break any laws, or stop and really case the place, or any other place that I could see. Anyway, it's the Russians who were being investigated about Mandy Mendel's death, not this Muslim kid. I'm going home.

Darrin disappeared into the cavernous tunnels of trains half empty with Sunday travelers, taking his uneasy spirit with him—uneasy about Margaret, Naomi, Chaya, and now once again, Omar. All challenges, each in their own way. Maybe he just needed to eat a quiet dinner in Teaneck with his father Lester and mother Velma, and then go to bed. Tomorrow would be a work day. For the first time in a long time, he was looking forward to it. Anything to take his mind off the last minute or two.

CHAPTER THIRTY-THREE

David Kaplan's health improved so rapidly that Lisa's visit to Kingsbrook Rehabilitation Institute that Tuesday was the last visit from anyone. Lisa was shocked and surprised to see her father walking full-stride down the hallway, wearing his black jacket and pants, and with his favorite black yarmulke fixed firmly on his held-high head. He walked even faster as he approached her, and gave her a firm enthusiastic hug.

"Lisa, my beautiful youngest daughter! See what the Eternal has done for me."

He released her and spun around like a handsome model on a runway. Lisa was still recovering from her initial shock.

"Look at you, Daddy. You're all better. Whatever the therapy was, it certainly worked. What did they do?"

"I don't know. Naomi said maybe it was just the *Mi-Shebeirach* prayer. You know, Lisa, our God hears that prayer. I prayed it. She prayed it. Maybe you prayed it?"

"Okay, Daddy. Whatever it was, I hope you just stay well. Between that stroke and the other one, you've had us all worried to death."

"So how are Marc and the children?"

"They're fine."

"That's good. I'd like them to come see me. And I want to give Noah and Lindsey a big hug. I haven't seen them in so long. They must have grown so much, I won't recognize them."

"You will, Daddy. They won't recognize you. The last time they saw you, you were very very sick. I'll try to bring them by tomorrow. They'll be so excited to see you well."

Lisa's plan, like the plans of so many families, didn't end up coming to pass. By the next day, David Kaplan was being wheeled into the elevator in a wheelchair he didn't need to be sitting in, by his oldest daughter, who had taken off work from the Macy's housewares department to take him home. She had ordered a cab—a luxury for Naomi—from the Rehabilitation Institute to their house. But in this case, it was a wise investment. When they got to the facility's entrance, David Kaplan arose from the wheelchair and entered the waiting cab. Naomi put his few belongings in the taxi, and they drove off. That morning, she had cleaned and straightened the house. Now she was about to welcome her beloved Abba back to the home they shared together.

When they arrived at the house, her father got out of the cab and stood facing the door he had entered and exited so often. He inhaled the sweet summer afternoon Brooklyn air.

"Home. My own *beis hamigdash*, my temple, my personal house of prayer, my holy dwelling…with you, my daughter."

"Let's go in, Abba. I'll make you your favorite tea. And then you can rest."

"I've rested enough. We'll sit and talk about the sages, even on a Tuesday."

"Okay, Abba. I've *so* missed that."

They entered the house. David proceeded to slowly walk through every room, downstairs and upstairs—as if he was inspecting it for purchase—while Naomi boiled the tea and put a few of his favorite *parve* cookies, ones that could be eaten with milk or meat, on a small plate. When he finally came down the stairs from marveling at his own bed— on which Naomi had placed fresh brand-new Macy's sheets—she waved him over to the kitchen table. His tea was ready to drink. And a small book sat on the table.

"Abba, I would like you to read the *Pirkei Avot*, the Sayings of the Fathers, to me, like you used to on Shabbat."

He pulled the book over to himself and began to leaf through it. All at once, Naomi began to feel the old safe and precious opportunity to ask the wisest Jew in the world anything she wanted. She thought she would never have that opportunity again, and yet here it was.

Whenever she had a concern in the old days, before his first stroke, he always said to her, "Well, my daughter. I see you have something on your heart. You may share it, whatever it is." At those times, she asked her deepest questions, and he always answered wisely and with no judgment. If he was looking into her eyes now, and not down at the book, he might say the same thing. And if he did, the question wasn't whether she would be safe. The question was whether *he* would be safe. He seemed well enough, sitting there leafing through the slender volume. There were no stroke symptoms whatsoever. He was obviously getting stronger every day since the "miracle," if that's what it was. But would he be able to answer the question that would most test his stable blood pressure? Naomi didn't know for sure, but she *had* to ask. There was nowhere else she could go, no one else she could turn to.

"Abba…um…"

He looked up from the book.

"I see you have something on your…"

"Yes, Abba. I do."

"Whatever it is…"

Well, here goes.

"Right. Whatever. Abba…what if Jesus…I'm sorry to use that name in this house so soon after you've come home but…what if Jesus…is the…the long awaited Messiah, God forbid?"

David Kaplan tried to control his newly restored face muscles, and to keep his eyes from widening in surprise. He knew he had to remain as calm as possible, so Naomi's heart would remain open. He breathed in and out as slowly as he could, to maintain his heart's resting state. Then—barely above a whisper—he asked his own question.

"Is there peace in the world, my dear daughter? After all, that is the sign of the Messiah's coming."

"Well…no…there isn't, Abba…you're right. I forgot that."

He nodded. But she wasn't quite finished.

"No, there isn't…except…in Darrin Brock's heart…I think."

She braced herself for his response. After all, his first stroke had been the primary reason she broke up with Darrin. Meanwhile, he tried to keep his tone at an even keel.

"I see. So he's trying to convince you of this possibility?"

"Oh, *no*, Abba! I haven't had *one* real conversation with him in months. I broke up with him, you know. I believe I told you that, while you were recovering from your first…your first…"

"Stroke. Yes, I remember. And he also told me you did that, mensch that he is. So, Naomi…what *is* all this? You *know* what we believe. Why are you asking such a question? Not that any question is off limits. But why?"

"Well…I didn't tell you everything on Sunday, after you woke up. I didn't tell you that Abrihet loves you very much…and…"

"Yes, I'm sure she does. I love her too. And…"

"Abba, your tea is getting cold."

She pointed toward the cookies.

"And see? I put out your favorite *parve* cookies. Please, take one."

"I will. I will. In God's time. And the tea can wait also. Please, go on."

"Well…I told her…I mean, after all, she was crying over your condition, and…you always say to respect the faith of others, so… Abba…you should drink the tea before it becomes iced tea."

"So? Isn't it summer? Naomi, if you're trying to make me nervous, it's working."

"I'm sorry, Abba. So…I told her she could pray for you…any way she wanted…even *her* way."

"So? That's it? So she prayed *her* way. So?"

"Well, remember when I told you I prayed the *Mi-Shebeirach* prayer?"

"Of course, Naomi. I remember. And of course, I wouldn't expect Abrihet to pray that prayer…unless perhaps she learned it in Ethiopia. But even then…"

"Right. She didn't pray that prayer. As a matter of fact, she just said one word. And right away, you woke up…all better."

"And I take it that word was…Jesus?"

"Well, no, Abba. It wasn't."

David tried to conceal his relief.

"Alright. Well, what was it?

"It was…*Yeshua*. His name in that Jewish version of the…the New

Testament."

"Oh. Well...there is a very reasonable explanation, my bright and inquisitive daughter. The word *yeshua* means salvation. She obviously was asking for God to save my life, just as we cry out during *Sukkot*, in the fall. And He did. That is the answer."

The *Sukkot* David Kaplan was referring to is the Feast of Tabernacles, a Biblical fall festival. And the *Sukkot* prayer that David Kaplan mentioned originated in Isaiah 12—*Therefore with joy will you draw water from the wells of salvation—yeshua* in Hebrew.

David could tell that Naomi wasn't fully satisfied with that answer, which happened to be the same one she had been telling herself since the "miracle." In her face, particularly her eyes, he could see a restless dissatisfaction with the *salvation with a small "s"* response. So he decided to call for some outside help—specifically, from a well known twentieth-century Jewish scholar. That scholar's name was Martin Buber.

Martin Buber was born in Vienna in 1878, to Orthodox Jewish parents. As a young man, he moved to Zurich, Switzerland to study philosophy. Eventually, he became an honorary professor at the University of Frankfurt, where he became close friends with the Jewish theologian Franz Rosenzweig, with whom he translated the Hebrew Bible into German. David had called on Rosenzweig for help the year before, when Naomi first asked questions about Darrin Brock's faith. Both Buber and Rosenzweig held much more liberal understandings of Judaism than David Kaplan. But they had important philosophical views in common with each other—views that might provide answers to Naomi's nagging questions. Buber's included his famous *I, and Thou* book, which investigated the relationship between two beings—human with human, and human with God. He received one of his several Nobel Prize nominations for that book. Buber ended up fleeing Germany in 1938, and moved to Jerusalem. He lived there until his death in 1965.

In all of Martin Buber's vast body of literature, there was only one short enigmatic paragraph that David decided to share with his daughter. He wasn't sure he—or anyone, for that matter—understood exactly what Buber was getting at. But he knew that others had quoted this short account to encourage Jews to stay within their own faith tradition. And that was good enough for him.

"Have I ever mentioned the great Jewish philosopher Martin Buber?"

"No, Daddy, I don't think you have."

Naomi knew, even with that short introduction, that for the second time in all their discussions, her father was about to quote a modern scholar, and not a traditional sage—the other time being Franz Rosenzweig. He continued by recommending Buber as a person worth quoting.

"Well…Martin Buber was just about the greatest Jewish philosopher of the twentieth century…maybe not Orthodox, but great nonetheless."

"I thought that Rosenzweig guy was, Abba."

"Yes, well, he also was. In fact, they were close friends in Germany, before the *Shoah*, the Holocaust. And they both thought about a lot of things…a *lot* of things."

David wasn't sure what all those things were. And he had never had much interest in finding out. But he did find one thing Buber said useful.

"So…he was once asked a question…a very difficult question. *Very.* Now, to be honest with you, I'm not exactly sure what the question was. But…I *think* it had to do with the attraction of other…other…you know…other religions…like for instance…Christianity."

Naomi's face muscles twitched almost imperceptibly upon hearing that word out of her beloved father's mouth. He noticed her response, but didn't let on.

"Anyway, this is what he said. I believe I can more or less quote the great man. Are you ready?"

"Yes, Abba. I'm ready."

He began the almost verbatim quote.

"There is something that can only be found in…in one place. It is a *great* treasure, *great*. A *great* treasure. The fulfillment of…of our whole existence. The place where this treasure can be found is…the place on which you stand…in your own back yard…so to speak."

He pointed down at the kitchen table.

"Right here…"

Then he pointed toward the kitchen window, which faced their small back yard.

"Or there, to be more exact."

"What does *that* mean, Abba?"

286

He nodded knowingly.

"It means…what it means. It's in your own back yard. That's where to look for your…your…*you* know…"

Naomi got up and walked over to and behind his chair, putting her arms around his shoulders, holding onto him tightly.

"I see, Abba. I understand. I'm so glad to be here with you, in our own house, with our own back yard, and our own synagogue in walking distance. There'll never be any man in my life but you, Abba. Never."

He put one of his hands on one of her arms and the other on her other arm. He considered encouraging her that there would someday be another man, a good Jewish husband. But he decided against it. It was enough for now that she understood what Martin Buber meant— or David Kaplan thought he meant—and that she seemed to be in agreement with it. Salvation was doing its job—David Kaplan's definition of salvation.

CHAPTER THIRTY-FOUR

Darrin Brock sat in his cubicle, swiveling in his cut-rate squeaky gray cloth office chair. He stared at the upper halves of his fellow officers, and the clerical staff that supported them, as they passed by on the well-worn taupe rug just outside his flimsy barricade. That included Margaret, who winked at him as she walked by—which was was far more expressive than the weak wave he gave her and Officer "Mack" outside the widow Chaya Mendel's home. But she tended to send signals whenever she passed him in NYPD's Midtown South Precinct building. And why not? They were engaged, weren't they?

As he leaned dangerously back in his chair, Darrin tried to mentally prepare for the meeting that was about to take place in Inspector Ralph Lewis' office. He had been considering this meeting with Lewis and Homeland Security expert Lawrence Schmidt for approximately two weeks. He had called for the meeting without explaining the exact reason for it. He didn't want Lewis and Schmidt to come up with answers beforehand. Instead, he wanted to lay it all out before them, and then let them respond. That way, they couldn't write off his concerns—and he *was* concerned. His experienced detective's sense told him something didn't make sense. And this time, he wouldn't be talked out of his suspicions.

He stared like a meditative Buddhist monk toward the aisle facing the main office door. Within two minutes, Lawrence Schmidt appeared.

What, is that ridiculously obvious gray suit and black tie glued to him, or what? What a career flunky.

Darrin didn't typically allow his thoughts to veer so negative. However, he hadn't been impressed by this HS guy the first time around, and he wasn't looking forward to seeing him again—especially along with Inspector Lewis. Yet he knew the meeting was necessary. He rose from his chair and left the cubicle, just as Schmidt walked by. The two locked eyes and then hands. Schmidt's grasp was decidedly firmer. Darrin greeted him, choosing an informal approach.

"Welcome to the Midtown Manhattan South Precinct, Larry."

"Yeh, yeh, Brock. What's this about?"

Darrin stiffened.

"You'll see. Just follow me to the inspector's office."

It was only a few feet away. He knocked, and Lewis yelled from inside.

"You're both late. Just come in."

Darrin pointed at Schmidt.

"*He's* late."

"Cut the crap."

Schmidt took it upon himself to swing the door fully open, as if he worked there, and not Darrin Brock. Lewis stayed seated, leaning back in his fine well balanced office chair, his feet firmly resting on his desk.

"Okay, take a seat, you two."

Darrin was glad that Lawrence Schmidt was about to suffer the same humiliation he was used to suffering—being seated in a shorter chair before the presiding inspector. When they were both seated, the inspector started in.

"All right. Your show, Brock. What is it?"

"Yes, well…I was visiting Chaya Mendel in Brooklyn…"

He turned to Schmidt.

"You don't know who she is."

"Yeh? Should I?"

"No. You shouldn't. But you might remember her husband Mandy, who was killed by the Russian mafia a year and a half ago. In the Diamond District."

"No. I don't remember. I *do* remember that they gave it to you in the subway. Anyway, that's your alley, isn't it? Not mine. I can't keep every lousy money-laundering murder inside my head. I got enough on my plate with *real* terrorism, domestic and foreign."

"Yes, well…"

Lewis sat up and then slapped his desk hard.

"Damn it! Get to the point, Brock. You're taking this busy man's time up, and mine too."

"I will. Right now, Inspector. I was leaving Chaya Mendel's house, after visiting with her little boy, with a security detail guarding the house…due to what seemed like a little business of an attempt on my life there a few months ago…which we are almost *sure* was another Russian mafia thing…which every lead points to…and is almost wrapped up… right, Inspector Lewis?"

"Well, we have someone of interest…more than one, actually. And we're keeping our eyes very open, and you safe. Let's put it that way."

Darrin nodded wryly.

"Right. I feel very safe in your hands. Anyway, I'm walking toward the subway, and who do you think I saw?"

"Is this twenty guesses? Come on!"

"Our very own Omar Shehadulah. Walking right in front of the house."

Schmidt looked slightly more interested.

"Casing it?"

"Well…I can't say that for sure. More like walking by. You know… slowly…I don't know, strolling. But deliberate…I think."

Lewis chimed in.

"Brock. Be reasonable. What's the big deal with that? People walk by houses all the time."

Darrin was ready for that answer, and became more assertive than he—or Ralph Lewis—was used to. He leaned forward in his low chair.

"Oh, come on! What are the odds, Inspector? Something just wasn't right about it. That's my detective's sense. But…why? *Why* would he have anything to do with Chaya Mendel? His family is of Pakistani Muslim descent, and about the farthest thing from the Russian mafia, or Kremlin spies…or anything Russian."

Schmidt stood up.

"Well, when you figure that out, let me know. We looked into this guy and...*nothing*."

Lewis waved at him.

"Sit down, Larry. For just a minute."

Schmidt smirked and sat back down. Ralph Lewis turned to Darrin.

"Brock, remember Stanley coming here to report Mahmud was missing?"

"Sure."

"Well, I don't know why, but I'd like to ask Stanley about Omar. Like I said, don't ask me why. I just know that Omar has been hanging around the midtown area a lot. I'm just curious whether, out of all the Muslims in all of Manhattan...and beyond...Omar and Mahmoud may have known each other. I'm probably wasting my time, and all of our time. And if that's true, I may just dock your pay, Brock."

Why hadn't Darrin mentioned Omar's name to Mahmud at Ben's Deli? Could he have known him at least in passing? Inspector Lewis picked up the phone.

"Could you come into my office?"

Schmidt got up again.

"Well, while you gentlemen play detective..."

"Sit down, Larry."

Lewis' executive secretary entered the office.

"Could you do me a favor? Connect with two officers in the vicinity of the main library, and have them call the Dewitt Wallace Periodical Room and ask about a guy named Stanley, an old Jewish guy. I've got his last name somewhere here. But it doesn't matter. Everyone there will know who he is. If he's there, just have them tell him we may have a lead on his friend. And have them bring him up here right away...in a squad car. You got it? Keep me abreast. Oh, and get me a picture of Omar Shehadulah."

"Yes sir."

As she left, Schmidt rose again.

"Look, this is obviously gonna take some time, and..."

"Sit down, Larry. It won't take time. Not in *this* precinct. Brock, even if he *does* know who Omar is, that doesn't mean the kid did anything."

Lawrence leaned back in the low chair.

"You said it."

Lewis leaned forward.

"*But*…he *would* possibly be a person of interest. Wouldn't you agree Larry?"

Schmidt sighed deeply.

"I suppose so."

"You're damn right, Schmidt. Hang onto your suspenders."

The secretary popped her head in.

"They're on their way here with Stanley, sirens on. One to two minutes to arrival. Here's the picture.

He grabbed it without looking at it.

"Good work."

As she left, he put the picture on his desk, and then got up and cracked his knuckles.

"Brock, did I ever tell you about the time I beat the mob bosses to a meeting at their own rendezvous point? I got the tip and was there with back-up before they got there. Of course, that was in the nineteen-eighties. I was a lot younger then. And the mob bosses were a lot more dangerous…back then when I worked for Rudy. I guess I met you not long after that."

"Yes, sir, you've told me about that before. I think I met you about six months after that."

"Right. Well…so where are these SOBs with that Stanley whatever-his-last-name-is? I would have had him here five minutes ago."

Schmidt shook his head.

"Just don't take forever when he gets here."

"Just settle down, Larry. I want you to hear this. Then you can go back to catching the bad guys."

There was a knock on the door. Lewis delivered his typical yell.

"Come in!"

Stanley slowly opened the door and entered.

"These officers who brought me told me you found Mahmoud."

Lewis sat back down.

"They told you wrong. Not yet. This is Lawrence Schmidt, Homeland Security agent. Darrin Brock you know. Sorry there's no extra chair."

Stanley raised one thick hand up.

"Mahmoud is no terrorist."

"Did I say he was?"

Inspector Lewis pulled the picture off his desk and flashed it at Stanley.

"Have you ever seen this guy?"

Stanley squinted, and then moved closer to the picture.

"Yeh. Yeh. I think so."

Lewis looked at Darrin Brock, and then Lawrence Schmidt, and then back to Stanley.

"What do you know about him?"

"Nothing. I may have just seen him once or twice in the Dewitt Wallace room. I think Mahmoud may have known him, or again maybe not. Maybe at Ben's Deli…but then again, maybe not."

Schmidt rolled his eyes.

"*He's* a big help."

Stanley looked in his direction.

"I know I've seen him somewhere. On the street. Somewhere. The face is very familiar. That's all I know."

Inspector Lewis went over and shook his hand.

"Okay. That's all. You can go. We'll update you when we know anything about your friend. Thank you."

"I don't get a ride back to the library? I can't walk all that way in this heat."

"What are we, a taxi service? All right, go out there, and my secretary will get an officer to take you back. But no sirens this time."

"When did I ask for sirens?"

"Good. She'll help you."

After Stanley left, Darrin turned to Lewis.

"Well?"

"Well, nothing. Maybe we'll interview the poor kid once more."

Schmidt stood up, and stayed up this time.

"Okay, now I'm leaving this time-waster. Contact me if you end up getting a *real* tip."

"Right. You can leave now too, Brock."

"I'm telling you, there's something going on with this kid, Inspector. You wanted me to assist in this area. I'm just saying."

294

"I hear you. But I'm not going to get into profiling here."

"But he was there…in Brooklyn…at her house…"

"Enough! Back to work."

When Ralph Lewis was finally alone in his office, he reached into his bottom-right desk drawer, grabbed a day-old jelly doughnut, and ate the whole thing in four bites.

CHAPTER THIRTY-FIVE

Naomi was awakened by the crystalline early-September sun, as it filtered through still green leaves before shining through her bedroom window, and dancing around her face. It took five or six seconds for her to realize that it was Sunday, and she didn't have to work. Simultaneous with that thought came a memory picture of her slowly walking arm in arm with her father under the Cherry Esplanade in the Brooklyn Botanical Gardens at Prospect Park.

She realized that the short early spring blossoming season had long passed. That's when, for the first time in years, she had visited the Esplanade without her father. She had run into Mahalia, Abrihet, and Javier, while David Kaplan was at the Kingsbrook Rehabilitation Institute. Suddenly, a pleasant thought crossed her mind. Why not walk under the naked Esplanade—arm in arm with her favorite strolling partner—on this sweet waning summer's day?

She quickly rose, washed, dressed, and descended to the first floor. There was David Kaplan, sitting at the kitchen table, drinking hot tea. She knew he had just finished his morning prayers. His blue velvet phylactery *tefillin* bag, with the Scripture boxes and straps for the forehead and arm, and his matching *tallit* prayer shawl bag were sitting on the table. His small *siddur* prayer book sat on top of them. Naomi went over and put her arms around her father's shoulders, and then kissed the top of his black yarmulke.

"Abba, let's celebrate your recovery by going to the Cherry Esplanade. We missed our early spring walk. We can take one now."

His eyes looked upward and at a ninety-degree angle, as if he was trying to see her as she stood behind him.

"You know, my daughter, that the Holy One has not promised us cherry blossoms in early September."

Naomi responded as the sages might, with a question.

"And where in all of Torah are we forbidden to walk beneath bare cherry blossom trees?"

She could feel his nodding head on her cheek.

"Hmm. I suppose so. After breakfast."

They spent the next few hours doing just that—eating a leisurely meal together, clearing and cleaning the kosher-for-dairy-foods plates, silverware, and other eating utensils—and preparing to leave the house and travel to the Brooklyn Botanical Gardens together. By the time they arrived there, it was about 12:00 p.m., and the sun was directing its warm midday rays on the summer green grass and blossom-less cherry blossom trees. Naomi took her father's arm, and they slowly walked to the Cherry Esplanade. They had never experienced the Esplanade with no blossoms above them. But even without the sweet pink ceiling, the miracle of their father-daughter stroll brought tears to Naomi's eyes.

"Abba...I thought I lost you. I was sure we'd never walk under these trees together again. I walked here myself in early April...alone. Now, when I think of how I complained to you last year under these same trees...about how I was in my late forties, and still husbandless and childless, like an old prune, like a leftover *tzimmis* carrot dish from someone else's wedding, that you should have had a son instead...I'm so ashamed."

"And what did I say?"

"You told me I'm better than ten sons."

"That's right, and in agreement with the esteem the Chofetz Chaim had for women. And even more so in your case, because you are *you*."

"And you're better than ten husbands."

"Well...actually, one would suffice right now."

"No, Abba! I'm through with all of that. *You* will suffice. My beloved father and personal sage."

When they arrived arm in arm at the end of the Esplanade, Naomi looked up as she patted her father's hand. There, not twenty feet from her, was the widow Chaya Mendel, with her five children. David Kaplan had never met sixteen-year-old Leah, thirteen-year-old Shimon, eleven-year-old Rhena, or eight-year-old Shmuel. But he had met six-year-old Natan, who immediately ran up to Naomi, stretched out his hands, and hugged her flowery summer dress.

"Is Darrin here?"

She knelt down and wrapped her arms around him.

"No, Natan. I'm afraid he isn't."

Then she pulled back and looked at him.

"My goodness! You've grown. You're such a *big* little boy."

She stroked his long Orthodox hair locks.

"And so handsome."

"Where's Darrin?"

Chaya just caught Natan's question as her other children left her side to play. She stepped up to Naomi and David.

"Natan, don't ask Naomi so many questions."

"It's okay. He just misses him. I…I guess I do too. Abba, this is Chaya Mendel. Chaya, this is my father, David Kaplan."

David smiled.

"I've met her. Sometime last year. And her adorable youngest."

Suddenly Naomi felt compelled, against her better judgment, to ask Chaya about Darrin. She spoke just above a whisper, even though she knew Natan's ears could pick up every word she said.

"So…has he visited you and Natan lately?"

"Who?" Chaya asked, as if she didn't know.

Naomi fidgeted with the straps of her small black cloth handbag.

"You know."

She became even quieter.

"Darrin."

Natan jumped up and down and answered affirmatively.

"Yes! Yes! He visited Ima and me, and we played with puzzles, and read books, and ate cookies. Didn't we, Ima?"

"Yes, we did."

Then Chaya's eyes found Naomi's.

"And he told me all about...you know...about him and Margaret. I congratulated him."

Naomi nodded.

"Yes, I know about that. Well...I was just curious."

"Well, it's all for the best. There are Jewish men just as eligible."

David had been observing the conversation. His empathetic heart bled for his daughter, and the awkward situation she was in—even if she *was* the cause of it. He didn't know quite what to say, but he had to say something.

"There's no one who is as eligible as Darrin Brock, notwithstanding the fact that..."

Chaya's eyes now found his.

"Certainly, Mr. Kaplan, you don't think...you couldn't be saying that...?"

"No. I'm not saying that. We all know the issue at hand. My daughter understands the importance of marrying from among our landsmen. Still..."

Naomi felt like her right foot could kick her left leg—which was impossible right now, as it would frighten Natan. Why did she even ask about Darrin? How utterly stupid! Now she had the obsessive need to let Chaya know she understood the importance of marrying someone Jewish, that her head was no longer stuffed full with unrealistic dreams. And not only that. She also felt the need to defend herself from the accusation that she would end up an *alte moyd*, an old maid. So even if Chaya intimated that there could be a Jewish man somewhere out there for her, Naomi needed to *convince* her of that...and right now. She reached into her handbag and started nervously fishing around. Finally, she came up with what she was looking for. She pulled out a small white business card.

"I understand the need to marry a Jewish man. I *do*. In fact...I met a very nice man...a dentist, and a very observant Jewish man. We really... we really hit it off, as they say. He asked me out...on a date...in fact."

David Kaplan could barely hide his consternation.

"What? You didn't tell me. I thought...just this morning, you..."

Naomi did something she had almost never done before. She rudely interrupted her father, as she handed Chaya the card.

"His name is Martin Cohen. He's quite dashing, really. He's a recent widower. And you should see how he fell for me. He told me it's unusual for him to be so forward. But he couldn't help himself, for some reason. And I believe him."

Chaya's eyes widened.

"What do you know! Martin Cohen's been our dentist for years. And a very good one...very gentle...and yes, very handsome. And it's true that he's a very nice religious *frum* man. I think this is *wonderful*. You've made quite a catch. Now don't you lose him. He's eligible...and he's *Jewish*. This is fate, Naomi...*bashert*. Don't you think so, Mr. Kaplan?"

Naomi avoided looking in his direction as he carefully answered.

"Well...yes...I suppose so...if it's God's will...and...if my oldest daughter is ready to...if she's open to meeting someone just now."

Chaya shot back.

"Well, if not now, when? She's not twenty anymore, Mr. Kaplan. And it's not everyday that she should get such a high recommendation from someone such as myself, especially when she thought he would be a total stranger to me. Isn't *that* bashert? Isn't it?"

Chaya had a point. Was this the hand of *HaShem* Himself? David Kaplan nodded his head in seeming agreement with Chaya.

"Well yes...I suppose that's true. It's just that I thought...she said just a few minutes ago that...but yes, I suppose it *is* a miracle. Yes, I suppose it is."

The rest of their time at the Brooklyn Botanical Gardens went pleasantly enough. Darrin Brock's name didn't come up again. And neither did Dr. Martin Cohen's. After Naomi hugged Natan, and said a cordial goodbye to Chaya and the other children, she and her father left Prospect Park for home. On the train, David felt it wise not to mention the disparity between Naomi's "celibacy vow," and her subsequent "dating arrangement" with the good dentist. Instead, they discussed an ancient second-century midrashic quote mentioned in the writings of the slightly less ancient eleventh-century sage Rashi—which Naomi of course loved every minute of. She kept her arm entwined with her father's the whole time.

When they arrived home, David Kaplan mentioned the need to take a nap. Naomi told him she thought it was a very good idea. Although it was true that David seemed to have fully recovered from the effects of his two strokes, it wouldn't be wise to test the God of Israel, who had performed such an obvious miracle—no matter which word He used to perform it.

Once David retreated to his bedroom, Naomi sat on the sofa. She watched the hazy end-of-summer late afternoon light through the front living room windows. She could just see a young Chassidic family passing by on the sidewalk outside—first the rail-thin young bearded father, fully clad in black, then the mother, just as thin in a long black dress, then two grinning preteen daughters in their own long dresses, and then a little boy about Natan's age, with curly sidelocks. She would never have a family like that woman, taking late summer Sunday walks with her devoted husband and obedient children. But at least she could just perhaps have a man—and a good one, according to Chaya Mendel. And he wasn't a stranger on the subway anymore. He was, in fact, the friend of a friend.

She pulled the card out of her handbag, along with her small flip phone. Then she bowed her head. What prayer would be appropriate? Perhaps the well-known *Shehechianu* prayer. She mouthed the prayer in English.

Blessed are you, Lord our God, King of the Universe, who has kept us in life, sustained us, and brought us…me…to this season…and maybe to Dr. Cohen? To Dr. Martin Cohen. Amen.

Then she took a deep breath and punched the numbers into the small device. She listened to the ring as she put it to her ear. After four rings, a recognizable man's voice answered.

"Yes? Dr. Martin Cohen speaking."

She hesitated almost long enough for him to hang up. Finally, she responded.

"Um…this is…I'm…Naomi…Naomi Kaplan."

She heard a gasp on the other end.

"Could it be you, my beautiful one? You have answered my prayer to HaShem. Your stunning eyes and perfectly straight teeth have kept me up at night."

He'd noticed her teeth? Well after all, he was a dentist.

"Yes, Dr. Cohen. It's me. I…I had your card in my pocketbook, and I just happened to see it, and…no, that's not true. Do you, by some chance, know a Chaya Mendel?"

He had been getting ready to attack a plate of pickled herring that sat before him. Now he put his fork down, and sat up straight.

"Do I *know* her? Are you *kidding*? I took care of her whole family, including her late husband Mandy…may he rest in peace. Of *course* I know her. And how is it that *you* know her, if I may ask?"

"Well…it's a long story. But…I happened to mention you to her, and she told me she knew you. She said you're a very nice man…and a good dentist. So I thought I'd call you, and…"

"It's bashert is what it is! Don't you think it's bashert? I'm already feeling like we should get together and talk about it."

"Yes…yes, I suppose it is bashert," Naomi responded cautiously, trying to sound as subdued as possible. After all, she had actually taken the initiative to call a…well, a still *somewhat* strange man on the phone— even if Chaya did know him. Not that there was any other choice. She hadn't given him her number, so he couldn't call *her*. It would have been too forward to have given that to him on the train. But still, *she* had called *him*. He interrupted her mental hesitancy by following up on the bashert remark.

"Do you know what? My heart is beating fast right now. And do you know why? God is matchmaking, don't you think? I want to see you again. When can I see you? I want to look at your *shayna punim*…your beautiful face."

Those Yiddish words prompted a surprising response, and she suddenly became a flirty schoolgirl.

"Well, I could text you a picture for now. But we'll see. Maybe. I think I have to go now. My father will be getting up from a nap soon, and I have to make dinner for him."

"Now, now, Naomi. You're playing with me, aren't you? Please don't hang up…at least not before I get your number. We don't have eternity to get to know each other."

"Yes, that's what Chaya says. She also says you're very handsome. And…and I told her she's right."

Naomi could hardly believe those words came from her mouth. But somehow she knew he shouldn't be the only one giving compliments. He didn't wait a beat before he responded.

"So what's the holdup? You're beautiful. I'm handsome. We agree. It's a match made in heaven, as my late wife used to say…of course not about you. But I know we have her blessing from above."

Naomi ignored those last awkward words and went in for the kill.

"Well…I suppose we could meet, in a public place. Yes, I would like to do that. I work in Manhattan, at Macy's, and I could see you some day during my lunch break. Do you know Ben's Deli on 38th Street?"

"Do I know it? Yes, of course. Who doesn't know Ben's Deli? A good kosher place with good food. What about tomorrow, Monday? When do you take your break?"

"Well, let's say 12:30 p.m. at Ben's?"

"Of course, Naomi. I won't sleep well tonight. But when I do finally get to sleep, I'll be dreaming of you. And your number?"

She gave him her number without hesitancy—which surprised her. But why not? This might just be God's answer to her lonely ache since Darrin Brock. Once he wrote down the number, he ended the conversation with a short goodbye.

"I wish it was tomorrow. Shalom, my love."

He hung up, and then she did. Normally, she would immediately second-guess herself. But she didn't have time for that. While she still held the phone in her hand, it rang.

"Hello?"

A woman's voice greeted her on the other end of the line.

"Naomi Kaplan?"

Naomi couldn't quite place the voice. She'd heard it before, probably in some kind of courtesy call. But this late in the day, and on a Sunday, yet? Maybe it was the receptionist at Kingsbrook Rehabilitation Institute, calling about some medical detail related to David Kaplan's release. Or maybe not. Whoever it was, she would get her off the phone fast, so she could spend some time processing the call that just ended.

"Yes?"

"This is Jody Goldberg."

Jody Goldberg…Jody Goldberg…Jody who? Oh yes, Jody. The messianic wife.

"Yes…hi…can I help you, Jody?"

"I hope you're not busy. I just wanted to take a few minutes of your time to tell you how much I…I…"

Should I tell her I'm busy? I suppose that would be rude.

"…how excited I was to hear about your father's no less than miraculous recovery."

"Oh, that. Yes."

"Abrihet told me all about it. I'm so happy for you..and your father."

"Yes. Thank you so much. If anyone deserves to be well, it's my beloved father."

Jody didn't know quite what to say in response to that remark. There was a short pause. She ended the awkward silence by continuing.

"Yes, well…I'd be so honored to meet him. I understand that my husband knows him…that is, he *knew* him as a child, when his father Irving would take him to the Linotype room at the *New York Times*. I guess that was a *second* surprise, after Abrihet spoke that word, and…"

"Word? Oh, *that* word."

"Yes, she told me she spoke the name *Yeshua*, in a kind of quick prayer…"

"You mean the *word* yeshua. It's a word, not necessarily a name. It means, God saves…that is, the God of Israel…"

Jody tried to prevent any edge from infecting her voice.

"Yes, Naomi, I know that. But when *Abrihet* used it, I can assure you…I can…*guarantee*…it was a name. And not just any name."

Naomi could feel her face begin to get hot, and she was sure it was turning red.

"Is that why you called me? To tell me that?"

Jody became, against her will, intimidated—and hence, somewhat timid.

"Well…no…but, in a way, yes. In a way. That is, I called to rejoice with you over your father's healing. But…it just seemed so obvious to me…after all, it was Abrihet, and…"

Naomi unbridled all emotional restraint, and released a full measure from her own personal deep reservoir of two-thousand-year-old Jewish pain.

"My father, I will have you know, told me the Hebrew word is just that…a *word,* and *not* a name! And according to him, it *was* in this case, may HaShem be praised! HaShem, and not…not…at any rate, *I* was there. *You* weren't. I think I need to go now."

Jody cast off her own restraint, and lost her own decorum. If she was being humiliated for calling to express thankfulness for a miracle performed in *His* name, she might as well take off the gloves herself and punch back—in spite of any admonition in the Sermon on the Mount.

"Well, excuse me Naomi, before you hang up on me…no, I wasn't there, but my husband *was* there. And he saw everything. And Abrihet was there. She breathed the *word,* as you call it, as a prayer. And yes, you were there too. I grant you that. *But*…your father *wasn't* there. He was out like a light. So I don't care how wise, and righteous, and whatever else he is. He wouldn't know whether it was a word or a name in that case… any more than you would know if it was a doctor's scalpel cutting you if you were under anesthesia…or it was a scissors. The only person who would know in what way she used the word 'Yeshua' would be Abrihet. So why don't you just ask her?"

By this time, Naomi was trembling. She tried to open her mouth to speak, but tears streamed down her cheeks instead. Jody waited for a response until she wondered whether Naomi had hung up—perhaps for good. Finally, she spoke up.

"So, did you hang up on me, or what?"

Naomi finally found her trembling voice.

"No…and…as a…matter…matter…of…fact…I will talk to that nurse's…attendant…"

"It's Abrihet…and she's more than an attendant. She's a highly trained therapist."

"Yes…I know that. You don't have to lecture me."

Jody made every effort to restore some semblance of gentleness to her spirit.

"Yes, well, why don't we have you over, and you can bring anyone you want, even your father…or your rabbi…or…anyone. And Abrihet will come. And you can ask her there. Your father can ask her there. We'll have a pleasant time. And we'll treat each other with respect. And you can agree to disagree, if you want. But at least you'll know what Abrihet's thoughts are. After all, she loved your father enough to pray for him."

There was another pause. Finally, a slightly calmer Naomi responded.

"Well...we might just do that. My father happens to respect all religions. He's that secure in his faith as a Jew. And he taught me the same way. That's why I allowed Abrihet to pray that day. I'm sure there's a reasonable Jewish explanation for this whole thing. Maybe my father and I will come over, or at least perhaps I will. Of course, we eat *glatt* kosher, so my father may not eat your food, even if you go out of your way to accommodate us, as you did for me."

"That's fine. That will work. You can eat before you come over. I'll talk to Sheldon about a time that might work, and we'll get back to you."

"Fine. I'll go now."

She hung up without waiting for Jody to say goodbye. Then she let out a heaving sigh, and flopped down on the couch. It suddenly occurred to her just how far she had come from her and Darrin reading the New Testament with intense fascination the year before, to this place of defensive anger. Everything had become so much more complicated since she had broken up with him—and even more so since her father's instantaneous recovery. Nevertheless, he had been healed, and that was something to thank HaShem for.

Now she would go up and check on her father, after which she would prepare her mind for her meeting with Dr. Martin Cohen the next day.

CHAPTER THIRTY-SIX

By Monday morning, the temperature had dropped ten degrees to 55, and the cloudless crystal-blue sky was as dry as Arizona. On this morning, the term summer was a mere technical one, considering fall's un-ignorable presence. And Naomi felt as cool, light, and clear as the day. She had none of the stomach-churning bowel-loosing nervousness that had accompanied the mornings at work before her lunch breaks with Darrin Brock the year before. Instead, she had a relaxed sense of humor about her upcoming Ben's Deli lunch date with Dr. Martin Cohen DDS. She could choose to be coy, evasive, and simply not care whether he was put off or not. After all, she didn't love him—at least not yet. In fact, she wasn't quite sure she was even doing this whole thing out of any romantic interest. Maybe she was just making a statement to Chaya Mendel that, yes, she could get involved with a religious Jewish man.

Even when Mrs. Lazar asked her to stay for an extra ten minutes before her lunch break, in order to assist her with an Internet sterling flatware order, Naomi stayed relaxed. Dr. Martin Cohen could wait. She would simply text him on the escalator, or on the way out of the Macy's Thirty-Fourth Street doors eight floors below.

The ten minutes turned into fourteen, and when the time to leave finally arrived, he simply texted back, *OK*—a lot more succinctly than the irritating Marvin would—and a lot more confidently. She maintained a similar confidence, breathing in the thin September Manhattan air on Seventh Avenue, as she held her forty-nine-year-old head high—complete with its newly washed curly brown hair.

When she finally arrived at Ben's, there was Martin Cohen, sitting in the same green upholstered booth that both Marvin and Darrin had sat in before him. He was dressed in a dark grey suit, with a crisp white shirt and no tie. As she walked into the deli, she thought, *Well, I just might marry this one. Maybe three times is a charm, love him or not.* As soon as Martin saw her, he struggled his way out of the bench seat, grabbing a long-stemmed red rose from the table in the process. He stood before her and bowed low, one hand on his abdomen and one behind him holding the rose, like a musical conductor with a baton. The crown of his Leonard Bernstein wavy silver-haired head completed the picture. Then he stood straight and brought his rose-holding hand forward, eliciting a wave of embarrassment in Naomi. Was anyone watching? What if they clapped, like they always seemed to when proposals are made in restaurants and ball games?

"For you, my spring…well, fall rose."

Naomi tried to be more overwhelmed than embarrassed—as overwhelmed as she had been the year before, when Darrin Brock first told her of the exotic dark brown-eyed Eastern European vision his eyes beheld. At that time, she wondered how Darrin could possibly be speaking about her. But he was serious, and he finally convinced her that she was, indeed, a beautiful woman. She wasn't overtaken in the same way with Martin Cohen's remarks, because she wasn't sure just what he was actually seeing before him. Were his eyes beholding what Darrin's were? Or was he just flattering her to try to win her—to gain her. And win her to what? One thing was sure. She was a virgin, and he definitely wasn't. Still, didn't Chaya say he was a good Jewish man? With that thought, she smiled, nodded, and took the rose.

"Thank you."

She didn't know what more to say. So she scooted into her side of the booth and waited for him to do the same on the other side. He obliged her. The same waitress who had waited on her when Marvin and Darrin were with her came with her order pad. She took one look at Cohen and raised her eyebrows. Then she gave him the once over. She was definitely acting flirtatious. Naomi quickly glanced at her. The waitress was about the same age as she was—a slightly oversized yet somewhat attractive Jewish woman with no wedding ring on her finger. Right then and there, Martin Cohen began to look more appealing to her. She was definitely dating a handsome Jewish professional—and a doctor, yet. Not bad.

"I only have a half-hour break, Dr. Cohen. Then I have to get back to work."

"Of course. This will be the first of many times, I hope…and perhaps the next time in a more, shall I say, intimate setting…one in which I might kiss those delicious lips of yours."

Naomi's face approached a shade of red matching the long-stemmed rose.

"Well…you *do* work fast, Doctor Cohen. Do you get down to the oral work on all your dental patients just as quickly?"

When Martin let out a loud blast of a laugh, Naomi realized she had been quite clever. She wasn't known for her wit, so she knew she was speaking self-protectively. She definitely had to follow up with something more sobering.

"Doctor Cohen…"

"Please. Call me Martin."

"Martin…I once kissed a man I truly loved, and…"

"Once?"

"Well…twice…and…I reserve my kisses for such persons."

"Of *course!* I wouldn't expect less. I am also quite selective. And that's why I selected you. I was faithful to my late wife all the years of our marriage, and all of my kisses…*all* of them…and, may I say, all other expressions of passion…were reserved for her. Now, I have been an extremely lonely man since her untimely passing. When I saw you on the subway, I knew instantly that God had provided a remedy for that loneliness. And so I will reserve my kisses…as well as those *other* expressions of passion…and I *am* a passionate man…for just you, and only you."

Naomi's eyes widened and her voice rose.

"Dr. Cohen…you are moving *entirely* too fast for me. You see, I need to get to know you first…if indeed we do happen to continue to see each other…which I'm not sure about right now, and I must say I'm almost doubting. So, could we please change the subject? Please."

Martin's mouth took on a remorseful expression, pursing in regret while obscuring his professionally whitened teeth.

"I am so very sorry. I must explain that I am a very religious man, and very moral. I observe strict Orthodox Jewish *halacha*, and have no addictive habits. I don't smoke, drink to excess, or have any other such liabilities. I am, in addition, a man of what you might call independent wealth, Baruch HaShem, and am ready to provide handsomely for the woman I love…for the rest of her life. You see, I tend to hide nothing. What you see is…not to put it too mundanely…what you get."

"I see. But *really*, you didn't have to tell me all of that, Dr. Cohen," she chided him, purposely returning to addressing him formally. He tried to ignore the return as he responded.

"And now, I would love to hear all about you. So I will listen, and learn about what I'm sure is a very remarkable person. I can see that in your extra-ordinary eyes."

"Well…Dr. Cohen…"

"Call me Martin, please."

"Martin. Dr. Cohen. Whatever. First of all, I'm in no way remarkable, and certainly not extraordinary. I'm just an observant middle-aged Jewish single woman who takes care of her truly extraordinary father, and works full time at Macy's…but not on Shabbat…and has a younger sister who is married and has two children…*and* lives in Englewood, *and* is not religious. And yes, I loved a man once. But he happened to be a Gentile, and a committed Christian. Don't ask me how that happened, because I won't tell you. And it didn't work out."

"I won't ask you, except, are you a…I mean, did he…with you…to you?"

"*My*, Martin Cohen, you are inquisitive, aren't you? No…not that. He happens to be a perfect gentleman, and I…I am, as I said before, a religious Jew."

"I see."

"Again, please don't ask how I ended up falling in love with him."

"Of course. I won't. Just one question, if I may. Are you still in love with him?"

She tried to limit the pause to a mere few seconds.

"I think the fact that we no longer see each other should satisfy your curiosity about that."

"You didn't exactly answer my question. But concerning his background, all I will say is that the heart can make unusual choices all its own."

She found herself agreeing with him.

"Yes, it can."

"Well, it's good for me that it didn't work out…and that I will be the first, if you understand what I mean."

She rolled her eyes, and whispered out loud.

"Martin! *Please!*"

He didn't hesitate to respond.

"But Naomi, you don't understand. I want to *marry* you. We are both in our golden years. And like gold, they are getting more precious by the day. As that precious time goes by, you will find me to be very romantic. And that's why I want to make love to you…after the wedding, of course."

Exasperated, she couldn't help but let out a slight giggle.

"My goodness. You certainly are different from…from…"

"From who?"

"I don't know. From everyone, I guess."

"And by the way, I'm an excellent dentist, too. Very thorough. And very gentle. Just ask Chaya. She will tell you."

"About that, I believe you. But we have a dentist already. A very good one. Dr. Sheib."

"Yes, he's good. Not as good as I am…but good. So tell me more about yourself."

"There's not much more to tell, Dr. Cohen. Except that there is a… well, some would call him a nebbish, or schlemiel…but I respect him enough to not call him that, although he is certainly a mama's boy…a man my age by the name of Marvin…also *frum*, very religious. And he also wants to marry me. But…that won't happen."

"Good. I would have had to challenge him to a duel," he joked.

"He would lose, believe me. And let's see what else. My beloved father and I study the great sages of Judaism regularly. And we go to the synagogue every Shabbat. And we're very close. He's the wisest Jew…and the wisest man…in the world. He was very sick. But he's all better now, Baruch HaShem. But that's another long story. And oh yes, you would very much like him if you met him."

Martin immediately interrupted.

"Then can I meet him soon…after sundown this Saturday, perhaps?"

Naomi instantly realized that it would probably make her father very happy to meet an Orthodox Jewish dentist like Martin Cohen DDS. And she could remind him about Chaya's strong endorsement. He would really like that. Even if Naomi *didn't* continue to see Cohen, just the smile on her father's newly healed face would be worth the visit.

"Well…that might be possible. I mean, yes, I think that might work."

"Good. Give me your address, then, and I will drive my silver Lexus to your house this Saturday at, say, 9:00 p.m. The *Havdalah* service ending the Shabbat will be over, and then I will arrive at your door with my heart beating. I hope I can sleep until then. It will be hard for me."

She raised her hands like a traffic cop.

"Now Martin, please don't make more of it than just a nice visit to meet my father."

He couldn't hide his expectant smile.

"Of course. I understand."

"Well, look. I've got to leave, or I'll be late getting back to work."

"I will phone you for your address."

"Right. I'll give it to you then."

They both struggled out of their sides of the booth. She took the rose. He took her by the other hand.

"Let me walk you back…at least partially. May I, please?"

"Oh…I guess so, if you wish."

She had to admit she was enjoying his gentlemanly demeanor. It certainly was the opposite of Marvin. They walked outside and began the trip back. A half a block up, he took her by the hand and gently pulled her into an alley between stores. Then he moved in close.

"May I just give you one quick kiss?"

"Martin! I told you…"

"Please. Please. I beg you. You are so beautiful…just one."

"Martin…"

He squeezed her hand as she looked into his eyes—sweet eyes, sad eyes, and actually kind eyes.

She sighed.

"You *are* a romantic, aren't you?"

She couldn't believe that she was allowing this—and that she actually wanted it, in some far off never-lived youthful adventurous way. After all, he was extremely handsome—like Leonard Bernstein, in fact.

"Okay, Martin. Yes, a small little one. But that's all. Just one quick one to help you with your…your loneliness…"

"Oh, Naomi! My Yiddish dove."

As she pressed close to him and he turned his head toward her, she noticed for the first time that he had the threads of hearing aids in his ears. *Well, he didn't say he was a young man.* Just after that, their lips met. She could feel his pounding heart through her blouse. In the middle of what ended up being anything but short—at least a minute, if not more—she realized she would be late getting back to work. She also remarked to herself that he was actually a surprisingly good kisser. A different good than Darrin—whom she had to admit she still deeply loved—but phenomenal in his own way. His lips were also smooth, and his breath was extremely fresh. *Not surprising for a dentist.* Somewhere two-thirds through, she found herself quite passionately kissing him back. And when they were finished, she was completely out of breath. Finally, she found her voice.

"Oh *my*, Martin. My goodness. That was…Oh, Martin. It wasn't short. But…I must say, it was…it was…sweet."

"Yes, very. *You* are sweet. I am, as I say, lonely, with a tender heart, and a recent loss. And I have *so much* to give. You will see. You will see."

"I've got to go now, Martin. Please, just let me run back now…or I will be very late."

With that, she exited the alley and quickly walked down the street. He watched her, with the same expectant smile on his face. As she began her fast-paced walk back to Macy's, a strong headwind of guilt blew through her blouse and penetrated her heart. From there, it invaded her conscience, bringing a kind of shame she'd never experienced before.

I've sinned! Oh, my! I've been loose! I've transgressed! Like a woman of the street! A very loose woman. I'm bad! A bad person, like those who hop from bed to bed. And I flirted with him, like Jezebel! Why did I do that?

Why? I actually kissed a man I just met! And a religious Jew, yet! And he's going to meet my father after this very Shabbat. He'll tell him! He seems to tell everything that's on his mind. Oh no. He's got a big mouth. A soft kissable mouth, like in the Song of Songs. But also a big mouth. A very big mouth! What am I going to do? What am I going to do? Well...at least Yom Kippur is just around the corner.

By the time Naomi ran up the escalator to the eighth floor, passing shoppers while excusing herself, she managed to quiet her unresolved conscience enough to focus on her afternoon's work.

CHAPTER THIRTY-SEVEN

Stanley missed David Kaplan, and he missed Mahmoud. On Tuesday morning at 11:00 a.m., he sat all alone in the Dewitt Wallace periodical room of the New York Public Library Manhattan branch, just as he had for the last several months. He didn't know that David Kaplan had experienced an unexplainable recovery. No one had told him. He had visited Kaplan a month before, but that was before the "miracle."

Stanley tried to read the *New York Post* that lay stretched out before him. There was plenty of room, since David's *New York Times* and Mahmoud's *Al-Ayyam* were no longer vying for space. But he couldn't concentrate on the front page articles, or anything inside the edition. He looked over at his bag lunch. He had prepared peanut butter on rye that morning. He was somewhat partial to peanut butter, and he loved New York Jewish rye. But he abhorred the combination. He chose the lethal lamination out of a lack of bread choices. And now that he was hungry for lunch, he had no interest in eating it, or the apple he included with it. What he *really* wanted was a pastrami on rye with coleslaw and Russian dressing, a kosher pickle, and chips—and a Dr. Brown's cream soda to wash it all down. He got up, walked to the garbage can in the corner of the room, and promptly dumped the bag, with sandwich and apple, into the receptacle. It hit the bottom of the almost empty can with a thud of finality. He knew he was wasting "good" food, but he had no interest in carrying the bag where he was headed.

The weather Tuesday was warmer than Monday, more like the late summer it actually was, and cloudy. Stanley walked out of the library and immediately hailed a cab for the eight-minute ride to the Second Street Deli in the Midtown East Side section of New York City. Once his large hulking frame was situated in the back seat, he looked into the rear view mirror to see a young man who looked like he might be a young Mahmoud.

"Where to?"

"Second Street Deli."

"Ah, yes. 33rd Street?"

That seemed obvious to Stanley. After all, this was the main location. The other Second Street Delis were many blocks away.

"Yes, of course."

"You got it."

For a quick instant, Stanley considered the possibility that he had placed himself in the hostile hands of an Islamic extremist. After all, he knew he clearly looked Jewish—somewhat like the lyricist Oscar Hammerstein, as David Kaplan liked to point out. Maybe the goal of this obviously Middle Eastern young man was to drive Stanley somewhere way out of his way, and then turn around and shoot or stab him before he could get out of the cab.

As soon as that thought entered his mind, he regretted having thought it. If Mahmoud were there in the taxi with him, he would say, "That is not right, my friend. I myself drove a taxi in this city before I retired. Would I harm you? No! And this man will not harm you either. Just because we disagree on Jerusalem, that does not mean we cannot be good friends." And Mahmoud would be right. After that thought, came another. *Speaking of Mahmoud, where in the world is he, anyway?*

The driver looked at the rear view mirror.

"Nice day, is it not?"

"Yes. But warm for September and a bit humid."

"That is so. Like my country, except that it was somewhat colder here yesterday. That would not happen."

"Yes, it can be changeable this time of year."

Stanley didn't want to talk about the weather any more, or the young man's country. So he maintained silence after that, until the driver changed the subject.

"Good place, that Second Street Deli. I have eaten there many times."

"Yes. I worked at a delicatessen many years ago myself…behind the counter. I know good delis, and I know bad delis. Some I wouldn't eat there if they paid me in gold bricks. But this is a good one."

"You make me hungry just thinking about eating there. And it is lunchtime."

The young man's comments put Stanley at ease. He figured that no one who ate at Jewish delis could be up to no good, Palestinians and other Arabs included. From that point on, the rest of the eight minutes went quickly. The driver pulled up to the curb, and Stanley got out and paid him. Then he gave him a firm handshake, and headed into the restaurant.

The original Second Street Deli opened in 1954 on Second Avenue and East 10th Street in the Yiddish Theater District of Manhattan.

Although Yiddish theater had all but disappeared by that time, a Yiddish Walk of Fame was created on the sidewalk just outside its doors, honoring the great Yiddish actors of the prior fifty years. Following the unsolved murder of its founder, Abe Lebewohl, in 1996, the deli closed briefly. Even Inspector Ralph Lewis, working under the Giuliani administration at the time, was unsuccessful in solving that crime. The deli closed again in 2006, and eventually reopened on 33rd Street.

Stanley walked straight to the dining area, where several pictures of the great Yiddish star Molly Picon greeted him. Then, hungry as he was, he took a detour and walked over to the spacious deli counter. He watched the deli workers slicing corned beef and wrapping lox, industriously waiting on a crowd of anxious New York customers. He had to admit, he missed the excitement of shouting over the crowd, and navigating past fellow workers from one side of the counter to the other. He never worked at this particular deli, but in so many ways they were all the same—the symphonic clink of plates and silverware, the cacophony of gossip, the smell of pickles, and pastrami, and matzoh ball soup. It was all so familiar. He even peripherally knew a few Second Street Deli workers, although not by name. But even if they recognized him, they were too busy to acknowledge it. He just stood there and took it all in.

Then, just in his sight range, he saw the young man whose picture he was shown at the NYPD Midtown South Precinct offices. He smiled to himself.

I guess he's another Arab who can't stay away from Jewish delis. That's what I love about New York City. It's everything Mahmoud says it is.

He pressed through the crowd and ended up next to Omar, who seemed very much engaged in staring at something in the opposite direction, toward the dining area. He gently tapped him on the shoulder. Omar snapped his head around, startling Stanley. When their eyes met, Stanley could tell there was something intense, and even frightening, about Omar's eyes. But perhaps not. Maybe the disruption just surprised him. Stanley remembered that he was shown the photograph of this man in relation to Mahmoud's disappearance. This was his chance to talk to someone who just might know something about where his Dewitt Wallace Periodical Room friend was.

"Excuse me, sir…young man…may I ask you a strange question?"

Omar instantly recognized Stanley from the library. With an obvious look of disgust, he responded.

"What…what is it, old J…what?"

Omar realized he needed to restrain himself from spitting in this filthy old Jew's face. For his part, Stanley was becoming less and less comfortable around Omar. But this was probably his last opportunity to ask anyone about Mahmoud's whereabouts.

"I know there are a lot of people in New York, and a lot of…well… people from your part of the…world…sir. But by some chance, do you know a retired taxi driver named Mahmoud? And if so, have you seen him recently, if I may ask?"

Stanley noticed that the young man's teeth clenched, and his eyed widened in a fiery blaze. He felt the need to glance away from Omar, and down, just in time to see his hand emerge from his pocket with a small silver blade. Instinctively, Stanley pulled back, like the Dallas sheriff when Oswald was shot. He stumbled backward and then turned and tried to lope away. Omar easily caught up with him at the close side of the deli counter. Stanley quickly hopped over a step-like barrier at that open end of the counter, and moved behind it. He pushed between two deli men and grabbed a round silver tray to use as a shield. A quarter pound of thinly sliced cheese slid off the tray and onto the floor. Omar quickly put the knife back in his pocket, but his eyes fixed on Stanley. Now that Stanley was onto him, it was obvious that he had to die before he could call the police. But how? He quickly realized that if he could get behind the counter, he could subtly pull the small blade out and thrust it below Stanley's ribs—and then flee.

Omar ran to the other side of the counter as two deli men were challenging Stanley about the tray. His seventy-six-year-old obese heart pounding, Stanley saw Omar going behind the counter from the other end. He clutched the tray and ran out the near side, as Omar stumbled and reversed direction. When Omar caught up with him, he pulled the blade out and tried to thrust it toward Stanley, who deftly—with the consummate skill of a deli man—raised the shield just in time for the blade to clink against it. This occurred three times, until Omar realized he was attracting attention. But the crowd around them was too focused on chopped liver and roast beef to realize what was going on. Omar looked both ways and then fled without killing his overstuffed over-tall over-aged Jewish prey. Stanley thought it best not to follow him. He knew he'd just escaped death. He also knew he had to use someone's cell phone and call the police—specifically Inspector Lewis, or Detective Brock.

Omar walked swiftly down the street. Suddenly, he felt his secure phone vibrate in his right pocket. He darted into an alley and pulled it out. He was hoping it was his Pakistani contact, but it wasn't. A familiar Russian voice spoke on the other end.

"Stupid Arab idiot! What were you doing in that deli, trying to kill the old man? We told you, do what we say. We pick you up next block."

"No!" an out-of-breath Omar insisted.

"Then we kill you before you kill infidel."

"You kill me. Okay."

"Even better, we have Mahmoud's body, who you murdered. It is preserved for evidence. We will make sure you go to American jail for life, like Khalid Sheikh Mohammed. At the next corner, get in car! We will hide you. Then you kill Darrin Brock for us. This time you succeed. Next corner!"

Omar left the alley and walked slowly forward toward the corner.

Before he could even choose to flee, two large muscular men in tight jeans and black long-sleeved shirts grabbed him and threw him into the rear seat of a late model gun-metal grey Hyundai Sonata.

CHAPTER THIRTY-EIGHT

Naomi was tired by the time she entered the subway after work on Tuesday. She was thankful to have found an unoccupied inside seat so she could rest her head against the window. There had been a flurry of customers over the last two hours that ended up being more like a snowstorm in late summer. She could never figure out why that happened. There were no special sales, and no holidays in sight. Maybe on this day, God was choosing to bless Macy's, resulting in a kind of curse for her—considering that she was working the department alone that afternoon. She tried not to think about her lurid "date" with Martin Cohen DDS, or the call and tense conversation with Jody Goldberg. The latter effort ended up being particularly impossible. She could just hear her cheap flip phone begin to ring in her handbag. And when she pulled it out, she recognized the same number that she'd seen a few days before—Jody Goldberg. *Oh brother!*

"Yes?"

"Naomi? This is Jody Goldberg."

"Oh," Naomi responded as nonchalantly as she could.

"Can you talk now? It sounds like you might be on the subway."

"I am."

Part of Naomi wanted to say she couldn't talk, and the other part wanted to get the phone call over with.

"But I can talk…for a few minutes."

"Good. Remember we talked about meeting with Abrihet?"

How could she forget? Jody continued.

"Well, what about Thursday night 7:00 p.m. at my house? We can have something light, if you'd like…dairy on paper plates with plastic utensils…and we can talk. Would that work?"

Naomi realized she would have to find some excuse to tell her father about where she was going. She had no intention of asking him to go with her, as Jody had suggested in the earlier phone call. But all things being equal, she supposed that Thursday evening was as good as any. The wisest Jew in the world—her beloved father David Kaplan—didn't have to be present in order for her to express his learned opinion. Yeshua was a *thing*, not a person—a thing meaning *salvation*.

"Okay. I will be there."

"Great. See you then."

Naomi felt even more exhausted after the call. She leaned against the window for the next half hour, and tried unsuccessfully to sleep. When she finally arrived at the Brooklyn home she shared with her father, he was in the kitchen cooking something. He hadn't heard her come in the house. For a few seconds, she stood there at the entrance to the kitchen and marveled at the continued improvement in his health. He was getting stronger day by day. Eventually, she cleared her throat so she wouldn't frighten him, and he turned around and smiled. She went over and hugged his shoulders.

"I love you, Abba."

"I've cooked dinner for us. Blintzes with sour cream, and potatoes."

"It smells wonderful!"

David turned the oven off while Naomi got the plates from the dairy side of the cupboard. She waited until all of the food was on the table, including iced tea. Then she broached the subject of Thursday evening.

"Abba…I have to be out with some friends on Thursday night. Remember Abrihet?"

"Of course I do."

"Well, she's one of them…and some others. Just some friends who happen to know her…you know, some people who kind of visit the Kingsbrook Rehabilitation Institute…sometimes…at someone's house.

Will you be okay here at home?"

"Yes, of course. You have your life. And you can see that I can cook my own dinner."

"*I* will do that beforehand, Abba. You can just heat it up."

"No. I like cooking. It gives me something to do."

That was easy.

"And guess what, Abba? That Jewish dentist is coming over Saturday night after Shabbat. He wants to meet you."

"Oh. That would be nice…very nice. I'd like to meet him. By the way, have you heard from Darrin? Does he know I'm home and feeling better, Baruch HaShem?"

She hadn't thought about whether Darrin was aware of her father's amazing recovery. After intentionally having no contact with him, she hadn't even considered who might have told him. But she had a guess.

"I'm sure Lisa must have let him know, Abba. And in time, I would think he would at least call you. Anyway, let's say the blessing before the blintzes and potatoes get cold."

They prayed the *barucha* blessing before the meal. That was the beginning of a lovely but short evening at home. It consisted of David quoting and then translating witty Yiddish jokes. This infrequent pastime of theirs convinced her that the joke she had told Martin Cohen about his dental patients actually did have some roots in these recitations of Jewish humor. But as enjoyable as the evening was, Naomi increasingly felt the effects of a very draining day, and decided to go to bed early.

However, after two listless hours, she sat up in bed and stared at the light from the street lamp as it bled through her window blinds. It occurred to her that this partial illumination perfectly represented her extremely partial view of truth and meaning in her life.

As much as she loved her father dearly, and had learned so much from him, she still had so many unanswered questions. What God did Darrin worship? If it was the same God as hers, then exactly who was the God *she* professed to worship? That year-old question still remained unanswered. Furthermore, what God did Abrihet worship, and how and why did that God answer her prayer for Naomi's father—whatever that prayer was about?

As her questions continued, they got deeper and wider, and

consequently more confusing. Why was she put on the Earth? Was it just to work at Macy's, to help her father until he died, and then to die herself, an old, single, and childless woman? Or as the mid-to-late-life wife of a dentist who seemed to be desperately looking for nothing more than a spousal replacement—like a new hearing aid battery? Even Jewish philosophers Martin Buber and Franz Rosenzweig couldn't answer *those* questions.

A lonely teardrop dripped from her left eye. She brushed it away with her left hand. Then she lay back down and tried to sleep. It took another two hours to accomplish that task. She woke up early Wednesday morning every bit as tired as the night before. She knew she would trudge through that day, longing for her pillow that night. Her only hope was a good night's sleep Wednesday night. And when that finally came, her desire was only granted because she took four Advils at 11:00 p.m. By the time Thursday came, her mind was fixed on that evening. How could she impress on Abrihet and the Goldbergs that she was right about the word "yeshua," and they were wrong? Although she didn't have that answer, she did know one thing. By that time, she had regained her spiritual equilibrium. So she was *sure* she was right.

By the sovereign hand of the Holy One of Israel, there were very few customers all that afternoon. And what customers there were just pulled small items like funnels and colanders off the wall—and items as large as toasters and mixers off the shelves—and brought them to the register for purchase. By the time Naomi traveled eight floors down the escalator and out the doors to 34th Street, she had a surprising bounce in her step. She would tell those people what her father told her. And she would thank Abrihet for being so kind to her father. And everything would be okay. She sat on the bench seat of the crowded subway car, alert and reading the back page of a young man's *New York Post*. The forty-five or so minutes went quickly, and within a few minutes after that, at 6:55 p.m., she was standing in front of Sheldon and Jody Goldberg's Brooklyn brownstone. She took a deep breath, and walked up to the front door. It opened as soon as she knocked on it. She might as well have heard a group of birthday well-wishers say "Surprise!" although she didn't. There, standing in the hallway, were Jody and Sheldon Goldberg, Abrihet, Mahalia Morse, Javier, Jeremy and Joshua, *and*—of all people—

Darrin Brock. She didn't see Margaret, because she was in the bathroom at the time. Naomi's face turned red. This was *not* what she expected. Nevertheless, she greeted them, one by one—Sheldon, Mahalia, the boys, everyone. When she got to Darrin, she held out her hand and then shook his firmly.

"Inspector Brock. I'm surprised. I came here to have a quiet talk with Abrihet and the Goldbergs. I'm…not quite sure why you're here."

Darrin didn't miss a beat. By this time in their severed relationship, he wasn't about to apologize for anything.

"I believe because I was invited, Miss Kaplan. I normally accept invitations from my friends."

He walked away, toward the living room. Naomi was taken aback. She was not used to a sardonic response from the kindest man she'd ever met—besides her father. As she turned around, Jody addressed her.

"I hope you don't mind my inviting some of our mutual friends."

"Of…of course not."

"I'm sure there'll be time to talk to Abrihet later…alone, or perhaps with a few others like Rabbi Goldberg and myself."

Naomi wasn't quite sure what the strategy was. Were they all planning to gang up on her, so to speak? Well, she could always insist on talking to Abrihet alone. Just then, her father's devoted helper came up and gave her a heartfelt hug. She felt a genuineness she couldn't deny.

"Abrihet. I'm actually here to see you. I'm so happy to see you again. My father is doing well, and I know he wants to see you soon."

"I think about him every day. I did not want to disturb him so soon. But I would like to visit him. And you and I will talk tonight. But come. We will all go in the dining room now and have something to eat."

She left, as did everyone else, except the boys. Naomi got on her knees and hugged Javier. Then she looked into his eyes.

"Javier. It's wonderful to see you again! Every time I see you since we met at Midwood Press, you get bigger and more handsome."

Javier didn't know what to do with that compliment. He looked down, and then gave one of his usual defensively humorous remarks.

"Well…you've gotten older too."

After she laughed as warmly as she could, she took Jeremy and Joshua's hands in each of her hands and looked up at them.

"My, you two boys are also growing. I wish you would visit me at Macy's sometime. We had such fun picking out carving knives for your father. Didn't we?"

Jeremy smiled.

"Dangerous ones."

Joshua, as the younger brother, giggled.

"Yeh."

Naomi didn't notice Darrin staring at her from the dining room. Margaret was still in the bathroom. If she was in the hall instead, she would unquestionably have been jealous to see him looking at Naomi that way. Naomi wasn't only oblivious to Darrin. She also didn't notice someone else coming in the still unlocked front door. Right after she finally *did* notice Darrin staring at her, *he* turned and noticed the latecomer. The stress in his voice was apparent.

"Omar? Why are you here?"

Naomi turned around. Omar looked frightened, nervous. This was his last and only chance to kill the infidel—albeit just a few of them, no thanks to the godless Russians. He opened his black lightweight fall trench coat. She could just see what appeared to be red sticks of some sort, and wires. *Could it be?*

He opened his mouth and said with a surprisingly weak cracking voice, "Allahu Akbar!"

Naomi screamed.

"Everyone get back!"

Then, while Omar was nervously fiddling with something in his pocket, Naomi grasped all three boys and fell to the ground, pulling them down and under her body in the process, and shielding them. Javier squirmed to free himself, but she held him tight. Finally, less than half of the sticks exploded. Like almost everything else Omar tried to do to kill the infidel—save the knifing of Mahmoud—he was sloppy and unprofessional in his work. Still, the explosion was strong enough to completely blow him apart, with one leg ending up in the foyer and another at the entrance to the living room. His severed head and part of his spine ended up just next to Naomi, although she was hunched over and barely conscious, and consequently didn't see it. She was bleeding from the head, with burns to her scalp. The boys were completely safe, uninjured. They remained under her, still in shock. The overall structure of the house remained uncompromised, although there was debris everywhere. Darrin ran over to Naomi just as Margaret, who had been fixing her hair when the explosion occurred, stepped out of the bathroom.

He took one look at his ex-girlfriend and shouted, "Call 911! Call 911!"

THE
SECOND FALL

CHAPTER THIRTY-NINE

David Kaplan sat in the inpatient surgical waiting room at Maimonides Medical Center. He had walked the halls of the center's pediatric cancer wing in the wintertime—every December 25th, to be specific—for the last several years. Dressed as Santa Claus, he had watched the smiles on the otherwise suffering faces of countless children. Now he was watching the pained impatient faces of his own grandchildren, Lindsey and Noah. Noah was fidgeting and flailing next to Lisa like any bored eight-year-old boy might—with the added dynamic of fear of death—not his own, but his aunt's. Lisa sat to his right, and her husband Marc to his left. And his eleven-year-old sister Lindsey sat to Marc's left, purposely separated from her brother. Noah whined as his arms reached around his mother's neck, threatening her perfectly curled late-summer/early-fall haircut.

"Mommy, how long will we be here? I'm hungry."

Marc responded, Lisa having performed that task a minute or so before.

"Stop it, Noah. Behave yourself. We told you. We don't know when the doctor will be finished. We'll eat soon."

"Is Aunt Naomi gonna die?"

Lisa did the honors this time.

"Noah, don't even think that!"

Lindsey peered around her father.

"But, Mommy, do you think she might not…might not…survive?"

Before Lisa could respond, Noah had another question.

"If she lives, will she be ugly?"

David, who was understandably in shock after hearing about the explosion, finally forced himself to find his voice. He got up from the orange fabric and plastic seat he had chosen, and walked a few orange seats over to his family. He leaned over and took Noah's hand. Then he stretched over to Lindsey and took her hand as well.

"My precious children. This is not your Aunt Naomi's time for HaShem to take her. And I believe she is even right now quietly praying the *Mi-Shebeirach* prayer for healing. Do you know the *Mi-Shebeirach* prayer?"

Noah shrugged. Lindsey brushed her hair aside and said, "I think so. You've prayed it with us, Grandpa."

"Well, Lindsey, she's praying it to God. And she's also saying to herself, 'I must get all better so I can see my wonderful niece and nephew, and tell them I love them.' And when she sees both of you, she will be more beautiful than ever."

Lindsey had a follow-up question.

"Like after Darrin fell in love with her?"

Lisa interrupted the conversation.

"We'll see. Now no more questions. Come on. We'll go to the cafeteria and get something to eat. Marc, take the alert thingy with you so they can tell us when the doctor wants to speak to us."

"You mean the pager?"

"Whatever. Are you coming, Daddy?"

"No, I'm not hungry. I'll just stay here and wait."

"You should eat something. They'll alert us down there."

"I think I want to stay here, Lisa."

"We can bring something back. They have some nice kosher meals."

"No thank you."

By this time, Noeh was pulling on his mother's arm.

"All right. We'll be back soon."

After his family left, David Kaplan stared at the clock on the wall opposite his chair and prayed his own personal prayers. He also thought

334

his own personal thoughts for the first time since he had been called by Lisa with the terrible news.

HaShem, I've prayed the Mi-Shebeirach prayer many times since I heard. But I wish I was as sure as I told my grandchildren...sure that she won't...won't...

David's prayers ended and his meditation started.

What was she doing at that Sheldon Goldberg's house? Every newspaper in the city...every TV station...mentioned what I know now...that Sheldon runs one of those messianic places right here in the middle of Brooklyn. And now everyone knows Naomi was there. Not that I should care what anyone else thinks about my firstborn daughter. But I don't think I should ask her why she was there. Not anytime soon, anyway. I don't want her to feel guilty for being in that house...to feel like God punished her for it. And I'm sure there must have been a good reason. Whatever the reason, she saved the lives of those three boys. That's the Naomi I know! That's a true mitzvah. And yet, there is something I must say to her when the time is right, if I only could. After all, she is the link God has given me to our Jewish legacy. But only if she lives, please God!

By the time Marc Silver's family came back with the flashing vibrating pager, David Kaplan had decided what he must do. And in order to do it, he had to get to the Linotype machine at the Midwood Press. But for now, he was as anxious as they all were to hear what the doctor had to say. Just as Marc returned the pager, right on cue, a nurse opened the door she had been opening all that day.

"Naomi Kaplan family?"

Lisa made an instant decision that Marc would stay with the children, and he was glad to oblige her. He had seen enough carnage in the last year, what with the violent death of his old "boss" Prima, which he had witnessed first hand. He had no desire to hear any potentially gory diagnosis about anyone.

Lisa and David followed the nurse back through the door and down the hall, to a small room that was designed to hold not more than four or five people. The nurse left them there for about five minutes. Then the trauma surgeon, Dr. Morgenstern, walked in. Lisa tried to read his eyes beneath his bushy black eyebrows—or to read the eyebrows themselves. But he was too professional for that. In his mid-thirties, and a conscientious physician, he had been trained to speak directly and answer all questions. He had also taken the class about taking bedside manner seriously—at least as seriously as his surgical training. Consequently, he was not easy to read before he spoke. And when he *did* speak, Lisa noted that he spoke words she had heard many times in real life, books, television, and films.

"She came through the preliminary surgery as well as could be expected. She's in recovery now. The next forty-eight hours are crucial. We did everything we could to staunch internal bleeding. We took her down to radiology and gave her a CT scan to pinpoint areas of cranial bleeding, which is to be expected in cases like this. And we set her arm, leg, and a few other bones. A special burn team will deal with her scalp later. She has a severe concussion. Right now, she is in a medically induced coma to insure she stays calm. We have also intubated her to assist with breathing. We will reevaluate that after those crucial forty-eight hours. We have an excellent staff of top-notch nurses and other highly trained technicians. And we will all keep an eye on her. I do suggest that those who know how to pray do that. As I say, the next forty-eight hours will tell."

Why is it always forty-eight hours? Lisa thought. Her eyes were fixed on Dr. Morgenstern's stethoscope as it rested over his own beating heart. Someday even this doctor's heart would be stilled in death, as would hers. Hopefully, her big sister's heart wouldn't be stilled anytime soon.

Just at that moment, it dawned on Lisa that her thoughts over the last year had become increasingly too serious—to be specific, too focused on things related to death. She longed to think light, frivolous, and frankly materialistic thoughts again. She ached to just sit on the backyard deck of her suburban Englewood, New Jersey house and sunbathe, while gossiping with her like-minded friends. But she realized that the fall would soon turn to winter. And her big sister Naomi would endure her own winter, taking months to recover—if she even did. And if she didn't, death would envelop Lisa's life like a permanent shroud. Doctor Morgenstern shook each of their hands, one by one.

"You can contact me at any time through my office. I try to stay in close contact with my patients. We will advise you of any change in status either way, and let you know when you'll be able to visit Naomi in

Intensive Care…hopefully as soon as possible."

Then he bowed slightly and left. As they walked out of the tiny room and down the hallway toward the waiting room door, Lisa put her arm around her father.

"Are you okay, Daddy? I mean, you just got over your own serious illness."

He shrugged.

"God has not forsaken us. He knows. He knows. How are *you* doing?"

"Not great. I think we'll take the kids home and get some rest. And if I know Marc, he'll want to go back the other way this afternoon and provide food to the Manhattan delis. We'll take you home on the way."

"No. I'll take the subway."

She stopped him on the other side of the door.

"Why? We have the car."

"I need to go somewhere."

"Daddy, it's been a long night and day. I don't think…"

"Lisa. Please…"

She sighed.

"Okay, Daddy. Please call me when you get home."

"I will."

He walked over and gave the children a hug. Then he shook Marc's hand.

"She'll be okay, God willing."

"And that means?"

"It means you should be a good Jew, and then you could pray and help her along."

"Please don't preach to me, Dad."

Noah chimed in.

"Yeh!"

Lisa put her hands out to halt further discussion.

"Enough. The doctor said the next forty-eight hours are crucial."

Marc sneered.

"Why do they always say forty-eight hours?"

"Let's go home. Dad, call me later."

Marc looked at him.

"Where's *he* going?"

"None of your business, or apparently mine. Let's go."

She practically pushed all three of her family members out the door to the main corridor. David was left alone. He waited until they disappeared around the corner, and then began his journey to the Midwood Press. It wasn't until he was the lone passenger on the inside seat of a half-empty subway car that he began to plan out his visit. He planned to write a letter to his oldest daughter. He realized that he could have written it longhand. But he wanted a more official communique. And he didn't have access to a word processing computer, let alone an old-fashioned typewriter. At any rate, it seemed appropriate for him to express himself to his beloved daughter using the machine he had typed on for so many years at the *New York Times*, before retiring way back in 1978—the machine that had been invented back in 1884 by Otto Mergenthaler.

That was settled. Now he needed to concentrate on just what to write his daughter. Overall, it needed to be positive. And it needed to communicate the legacy—his legacy and the legacy of the Jewish people—that she would carry into the future. Maybe it wouldn't be a legacy she would leave to her own natural children. But nevertheless, it needed to be one she would…would what? To whom would she leave it? After a few minutes of thought, he finally decided that he must impress upon her something about the impact of her commitment to traditional Judaism on the next generation—a commitment worthy of the sages, one that awaited the Messiah who was yet to come, and one that honored the Judaism of her ancestors. But how could he do that without making her feel pressured, or guilty about anything she might have already been considering—with or without Darrin?

When David arrived at the Midwood Press, Ben opened the door.

"Mr. Kaplan! How are you? The last I heard, you were laid up with some serious stuff."

"Well, Ben. Let's just say God had other plans. Hmm. It's quiet here today."

"Yeh, well, I'm kind of holding down the fort for the time being, so to speak. And this isn't school visiting Thursday, so…I guess this is what it looks like when there's not much going on. Even the old Linotype machine is quiet…which isn't normal, considering what a noisy contraption it is. How's your daughter? She seemed to have such a great time in the spring, watching you work that thing."

Apparently, Ben hadn't heard about his daughter's injury, even though it took place in Midwood, not far from where they were. It seemed odd that a printer like Ben wouldn't even have read about it in the newspaper. But David didn't want to discuss that now. He chose a vague answer.

"She's been better, but...um...Ben. Do you think maybe I might make a bit of noise with the Linotype machine? I just want to print a little something. I realize this is a business, and the children aren't here today. But...if you don't mind..."

Ben put his hand on David's shoulder.

"For you? The greatest Linotype operator in the history of the *New York Times*? Are you kidding? Be my guest. You know how to fire it up. It's all over there, including printer's ink and paper. I'll be in the office doing some paperwork."

After Ben walked away, David approached the machine. He flipped the switch. It began to hum and click, as its various parts swung into position. He sat down and closed his eyes. He laid his right hand over the oddly shaped keyboard, without actually touching the keys—and then moved his lips without actually speaking aloud.

"HaShem, you gave Israel the Torah that sustains our people to this very day. Could you not give me a few meager words to encourage my daughter...who is healing at the hospital which is named after one of our greatest sages...that she might follow that sage's admonishment to keep Torah?"

He opened his eyes and looked up at the magazine that held the many matrices, the metallic letters that would be used to mold the lead sentence slugs. The escapement patiently and obediently waited for him to release the matrices down the channels like quicksilver messengers, as he delicately tapped on the keys. He had already decided to keep the letter short, but was still considering just what to say. He could have written out notes beforehand, but decided to just edit the thing in his head. He knew pretty much what he wanted to say. And he knew that as he typed, the Linotype machine would respond to his every command. Still, as he started, the first sounds of clinks, clicks, and metal-sprocketed chains strangely startled him.

My dear and beloved daughter Naomi,

As I type this on the Linotype machine where we sat together not long ago, you are lying in a coma, after saving the lives of three young children. I can't tell you how full my heart is that you performed such a mitzvah. You obeyed Moshe, who told us to preserve life.

David had used the space band lever for spacing the letters while he pressed the keys that released the letter matrices, and sentences began to appear in the assembler. He had triggered the caster at the end of each line, so that hot lead could be released to create the slugs. Now he paused. The first lines seemed acceptable. If, by God's design, he never got a chance to speak to his oldest daughter again in person, he wanted, if possible, to let her know how proud he was of her before she passed from this world. He took a slow breath and hesitated before finally continuing:

I know you have an inquisitive mind, and have asked many excellent questions worthy of the sages. No one on Earth has the answers to all of those questions. But I want you to always ask them, like our father Abraham did when he stood before HaShem in the matter of his nephew Lot. Yet, as your loving father, whom I'm sure you will outlive by many years, I want you to always remember that the answers are in our Jewish tradition, even as you respect the faith tradition of the other...as I've always taught you. It's true that you may never have your own natural children. But in God's wisdom and God's way, you will carry the legacy of our forefathers into the future, even for your niece and nephew, and many other nameless Jewish children.

He paused. Should he say the one last thing that was on his mind? Yes, and then he would finish.

That legacy includes the words of our great sage Maimonides, who said he believed with perfect faith in the coming of the Messiah...by which he meant our Messiah. By keeping our legacy, you will usher him in.

Your loving Abba

As David Kaplan watched the distribution mechanism return the matrices to the magazine section like soldiers returning to their barracks, he had second thoughts. Perhaps he should similarly return to his imagination what he just wrote, before he ended up arranging the lead sentence slugs on a tray for printing. But instead, he pounded his fist just to the right of the keyboard. *No!* He would prepare the letter, put it an envelope, and wait for the right method and moment to give it to Naomi. Until then, he would visit his daughter and stay devotedly by her side, praying to a compassionate God for her recovery.

CHAPTER FORTY

What color is black? Or is it?

The altered logic in that blurry meditation echoed through the ink-black darkness of a narrow path somewhere in the folds of Naomi's brain. It was dull, circular, perseverating, obsessive. If her "sight" was a formless void, her hearing was anything but. Even after such a concussive explosion, it was miraculously crisp and sharp, and very clear—picking up the random buzz of a monitor, the rhythmic thud of her heartbeat, the amplified whisper of the medical team, led by Dr. Morgenstern.

"We'll have to deal with the cervical plexus in the back of the neck."

"Yes. I see that."

"Fortunately, she covered her face. But…there may still be issues there. Later."

Another voice.

"Like almost everything comes later."

Dr. Morgenstern responded.

"Right. But not the significant brain swelling with a large hematoma, and the attendant cranial blood. But fortunately, no skull fracture."

He continued to diagnose and instruct.

"Amazing, I would say. But of course, we will need to address fractures in C5 and C6."

"Yes."

"Permanent paralysis below that?"

The doctor lowered his voice pensively.

"I wouldn't say categorically. But there's a definite chance."

A third voice.

"And grafts to the significant scalp burns. Right."

"Yes, but later, of course. Prepare the Silvadene cream, and adaptic dressing and gauze. The burn team will evaluate for skin grafting in a few days."

A young ambitious intern chimed in.

"Her face is pretty swollen from the bomb's impact. There could possibly be some significant damage to the facial muscles, don't you think? But it could have been much worse. Still, I hope she wasn't too pretty."

A fourth voice jumped in before Dr. Morgenstern could—this time, a woman's.

"Shh. Don't say that."

"Who's listening?"

"Maybe she is."

"Yeh. Right."

"Well, let's just hope she lives. Okay?"

The intern continued.

"Well, if she *does* live, she may need a wig, what with those scalp burns."

"My, aren't we putting the cart before the horse."

"I'm thinking ahead."

"Well, some people's hair grows back."

Doctor Morgenstern broke in on the banter.

"Increase antibiotic drip, and hope for no pneumonia."

"Of course."

"Continued induced coma with pentobarbital. Keep an eye on the dosage."

"Check."

"All right. We'll keep a very close watch, especially here in ICU for the next forty-eight hours."

"Check."

Check is a funny word, like black. Now I'll really be ugly. Check. Help me, God. Help!

Over the next few hours—or maybe it was days—Naomi sensed the bustling and fiddling of aides and nurses, as they seemed to be applying something wet to her head, and what she supposed was some kind of brace around her neck. She was sleeping when she was taken to radiology for the CT scan. When she finally woke up, her perceptive ears picked up the stray words of a distant conversation.

"Only five minutes. Are you family?"

"Um…family…yes, oh yes. Sure, I'm family. We have plans, she and I…we do."

A familiar man's voice. An unpleasant-feeling one.

"Will she die?"

A "shhh," and the same voice, mumbling.

What color is black again? Blood red? Death, dying? Am I?

The irritating man's voice came close—too close.

"My mother told me to forgive you for visiting that messianic place."

Marvin!

"I said a *Mi-Shebeirach* prayer for you at synagogue. And I told God I would marry you, even if you're crippled and your hair doesn't grow back, and you have to wear a wig like the Chassids. So I…I…hope you will love me now. My mother says we're a match made by HaShem. So… will you marry me and make a kosher home for me? I forgive you for going to that place, and for that goy Darrin, may God forgive him for whatever he did to you. Will you? You don't have to answer now. I mean you can't…yet. But when you can?"

No! No! No! Never! Go away, Marvin! Go away!

"I think you can hear me, and you're saying yes. They say people in comas can hear, and they told me you were comatose right now, which I think means you are in a coma. So you are saying yes? I hope so. I will come back, and maybe you will tell me then."

Never! Leave and never come back! Just…Go! Go!

"Well, I'm leaving now."

Good!

"I'll say hello to my mother."

Don't do me any favors.

"Well, I'm leaving. I'll pray the *Mi-Shebeirach* prayer everyday. And I'll see you soon."

Marvin, I do appreciate the prayer. But I don't know what color black is, and you're the last one I want to tell me. Now go away!

Silence, save hypnotic periodic beeping and clicking. Another man's voice, another *Mi-Shebeirach*.

"*Mi-Shebeirach Avoteynu, Avraham, Yitzchach, v'Ya-akov*…May the One who blessed our ancestors Abraham, Isaac and Jacob, bless and heal the one who is ill…"

"*Abba! Abba! Oh, Abba!*"

"My precious Naomi. My precious daughter."

He was glad she couldn't see the tears streaming from his eyes like water from the rock at Horeb in the Torah. The Linotype legacy letter was hidden in the inner pocket of his black jacket. And it would *remain* hidden—for now.

"Naomi, you have saved the whole world."

I'm confused, Abba. What color is black? And how could I save the world? Maybe it's not you. Maybe it's only your voice telling strange things.

"You saved the lives of those three boys. You have fulfilled the greatest mitzvah, my daughter, whether you saved one of ours, or one of the other's. He who saves one soul, it is as if he has saved the whole world."

Oh, I understand, Abba.

Then David suddenly started to weep in jagged heaves, and began moaning and wailing. She could just feel his folded hands stirring the sheets next to her leg.

Abba. Why are you crying so much? Maybe because you know where I was, at the messianic place?

He repeated the prayer for healing.

"*Mi Shabeirach Avoteynu, Avraham, Yitzchach, v'Ya-akov*…"

Then he arose.

"I'm sorry. I didn't mean to cry."

She could just hear him blowing his nose.

"I will let you rest now. I just…just want to say that…you have to live, Naomi. You have to *live*, and carry on our legacy as a people. I know you can't hear me now, but I will give you a letter when…but that's for another time. I will be back."

She could feel his lips just touch the gauze over her scalp. Then more silence, not even a beep or a click. She lay completely still, listening to her own breathing. She drifted off to a fever sleep without the fever, where distorted reality continued in a dream state, along with comatose perseveration.

Darrin! Is it you? Is that you, Darrin? Yes, There you are, with your wonderful porcelain nose and electric blue eyes, and your shock of yellow straw hair. I love that hair. Can you tell me what color black is? Can you? What color is it? Wait. Don't leave. Kiss me like you did at the Channel Gardens, in the pouring rain, under your big black umbrella. No! Don't! We can't ever marry. You have to go! Leave! Wait! Please! Don't go! Can you tell me what color black is? Don't go! Don't...go!

The real Darrin Brock was at the Manhattan Midtown South Precinct station. He had every intention of visiting Naomi at the Intensive Care Unit of Maimonides Medical Center. He knew she was in an induced coma in guarded condition. But Inspector Ralph Lewis had asked for an immediate meeting with him and Homeland Security agent Lawrence Schmidt. Margaret, dressed in her full police uniform, her blonde hair protruding from her cap, entered Lewis' room—uninvited. But the inspector saw no harm in letting her stay. He didn't offer chairs to any of them, as he normally would. They all stood. Lewis' agitated state was obvious. He began by addressing Schmidt.

"Well, Schmidt, you and I were wrong. And Brock was right. Frankly, Schmidt, it should cost you your job."

Schmidt responded defensively.

"We partner with the NYPD. Remember? What about *your* job? Anyway, everything points to a lone actor. A good kid gone bad. Just influenced by the Internet, from what I understand so far."

Darrin was surprised by Schmidt's confidence. His long-time hunch, which Schmidt still seemed to be ignoring, told him something else.

"That's a little premature, isn't it?"

"That's what they pay me the big bucks for, Brock."

As Margaret grabbed and squeezed Darrin's hand supportively—and sensually—Lewis fired back at Lawrence.

"It looks like someone *else* paid, Larry. Someone by the name of Ms.

Naomi Kaplan."

As soon as Naomi's name was mentioned, Margaret let go of Darrin's hand. He had endeavored not to accuse either Ralph Lewis or Lawrence Schmidt. But he couldn't restrain himself any longer. He turned to Ralph Lewis.

"Thank you for remembering that, Inspector Lewis. I hate to mention it, but if you'd both listened to me, Na…Na…omi…"

His voice cracked and shook as he spoke her name.

"…Kap…plan…wouldn't be…"

The shaking in his voice increased, as his eyes unexpectedly and unprofessionally moistened.

"…hanging on to…to…life right now."

He cleared his throat.

"And I believe…I admit without direct evidence…that there's some kind of connection between those who tried to take my life… the Russians last year, and this year…and Omar's attempt at Sheldon Goldberg's house. Don't ask me why I feel that way. I just do."

This time Inspector Lewis responded, while Margaret put her hand on Darrin's shoulder to comfort him.

"You're crazy, Brock! This was obviously an Islamic radical terrorist act. The kid as much as declared it. The other was clearly a Russian connection related to your prior investigation of the mob boss Prima and the whole Mandy Mendel Diamond District thing that's still being investigated. Maybe I shouldn't have asked you to get involved with Omar Shehadulah in the first place. Then you wouldn't be so mixed up. Do me a favor and let us handle this investigation. You stick with the Russians and the Italians, or what's left of them."

"So that's a demotion, then?"

"I didn't say that, Brock."

"Yeh, well…maybe now is the time for me to *finally* quit and start that children's ministry like I was going to last year when you threw me the bone of visiting the widow Chaya Mendel and her son Natan."

"That was a bone? I thought you loved that little Chassidic kid? You want to quit, quit, damn it! I'm not gonna beg you to stay this time. There's the door!"

He pointed to the closed door, as if no one knew where it was.

Margaret saw where things were going, and spoke up.

"Darrin. Please. You don't want to do that. Let's all just calm down. Inspector, he's just upset about Naomi Kaplan probably being on her deathbed. That's all it is."

Darrin pushed back on her presumption.

"Don't say that, Margaret. She can't die. She can't, and she won't."

Margaret tried to finish any discussion about Naomi by agreeing with Darrin.

"She won't. I'm sure she won't. I bet she even attends our wedding."

Darrin nodded obligingly. Ralph, for his part, wasn't finished with his tirade against Darrin.

"I'll tell you what, Margaret. I'm tired of Darrin's bellyaching. How about if I promote you to his detective position? How about *that*? Then you can be the breadwinner, and he can chase little gang-bangers around, and blow their noses."

Lawrence Schmidt hadn't been paying attention to any of the back-and-forth arguing. Instead, he had been trying to rationalize his strategic failure. And he had come up with nothing. But he felt compelled to say something.

"Look...if we're finished, I've got to get back to my office. But...I will admit this one fell through the proverbial cracks. Okay. It happens. So we learn for the next time. But...we can't use this kind of example to suspect *every* Muslim. And anyway...it could have been much worse."

Darrin shot back.

"No, we can't necessarily profile. For instance, in the case of the missing Mahmoud. And it *would* have been worse, except for...for..."

He found himself unable to repeat Naomi's name again. So he just stood in silence. Ralph Lewis took note. He was beginning to feel regret for losing his temper, and ended up exposing his unguarded heart—which was very unusual for him.

"Look. I got kind of carried away. My reason for calling both of you in was just to debrief with you. But I...I guess I kind of let things get away from me. Larry, just keep in touch about what our team of HS and NYPD guys are seeing forensically. And Darrin, why don't you go visit Naomi Kaplan in the Maimonides ICU? That's all. Would one of you please close the door on the way out?"

Everyone left the room. Margaret began to feel insecurities she was working overtime to hide. She once again took Darrin's hand.

"Are you…I mean, are you okay, darling?"

"I think so. It's not gonna be easy seeing Naomi in her condition, but I think Inspector Lewis is right. They said visitation is restricted to immediate family and clergy right now…and I'm sure law enforcement. I'll probably try to go late this Monday night after work. Why don't you come with me?"

Part of Margaret wanted to go and stand with her intended as he grieved over Naomi's serious condition. Another part of her hesitated, not wanting to watch him crying over someone he had once professed love for. The hesitant part won out.

"Maybe I'll visit her with you in a week or so. Why don't you go without me on Monday?"

"Okay."

Darrin was glad Margaret was there to comfort him. He felt a particular need for her companionship just now. But he was also relieved she decided not to come with him to the Maimonides Medical Center. He knew that feeling had something to do with confusing complications inhabiting his mind and heart, which he was in no condition or mood to try to untangle.

Chapter Forty-One

Black was the night, and black was the day. Naomi was suspended between the two, chilled and shivering. Approaching voices increased in volume like a slow fade-up. Finally, the words of medical authority registered in her semi-conscious mind.

"She's 102.5. Time to watch out for respiratory complications. Increase the antibiotic drip. We'll wait one day and then revisit intubation."

"Very good, Doctor."

Good?

Naomi was swirling and spinning in nauseating rotisserie-like rotations. She could somehow tell she was extremely sick, maybe even dying. If HaShem took her, what color would black be then? Would it be a grey void?

Oh, Abba! Abba! Help, Abba! God, help me! Help me!

After an undetermined period of time, she heard two familiar voices.

"I'm her aunt. Well, technically, I'm not. I'm her friend Marvin's aunt. But to the nursing station, I'm Aunt Ida. How did you get past the border guards? I don't think she has any black relatives."

A short laugh.

"No, I'm not related. But I'm clergy…of sorts. Mahalia Morse. It's a pleasure to meet you. I think she may have mentioned you to me once or twice."

"It looks like we both broke through enemy lines. It's nice to meet you as well. So how do you happen to know the patient?"

"I met her at a synagogue in Midwood. Beth Yeshua."

"Hmm."

Aunt Ida and Mahalia. Mahalia and Aunt Ida. I love you both. I do. I love you, Mahalia Morse. I love you, Aunt Ida. Oh, I love you both. I want to tell you before I die. I know you both love me. I know that now. And I'm so glad you met each other.

Aunt Ida's curiosity prompted a question for Mahalia.

"By any chance, do you happen to know a very handsome Gentile man by the name of Darrin Brock?"

"You mean that fine man she tossed out of her life like he was some lazy good-for-nothing womanizer?"

"Yes. That's the very man...the very man she loved, and dropped because her father had a stroke. Ridiculous! And now he's gonna marry that...well...that police woman. I guess they'll have several Waspy blonde babies."

"It don't make no sense. No sense at *all*. See, I happen to know her father really liked him, and I believe he would've come around to accepting him into the family."

"Oh."

Aunt Ida paused, and then followed up with another question.

"Have you met her father?"

"No, I haven't, Ida. I haven't had the pleasure."

"Oh. Well then, how do you know he liked Darrin Brock? Did she tell you that?"

"Let's say someone whispered it in my ear. May I pray for her?"

"Well, this wouldn't be a clergy visit if you didn't."

"Amen."

Naomi, even in her fevered state, could sense Mahalia coming close to her bruised and swollen forehead. She began to speak almost melodically in some kind of strange foreign language. Naomi could tell that she was somehow crying through the syntax of the unusual words. Of course, Naomi couldn't see Aunt Ida's face registering a question mark about Mahalia's sanity, and then settling for an acceptance of her Christian "holiness" religious fervor. The prayer didn't end up achieving the same immediate results as Abrihet's. The only consequence was a sharp pain in Naomi's heart—or maybe her chest—and a deep cry bypassing her dormant vocal cords.

Darrin! Darrin! What have I done? What have I done! Darrin!

Then there was some nurse-sounding mumbling, after which Aunt Ida spoke first.

"Naomi, you know you have to get better so we can have dinner in the Applebee's in Newark, and I can give you a good talking-to. You can bring some kosher kugel in a napkin. So you get better."

Her voice cracked as she spoke that last sentence. Then Mahalia Morse spoke.

"*When,* not if, you get better, your scalp burns will be all new skin… like you."

What do you mean?

There was no answer. Naomi could tell they were gone. She begged for sleep, and within a minute or two, she got her wish. But it wasn't a restful sleep. It was more like a visit to the spin cycle of a rocking washing machine, which seemed to border eternity in length. She was hot and nauseated, and then cold and sweaty. And it didn't end by itself. It took another visitor to flip the switch. And this time it definitely wasn't family or clergy. This guest wasn't on the hospital's "list." It was after-hours, and the rules were a bit lax at those times. A man's voice woke her from a deep sleep to her usual comatose state.

"Um…Naomi…um…this is Martin Cohen, the dentist. I've come to wish you a…hopefully…a…full recovery. And if you try really hard, and you do get better, you have a free dental check-up waiting for you. I promise you that. And if your teeth are damaged, I have a surgeon friend who does great work."

He hesitated for almost a minute before continuing.

Well, Dr. Cohen, is that all

Finally, he broke his own silence.

"Look, I know you can't hear me. But I have something to say anyway. And I'm glad you're the way you are, because it makes it easier to say it. See…I just lost my wife seven months ago, after a long illness. And…I'm sure you understand. I'm just not ready for another convalescing person, who may or may not…that is, I'm sure you will. But…"

So what happened to bashert? And you kissed me on the mouth, and told me you loved me! What am I? A call girl? I thought you were observant. Some observant!

"…but…I can't. I just can't. So…I wanted to pay my respects…I mean, not that you won't…I mean…recover. But I won't be back again to visit. But later…if…I mean when you are all better, I promise to contact you for the purpose of a free dental appointment…totally free services. I mean, bridges, root canals, even implants, whatever you need after this…this tragedy. It's the least I can do. And any surgery beyond that, I have a friend in the business who I'm sure will be generous as well. I know him, and I'm sure…well, anyway, I know you can't hear what I'm saying, but…goodbye, Naomi, my Yiddish dove. It was such a pleasure knowing you. I thought you were the next wife HaShem had planned for me. But, I'm sure you would understand, my having just lost my late wife. God must have other plans. So…"

His voice lowered.

"I'm sorry. I'm so sorry. I have to leave now. I hope to have the courage to tell you this someday when you can hear me. But…for now, goodbye."

What nerve! I have a perfectly good dentist as it is. And he's very Orthodox, no treif…no pork or seafood ever on his hands, like you probably have, you phony. You entered my life on that train, Martin Cohen DDS, without my asking. And you're leaving me like this, just when I need you most. I'll never forgive you for treating me this way. Never! So why would I ever accept your stupid dental services?

She never would have guessed that someone could get so emotionally worked up while in a coma. And she didn't know whether it was good or bad for her prospects of recovery. But she couldn't help it. Chaya was wrong about him. It was a shame about his late wife. But still, this man was no mensch. Darrin Brock was much more of a mensch than he was. And Darrin wasn't even Jewish! She was glad Martin Cohen was gone. Now she could go back to the spin cycle again.

What color is black? Is it getting blacker? I hope not.

CHAPTER FORTY-TWO

The black of the previous night was gone, and a clear fall Sunday dawned. Of course, Naomi didn't know that, just like she didn't realize that it had been night during Dr. Martin Cohen's visit. During the morning hours, she went in and out of a blurry coma-consciousness. In the morning, Abrihet called David Kaplan to make sure he was doing okay. In the early afternoon, she was on the phone with Javier's mother, updating her by explaining that, from everything she'd heard, Naomi was doing as well as possible.

Javier hadn't been his usual comedian self since the night Naomi shielded him. He didn't have much of an appetite, and spoke little. And he had a hard time getting to sleep and staying asleep. Physically, he checked out fine. But arrangements had already been made for him to get counseling from a child therapist. Abrihet made sure to emphasize to his mother that everything possible was being done for Naomi, including much prayer. She asked if Javier wanted to speak with her, but he told her he didn't want to speak to anyone—at least not yet. Then Abrihet called Jeremy and Joshua's parents. Their father ended up answering. Apparently, the brothers were faring a bit better, since they had each other. In contrast to Javier, they wanted to speak to Abrihet—actually, both of them at once, on the speaker mode of their father's iPhone.

"How is she?"

"Joshua, let me ask!"

"I asked first! Is she walking yet?"

"Can we talk to her? She's probably all worried about us, asking how we are."

Abrihet had determined not to go into great detail about Naomi's condition. She just wanted the boys to know that she was slowly getting better.

"Well, boys, she's still sleeping a lot, but that helps her get better. I'm going over there today, and I'll tell her you're both perfectly fine. She'll be happy to hear that."

"And tell her about Javier too," Jeremy interrupted. "Tell her he's doing well too."

"I will."

"Is he?" Joshua blurted out.

"He is. But, he's having a little problem getting to sleep."

"We're sleeping great! All night!" they spoke over each other.

"That is so good, boys. And I know you'll be praying for Javier. He doesn't have a brother like you boys have, or a father to pray with him."

After the boys agreed to do that, Abrihet said goodbye to them, and then their father. Right after she hung up, she prepared to visit Maimonides Medical Center to see Naomi Kaplan. She had kept in touch with her father David, and she planned to tell her that she was looking in on him and he was doing well. And then she planned to pray with Naomi—at least a short prayer. She prayed all the way on the subway, while leaning on the window with her eyes closed. When she got to the hospital, she remarked to herself that she was as ready as she would ever be to see Naomi and believe for the best for her. But when she arrived at her room in the Intensive Care Unit, and saw Naomi lying unconscious on the bed, with obvious serious injuries to her scalp and torso, doubt throttled her like a strep throat. Her voice quavered and quaked as she spoke close to Naomi's ear, all the while doubting that any of what she said was getting through.

"Naomi, it's me, Abrihet. Um…I've come to tell you your father's doing well. I keep in touch with him several times a day. This morning he told me he visited you. He'll be back again soon. I make sure to ask him if he eats, and takes good care of himself. And I plan to visit him at his house very soon."

May the God of Israel bless you, Abrihet. May He bless you.

"I know the doctors are doing all they can. And soon you'll be as good as new."

She didn't sound as convincing as she wanted to, because she wasn't totally convinced. She didn't know much about Naomi's condition, but she was aware of the swelling of her brain, and the possibility she might have some paralysis. And she knew about the induced coma. Still in doubt's grip, but with faith possibly the size of at least half of a mustard seed, she took a deep breath and began her prayer. She spoke the word she had spoken over David Kaplan, but this time it came out more like a question.

"Yeshua? Yeshua?"

She paused and then repeated it.

"Yeshua? Um…God, I pray you heal my friend Naomi. I pray you hear this prayer, and…do something for her. Please?"

She continued to pray somewhat anemically for another minute, and then held Naomi's hand. Tears filled her eyes, and Naomi could hear her weep.

Don't cry, Abrihet. I don't mind that you said that word that means salvation. And I know you care about me. I wish I could dry your tears. But I can't. I don't know if I'll live or die, but I know I love you. Thank you so much for taking care of Abba. I know you'll watch over him.

Abrihet stayed another few minutes, and then kissed Naomi's forehead like her father had and left. Naomi knew she was alone. But Abrihet had left some kind of sweet blessing behind, despite her timid prayer. Somehow, Naomi could sense that. And the peace associated with the blessing enabled her to fall into a more peaceful sleep than the spin-cycle sleep of the night before.

CHAPTER FORTY-THREE

When Naomi awoke, the perseverating obsession with the color black was gone. Something else replaced it—an infinitely brilliant more-than-white light that filled all of the space around her. This puzzled her, because she somehow knew that her eyes were shut. She spent the next several seconds pondering about the scientific possibility of that, like Moses pondered about the natural impossibility of the burning bush. She was amazed that the light didn't seem like a vision or dream, but was instead very much real and present.

Next, she heard a gentle clinking sound that reminded her of only two other similar sounds—the Linotype machine when the letter matrices hit the bottom of the channels, and an Internet audio clip she had heard of the first-century high priest's bell that apparently fell from his garment hem and was discovered at the Temple site in 2011. As the clinking increased in volume, the light became almost unbearably bright, as if she had opened her eyes in the face of ten suns. But she hadn't. She was so overwhelmed by these "sights" and "sounds" that she barely noticed her medically sedated heart, which had begun to beat furiously.

After what seemed like minutes, but she knew was more like seconds, a figure as white as the light began to emerge. She knew that was also implausible—like the concept of a blank canvas supposedly of a white cow in a blizzard. Just then, the blinding light gave way to a shape. But it wasn't a white cow. It was some sort of human, with arms she could just make out. They were also brilliantly lighted, but not as brilliantly as the face that emerged, with curly hair that seemed to be on fire, and a small beard that she could tell should be brown, although it was too bright for her to be sure. Then the being began to open eyes that had been shut, and her heart beat even faster.

Oh no. He's going to look at me!

He focused right on her and almost through her, even though her eyes were in reality—if such a thing as reality still existed—still shut. His eyes were dizzyingly three dimensional, and the depth was all love. She didn't know what to say in the face of a being such as this. But she thought she'd better be polite.

Um...can I help you, sir?

A male voice that she could only describe as a combination of every voice of every tender man she'd ever been exposed to in her life—from Fred Rogers, to David Kaplan, to Darrin Brock—spoke from the center of the whiter-than-white light.

"Your sins are forgiven."

She could only surmise that she had been caught. Someone from Heaven had taken note.

Um...I'm so sorry. But Dr. Cohen kissed me first. Still, I admit I enjoyed it. So I apologize for that...

"Naomi..."

When the voice spoke her name for the first time, she felt totally seen through, completely transparent, fully known. And for the first time since the visit began, she was convinced who it was, although she had been doing her best to deny it until then. He continued.

"Let me show you something."

He lifted his right arm until she could see the inapproachable light through an undeniable hole in His wrist.

"What does that say to you, Naomi?"

Um...since you asked, Saint Patrick's Cathedral is the first thing that comes to mind. They've got a lot of crucifixes there, you should excuse the expression. But isn't it in the hands, not the wrists? Not that I've ever paid much attention. Anyway, that's what it reminds me of.

Just then, when she half-expected Him to get angry at her response, she detected a pure and innocent grin.

"That was not the intention of the God of Israel, Naomi…or the former slave Patrick, for that matter. I desire that it say 'gift' to you."

By this time, His eyes told her she was in the presence of some sort of pure holiness…HaShem's holiness. And she began to do more listening than speaking.

Oh.

"The gift of forgiveness. And the kind of gift you can give others, Naomi. Like Joseph did his brothers."

Oh.

"For example, Martin Cohen."

She thought He meant for kissing her. Forgiveness for that didn't seem like a great stretch to accomplish. But He read her thoughts.

"No, Naomi. Not for that. For rejecting you…last night."

Her unforgiving heart played back to her like film in reverse, along with the words, *I'll never forgive you.*

Oh, I see. I…I…forgive him. I totally forgive him. I do. I do.

"And what about Marvin?"

Um…you mean…I have to…marry him?

"No. I mean, what about forgiving him for not taking no for an answer?"

Oh, I do…I mean, I do forgive him. I know it's hard for him to let go.

"See? When you're forgiven, it's easier to forgive. And your sins are forgiven, Naomi."

The words began to sink deeply into the very depths of her being, to such an extent that she found she had the courage to ask the hardest question of all.

Um…are You…are You…the word…Abrihet spoke?

"I am."

Oh. Yeshua, then?

"Yes. My name."

She knew He was alluding to her father's idea of the word as a salvation concept only. She wanted so much to ask Him more about David Kaplan, the greatest Jew who had ever lived…until just now. But before she could speak her thoughts, He broke in.

"Naomi. I love you."

With those words, her heart totally melted, like the wax candles on the Kiev menorah in the little Brooklyn home she shared with her father. From all she could tell in her comatose state, her closed eyes began to water, and salty tears streamed down her face. Time stood still, as she wept. But she realized they were tears of joy. The silence continued. Perhaps He had left.

I…I think I'm crying. Are You…are You still there? Did You leave me? Please don't leave me.

"I'm here. I'll always be here, even when I'm not visiting you like this. Do you understand?"

Sort of. I think I do.

She didn't have any theological basis for it within her deep One God Jewish conviction, but somehow she knew that he was He. But she didn't feel the need to ask about something that was so obvious to her now. She hesitated, and then laughed to herself as she addressed Him by name for the very first time.

Yeshua, I love Your words in that sermon on that mountain, that… that…my…my…friend…a friend of mine…hey, I never thought I'd get a chance to tell You how much I liked it in person. I told my father I did. But not You. Anyway, that my friend…Darrin read to me. You know. Darrin? Darrin Brock? Oh, what's the use? You already know him, and how much I love him. But he's gone. He's found someone else, someone who loves him. So I'm not going to ask…anyway, maybe I could ask You something else, if You don't mind. Could You heal me like…You…I mean, I realize it was You…healed my father? Maybe?

"That will come along with another gift. I'm going to leave you now. But I'm not really leaving. My Spirit will remain. Be strong, Naomi. And trust in me. Everything will work out."

I will. I will. I love You. I love You. I…I…don't mean as…as…the other. No. You're…You're one of us. I see that now.

She smiled to herself, although her comatose lips remained unchanged.

And I guess also…I'm one of Yours.

All at once, His face drew closer and closer, increasingly covered by a newly formed shadow as it did. He reached all the way to her upper forehead and kissed it on the bandage exactly where her father had. Then He withdrew into the light, which quickly diminished as if it had been swallowed up by a black hole. And the pitch black returned. But she didn't ask what color it was. It didn't matter any more.

CHAPTER FORTY-FOUR

Darrin Brock was on the line with the Maimonides Medical Center patient information center at just about the same time a nurse came into Naomi's room—which in turn was right after her Divine Visitor left, taking the brilliant light with Him. However, the nurse wouldn't have noticed that. What she *did* end up noticing were Naomi's vital signs, which were at least somewhat improved over the morning readings. She was able to contact the doctor right away, who, among other things, upgraded Naomi's visiting status to include close friends—although the five-minute time restriction remained. So when Darrin asked about visiting that night, he was given a clearly affirmative answer. All afternoon, he tried to prepare himself for what he would see. Naomi had appeared on the verge of death when he called 911 at the Goldberg's house. He was aware that she'd improved. But he understood that she was still in danger, and he knew she was still in an induced coma. Just that fact alone broke his heart. Watching her in that state would be extremely painful for him. But she had visited him when he was in a coma the year before. So he could do no less for her. Of course, unlike those visits, he would avoid any reading of Scripture, discussion of God, or prayer. After all, she had ended her relationship with him as a result of her father's stroke—and her conviction that by going with Darrin, she had broken his observant Jewish heart.

After work, he decided to take the cruiser to the hospital. As he got out of his car to walk toward the massive complex, he realized that he probably looked like any other visitor, although perhaps a visitor on official business. He always felt that way because, as a detective, he usually *was* on official business. But he knew his business in this case was also personal, more personal than even he wanted to admit. For that reason, to try to remain in his professional role, he would visit her for only the allotted five minutes, and then head home to a waiting dinner with his parents Lester and Velma in Teaneck. At least he would be safer driving home in the cruiser late at night than if he was in an unmarked car—considering the dangers that remained. It was sort of like having Margaret as a police escort without Margaret having to be there. He followed the familiar signs to the Intensive Care Unit, room five. When he arrived, a nurse met him at the door.

"How is she?"

"And you are?"

He pulled his police rank strategy to get the information he wanted.

"Detective Darrin Brock, NYPD. I was part of the life-saving team."

With that information, the nurse could disclose information.

"I see. Well, believe it or not, she's doing a little better than this morning. The doctor says if things continue like this, she won't have to be intubated again, which is good news. And a recent CT scan shows that the cranial blood is definitely being absorbed...slowly. Also, any kind of permanent paralysis is out of the question now. That is very good news as well. But the doctors feel she's by no means out of the woods. So we're asking for just five-minute visits. Okay?"

"Yes, of course."

"You may go in. She's not able to respond, as she's still in an induced coma. That's a good thing at this point. She needs rest."

"I understand."

Darrin walked slowly into the room. Immediately, he could sense the presence of something, and that something felt positive. At least that was a good sign. He walked up to Naomi, and almost had to look away. Her eyes seemed sunken and swollen at the same time. Her breathing wasn't exactly labored, but it wasn't steady either. The bandages on her scalp were thin enough to reveal what looked like burned flesh and missing hair underneath. And of course she was catheterized, with the bag of urine at Darrin's side of the bed. One arm and one leg were in a full cast, and he knew there was a question about her future walking ability. But the nurse had told him there was some improvement since that morning, and visitation had been widened. All of these were hopeful signs. In spite of her appearance, his love for her was as great as ever—even greater now that he saw her in this helpless state. And then there was that presence. He knew he had just a few minutes. So he might as well let her know he was there. He spoke in a low tone, almost afraid in some irrational way that he would wake her up.

"Naomi? Naomi Kaplan? This is your old...old friend Darrin, just coming to see you for a few minutes. Um...they're only giving me a few minutes."

Darrin! Darrin! You're really here! Wait. Don't leave! Darrin!

"I just want to tell you that...everyone's pitching for you. Um... Chaya Mendel told me to say hello. What with all of those children of hers, she can't get over here just yet. But she told me she's saying prayers for you. Well...I don't know what more to...to...say...I..."

She thought she could hear him beginning to cry. He sniffled.

"Oh, brother."

Then he sighed deeply and paused before ending his very short visit.

"Listen. I'm gonna leave now."

No Darrin. No! I saw Him! I saw Him, Darrin! Don't leave. He talked to me, right to me! Please don't go! Please! Move, stupid body! Don't let him leave. You useless, worthless body! Help me, God! Yeshua! Help! Help!

Darrin arose from a bowing position and looked intently at Naomi's face.

"Lord, the nurse said Naomi isn't out of the woods. Please, will you bring her through this? Please?"

Her sunken swollen eyes and unsteady breathing seemed to weigh his prayers down and drag them from the ceiling to the floor. A doubting dire expectation mingled with his aching heart, as he spoke directly to her.

"I know you can't hear me, so...before I leave...maybe for the last time, if you don't make it...which some people wonder if you will...I'll just tell you that...I love you deeply...and *madly*, Naomi Kaplan. I know

I will learn to love Margaret, and be a dutiful husband. But learning came easy with you, Naomi. And I so wish things had turned out differently. But they didn't. Still, the truth I will *never* share with anyone ever again is that as of right now, *you* are the love of my life. I know that's wrong, what with my engagement. But I believe God will forgive me, and I'll move on. And I do respect your wishes, as a traditional Jew, and your love for your father. But still, right now, it hurts deep inside me. That's why I have to leave now and not come back. But I just had to say it...."

Just then, the dam broke loose. He began to weep, and fell to his knees. Then he began to pound the side of the bed.

"God, help me! Help me! Help me not to feel this way!"

The nurse came rushing in.

"Sir, I'm sure you're concerned for her. But perhaps you should go somewhere and compose yourself."

He stood up and sighed deeply.

Don't make him leave, stupid nurse! Please, don't!

"I'm sorry. I'll be alright now. Please just give me thirty seconds, and I'll leave."

"Okay. But she needs rest, not agitation. Do you understand?"

"I understand."

Body, if you don't do something now...anything...he will leave and I'll never see him again. It's now or never!

Darrin took one last long look. He turned around to leave, intentionally keeping her in the corner of his eye. Just then, he thought he saw her left eye twitch slightly. But like an imaginary wink from a master's portrait painting, he paid no attention to it. Then, almost imperceptibly, the other eye seemed to twitch. That was enough to encourage him to turn toward Naomi, and then to come close to her.

"Naomi? Naomi?"

She finally worked up enough strength to raise both eyebrows slightly.

"Naomi!"

The mouth was next. She had to tell him what happened to her.

That was harder. She hadn't said a word since the explosion, and she was highly medicated. But Darrin made things easier. He turned around to make sure no one was watching, and then came close and put his lips against hers. He kissed her full and deep, his tears softening both of their lips in the process. That did it. The induced coma didn't have a chance. One of her eyes fluttered open, and then the other. He felt them with his eyelashes, and pulled back.

"You're awake! They'll kill me! They want your brain to rest."

Her tongue wasn't exactly loosed, but it did start to wiggle a bit against her teeth. And she had her breath.

"Yesh…I…Ye…shu…"

"I know. I'm sorry. I should never have read those things to you. We come from different backgrounds, and I'm so sorry about all you've been through with your father. At least he's better."

"N…n…n…o…n…o"

"You were right. It's best the way it is. I will marry Margaret. She's a… good woman. You will find the right one for you. Now you should rest that pretty brain of yours. Doctor's orders. And I'll be going."

"St…st…"

"St…what?"

Suddenly, her tongue was loosed.

"Stop. Stop, Darrin. You're…you're…being…an…an…*ass*!"

He couldn't help but giggle.

"What?"

"St…st…op and listen. I saw…I saw…"

"You saw what?"

"I saw *Him*."

"You saw who?"

"*Yeshua*, you goose. I saw Him. He talked to me. It's true! It's all true! And…and…"

She ran out of breath and closed her eyes. She had to rest a minute. It was all too exhausting for her. He thought perhaps she was sinking back into a coma, just as she was getting to what sounded like the good part.

"Naomi? Are you…still conscious?"

She popped her eyes open.

"Of course, you idiot!"

He didn't realize that the name calling was at least partly the result of impulsivity related to her quickly healing brain injury, and partly the result of overwhelming joy.

"He's wonderful! And He told me my healing would come with a gift. And you know what? I realize now that…*you're* the gift!"

"But…"

Her neurologically impulsive behavior was beginning to work in her favor.

"I heard everything you said, Darrin. *Everything.* You have a pretty big mouth. I'm the love of your life. You love me madly and deeply, and so much it hurts deep inside. Every word. So I'm here to heal your pain, like you're here to heal mine. And Yeshua is here to heal us both. So…"

His eyes widened. He could hardly believe what he was hearing. Still, wasn't this too good? Didn't he have to think like a responsible adult—responsible to others beyond himself?

"But what about everyone else, Naomi? We have to take other people into account. We can't just think of ourselves."

She was getting bolder, as her voice got stronger.

"Yes, Darrin Brock. But you know what? In this case I think we *can.* And like *who*, Darrin? *Who* do we have to think about? God will take care of my father. He always has. I was so stupid not to see that. And He'll take care of Margaret. She'll marry someone who *really* loves her. So…"

"So?"

She had been gaining strength by the second. Now she pulled herself up, to such an extent that the buzzer went off and the nurse headed toward her room. She had limited time.

"So…marry me! *Marry me*, Darrin Brock, and love me like Yeshua does. You are also the love of *my* life, you know. Don't forget about me!"

He began by kissing her upper forehead where the bandage covered her scalp—right where her father and Yeshua had kissed her. And just as he returned to her mouth, the nurse arrived. She pulled him off her with the strength of a trained health worker.

"Just *what* are you intending to do to her, sir? I'm going to call security *right now*!"

"I'm going to marry her. That's what I'm going to do."

Just as the nurse reached for the call button, Naomi shocked her to her toes with her own one-word answer.

"Yep."

CHAPTER FORTY-FIVE

Lawrence Schmidt was standing before his small team of investigators in an undisclosed location on the third floor of one of the more generic office buildings that dot Midtown Manhattan. Like a stoplight, his face had been turning periodically red as he lectured and lambasted. His audience, on the other hand, was exhibiting various expressions of uncomfortable body language, from the head-in-hand kind to the pencil-eraser-chewing variety. He was presently back in the crescendo side of his performance.

"The only reason heads aren't rolling here is because mine is the one on the chopping block. Among other skilled personnel, I rely on *you* to provide me with up-to-date human and electronic intel so that I can give my best assessment to the NYPD, the FBI, the CIA, and every other bureaucratic behemoth that depends on HS. And guess what?"

His face reddened more.

"You've failed! You've all failed! You've failed yourselves, me, and all of New York! Not to mention our whole nation! You all better be thankful this idiot blew himself up in some rabbi's two-bit Brooklyn brownstone instead of a crowded Manhattan landmark...and that the bomb he had strapped to him pretty much...well, bombed. What in this *insane* world happened that you missed this? All I can tell you is you'd better find out, so it never happens again. And I want to know *who* he answered to, if anyone. We should have uncovered any information a long time ago, including the lone wolf kind. Instead, we interrogated him *ten* times, and…nothing! I walked into some of those with information *you* provided. And now I've got morons investigating *me* for incompetence! Unbelievable!"

A skinny, curly-headed, eager young agent sitting right in front of Schmidt had been waiting for just this moment. He was a high-tech security expert whose gift had yet to shine. But it was about to. He had dedicated hundreds of hours since the explosion, and this was the time to reveal what he'd found to his only partially aware fellow agents. He had held back key findings until now, which he wouldn't have done if he thought present danger was still imminent. But the time was now ripe. He raised his hand halfway up, as if he were concerned it might be shot down if it rose any higher—which often happened, since he usually asked more questions than the others. Schmidt took note of the hand.

"What is it, Kress? Make it quick. I'm not finished."

"Sir…um…I've been working on something for the last few weeks, and…"

"Yes? Yes?"

"Well…I've been doing some detailed forensics on Shehadulah's phone, and…and…I've been analyzing it. I've detected something quite surprising."

He paused theatrically, as he knew he had everyone's attention—especially Lawrence Schmidt's. Then he continued.

"It seems that the phone has been the recipient of what could only have been very sophisticated Russian technology."

Schmidt couldn't help but interject.

"Russian!"

"Yes, sir. It seems, if I have diagnosed things properly, that they have targeted his phone for hacks even more sophisticated than the ones we've been familiar with. In fact, it's been challenging keeping up with them. But this is what I've uncovered."

"Go on. Go on, Kress. And don't take so long."

"Well…They seem to have been able to break into his apparently highly secure phone, *real time*. The only way I can describe it is by referencing those old 1950's sci-fi movies where the aliens break into TV signals in the middle of broadcasts to speak to viewers. So…the point is, they seem to have been able to break into his phone usage at any time to give him direction, threaten him…and also listen to his calls, including those he talked to. And of course, they could text him at any time, and view all of his texts."

"Are you sure?"

"Yes, I'm sure," he shot back confidently. "Here's an apparently old text I've intercepted, from maybe a few months ago…or more. 'Forget the Flatiron Building.'"

"The Flatiron Building! Sorry. Go on."

"'Go only where we tell you to go. Follow Brock when we tell you to.'"

"'Brock!'"

Schmidt couldn't help but recall Darrin Brock's warnings, not only about Omar himself, but also about Russian involvement in this whole mess. It only served to sour his mood further.

"Why are you stalling, Kress? Continue!"

"Because you keep…never mind. 'You'll never live to honor Allah with any infidel deaths if you don't do exactly what we tell you to. If you don't, we'll just kill you now before you kill anyone.'"

He paused again.

"And?"

"Here's another one. 'We have Mahmoud's body, who you murdered. It is preserved for evidence. We will make sure you go to American jail for life, like Khalid Sheikh Mohammed. At the next corner, get in car! We will hide you. Then you kill Darrin Brock for us. This time you succeed. Next corner!'"

"Well, that answers that mystery. I guess that Stanley fellow will want to know that."

"Well, I don't know who Stanley is, or who Mahmoud is…or was. But…that's it. I'm working on other texts, and even possibly some voicemails. The other live voice transmissions are gone, of course. We do also have records of calls from Pakistan, but no content."

"Hmm."

A fellow agent jumped in.

"You know, we could help you, if you'd just communicate with us."

Bill Kress nodded.

"Either way, I'm sure there are promotions for all of us, including you, Mr. Schmidt."

Lawrence Schmidt barked back.

"Oh, shut up! I'm not thinking of that right now. Unbelievable! The Russians seem to be using him to shield their identity, like a parasite uses a host. We're nowhere near done with this. But…good job, Kress. Listen to me. Follow the Pakistan lead, and keep working on the phone forensics. I'll get hold of Ralph Lewis and the NYPD…and this guy Brock, of course. And…work together to get this done quickly, before the Russians do something else…let alone Shehadulah's Muslim radical contacts in Pakistan. *Unbelievable*."

As the meeting drew to a close, an oblivious Darrin Brock was driving back to his parents' Lester and Velma's house in Teaneck, New Jersey. He crossed the George Washington Bridge and entered the State of New Jersey. He was in a particularly positive mood—more positive than he had been since before Naomi broke up with him months earlier. And he was looking forward to sharing some very good news with his parents.

When he finally entered the house on West Forest Avenue, there were Lester and Velma, waiting for him in their living room chairs. Velma seemed to take less notice of him than ever. She stared straight forward, and he had a harder time thinking he detected any visual or cerebral response. Perhaps he had been kidding himself about her attentiveness over the last year. But now he couldn't kid himself any longer. Lester smiled from his chair. He didn't get up.

"How are you, son?"

Darrin smiled broadly.

"Dad, I can't tell you how well I'm doing! A miracle has occurred with Naomi, like the miracle you witnessed with me last year. She woke up even from an induced coma, and she's getting better even as we speak. I'm sorry I haven't told you before, but I've been so busy. I'm in love with her, Dad. And she is in love with me. We're going to get married."

"And her faith? And her father's faith?"

Darrin did something he rarely did. He got down on his knees in front of his father's chair and took his right hand. Tears filled his eyes.

"Dad. You won't believe it. Naomi saw a vision…no, that's wrong. It wasn't a vision. Jesus visited her. He spoke to her, Dad. She responded. And now He's healed her. Or He's healing her."

Lester nodded.

"I knew such a thing might occur, but maybe not this soon. I've always seen something in Naomi's heart…an open heart for the Father, like her heart for her own father. I'm thankful for that. I'm thankful for her. I'm thankful for you. But…"

Darrin could see a shadow pass over his father's face. He knew there was something concerning him.

"What is it?"

"Well, what about Margaret? Have you told her?"

"Well…not yet. I'm not quite sure how to do that."

"Hmm. Well…do it wisely. You mean so much to her. Perhaps too much. She is not mature in her faith. And her heart is vulnerable. Do it wisely. But do it, and do it soon. Don't delay, son. Don't let her hear it from someone else."

Darrin appreciated these admonitions from his father. He wished his mother could weigh in. But now he couldn't even look for a visual assent. He knew Lester was right, and he was just about to respond in agreement when his phone vibrated. He didn't want to answer it, but something told him he should at least look at the phone. He reached into his light fall jacket pocket and took it out. It was Inspector Ralph Lewis.

"Yes, Inspector?"

"Get in here now, Brock. It's important."

"But I'm in Teaneck with my parents, and we haven't eaten."

"So eat fast and then come in, say within the hour. And watch yourself. Keep an eye out for anyone tailing you. I'll fill you in when you get here."

"Okay."

Darrin put the phone in his pocket and turned to his father.

"I'll help you get Mom to the table for dinner. I guess it's about done? I can smell it. It smells good."

"Yes, we're about ready. It's in the oven."

"Right. I have to eat quickly and then go in to the office. I don't know what it's about. But Inspector Lewis wants to see me."

Lester got up, and together they assisted with Velma. Darrin could tell she wasn't helping as much as she had been. But he thought he detected at least some cooperation as they each took a side.

CHAPTER FORTY-SIX

Darrin's detective's instincts had slowly begun to resharpen since the turn-around with Naomi. He recognized that a certain passive sloppiness had crept into his work over the last several months, resulting in a diminishing of his well-trained observant eye. Along with that realization came a sudden remorse for his entire life-attitude since the break-up. His conscience was roused from its dormant state, as if a numbing anesthetic had worn off. He was ashamed and embarrassed. His father had warned him about this pouting schoolboy response to something he couldn't obtain, but he hadn't listened to him. Now that the most important treasure in his life—next to God—had been returned to him, he was face to face with his immaturity—an immaturity that had actually existed through his entire adolescent and adult years. As he drove out of the Lincoln Tunnel and into Manhattan, that reality began to hit him as well. Perhaps it was even the reason for the fact that he had never found a healthy dating relationship with the opposite sex during his Christian high school and criminal justice college years—let alone a spouse. Why hadn't he addressed these issues earlier? He found himself confessing out loud to God, as he drove toward the Midtown South Precinct station on 35th Street.

"Please oh...I'm so sorry...I've been a jackass, God. A total jerk. A spoiled brat. I don't deserve Naomi. How can I be the husband she needs me to be, when I acted like such an idiot? And…oh, my goodness! I've also sinned against Margaret. She may have come off desperate and strong, but I've caused her to stumble by encouraging her when I *knew* I wasn't helping her. I was *hurting* her, and her newfound relationship with God. What's the matter with me? Please…forgive me!"

As he confessed, his eyes continued to sharpen, and the mist of oblivious inattentiveness cleared further. He suddenly became aware that he was being tailed by a black late model Honda Accord as he drove up Ninth Avenue in the late evening illumination of streetlights and headlights. His heart began to thump in his chest. Would shots rip through his body next, as they did the previous year? He chose his secure cell phone over the police radio, and dialed headquarters. Of all people, Margaret answered.

"Margaret, listen to me. I'm almost at the station. I'm being tailed, maybe by Russians. Tell Inspector Lewis to post an armed detail outside, near my parking space and up to the building."

"Oh…oh…okay. Be careful."

Margaret was obviously flustered. She didn't want to lose someone she didn't realize she'd already lost. While talking to her, Darrin had been glancing in the rear view mirror, watching the man in the front passenger seat of the tailing car. He was listening on his own cell phone, and then—right after Darrin stopped talking to Margaret—the man turned to the driver, and then back again. Could he actually be listening to Darrin? How could that be possible? The Honda took a sudden turn onto 33rd Street, and was gone. Darrin took a deep breath, and finally arrived at the precinct station. As soon as he got out of the car, four policemen surrounded him, guns drawn, and escorted him into the building. When he got to the second floor, Lawrence Schmidt and Ralph Lewis were waiting for him. Lewis was leaning back in his swivel chair with his feet up on his desk, and Schmidt was sitting on the front of the same desk with his feet dangling over the side. Lewis motioned for Darrin to sit a foot or so from Schmidt in his usual lower seat, with Lawrence towering over him. The only consolation was that Margaret wasn't in the room.

"Larry, tell him what you've found."

Schmidt proceeded to tell Darrin about the discovery of Russian texts on Omar's cell phone, as well as evidence of them breaking into the phone's voice signal. After he finished, Darrin realized why he was in the low seat, with Ralph Lewis' feet up on the desk and Lawrence Schmidt sitting there towering over him. The configuration minimized the chances of him saying "I *told* you." But he didn't have to. He had other possible evidence to discuss.

"Hmm. I was watching the tail car in the rear view mirror when I called in, and I swore the guy riding shotgun was listening to me on his phone. At least it seemed that way."

Schmidt jumped off the desk and almost stepped on Darrin's toes. He walked behind the desk and stood next to Lewis with an air of investigatory confidence.

"With what we now know, that could very well be. We'll look into it. Ralph. Put a protective detail on Brock…a serious one."

Lewis leaned forward and looked up at Schmidt with even greater confidence.

"You don't have to tell me that. We know what we're doing here."

Darrin wasn't finished. He was back in action as a detective, and his tone of authority even exceeded theirs.

"Also, after they took shots at me at the Mendel house, two men dressed as Chassids ransacked the upstairs master bedroom. We need to find out who they are."

The inspector jumped in immediately.

"We will. We will. You just do what we tell you, so you don't get killed. Stay with the detail. Don't go to the *bathroom* without them. Now get out of here. I gotta get some sleep."

That ended the meeting, Two police cars escorted Darrin to Teaneck, with sirens off. They returned in the morning to escort him to work. And from there, they escorted him to the Maimonides Medical Center to visit Naomi. He parked in a handicap space, with two cop cars following him there, and then they walked him to the main entrance. He wanted to tell them that wasn't necessary, but Inspector Lewis had told him to cooperate with the program for his own safety. Besides, he was too busy preparing his heart for the visit with Naomi to complain. Fortunately, they didn't follow him up the elevator and into the Intensive Care Unit. He prayed under his breath the whole time. When he entered the room, she was sitting up in her bed, with fewer bandages covering her scalp and a healthy rosy color in her cheeks. She responded to his surprise entrance with a broad sunny smile.

"Darrin! I get my own room today, and I may get released in the next few days. I told them...my heart, and everything else is...is..."

He prepared to hear a new diagnosis. Fibrillation? Infection from her skin grafts, to which calcium alginate dressing had recently been applied to promote healing?

"...is...so...*full*."

Large round tears spilled from her eyes, down her cheeks, and onto her neck brace, like the overflow of King David's cup that *runneth over*.

"I love you so much. And I love...you know..."

She mouthed the next word without any sound at all—not even a breath. He began his response with carefully rehearsed words.

"Naomi...Naomi...I understand more about God's love today than I did last year. Since then, He has helped me to see just how ungrateful I could be...how childish and selfish. I'm ready to love a woman now more selflessly than I could last year. I'm ready to love *you*. I know it sounds like I'm reciting my wedding vows before the wedding. But..."

"Darrin, I never saw a man as selfless as you were last year. That's the man I fell in love with at first sight, when you made that long line of returns customers at Macy's wait while I went to the bathroom."

Her face lit up fully as she giggled like a little girl.

"I guess if I was catheterized then like I was yesterday, we wouldn't be in love today."

She giggled again, and he joined her. Then he responded to her mouthed word. He knew she was concerned with keeping her secret from her father, even if he was nowhere near enough to the hospital to hear her pronounce the name *Yeshua*.

"Naomi. My heart is full too. It seems like God is watching over us, and has some wonderful plans for us. I believe those plans include the deep love for Israel the land, and Israel the people, that we both have. But I also know how deeply you love your father, and how hurt he will be when he finds out that you...well, that you...you know...believe. But... well, my guess is that you haven't told him. We both know you need to. Somehow, some way, he needs to know before he hears it from someone else."

Naomi paused. Then she nodded.

"I know. I know. I think maybe I want you with me. Maybe. Darrin, can I ask you something?"

He nodded as he dabbed her cheeks with a tissue.

"I was just wondering. Did you tell Margaret yet?"

"No. I...I...but...there's something else. I don't want you to worry, but...things aren't over with me."

She pulled his hand away from her cheek and sat up straighter.

"What do you mean, it's not over? Are you giving me a reason to be jealous? Please don't tell me you're still...still in love with..."

He cupped her cheeks with his hands.

"No. No. I mean, I'm being followed by Russians. It's not over with *them*. We've discovered a number of things, including...believe it or not...Russian connections with Omar. We need to crack this thing once and for all so we can both be safe. I've been so busy with that, I haven't had time to talk to Margaret yet. But I will. I will."

He saw the worried look in her eyes, and sought to comfort her.

"God will protect us. He will."

His face drew near hers as he sat on the bed, and their lips touched. Then he pressed them to his, and gave her the longest and most passionate kiss yet, purging both of their lips of any leftover memory of Margaret and Dr. Martin Cohen.

All she could say when he finished was, "Mmm...I'm home." He had no idea how she had strayed from that "home" with Martin Cohen DDS—and he didn't need to know. He stayed another half hour. They didn't kiss again, but his right held her left hand like teenagers on their first date. And then he left to go into work, followed by the detail that was waiting at the main entrance to take him to his car. Not two minutes after he left, her sister Lisa walked in with Lindsey and Noah. She was smiling wryly, and Noah revealed the reason, accompanied by a few short jumps.

"We just saw Darrin in the hall!"

Lindsey played it down.

"So?"

Lisa raised her eyebrows.

"Wow! I heard you were doing better, but you *really* look good, much better than the last time I was here…what, a few days ago? You're awake, and sitting up. And see? They even let the kids visit. And…was he just visiting you? He was, wasn't he? What was that about?"

Naomi rolled her drying eyes benignly.

"Questions, questions, questions."

"You're back together again!"

"What do you think? Anyway, you were right months ago. And we're more in love than ever."

"I told you! I'm so happy for you! And Margaret?"

Lindsey and Noah were listening carefully. Noah wasn't even fidgeting. Naomi looked their way.

"Lindsey, Noah, can you keep a secret?"

Noah answered right away.

"No. Not really."

Lindsey poked her brother's shoulder.

"Shut up! Yes, we can."

Noah got the point of the poke.

"Okay. Okay."

For some reason, Naomi was in the secret-revealing mood. Maybe it was related to her healing brain. Perhaps something within its recovering grey folds itched, and needed one or more secret-revealing scratches. Or maybe it was just concussive impulsivity—the kind that likes to blurt out, *did you hear?* Whatever it was, she chose to trust Lindsey and Noah's word. After all, they were getting older every day.

"Well, he hasn't told Margaret it's over yet. But he will, and soon."

Lindsey expressed tragic romantic empathy on Margaret's behalf.

"That's so sad."

Lisa chose Lindsey's response as a teachable moment.

"Well, honey, sometimes what hurts at first is for the best later. When you grow up, there may be times you'll have to end a relationship, or maybe the boy will have to. If it's not the right one, it's better for it to end sooner rather than later…that is, after marriage."

Noah had a less teachable response.

"I'm glad Darrin is ditching her. Too much blonde hair between them."

Naomi shook her head and smiled.

"I don't know what that's supposed to mean, Noah. Just don't say anything to anyone until Darrin tells her. Okay?"

He nodded. Lisa refocused on Darrin.

"So…what about Darrin's faith? Not that I'm suggesting you don't see him, or anything. You *know* I was never for that, Naomi. I told you not to break up with him, and you didn't listen to me. But I'm just curious how you plan to deal with that. After all, you were so concerned about Dad's stroke having something to do with it. Not that it did. But you got it into your head that it did."

Naomi's brain folds were still itching, and in need of a good scratch.

"Well…can you all keep another secret? And *really* keep this one?"

Noah acted exasperated.

"Oh, no. Not another one."

"Promise?"

Lindsey and Noah responded at once.

"Promise."

"Lisa?"

"Of course."

Naomi lowered her voice, although not as low as she had with Darrin.

"Well…I had an experience while I was in the coma."

Lisa's interest was piqued.

"What kind of experience?"

"I…I…"

She got quieter.

"I saw Him. He talked to me."

"Who talked to you?"

"I can't bring myself to say His English name. Only His Hebrew one. But it was Him. And he told me my…my sins were forgiven."

"What! You're crazy. You're talking about Jesus…Jesus Christ, for God's sake!"

"Well…if you put it that way…"

"It was the medication…your hidden love for Darrin…dead brain cells. Sorry, but…"

Noah's interest was piqued too.

"Naomi's a Jew for Jesus! Can I tell Grandpa?"

Now it was Naomi and Lisa who responded at once.

"No!"

Lindsey was visibly disturbed.

"That's creepy, Aunt Naomi. Like a visitor from beyond the grave in a horror movie. I don't *want* to tell anyone. I don't want any of my friends to know."

Naomi had always loved her niece. But now she looked at her with a new level of compassion.

"I understand how you feel, Lindsey. But I don't feel creepy. I don't. I feel love. The God of Israel kind of love. I think you'll understand a little more later."

Lisa jumped in, trying not to sound defensive. She didn't want to be argumentative with her recovering sister. She intentionally chose a smile.

"No offense, Naomi, but please don't preach to my children. Remember, they're Jewish."

"I wasn't, really…and I *know* that. I'm Jewish too. But I understand how you feel. I was only trying to comfort Lindsey."

Lisa took a deep breath.

"It's okay, Naomi. You're getting better. That's what counts. And I'm still all for Darrin. When you're *all* better, maybe you'll see this in a different light, a clearer light, the light Dad taught you about. And you'll be the same Orthodox sister this Reform girl knows and loves. And I *do* love you."

Naomi wasn't in the mood to argue either.

"Of course I'll still be Orthodox. And I love you too."

"Well, we should go now so you can get some rest. Not a word, kids. Right?"

"Right," they responded.

After a short hug with each one, Naomi was left alone. Why did she have to tell them? What possessed her? Well, one thing was for sure. This wouldn't be the last time she elicited a startled and skeptical response from others.

Chapter Forty-Seven

Darrin felt like the president of the United States, and he didn't like it. He had his own Secret Service, and he couldn't shake them. But he had to admit, since he had his own security detail, no cars had tailed him. And since Ralph Lewis had also declared buses and subways off limits, and restricted his cell phone use, Darrin felt relatively safe. But not completely safe. *Then again, who is,* he thought as he pulled into the NYPD Midtown Manhattan South Precinct station. His armed guards escorted him inside and up to the second floor.

Margaret greeted him as he was headed for his cubicle. He noticed that her hair was different. It was stylishly shorter, and swept across her forehead in a gentle breezy wave. Her eyelashes were longer, and the mascara around her eyes accentuated their extraordinary beauty. Her lipstick was a glossy and slick pink, and her cheeks were more rosy than he remembered. She seemed to wear her standard issue police uniform better than he'd ever seen. Had she lost weight? She came close enough to touch his nose.

"Hi."

"Um...hi."

Ralph Lewis appeared from somewhere beyond them.

"Brock, Margaret will ride with you. You need someone inside the car, not just outside."

"But…"

"She'll accompany you home every night, and then ride back with the detail."

"I don't think I need…"

"You know, Brock, I don't think you know *what* you need. Leave that to us. We'll have this thing cracked soon, and then you can play tennis with the leader of MS 13, for all I care. For some reason, Russians want you dead, or worse. And as long as that's the case, we need to make sure you stay alive."

Darrin gave up.

"Yes, sir."

He spent the rest of the day trying to ignore several obvious advances by Margaret, while at the same time dispatching his various desk work responsibilities. The most obvious example consisted of her standing in front of him while he was seated, with her shirt unbuttoned to the third button. He couldn't wait for work to be over. When it was, he went from a portable hot plate into a closed oven—in the form of his cruiser. As soon as they were on the road and headed for Teaneck, Margaret grabbed his steering hand and squeezed it.

"I've been thinking about you constantly…thinking about you, and me…and our wedding night."

He began to sweat, even though the car was by no means warm. He wanted to wipe the sweat off his forehead, but his right hand was trapped under hers, and his left hand was doing the steering. Margaret could sense unease.

"What's wrong?"

Darrin felt as trapped as his hand.

"What do you mean?"

She raised her voice.

"I mean, why didn't you tell me what happened with Naomi at the hospital?"

"Margaret…"

Anger crept in, raising her volume even more.

"Don't Margaret me! I understand she's better now."

"Isn't that a good thing? I mean…"

"Do you still love her? That's what I want to know!"

"Margaret…"

"Do you?"

"Please…"

Margaret squeezed Darrin's hand harder.

"You know, Jacob had two wives, Leah and Rachel. He loved Rachel, but not Leah. What about you? Who do you love? Anyway, if I'm not mistaken, people don't marry two women in the West since Jesus walked the Earth. Am I right, Darrin? *Am* I?"

Darrin pulled his hand out from under hers. The car swerved out of its lane, and then back.

"Margaret, stop!"

"Do you love me, or not? That's what I want to know. Me and only me."

Darrin realized that this was no time to tell her the truth, or she might be just angry enough to grab his hand and destabilize the vehicle. Instead, he had to de-escalate the situation.

"Can we talk later? You're supposed to be on the job protecting me. Maybe we can go out to dinner somewhere in Manhattan tomorrow night after work."

"No! I want to talk now! I worked so hard to look pretty for you today. And you didn't say *anything*!"

"I noticed."

"Why didn't you say anything? Why? I think I know why. Your heart has already gone astray. You know, the Bible has a lot to say about that."

"Margaret, I'm not talking anymore until we're parked outside my house."

She folded her arms and clenched her teeth for the rest of the drive. When they pulled up in front of the house, the other cars arrived and parked a half a block away so they wouldn't alarm his parents. They waited for him to get out to go into the house before one of them drove by and picked Margaret up. This was her chance.

"Prove you love me. Kiss me like you've never kissed me before. I want you so bad it hurts all over."

She tried to pull him to her side of the seat and straddle him. He resisted, and pulled back to the driver's side.

"Stop, Margaret! Okay. Okay. I admit it. I love Naomi. I can't go through with this marriage. I was going to tell you, but I guess you figured it out."

"What? You rotten...! Some Christian! You led me on real good! Real good! Oh my God! I can't...I can't...breathe. Oh my..."

She began to scream, and then wail. Her tears marred her perfect mascara job, which, mixed with the rouge on her cheeks, created the appearance of a grieving clown.

"Here's your stupid ring!"

She pulled it off her finger and and threw it against the windshield. It bounced off it and landed in Darrin's lap. She continued to wail for a good minute. He forced himself to turn to her. By this time she was spent, and began to pout like a child, as she looked fully into his eyes. He reached out and cupped one painted cheek. Compassion filled his soul like a warm flowing salve.

"Margaret. Listen to me. Listen to me. God won't leave you alone. In time, after you've grown a little stronger spiritually, He'll provide a godly man who will love you like He does. I absolutely know that. It's not me, and I should have realized that and told you a lot sooner. I've been weak and selfish. But I was hurting myself, and hurting you. Please Margaret, don't give up...not on God, and not on yourself. I'll be praying for you. You'll get through this."

She cried some more, and then sighed a deep sigh.

"Well...it was nice while it lasted. It really was. But I knew it wouldn't last. It never does. Never. Oh well."

"The next time it will."

"How do you know?"

"I know. Somehow I know. I need to go in now."

"Okay. Please...please...pray for me. And...pray I don't come on so strong. I was too forward, Wasn't I? Wasn't I?"

"Sometimes, Margaret. It's because you want a lasting relationship. But you'll have one anyway, even without trying so hard. You'll see."

As he got out of the car and walked toward the house, he wondered how he could sound so confident when he had no evidence. One of the police cars drove up, and Margaret pulled out a tissue before she got in.

At the exact moment the police detail pulled away and drove back toward Manhattan, Naomi lay in her hospital bed whispering out plans, unaware that Darrin had already completed his part of the bargain with her.

"I'll be first, before Darrin. Abba will be here sometime tomorrow morning. I don't know how, but I'll tell him then. I've *got* to tell him. I promised Darrin. Please God, don't let him have another stroke when I tell him. I know you can keep that from happening. After all, you healed him from the last one."

It took her two more hours to drift to sleep, aided by a high dose of Tylenol. Her anxious thoughts morphed into an extreme anxiety dream, in which her father's face appeared before her. She opened her mouth to begin sharing her spiritual experience. As she watched his expression, it began to become more and more contorted. Within seconds she realized something was blocking his trachea, and he couldn't breathe. He gagged, but she felt powerless to help him. Oh, if she had only been trained in the Heimlich Maneuver! His face became redder and redder, until finally his head exploded like a squeezed tomato, leaving nothing but a bloody stump of a neck, and a gurgling sound. Her eyes popped open. Sweat was dripping down her face.

"Oh my. Oh my. Not this morning. I can't. I can't tell him this morning."

She spent another few waking hours before sleeping another tentative few hours. After she was awakened by the nurse for vital signs, she slept again through breakfast. When she next awoke, the face in her nightmare appeared before her in the flesh.

"Abba?"

"Baruch HaShem. You're healing so fast, my precious Naomi. God is with you. The doctor told me it won't be long before you can come home, and we can read the sages over dinner, and on Shabbat. I miss you at home. You nursed me when I was sick. Now I will do the same for you, until you're ready to go back to work."

He reached over to the top of her head and stroked the curly patches of hair protruding from the gaps in the graft protection that still remained. She knew she should tell him everything that happened, but she still had visions of his head exploding like a squeezed tomato. She made an on-the-spot decision to at least tell him about Darrin.

"Abba. I just want to tell you. Darrin and I are seeing each other again. I just wanted you to know that."

David Kaplan made every effort to keep every muscle on his face calm.

"Hmm. He is a good man. But what about his policewoman friend?"

"Well…I happen to know that's not going to work out."

"I see. Well…you know I've always taught you to love the other. But certain kinds of love would not work well for us as Jews. I know you understand me."

"Yes, I do, Abba."

Was she now *the other?*

"The other. I understand. Still…I love him deeply. I will always love him. And he will always love me. When I get better….when that happens…we are going to…"

"I understand. You don't have to tell me. We will talk about these things later. I will have something to give you then, to help you remember who you are. Until that time…you're tired. I woke you up. And I'm tired. I didn't sleep well last night."

He reached over and kissed her on her forehead. Then he slowly walked out of the room without looking back, feeling the Linotype legacy letter in the pocket of his black jacket. Naomi bit her lip. Then she prayed one short prayer.

I hope you know what You're doing, Yeshua. Forgive me. I know You know what you're doing.

CHAPTER FORTY-EIGHT

As he and Darrin waited for Inspector Ralph Lewis, Lawrence Schmidt was either agitated, anxious, or excited. Such was Darrin's imprecise assessment. He studied Lawrence's round Hemingway face as they stood in Lewis' office. It had very few lines for a man in his early fifties—really none. Apparently, the dangerous world of terrorist activity didn't keep the Homeland Security agent up at night. Maybe that was a good thing. Who needs a nervous Homeland Security agent? His thick brush mustache was extremely well groomed, as was his thick straight brown hair that covered his head, except for a typical small bald spot in the back. He had no ring on his finger. He either was never married, was widowed, or was divorced.

It turned out Schmidt was excited. As soon as Ralph entered the office, the Homeland Security agent clapped his hands together so loudly, it sounded like a firecracker on the Fourth of July.

"Okay. I've got something. As you know, since we found a Russian connection with Omar Shehadulah, we've been working overtime with the NYPD at the Diamond District's crime scene of last year's Mandy Mendel murder."

He found himself out of breath and overwhelmed, trying to get all the revelations out. After a short pause and one inhale and exhale, he continued.

"Boy, those vendors don't like to talk about *anything*. It's like they're trying to hide the fact that they sell diamonds at all, like they want us to think they sell kosher hot dogs from push carts, or something. Every transaction, every import, and everybody else's import...or export...is nobody's business. I don't know if they've got a code tighter than the mafia, or what. Anyway, we finally got one of these guys to talk about Mandy Mendel to an undercover cop posing as a Chabad Chassidic diamond merchant from Israel...with the accent, the outfit, the beard, the whole bit. *Finally,* and I mean *finally,* he started spilling about a street rumor he swears is true. From what he says, Mendel himself confided in him about it. And the guy never told anyone. He was even uncomfortable mentioning it to anyone after Mendel's death. Anyway, it seems Mendel was expecting, or had received...he doesn't know which...a shipment of diamonds rescued years ago from the Holocaust. They had been hidden by a family in Crimea. The family perished in the camps, and the diamonds were considered lost...particularly two very large perfect diamonds, like maybe twenty carats each. These are so perfect that they are rumored to be worth like thirty million apiece. At least that's what the guy I talked to says. I have no information on the cuts, or shapes, or anything like that. But apparently, these importers of rocks like that tend to hide them in crazy and unexpected places, often somewhere in their own houses, until they can export them to their next destination safely. Brock, the first thing I thought of was the two Chassidic men, or men dressed as Chassidic men, who ransacked Mendel's bedroom after the attempt on your life. They were definitely looking for something."

Inspector Lewis sat in his desk chair, leaning back and swiveling at the same time. He was sucking on the kind of cheap lollipop that banks keep on hand for fidgety children. He took the lollipop out of his mouth.

"Brock, this is your investigation. You once complained to me that you were stuck with the remnants of the Italian mafia. Well, I put you on the Omar Shehadulah investigation, and all you did at first was complain about that. But your instincts about Omar were right. Now I let you get involved with the Russian connection again, a connection that could rise as high as the Kremlin, what with their sophisticated technology. That's where we are right now. I don't want to hear you bellyaching about this one. It seems like they might be looking for these diamonds. So I'm sending you over to the widow's house with a heavily armed detail. They won't dare expose themselves to a police fire fight. And we want them to know we stand behind you. Interview her and check out the house. Use every detective skill you've been trained in. We'll call her and let her know you're on your way. Do you want Margaret to ride shotgun?"

"Um…no, I don't think so."

Lawrence broke in.

"I agree with Brock. I think she should stay here with me."

Lewis gave him a quizzical glance. Just then, Margaret knocked on the closed door. Lewis shouted.

"Who is it?"

She walked in and stood close to Lawrence Schmidt. Darrin eyed them both intently. What was it about their body language? Was Margaret flirting? Was Schmidt? She put her hand on his shoulder, looked at him, and smiled. Darrin thought, *I've seen that before. So soon? I told her to give it time, to give herself a chance to grow spiritually. And besides, I can't believe the inspector is ignoring what she's doing. It's one thing for him to have looked the other way when Margaret did that with me. After all, it was convenient. He wanted me to get over Naomi. But Schmidt?* Just then, Ralph Lewis—who was too focused to pay attention to the infraction— slapped his hand on the table.

"Okay, all of you. Get going. Schmidt, get back to your office and dig up more information."

He left first, and began to walk through the outer office. Margaret left next, and Darrin after her. Outside of the inspector's office, she stopped him.

"He goes to a good church. He's believed since college. And I'm going to his church with him this Sunday. I *love* his cute thick mustache. And I think I could love *him* too. I hope he'll fall in love with me. We have a dinner date Friday night. I guess you were right when you said God won't leave me alone."

Darrin nodded.

"But it's a bit soon."

She bowed her head and whispered.

"It may be my last chance, Darrin. I'm almost fifty. You have Naomi."

He appreciated her honesty. She was never that honest with him. He lifted up her chin and looked into her eyes.

"One word of advice."

She struggled to look directly at him. He detected the shame she was trying to conceal.

"Margaret. Listen to me. Take it slow. Very slow. Get to know him first without…getting to…*know* him, if you know what I mean. Leave a whole lot for the wedding…and invite me…to the wedding, that is."

She grinned and winked at him, and then proceeded to her cubicle. Ralph Lewis opened his office door and stuck his head out.

"Get going, Brock. I just called Mendel's widow, and the detail is waiting for you outside."

"I'm going. I'm going."

He walked down to the first floor and out the door. One of the fresh-faced rookies was in the parking lot standing next to Darrin's car.

"I'll drive us in my marked car. You can leave yours here, sir."

"Are you sure? I mean…"

"Yes, sir. I think the inspector would want it that way."

"I don't know if he would or wouldn't. You know how to drive this thing?"

"Yes sir."

"Just kidding."

"I understand, sir."

They both got in and drove off, with three marked cars escorting them as they traveled the half hour or so to Brooklyn via the Manhattan Bridge. Darrin didn't feel like talking, so he let the rookie know.

"I'm going to get some rest. Let me know when we get there."

He shut his eyes and leaned his head back. Then he prayed to himself.

Oh God, help me to ask the right questions, and get the right answers. We've got to solve this case, for Chaya's sake, as well as mine and everyone else's. And oh…please keep us safe.

He was actually glad he had a driver, because he did doze toward the very end of the ride. He woke up just as the three escorting police cars pulled in front and behind the rookie's car. They all double parked in front of Chaya Mendel's house. The other policemen got out of their cars and put their hands on their holsters. With two cops per car, it looked like a drug bust. Two neighbors opened their front doors and stared at them. Darrin got out and walked up to Chaya's front door. The rookie stayed in the vehicle. Chaya let him in immediately. Then one of the cops asked a neighbor if he could use their bathroom while the others got back in their cars. Once inside Chaya's house, she asked him to sit on her pristine white couch, while she sat in the dark red upholstered armchair adjacent to it. She was dressed in her usual long black skirt and white blouse. Her traditional Chassidic wig, or *sheitel*, was fastidiously styled. Darrin looked around, and asked a question he'd often asked before.

"Where's Natan?"

"He's playing with the other children upstairs. It's better this way, and safer, notwithstanding the fact that half the NYPD is outside."

Darrin felt a bit disappointed that the children were right upstairs, and yet the one who called him *Abba* and loved to jump in his lap wouldn't be spending time with him. But Chaya was right. That was not the purpose of this meeting. Earlier, her heart had jumped in her chest when the inspector had called and mentioned her late husband's name. Now she was trying to keep it from further jumping by starting with small talk.

"So…how is your fiancée?"

"You mean Margaret, I suppose."

"Yes. She's a lovely woman and a good match, I think."

"Yes she is, for someone. In fact, she's seeing a Homeland Security agent named Lawrence."

"Really. I'm sorry it didn't work out."

There was an awkward few seconds, after which Darrin spoke up.

"Um…I'm not sorry. I'm seeing Naomi Kaplan…again."

Chaya tried not to sound surprised, or disappointed.

"Oh."

There was more silence, which she broke this time.

"So which one is changing religions…or is neither one?"

"Perhaps you should ask Naomi that."

"Perhaps I will. I do realize that you are fond of each other. I can understand that. You are both wonderful people, as well as good friends of mine. That won't change. But of course, you realize there are other important factors."

Another pause.

"However, we're not here to discuss that. So…I understand you have some news about my late husband's…murder."

Darrin was glad they were moving away from the last subject, and getting down to the reason he was there. He needed to keep this professional, and focused. He had spent enough time the year before trying to question Naomi about her brother-in-law Marc's possible mafia connections, only to be constantly distracted by his growing love for her. That was so unprofessional. A professional approach was important in this case.

"Chaya…we may have found some connections…to some diamond imports. I mean, I know your husband was in that business. But I'm referring to some specific imports. Did he ever…discuss anything about some jewels retrieved from Eastern Europe…specifically recovered from someone or ones who hid them in the area of Crimea during the… Holocaust?"

"He never discussed his work with me, Detective Brock."

She normally called him Darrin. Did she call him Detective Brock because this was in a different context than his visits with Natan? Or was it because she was distancing herself from him now that he was back with Orthodox Jewish Naomi? Maybe it wasn't that. She said they'd always be friends. She continued.

"Our husbands *never* discuss their work with us…that is, especially their work in the diamond business. They make a living so we can follow Torah and serve God as a family. That was his work's purpose. My husband was a good man, and was filled with good works. But some of those works he didn't share with me."

"I see. Do you mind if I ask you something?"

"Of course, Darrin. You can ask me anything."

He liked hearing his first name again, even though it was less professional.

"Can we go up to your bedroom for a few minutes? I mean…I know that it's your private quarters. But…we feel that there's a connection in all this with those two men dressed as Chassidic Jews who…who left that room in disarray. I know you've wondered about them."

"Yes, you can examine the room. But I don't think you'll find anything. After all, something tells me that if they *were* pretenders, they

396

didn't find whatever it was they were looking for."

"That may be true, Chaya. But I'm a trained investigative detective. I just want to take a look."

"Okay. I'll take you up there. But please be quiet. I don't want Natan to see you. He's playing with his brothers and sisters in a room down the hall."

They walked upstairs and entered the Mendels' master bedroom. Chaya kissed the mezuzah on the door on the way in. All the rooms had them, not just the front door. Once inside, Darrin was struck by how tidy it was, and how sparse. Of course, he hadn't investigated the closet or bureau drawers. There were two unassuming twin beds. Very few items were on the night tables. The most prominent item was the white basin Mandy had used to wash his hands and face upon arising in the morning. Darrin then looked across the room at the dresser. On top were two worn blue velvet bags. Darrin went over and picked them up.

"May I?"

"Yes. I'm sure you know what those are."

"Yes, I do. This one has the *tallit*, the prayer shawl."

"Yes. We say *tallis* in our community."

"Right. And this one has the *tefillin*, the leather boxes worn on the forehead and arm, with Scripture in them…Scripture that directs one to wear them."

"Very good."

He zipped the bags open one at a time, feeling them for anything sewn into them, and quickly examined the contents. After he zipped the bags closed, Chaya shared more about them.

"Those were the holiest items in Mandy's life…that and his prayer book. That's downstairs, if you want to look at it. But these were even more holy. They were his father's, and his father's before him. His father brought them from Poland when he came early in the twentieth century. Neither bag left his side in the morning. That is, rarely. The *tefillin* went in for repair a while back for only two days. He borrowed someone else's then. And he brought the *tallis* with him to synagogue every Shabbat. *Tefillin* aren't used on Shabbat."

"I see."

He placed the bags back on the bureau.

"Thank you for allowing me to handle them. I hope you don't mind my looking in some drawers that may have some unmentionables."

She nodded.

Then he proceeded to pull out every drawer and examine the bottoms, sides, tops, and the inside of the bureaus and night tables for any unusual compartments or other hidden areas. He looked in the closet, and checked the drapes for any unusual hidden areas. Then he turned to her.

"I'm sorry for the inconvenience, but our Homeland Security contact…"

"Margaret's new boyfriend."

"Yes, that's right. He told us that diamond merchants like your husband sometimes temporarily store things in unusual places, and possibly places close to home. Well, I'm finished here."

She led him back downstairs. As he approached the front door, he turned to her, being careful not to touch her, which was forbidden for any man but her husband.

"Well, we'll stay in touch. I know we'll get the answers you…and all of us…want. The police will continue to keep a protective eye on you and your family."

"Thank you. You have always been very kind to us…to Natan, myself, all of us. Please give my regards to Inspector Lewis."

"I will."

With that, he left. The police exited their cars and escorted him to the car he came in, with hands on their holsters. One even had his gun drawn. They all got in their cars and drove down the street in close proximity to each other. As soon as the rookie rounded the corner, Darrin's phone rang. There was no caller ID. He put it to his ear and listened. Someone with a clear Russian accent spoke.

"We saw you, and we see you now. Don't play with us. We are always listening, and always watching. Your investigations are nothing. We will investigate you, and find all you look for. Don't bother tracing this call. You will not be able to."

The voice hung up. Even though he knew it was useless, he shouted the typical, "Hello! Hello!" Then he mumbled to himself.

"I'm so sick of those Russians."

He turned to the rookie.

"Take me back to precinct headquarters."

"That's where I'm going, sir."

"Right. Of course."

He knew this whole mess wasn't over yet. That was for sure. He found himself once again praying for himself, Chaya, Naomi, everyone—even the policewoman Margaret.

CHAPTER FORTY-NINE

Darrin sat on the edge of Naomi's hospital bed, holding up her toothbrush.

"Don't forget your friend here."

She smiled as she sat in a hospital-provided wheelchair, waiting for the nurse to come and release her. Darrin then softly spoke words she had been waiting sleepless nights to hear.

"I told her. She's already showing interest in a Homeland Security agent. You're the only one, Naomi. You always will be."

Naomi responded thankfully, but also sheepishly.

"Baruch HaShem. But I haven't told Abba about me."

"In God's time."

She was making real progress walking, but she wasn't yet ready to navigate freely. The casts on her arm and leg were smaller now, but she still had a few weeks until they came off. And the same was true for her neck brace. A small blue silk scarf covered the still healing areas of her scalp, giving her the appearance of Tevya's wife Golda in *Fiddler on the Roof*. But with Darrin by her side carrying her small suitcase, she felt more like one of their five daughters. The fact that one of the daughters married a Christian man didn't enter her mind.

Finally, the nurse came. She asked Naomi to sign a form, gave her crutches to hold, and wheeled her out of the room, with Darrin by her side. They passed an NYPD sentry in the hall, and he followed them down the elevator and out of the Maimonides Medical Center. There were two police cars waiting, and Darrin's car as well. He placed Naomi in the passenger seat, and then put the crutches and suitcase in the back seat and got in the driver's seat. He drove her toward her Brooklyn brownstone, escorted by the two marked cars. When they arrived there, an anxious David Kaplan was watching them through the living room window. He hurried to the front door and opened it. Naomi waved at him from inside the car, as she waited for Darrin to get her suitcase and crutches out of the back seat. David went out to help with the suitcase.

"My precious Naomi, welcome home."

He leaned over and gave her a quick hug.

"You are doing so well, and you're more beautiful than ever. Hello, Darrin. I'll help with the suitcase."

"Hello, David."

Darrin gave him a hug, and then gave him the suitcase. He assisted with Naomi, and helped her adjust her crutches as she stood up. His experience helping his mother Velma gave him training in gentleness that matched his sweet personality. And it wasn't lost on Naomi. David Kaplan watched ambivalently as she gave Darrin a quick kiss on the mouth. Then Darrin and David slowly accompanied Naomi as she made her way toward the house. When they got inside, an NYPD policeman closed the door behind them and retreated to his car. Once inside, Darrin escorted Naomi to a kitchen chair.

"Is everything good?"

"Everything's good. Especially with my two favorite men here."

David stood over her.

"Can I get you something?"

"No, Abba. I'm not hungry or thirsty. I just want to sit here for a few minutes and thank HaShem for bringing me to this season."

David Kaplan thought, *bringing her to the season of marrying a Christian, even a good Christian*? But he held his tongue. She, on the other hand, had only gratefulness to the God of Israel. She quoted the *She-hechianu* prayer as her father mumbled it half-heartedly along with her.

"*Baruch Atah Adonai, Elohaynu Melech Ha-Olam, She-hechianu,*

V-Kee-yemanu, V'Higianu, Laz-man Hazeh, Blessed are You, Lord our God, King of the Universe, who has given us life, sustained us, and enabled us to reach this season."

She turned around and noticed an envelope with her name on it sitting on the kitchen table.

"What's this, Abba?"

"It's just a letter…from me. I'd like you to read it now, if you would like to."

"Of course, Abba."

As she picked up the letter, he reached out and put his hand on hers.

"As you read it, I want you to remember all the times you asked me questions, and listened intently to my response. I'd like to think that this is one of those times."

"Okay. I loved those times. I did. Well…I'll open it."

She opened the letter, and unfolded it.

"It looks like this was printed on a Linotype machine. That alone makes it special, Abba."

"Yes, it was."

Then she read the letter. Both David and Darrin could hear a nervous quaver in her voice.

"My dear and beloved daughter Naomi,

"As I type this on the Linotype machine where we sat together not long ago, you are lying in a coma after saving the lives of three young children. I can't tell you how full my heart is that you performed such a mitzvah. You obeyed Moshe, who told us to preserve life.

"I know you have an inquisitive mind, and have asked many excellent questions worthy of the sages. No one has the answers to all of those questions. But I want you to always ask them, like our father Abraham did when he stood before HaShem in the matter of his nephew Lot. Yet as your loving father, whom I'm sure you will outlive by many years, I want you to always remember that the answers are in our Jewish tradition, even as you respect the faith tradition of the other…as I've always taught you. It's true that you may never have your own natural children. But in God's wisdom and God's way, you will carry the legacy of our forefathers into the future, even for your niece and nephew, and many other nameless Jewish children.

"That legacy includes the words of our great sage Maimonides, who said he believed with perfect faith in the coming of the Messiah…by which he meant our Messiah. By keeping our legacy, you will usher him in.

"Your loving Abba"

Naomi looked at her father as tears filled his eyes. Then she looked at Darrin's soft yet electric blue eyes. They seemed to say, *this would be a very good time, Naomi.* Then she turned to her father again.

"Abba…Abba…"

She froze for several seconds, and then jumped up.

"I…I…think I have to go to the bathroom."

She grabbed her crutches and walked slowly out of the kitchen, and down the hall into the first floor bathroom. David and Darrin sat at the kitchen table in awkward silence. They could just hear Naomi, who was weeping softly. Finally, Darrin broke the silence.

"Mr. Kaplan, while we wait for Naomi to come out of the bathroom, may I get your advice on something?"

David saw an opportunity to further explain the legacy letter to Darrin. But as soon as Darrin asked his question, the opportunity dissipated.

"I must ask for your confidentiality, because this relates to my work, specifically concerning the Mandy Mendel case. I believe you're familiar with that crime, and his widow Chaya."

"Yes. A great tragedy. I'm sure you and your friends are working hard to solve it, if you haven't solved it already."

"We haven't. In fact, that's the reason I have police protection at the moment, including outside your house."

"I see."

Darrin hesitated, and then shared the most sensitive information.

"At any rate, my question has to do with a certain shipment of precious jewels that Mandy may have stored…or hidden somewhere, before planning to export them. We have reason to believe that these belonged to a family who perished in the Holocaust. I was told by dealers in the Diamond District that Chassidic Jews who act as importers and exporters sometimes store these items temporarily, often in unusual places, close to their person in some way. If you were Mandy Mendel,

404

where do you think you would...store...such things? And I must tell you, before you answer, that certain Russians seem to be obsessed with his bedroom."

"Diamonds, I take it."

"Yes, two of them. Big ones."

David would have rather discussed the letter, and Naomi's Jewish legacy. But Darrin had asked about where Mandy Mendel would hide diamonds from the Holocaust, so he answered him.

"What is the most precious and holy item Mandy Mendel owns, even more precious than diamonds?"

The answer to that question was easy. Chaya Mendel had just shared that information with him.

"Um...his *tallit* and *tefillin*. But, the bags have nothing sewn into them. And he wouldn't..."

"Wouldn't he?"

"But it wouldn't be kosher, would it? I mean, the holy Scripture is enclosed, on holy parchment. They are to be used on the forehead and arm in accordance with Deuteronomy 6:8, and for no other purpose. I know that much. As you said, it's a *very* holy item."

"That's true, Darrin. But if I were Mandy Mendel, I believe I might consider jewels which belonged to an entire family whose blood was shed in martyrdom for their faith...after they hid the diamonds...to be quite holy. Wouldn't you? You see, observant Jews can be quite flexible, sometimes...about some things."

Darrin paused as he looked down at his shoes. Then he lifted his head and his eyes met David Kaplan's.

"Crazy. It reminds me of that movie *The Maltese Falcon*."

"I never saw it."

"That's okay. It's not worth explaining. Let me ask you just one last thing. Something Chaya said got me thinking. She told me that the *tefillin* left Mandy's side just once recently for a repair that took a day or two. I believe he may have borrowed a friend's during that time. How often might *tefillin* that have not been damaged in a fire, or the like, be taken somewhere for repair?"

"Never that I know of. I mean, if the leather straps are well wrapped... and they usually are...and they are stored in the velvet bag, often with caps over the boxes, why would they? I still have my grandfather's, in mint condition, so to speak."

"Uh-huh. Hmm. Hmm."

Just then, a red-eyed Naomi hobbled into the room. She stood between Darrin and David, faced her father, and began to speak. Her speaking pace was quick, her heart was pounding, but her voice was clear.

"Abba. I have to tell you something. When I was in a coma…well, I know, you'll say it's because I was in the coma. But this was different. Besides, I could hear everyone *else* who walked in the room, including you…"

David held up his palms to slow her down.

"Naomi, my daughter, you're not making sense."

She knew she had to tell him plainly.

"Okay. Abba. Everything was dark. It was blackness all the time while I was lying there…when you came in, when Darrin came in, when Aunt Ida came in with a woman named Mahalia Morse, when others came in. I heard everyone, but didn't see anything. But then…"

She closed her eyes and concentrated, trying to remember what it was like.

"Then, a light as bright as the sun filled the room, and a man came in. It was like he was on fire, like his eyes were on fire, he was so bright… but he wasn't…like the burning bush."

She opened her eyes. David Kaplan looked at her and reacted to the direction he perceived things might be going.

"Like an evil presence?"

"*NO*, Abba. No. He spoke in the kindest voice I've ever heard, almost like your kindness, but beyond any kindness in this world. He said, 'Your sins are forgiven.' He told me some other things, like when I would wake up from the coma, and start to get better. And He showed me holes…in His wrist. They were in His *wrists*, Abba. Not in His hands. That's *wrong*. I know that…I know that…for a…a…*fact*. He showed me. I *know* it. And the *love*. Wow! I can't…I can't describe it, except…it was *God's* love. The God of Israel."

Tears began pouring from her eyes. She shut them and then tried to wipe them with her forefinger. When she opened them, she saw—

through blurred vision—David Kaplan sitting on the chair, staring forward, ashen. At least thirty seconds passed. Maybe a minute. Darrin stood perfectly still, his eyes fixed on her. Finally, she spoke just above a whisper.

"Abba…Abba…say something. Do you still…? Tell me you still…love me. Please, Abba."

His gaze stayed fixed forward. He spoke in a monotone.

"Of course I still love you, Naomi. How could I not love you?"

He turned to face her.

"I love you very much…but as the *other* now. You are now one of the others that I love…as I love myself. I love you like the little Gentile children with cancer that I visit as Santa Claus at Maimonides on December 25th. I love you…but as the other."

A look of absolute and desperate horror appeared on Naomi's face—a look Darrin had never seen, and actually frightened him. Then she began to scream and wail so loudly that Darrin was sure one of the policemen would rush the house.

"No, Abba. NO! NO, ABBA! *No*! I'm *not* the other! Don't say that! Don't you *dare* say that! Please! Don't! I'm NOT the other! I'm ME. I'm your eldest daughter Naomi Kaplan, who will carry on your Jewish legacy. I WILL! You'll see! You'll see. I will. Won't I, Darrin?"

Her face, which had grown as red as the blood that had rushed to her head, began to return to its original color. Darrin spoke as quietly as he could.

"You will, Naomi. But perhaps we shouldn't keep talking about this now. Emotions are raw. Hearts are broken. It's enough for now that love is being expressed."

David turned to him.

"You're right, Darrin. That is wise, like the sages. You are a good man. You are one of the best men I've ever met, Jew or Gentile."

He stood up and shook Darrin's hand. Then he went over to Naomi, and kissed her on the forehead for a good ten seconds. He looked into her totally bloodshot eyes.

"Darrin is right. Remember that I still love you deeply…and yes, as your father. Many children convert."

"But Daddy, I haven't…"

"Shhh. Be still. That's how it feels to me, Naomi. That's how it feels to *me*. Feelings don't just change to other feelings. This is the hardest news a Jewish father could hear. But…we'll get through this, one way or another. Right now, we should both rest. After all, we've both just recently recovered from very serious conditions. One of us is still in the early stages of recovery, as your crutches make clear. Let's just love each other, and get along. God will take care of the rest. I'll take the legacy letter and throw it out."

As he reached for it, she put her hand on his.

"No, Abba. I want it. I want to have it."

As she took it, he nodded.

"It's yours if you want it."

He got up and slowly walked out of the room.

Darrin turned to Naomi.

"Your father is a great man, a truly great man."

She wiped more tears with her forefinger, and nodded in agreement.

"He's one of two, and the other one is you."

"Well, he also gave me some incredible work advice. And that's why I need to leave right now, and get over to Chaya Mendel's. I'm so sorry, my beloved Naomi. But it's urgent. Can I borrow your phone?"

"Well…sure. Is yours broken?"

"Sort of. Let's put it this way. It's broken *into*."

She handed him her phone. He called Ralph Lewis.

"Inspector, it's Darrin Brock. This is Naomi's phone. I've got a hunch. I'm headed back over to Chaya Mendel's. I need more backup than ever. Please call her and tell her to be careful."

He gave the phone back to Naomi, and then gave her a quick kiss and a hug. Then he walked out the front door.

CHAPTER FIFTY

The rookie was three-quarters to Chaya Mendel's house when Ralph Lewis called Darrin on his phone. He was surprised that Lewis was calling on what was obviously a compromised phone that had been hacked using technology that might be traceable to the highest authority—the Kremlin.

"Inspector? This isn't safe."

"Who the hell cares about that now? We've got our men in position across the street. There's been an intrusion. We're dealing with a hostage situation."

"What?"

"You heard me. The whole Mendel family. The neighbors saw it happen. And you know these Russians."

"Oh no. This is obviously a very dangerous situation. I don't suppose I could ask you to pray for the Mendel family, Inspector."

"*You* pray for them...and yourself. I'll cross my fingers."

He hung up. Darrin turned to the rookie.

"Park down the street. I'll walk from there. I'll be okay. These morons are too busy, and too greedy, to think of me just this minute. Anyway, I believe things are beyond that now."

"Yes, sir. Whatever you say. But I'll cover you."

"Thank you. You do that. Park here."

As the rookie pulled up and parked, Darrin got out, and pulled out his gun. He arrived across the street and asked for a briefing from the detail posted there.

"What's up?"

"They've been in phone contact. Three of them, we think. They're holding the mother and children at gunpoint. They're telling us they'll slaughter all of them in a hail of bullets if we make a move. They told us that way the deaths of the children will be painless. Such hearts. They also reminded us about Mandy Mendel, as if they had to."

"Oh boy. Cover me."

"Where are you going?"

"I'm going to the only place I *must* go."

He walked down the street, and then crossed it. The head of the police detail tried to catch his attention without attracting anyone else's.

"Wait a minute. Wait a minute."

Darrin disappeared around the corner. The cop shook his head.

"How can we cover him if we can't even see him?"

Just then, Darrin turned the corner again and walked back toward the house, clinging to the brick front of each house on the block. He climbed over each porch, and stayed as close to each house as he could. When he got to the near side of the Mendel house, he closed his eyes and prayed to himself.

Well, I think I'm totally healed of that shotgun wound last year. But if I'm not, I'll certainly find out now. Please, God. Cover me.

He took a deep breath, put his gun in its holster, and then climbed up the right side of the first-floor window. His feet slipped once or twice, but finally he climbed onto the ledge above the window. He was thankful Brooklyn brownstones were built that way. He was now just to the right of the master bedroom window. He was also thankful that the curtains to that room weren't fully drawn. He could just see into it. One of the three Russians, who were all dressed as Chassidic Jews—in black, with white shirts, and sporting curly beards—seemed to be tasked with looking out the front window from time to time. He did it from an oblique angle to avoid being in the line of fire. But that angle also obscured Darrin from him, which was another blessing. Darrin could just see the other two training their guns on the Mendel family. One seemed to be aiming his gun right at Natan, which particularly disturbed Darrin. But he was doubly thankful that the Russians' backs were to him, and the family were facing him, hands in the air—that is, until Natan saw him through the window. Darrin saw Natan mouth "Abba" and was sure he'd spoken it out and that everything would be exposed. He shook his head *no*, even though it would have been too late if Natan had spoken. But it soon became apparent that Natan hadn't. He had merely mouthed the word to let Darrin know he saw him. What a bright little boy! Darrin then noticed that one of the Russians had the *tallit* and *tefillin* bags in one of his hands. They must have figured out the same thing he had, and perhaps had even grilled the "repairer." Darrin also realized it must have been obvious to the Russians that they were trapped. But he knew they weren't going to give up the bags at this point. And they were certainly capable of shooting the family. He had practically no time left to act.

In all his years of service, Darrin had never killed a man—or a woman, for that matter. And it was his intention and goal to leave the force with that record. However, he realized now that such a goal would be impossible. In fact, like Gary Cooper in *High Noon*, or Alan Ladd in *Shane*, he knew he was going to have to kill all three men. He waited for the "safest" moment—that is, safest for the Mendel family. One thing he settled in his heart was that he *had* to do it, not just for Chaya and her children, but for all the victims of the Holocaust who were slaughtered like cattle —including the family who had hidden the diamonds. He waited until the Russian with the bag glanced at it.

NOW.

He aimed for heads and started with the undistracted one. He had been at the top of his class in target practice, with one hundred percent bullseyes, and that came in handy now. He pulled the trigger, and the window glass shattered. The Russian's head was propelled forward before he collapsed. Then he quickly shot the one with the bags. The window was open, and the Russian's head exploded like a shattered egg. He didn't have time to watch the blood and brain matter spew from its open top. Finally, he turned to the third man, who was in shock. He regained his faculties and swung his gun toward Darrin. At least the family was safe. Now it was a duel, and Darrin had the better of him.

He squeezed the trigger and shot him in the face, caving his nose into his brain. He, like the others, collapsed to the floor. The children were all screaming, and ran into their mother's arms. Natan, however, ran toward Darrin, and the shattered glass window. Darrin dropped his gun into the bushes below, and held out his arms to stop Natan, while screaming "Stop, Natan!" Natan obeyed, but Darrin lost his balance, and fell backwards off the ledge, and down the one story to a combination of bushes and pavement. When he hit the ground, his ankles snapped. Before he fainted, he shouted as loud as he could, "I got all three. They're all dead. The family's safe. Help me! Help me! And bring those velvet bags to the lab."

When he woke up several hours later at none other than the Maimonides Medical Center emergency room, Percocet was being pumped through his veins. Naomi was telling him how proud of him she was, how he was her hero, as well as Natan's, and how there was one large diamond inside each lead-lined *tefillin* box. A rabbi had even observed that operation, although such was not the case with his ankle surgery, she added with a smile. He didn't remember any of that later—or her gentle kiss.

THE
THIRD WINTER

CHAPTER FIFTY-ONE

The fall passed slowly for Darrin Brock. Both of his ankles were cast. The damage to one of the more complex bone structures in the human body ended up being considerable. After a week or so, he refused Percocet and other opioids. So he was left with Tylenol, Advil, and earnest prayer. The winter made an untimely New York entrance on Thanksgiving, depositing five inches of powdery slippery snow that made it challenging for Darrin to go out. Although the snow melted two days later, the temperatures were well below freezing by the first night of Chanukah, in mid-December. And there were large patches of ice on sidewalks and any uncleared walkways in front of Brooklyn brownstones like the one where the Kaplans were hosting a party, as they had the year before. The streets, however, were mostly clear.

Darrin wished it was already spring, and he could walk down the aisle with Naomi at his just planned Beth Yeshua wedding. He sat in an armchair in the Kaplan living room, with his crutches at his side. Naomi was at the kitchen table, polishing the old Kiev menorah that had been in the family since the 1800s. Darrin could see the kitchen light reflect on her diamond engagement ring—one that was a lot smaller than Mandy Mendel's hidden treasure, but bigger than the ring he had given Margaret. That seemed so long ago, although it wasn't. It felt like he had stepped out of a fog since then. And not only that. He also seemed to have truly grown up—at forty-nine years old, as ridiculous as that may seem. He realized that, as much as he was deeply in love with Naomi the year before, he was more prepared now to be the caring, emotionally intimate husband God had called him to be. And he was more circumspect in his life. *It's funny how killing three men can do that to a man*, he mused.

Marc Silver was sitting on the couch reading a newspaper. He looked up to see his father-in-law David Kaplan, and his wife Lisa, come down the stairs with their children. David was holding his Santa hat.

"I was showing them what I do on Christmas, visiting the children in the cancer ward. I was explaining what a mitzvah is. It's why what Lindsey will have is called a bat mitzvah, and Noah's is called a bar mitzvah. How many Jewish children understand that? *They* understand. Maybe they'll come with me to the Maimonides Medical Center children's ward this year."

Noah felt compelled to say something.

"Grandpa says they're *the other*. That means they're not like us, but we should treat them like we treat us. Right, Grandpa?"

He coughed nervously. Naomi's polishing skipped a beat. Then he answered Noah.

"Yes, you understand, Noah."

Just then, the guests started to arrive. Aunt Ida came practically arm-in-arm with Mahalia Morse, and was as gregarious as usual.

"Look who I brought. A perfect copy of me, and my new best friend. I haven't had a best friend since my old pal Zelda died ten years ago. I've just been stuck with all of you who call me *Aunt* Ida."

Mahalia reciprocated.

"Yes. Amen! You all know, God works in those *mysterious* ways of His, His…well, you all know the line…wonders to *perform*. I met this twin sister while visiting Naomi in the hospital. We talked about…"

Naomi stopped polishing and interrupted.

"I know. Both of you talked about what a fool I was to have rejected Darrin. I heard the whole thing. I heard *everything*, in the dark and in the…light. The light too."

She glanced at her father. Mahalia jumped in.

"I *knew* you were listening. The Spirit told me that. I'm glad you took our advice."

"I did…shortly thereafter. I heard you too, Abba, when you talked about legacy, and the letter, and *everything*… I heard you weep, and felt you kiss my forehead. I love you so much, Abba. So much. I love everyone who visited me. *Everyone.*"

David Kaplan smiled, as his eyes twinkled.

"Remember, Naomi, I will always love you…regardless. I told you that. Regardless."

"Thank you, Abba," she responded from across the room. "Thank you." She knew that, for now, she couldn't expect more than that.

After that, the door flung open and in came Marvin, accompanied by a plump round-faced woman in her early fifties. She was a few inches taller than Marvin, with a Chassidic silver *sheitel* wig, and a long black bulging button-down dress beneath her open black wool coat. Marvin wasn't about to introduce her, so she introduced herself.

"I'm Leah. And I suppose you all know my future husband Marvin."

Naomi, who had been holding a knife, dropped it on the table. Leah continued.

"We met at synagogue. He looked up at the balcony, and there I was. He just kept staring. I couldn't wait for the service to end. Of course, we had to meet his mother. And that was it."

There was silence for a few seconds, after which Mahalia shouted in Pentecostal style, "Now *that's* what I'm talking about!"

Ida added, "A-men! It's about time." And then everyone clapped and congratulated them. Leah waited for the applause to stop.

"May I ask where the restroom is?"

When that was explained and she left the room, Marvin stepped up to Naomi and spoke just above a whisper, which wasn't easy for him.

"God wanted this Jacob to have his Rachel…I mean, *you*…but I had to settle for a Leah. At least she's *frum*…very Orthodox, unlike your future husband."

Naomi whispered back. The anger in her voice was palpable.

"How *dare* you, Marvin! Don't you *ever* say that again!"

"I mean, you're marrying that Christian Darrin, aren't you?"

"That's not what I meant! You'll hurt her if you ever talk like that and she hears it. *Never never never* call her second best, or treat her as second best…*ever!* Do you hear me? Marvin? Do you hear me?"

He was taken aback. He had never seen Naomi so angry, except that one time at Macy's. But she was even angrier now.

"Marvin! Tell me you will love her and cherish her as your first choice. Tell me now or I'll tell her you don't deserve her and not to marry you. *Now!*"

He fumbled with the orange sock hat in his hand, and then he spoke up.

"My mother told me the same thing."

"Well, she's *right!*"

Naomi walked across the room just as the door opened again. Abrihet came in with Jeremy, Joshua, and Javier. Jeremy and Joshua ran over to Darrin, who was sitting in the armchair with his crutches leaning at its side. The older, taller Jeremy looked at his casted feet.

"You really did it *this* time."

Younger, rounder Joshua added, "You did! We really miss you. But we're really glad you dumped that Margaret and you're back with Naomi. We're so excited!"

Jeremy shook his head.

"Don't say 'dumped,' Joshua. It isn't nice."

"But he did."

Darrin reached his hands out and took both their hands.

"Well, boys, I did essentially dump her. But she's got a new love already, and I have the love of my life. So all's well, as they say. You are both growing so fast."

"Not me," chubbier, shorter Joshua said.

"Yes, you, Joshua. I can see it starting. You'll be as tall as your brother when it's over, maybe taller."

Javier had already run over and pulled Naomi down from a standing position to hug her. She was at a loss. She looked at Mahalia, who mouthed, "His heart has softened a lot since the attack."

Naomi mouthed back, "I can see that."

He snuggled against her, and said, "I love you. I love you so much. I'm so happy for you and Darrin. And you're all better. Thank you... thank you for saving me."

They both began to cry. He refused to let her go. Finally, after she got on her knees and hugged him tightly, he smiled and walked off to play with the other children.

When Chaya and her children came, Natan climbed onto Darrin's lap and stayed there for the rest of the night, falling to sleep nestling his angelic face—with cherubic side curls—against Darrin's shoulder.

The final guests were Rabbi Sheldon Goldberg and his wife Jody—and Stanley, who proceeded to spend much of his time reminiscing with David Kaplan about their late friend Mahmoud. Jody Goldberg gave Naomi the longest hug of the night.

"My precious Naomi. Engaged! I knew it would work out. I told you. Remember?"

"You did! You did! Oh, Jody. I hadn't felt a mother's kind of love for years, until I wept in your arms in Devorah's room. Please forgive me for all the unkindness…"

"Oh, Naomi. I understood what you were feeling. But look at you. A blushing bride at Darrin's side! I'm so, so happy for you. And my husband is officiating. So exciting! Get ready for me to fuss over you, including finding a dress, and paying for it."

They both cried and hugged again. And then everyone ate. When they had had their fill of *suvgan-yot*, Chanukah donuts, and of potato latkes, Naomi lit the candles for the first night. They all sang the two familiar Chanukah blessings that are chanted every night, and the special first-night *She-hechianu*.

"*Baruch Atah Adonai, Elohaynu Melech Ha-Olam, She-hechianu, V-Kee-yemanu, V'Higianu, Laz-man Hazeh, Blessed are You, Lord our God, King of the Universe, who has given us life, sustained us, and enabled us to reach this season.*"

As Naomi watched the flames of the servant candle and the first-night candle flicker, she considered those words about enabling us to reach this season, as well as the written words of the greatest Jew that ever lived—well, the second-greatest Jew—her beloved father.

In God's wisdom and God's way, you will carry the legacy of our forefathers into the future.

She repeated those words to herself, and then spoke her own words deep down in her heart—right then and there, on the first night of the Feast of Dedication—on Chanukah.

"If the saving, caring God who put such love for Israel in Darrin's heart is also *my* God…and *my* God is also the God of Israel, the God my father believes in…then I can carry on the legacy. I *must* carry it on, and I *will* carry it on."

She looked over and saw Natan sleeping in Darrin's lap. Somehow, her father's legacy was evident even there.

Michael Robert Wolf was born and raised in Philadelphia, Pennsylvania. He graduated magna cum laude in English and literature from Temple University. Eventually, he moved to Cincinnati to serve in ministry related activities. In 2012, he released his first novel, *The Upper Zoo*, published by Destiny Image Publishers. It rose to number three across all genres at Amazon.com. *The Linotype Operator*, published by Finishing Line Press, was released in June of 2016. New York Times number one bestselling and first Oprah selection author Jacquelyn Mitchard has written about *The Linotype Operator*, "It enchanted me in a way I've been enchanted by only a handful of stories over the last ten years. When I finished it, I wanted to read it all over again." *The Other: The Linotype Legacy* is his third and latest novel. He lives in Cincinnati with his wife Rachel, author and editor of North Light art books.

CPSIA information can be obtained
at www.ICGtesting.com
Printed in the USA
FFHW020043040619
52817573-58355FF